THE STONE GARDEN

Mary Rosenblum

A Del Rey® Book
BALLANTINE BOOKS • NEW YORK

For Greg

A Del Rey® Book
Published by Ballantine Books

Chapter One originally appeared in a slightly different form in *Isaac Asimov's Science Fiction Magazine.*

Library of Congress Catalog Card Number: 94-94649

ISBN 0-345-38958-1

Manufactured in the United States of America

First Edition: January 1995

10 9 8 7 6 5 4 3 2 1

I'd like to thank Sage Walker for her usual perceptive and invaluable critique.

Special appreciation goes to Greg Abraham, who created Margarita's poetic voice, and whose artistic input added a lot to this novel.

Theresa

HERE'S WHAT CRITICS, EDITORS, AND PROMINENT AUTHORS ARE SAYING ABOUT MARY ROSENBLUM AND

THE STONE GARDEN:

"The nineties wave is here, and Mary Rosenblum is riding its crest."
—Walter Jon Williams,
author of *Hardwired* and *Aristoi*

"A moving adventure of life and love, kinship and alienation, art and survival. It will take you from Earth to outer space, from a fully realized future society to the workings of its characters' hearts."
—Vonda N. McIntyre

"One of the most eloquent new voices of the nineties. What really distinguishes *The Stone Garden* is its keenly observed artists. Rosenblum rings some dazzling technological changes on the world of high art while reexamining the eternal verities of inspiration and transcendence."
—James Patrick Kelly

"An honest, searching journey to the farthest reaches of what makes us human—without once sacrificing a concrete future of asteroid mining, economic power, and urban violence. I recommend Mary Rosenblum to you."
—Nancy Kress

"*The Drylands* marks one of the strongest debuts in recent science-fiction history. Clearly the work of a major new talent."
—Lucius Shepard

By Mary Rosenblum
Published by Ballantine Books:

THE DRYLANDS
CHIMERA
THE STONE GARDEN

Chapter One

Dear Mr. Tryon . . . The opening words of the letter ran through Michael Tryon's head again and again, as if they had been engraved on his cortex. *You don't know me. My name is Margarita Espinoza. My mother was Xia Quejaches. You are my father.*

"Of course I could get someone else to restore the Stone," Chris was saying. Her sandals tapped an impatient rhythm on the baking Old Taos sidewalk. "I could call Prosper. This isn't just *any* Major Stone, Michael. This is an Estevan."

Dear Mr. Tryon . . . "Prosper's very good." Michael made an effort to pay attention. "I sculpt Stones; I don't restore them," he said. "Get Prosper." Tourists cluttered the street, decked out in the latest expensive version of southwestern chic. Their enthusiasm made his head ache.

"It's because of Xia Quejaches, isn't it?" Chris caught at his arm. "Is that why you won't do it?"

"No." Or was it? He'd banished that ghost a long time ago. Or so he'd thought. Michael paused, looking down at Chris: pale-haired, brown-eyed Anglo, gallery owner and young enough to . . . "No. It's not because of Xia." He avoided her anxious, angry eyes. "It's because you don't need a sculptor to restore the Estevan. Xia was long ago." *Dear Mr. Tryon . . .* The letter mocked him. "Xia was a long time ago."

"I'm sorry." Chris flushed. "But I *do* need you to do this, Michael. Because you're the best. Because the Archenwald-Shen Stone is damaged. Estevan Majors are masterpieces, and Prosper is a *technician*, damn it."

There was truth there, and that truth snared him. "All right,

Chris." He sighed, his shoulders drooping beneath the dry afternoon heat. "I'll listen to the Estevan. If I tell you that it's nothing worse than superficial distortion, you call Prosper. Agreed?"

"Agreed." Chris stood on tiptoe to kiss him lightly on the cheek. "Thanks, Michael. I appreciate it."

It was hard to say no to her when he hadn't given her anything except Minors and mood groups lately. Majors brought the big money. Struggling with old anger, Michael watched her hurry back toward the gallery. Yes, Xia was part of it, never mind what he'd told Chris. We were close, Estevan and I. Michael swallowed, tasting old bitterness. You wrecked us, Xia. You destroyed us. Her blame, not Estevan's. Once he had blamed them both. Before Estevan had died.

Death, Michael thought bitterly. It forgives so many of our sins. He watched the tourists shuffle past, staring at the smooth adobe walls of the Main Street stores, ogling real leather vests, necklaces, and belts heavy with conchos of silver and rough nuggets of real turquoise. Dressed in newly purchased southwestern clothes—cowboy jeans and chambray shirts this year—they sweated in the dry heat. The streets of Old Taos, property of the Federal Historic Registry, were *hot*. And carefully regulated to the last lizard sunning itself on the plaza stones. No hovercraft overhead, no virtual parlors, no public terminals on the streets. In Old Taos you still got a glass of water beside your plate instead of having to order it from the menu. It was imported iceberg melt, not local of course, and you paid for it when you paid your entry fee. You paid even more for a resident's license, unless you were a desirable artist, in which case the Registry gave you a grant to keep you part of the local scene.

Back in the early years, back when Michael and Estevan had sat on the patio at the inn, drinking beer and ignoring the tourists, the water and the residency had been free. Or at least cheap. That had been a long time ago—long enough to make him feel old. Michael focused on a beautifully muscled youth who was staring with horrified fascination at a Victor Lopez vest woven of goathide and stone beads. Victor had an artisan's license to raise animals for leather and bone.

Judging from his dress, the kid belonged to an inside node—a son or a lover. Michael eyed his natural-fiber singlet, inlays, and makeup. The offspring of some corporate junior exec, perhaps? All set to inherit a position, assured of life with credit and private medical benefits. You want that vest, Michael thought as the kid scuffed his feet. You pretend to be disgusted, but you really want to feel those strips of once-living skin flick against your own perfect hide. You want to savor the hint of blood and death that they will whisper to your body. You want the envious shock that the dead-goat vest will bring to the party faces of your friends.

Death. He'd been searching for hints of it lately—in the grieving of an accident victim's relatives or the tears of a new widower. But grief wasn't death. Grief was a shallow human emotion, muddy with resentment and anger. Michael shook his head, not sure why he was so drawn to it—death. *You're getting old,* a tiny voice whispered in his ear.

No, that wasn't it. The body shops could give him many more years, could keep his own death at bay for a long time. Michael scowled at the node's kid, then moved closer. That horrified, narcissistic lust might be just the note for Small Stone, his youngest Major. He shrugged, then touched the youth lightly on the arm and proffered his small, old-fashioned paper card to the kid's sulky stare.

"Would you be interested in modeling for me?" The kid probably didn't know a Major from a geode. "This isn't some come-on," Michael said as the kid recoiled. "I'm not after your body, just your soul."

The kid's lip curled at this corny line, but it hooked him, and he looked at the card instead of throwing it in Michael's face. Michael waited patiently as he turned the small rectangle over, twisting it, fingering it, waiting for a sound chip to kick in or a holo to appear.

"You're really one of those asteroid artists, huh?" The kid gave up on the card at last and looked up. "Are the rocks really alive? What does a model do?"

A slick accent and a trace of excitement beneath the attitude. Multilingual private school, probably. "I suppose it depends on how you define life." Michael spread his hands. "You relax beside a Stone. I ask you a few questions, and the Stone absorbs some of your emotional broadcast."

"So if someone listens to it later, they'll know what I was thinking?"

Was he wary? "No, no." Michael made his smile reassuring. "A listener is aware of nothing more than a complex harmony—a blend of emotion and sensory input from all the models used." Unless the listener was an untrained sensitive or another sculptor. "The Minor Stones absorb only sensory perceptions. The Majors absorb emotion plus the senses."

"Weird." The kid considered, fingering the expensive dermal inlays that decorated his hairless scalp. "Sure, why not?"

Anything for a thrill. Taos probably bored him to tears. "How about tomorrow afternoon?" Michael kept the smile on his face as he pointed. "Go down Le Doux Street. The studio is at the very end, by the perimeter fence."

The kid nodded and walked away, his narrow hips swaying to the inaudible rhythms pounding through his implanted audio link. Was he right for the Small Stone, after all? Michael sighed, doubting. The slick, plugged-in tourists seemed alien and unreal—untouchable. As if they weren't quite human anymore. Perhaps humanity was evolving into something else, Michael thought. And he had gotten left behind—was that it? Oh, hell. He started down the sunbaked sidewalk. He'd borrow the vest from Dolores—she'd give it to him after closing—and let the kid play with it and see what happened.

Left behind . . . Is that why the Stones aren't working? They're working, Michael told himself, but the resonances he'd added lately all sounded thin and superficial. It was a phase. He was out of sorts because of the dust and summer heat. Things would go better in the fall.

Why death? Why did that elusive note keep drawing him?

Michael tossed the thin gray braid of his hair back over his shoulder, hurrying as if he could outrun the doubts that fluttered in the still afternoon air. The hardcopy printout of the general delivery letter crackled in his pocket, and he flinched.

You are my father. Xia told me last spring. She said that it was a long time ago. That's true. I'm twenty-two . . .

Yes, a long time ago. Xia wasn't pregnant when she left, Michael told himself. If she was, it would have been Estevan's, not his. He should go listen to that Estevan. It would make Chris happy, and then she'd call Prosper. He crossed the dusty street in front of a tour bus. The driver leaned on his horn and glared, but Michael ignored him.

The man who owned the Major, a web node named

Archenwald-Shen, had leased a late-period guest residence out behind the Fechin House. Michael shuffled up the dusty driveway—authentically unpaved and unstabilized. The best of the best hung in the Fechin House Museum: old masterworks in oil and acrylic, kinetic sculpture, scent compositions, and even one of his own Majors. Mr. Archenwald-Shen must be impressively connected to have obtained the lease to the guest house; mere credit wouldn't suffice.

The dappled cool of the real-grass lawn behind the main house welcomed him, and Michael wiped dusty sweat from his face. It had been cooler in the old days. Perhaps the Registry would cover Old Taos with a dome if the climate kept worsening—no expense spared for verisimilitude.

"Mr. Tryon?" A scrawny man with Caucasian features and polished Afro-dark skin popped his head out of the studio door. "I'm honored." He beamed and brushed invisible dust from his badly cut real-silk tunic.

The dark skin was body-shop work. "A good restorer can do a marvelous job with a Major." Michael walked past the man's gloating eyes, not trying to keep the grumble out of his tone.

He knew this man, knew the men and women like him: the ones who ran the Worldweb, living and dying by points made and lost against rival nodes—both economic and social. And this visit would score the man social points. *Ah, yes, my dear. I had Michael Tryon out to touch up my Estevan Major . . .* Michael swallowed a surge of irritation at Chris. Just do this for her. She didn't nag him, even though she had buyers waiting for Majors. Michael glowered at the little exec, whose jowly face seemed too large for his soft, skinny body. *Power,* his face and flab proclaimed. *I'm so Inside that I don't have to be fit and pretty. I can do what I want.* That polished, beautiful skin created a jarring dissonance with his flaccid, unimpressive body.

"If you'll show me the Stone?" Michael snapped.

"Right this way." The small man put a hand on his arm. "I met Mr. Estevan years ago," he said. "Wonderful fellow. He asked me to sit for one of the Stones—a Major. Marvelous experience."

You need a few sour notes in any Major, Michael thought but didn't say. He stepped pointedly from beneath those possessive fingers and followed Archenwald-Shen through the small, low-ceilinged adobe rooms of the guest house.

"I'm thinking of purchasing a Major for my office on New York Up." The exec flicked a whiplash glance over his shoulder. "I find them stimulating and relaxing. One of yours, perhaps?" He bowed as he ushered Michael into what had been decorated as the living room. "I'm afraid I must have missed your latest unveiling."

He hadn't *had* a recent unveiling. Not of a Major. Michael walked past him, wondering if he had underestimated this greasy little node. Maybe that tunic and the dissonance between skin and muscle were intentional. If so, the man was subtle. Michael wondered just what his game was.

The Stone stopped him just inside the door, banishing all thought. Nearly five feet tall, it dominated the room from its carefully lighted corner. Michael sighed and let its broadcast sweep him away—the weary pleasure of twilight, the press of a rock against his thighs, sweet fatigue, graced with the high, clear energy of young eyes watching morning sunlight.

Tree Stone. He recognized it instantly.

Michael closed his eyes, Estevan's folded, weathered face vivid against the screen of his eyelids. Sometimes, in the presence of a Stone, he felt as if he could reach through the barrier of time itself to touch yesterday—not the memory of yesterday but the moment of love, or fatigue, or grief itself. If he reached out right now, this minute, his hands would find the familiar down-curving shoulders and he would hear Estevan's soft chuckle as Michael kissed him on both cheeks. *Such passion, M'kile. You make me feel old.*

Michael's eyelids fluttered, and the moment fled. You weren't old, Estevan. He struggled against the grief that threatened to choke him, grief as sharp and bitter as it had been on the day he'd gotten the call. You weren't much older than me—such a waste, our silence. Such a terrible waste.

Do we know the value of what we discard only when it's too late? Michael opened his eyes, putting that grief aside, wondering if its jagged edges would ever wear smooth and familiar. Focusing, he groped for the distortion that the little exec had complained about and winced as a shrill echo pierced him. Raw, unfiltered emotion disturbed the perfect harmony of the Stone, rasping against mental nerve endings like fork tines across a china plate. Michael laid his hand on top of the mottled gray curve of the Stone's surface. It felt dense, alive, not like dead rock at all. Petrified flesh. That's what he had thought the first time he'd touched a Stone—an alien, Medusa-frozen soul set adrift in the void.

Archenwald-Shen cleared his throat. "Is it all right?"

Michael started and took his hand away. "Of course it's not all right."

"When we bought it, the agent assured us that they wouldn't distort on display."

He was poised for righteous anger, waiting for Michael's cue to storm, and rant, and threaten a lawsuit. Michael wondered if Archenwald-Shen would offer to pay him to testify as an expert witness. His lip curled. "Stones don't distort seriously if they're not wakened by a sculptor. Casual contact doesn't have much effect, although a natural sensitive can accidentally waken a Stone and allow it to absorb some amount of local emotion." No one had ever defined that ability. It wasn't hereditary, couldn't be tested for. Except by a Stone's response or lack of it. "Are you a natural sensitive?" he asked.

"No."

Michael felt rather than saw the exec's small flinch. Ah, so? "Please leave the room while I evaluate the Stone," he said abruptly. "I need total privacy."

The little man flushed at Michael's tone, dark skin darkening still more, his Adam's apple twitching with swallowed anger. "How long will it take?" he asked in a tightly controlled voice.

"I don't know. If you'll excuse me."

The exec's stiff-legged exit broadcast stifled affront. Was he weighing the cocktail-party points against Michael's insolence? Trying to decide if he was worth it? Well, to hell with him. Michael shrugged, banishing him. He closed his eyes and breathed in and out once, slowly, focusing on the Stone as he passed his hands gently across its fine, dense grain. Estevan had spent twenty years creating Tree Stone, blending perfect moments of human emotion to create a symphony of human peace. Michael himself had leaned against the awakened Stone for Estevan one sunny afternoon, letting it absorb his drowsy lethargy after a passionate noon of lovemaking with Xia.

You don't know me, but Xia Quejaches was my mother . . .

Wisps of blue-green and amber seemed to swirl, coalesce, and dissolve on the Stone's surface. The room faded. Michael caught a glimpse of a Hispanic face, a boy, shadow-eyed and sad; he felt the cool touch of lotion on sunburned skin, smelled the tang of horse manure drifting on hot afternoon air, felt a twinge of bittersweet pain: *Do I have to throw things, Estevan?* A woman wept in the Stone's song. *Do I have to kill him to make him realize how much I love him?*

"Xia?" Michael's eyes snapped open, but her voice was gone, drowned by the screech of discord that he had noticed earlier.

Distant shouting echoed in his head, barbed with violence. Michael clenched his teeth, picking out the individual notes of harsh dissonance. An ordinary listener would feel only the fingernail scrape of discord; he was a sculptor. Holding his anger in check, Michael unraveled the blaring notes from the whole. They resolved into physical pain and a dark, twisted thread that might be hatred or even love. For an instant a face took shape in Michael's vision, male and mostly Asian with exquisitely molded cheekbones and grass-green eyes. This was Old Taos, and Michael knew Archenwald-Shen's lover when he saw him, had heard the rumors about their fights.

Michael lifted his hands from the Stone's warm surface, breathing too fast, feeling sweaty and light-headed with anger. Slowly the Stone's resonances faded to a subtle whisper again. Twenty years Estevan had spent creating this song of the human soul. For what end? So that some greedy little web node could treat it like so much bric-a-brac?

Why had Estevan worked with Stones? What had they meant to him? It came to Michael suddenly that he'd never asked Estevan. Or himself.

But this wasn't the time. As Michael stomped out of the house, Archenwald-Shen scurried down the dusty driveway after him. "Well?" he panted, his composure lost in the hot afternoon glare. "Is it all right?"

"The Stone has been damaged." Michael rounded on him, strangely light suddenly, full of words like hot gases that threatened to lift him from his feet or explode, shattering him into a million pieces. "I'm going to fix it. I'll be coming in and out with models." Xia had modeled for that Stone. *Do I have to throw things, Estevan?*

No, no, she couldn't have said that. That wasn't how it had happened.

"You mean in here? What kind of models? Security has to run a check on them first, and we're giving a dinner party next Thursday. Will you be finished by then?"

"To hell with your party." The hot, light words seemed to lift him from his feet. "This is *Tree Stone*. Beat your damn lover somewhere else." Michael turned his back on the man, drunk and dizzy with the freedom of his words, while a small part of his mind screamed that he'd been a fool, that the node would fire him and Tree Stone would remain forever damaged or patched by a technician like Prosper.

And did it matter? Estevan was dead. Did he care who did or didn't own his Stones or what they did to them?

Michael cared. He marched down the drive beneath Security's invisible stare. He'd fix Tree Stone, and Security be damned.

Do I have to throw things?

Xia's whisper pursued him. The letter might have been a spell, conjuring ghosts and this craziness from the depths of Estevan's stone. You didn't love me, Michael thought. You were jealous of the Stones. I *remember*. Michael shoved his hand into his pocket, savagely crumpling the hardcopy. The air smelled of dust and no rain as Michael headed for the Taos Inn. It always smelled of dust this time of year. The Registry wouldn't have it any other way.

Chris tracked him down in his corner booth. She twisted her way between the crowded tables, her short-cropped hair shining in the dim light like a stray shaft of afternoon sunlight. Two beer bottles and a single glass clinked in her hand.

"Thank you. For going to see the Estevan." She plunked the dewy bottles down on the table and slid onto the bench across from him.

So the node hadn't complained. Maybe he didn't want to admit that Michael Tryon had told him to fuck off. "*De nada.*" Michael picked up one of the bottles.

The adobe walls of the inn, sunbaked mud flecked with golden straw, held in a faint echo of the morning cool. No air-conditioning for the inn. Nothing had changed in the decades Michael had lived here. Xia could be out on the patio, silver earrings gleaming against her dusky skin and the dark curtain of her hair, laughing at one of Estevan's sly jokes. Michael twisted the cap from his beer. "Archenwald-Shen is a prick. Did you know that?" He drank from the bottle, belched. "How did *he* end up with Tree Stone?"

"He paid for it. Yeah, he's a prick, and a very rich one. What's with you?" Chris eyed the already-empty bottles, then poured amber and foam down the side of her tilted glass. "He wants to buy one of your Majors, by the way."

"He told me." Michael laughed sourly. "I thought he might have changed his mind."

"You're in a mood today." She made her voice light, but her eyes were worried. "That Minor you brought over is wonderful. If I close my eyes, I'm sitting in the sun on the bank of the Hondo. The brewing thunderstorm is a masterstroke, Michael. You keep getting better. I can't wait for the next Major."

She was trying to make him feel better, cheer him up. Keep the golden goose laying . . . But that was unfair. Chris cared about the art she sold. She cared about the artists. "I'm sorry." Michael set his beer down and sighed. "I think I'm a little drunk. You want to know if Sun Stone's finished, right?"

"Well . . . yes. Buyers are not patient people, and you said it was getting close."

"It is." He'd been saying "close" for a year, and they both knew it.

Chris tilted her head so that her white-blond hair fell down over one eye, and Michael looked away, stabbed by sudden memory. Xia had tilted her head the same way. Sometimes Chris reminded him of Xia, even though her silver hair and ivory skin were the opposite of Xia's darkness. Xia had claimed to be from Guatemala, a Lacandon Maya. The LA barrio was more likely. It's the eyes, Michael realized suddenly. Chris's were brown and depthless, like summer pools in the Hondo. Like Xia's. "Sun Stone might be ready next month." Chris's eyes dragged the words out of him.

"That soon? That's wonderful."

"I said it *might* be ready." Michael drained the last of his beer and signaled for another. "I'm not satisfied with its upper-end grace notes."

She said you didn't know, that it was a long time ago . . .

So Xia was still alive? He had come to assume that she was

dead, like Estevan. If she was alive, she would be in her forties. He couldn't imagine Xia aging; he wondered if she had purchased perpetual youth from the body shops. He pulled the crumpled letter out of his pocket and tossed it onto the table.

Chris picked it up, smoothed it out, and read it, her eyebrows arching slowly. "Oh, Michael." She laid the paper down as if it were made from butterfly wings or as if it were a bomb ready to explode. "Could it . . . be true?"

"No." Michael looked away from her dark, shocked eyes. "She's Estevan's," he said. "Or someone else's." Margarita Espinoza. A father's name?

"She's rather abrupt." Chris frowned at the letter. "Staying at the Albuquerque Hilton until Sunday, huh? Are you going to go see her? It's probably some kind of scam, Michael. You're pretty famous. I bet she didn't bring along her gene scan."

Chris was angry. Michael frowned, wondering where that anger came from. "I don't know if I'll go. I can't work for a week after I've been in the city." The city had eaten Estevan, chewed him up in its metal and plastic jaws. His wasted talent stained its streets like old dry blood. "I'll call her and tell her she's mistaken." He folded the flimsy sheet of hardcopy. Why now? Why this, after all these years? What do you want from me, Xia? he asked silently. Are you alive? Are you a ghost, sending this child to haunt me?

"I'm sorry." Chris's hand closed on his. "I'm sorry this came down on you out of the blue. Even if it's a scam, it's got to hurt. Do you want me to have the gallery lawyer handle it?" Her eyes sought his. "It might be better. I can call him right after lunch."

That might be best. Michael hesitated, then shrugged. "No, I'll handle it. She's not threatening to sue."

"Not yet." Chris glared at the beer bottles that littered the table. "Let me know if I can do anything, okay?" She slid out of the booth, her posture stiff, still resonant with anger. "I have to get back to the gallery. Aretha's learning, but she still can't tell one Barkenson from another."

Who can? Michael thought irritably. The damn light shows all looked alike. "Go save your assistant from Barkenson confusion. I'll work on Sun Stone," he said without enthusiasm.

"Great. I'm waiting." She touched his cheek lightly and hurried away.

Michael felt a twinge of guilt as he left the inn. Chris's gallery wasn't doing well, no matter that she busted her ass. It wasn't entirely her fault, although she had made one or two bad bets on local talent. The people who had the money for art seemed to be getting more and more conservative as the years went by, less willing to risk money on new names. And Chris was young. Truly young, not body-shop young—as young as Xia had been when she first arrived in town, a performance artist working with a mixed-media troupe.

Nearly as young as Margarita Espinoza.

Michael passed the last of the adobe shops and turned down the cracked asphalt path that led to his studio. The squat adobe building stood a scant five meters from the chain-link and razor-wire perimeter fence. The red and black seal of the Federal Historic Registry glared out at the dry hills and the waterless *acequia* that had been hand-dug centuries earlier. No entry here. Not to the present. Walk around to the gate, surrender your video equipment, pay your fee, and you can visit Old Taos.

"I live in an egg," Michael said out loud. "Full of the yolk of the past." A thousand-year-old egg buried in the manure heap of the present. Two magpies lifted from the shade of the old cottonwood that shaded his tiny adobe studio, flapping heavily into the branches. "This fence is a shell," he told them, but they preened without answering, not interested in shell or egg unless it cracked and stank in the sun.

This petrified egg had hatched a cuckoo's chick—Xia's anguished whisper from the past. When had she wept those words to Estevan's Stone? When?

No, the cuckoo's chick was Margarita Espinoza. Who are you? Michael asked the cottonwood shadows. My DNA, wrapped in a stranger's flesh? And does it matter after all this time? The crows flew away with a disdainful croak, and the cottonwood didn't answer. I *am* in a mood, Michael told himself, and veered toward the back of the studio and his Stone garden, where sun and cottonwood shade dappled the rocks and wiry grass. The Minors were grouped by themselves, in singles or chords of contrasting moods, small and silver gray, like strange eggs themselves, drowsing in the hot sun. The Majors stood apart, shadows of Stonehenge, dreams of Easter Island, individuals. They aged and matured as the sun wheeled overhead, absorbing the hopes and dreams and fears Michael wove into them, note by human note.

Michael sighed as the subtle harmonies of the Stones enveloped him. He spent hours here, listening to the unawakened Stones, letting their sensual and emotional resonances suggest new themes and counterpoints. Now he dropped his tattered cushion in front of Sun Stone and knelt slowly, wincing at the stiffness in his knees, his inner turmoil dissolving in the soft murmur of the Stones. Gently he stroked Sun Stone's smooth surface, felt its ripple of response.

Not everyone could be a sculptor—it took more than a pat to wake a Stone, to weave the themes of love and pain, the variations of summer heat and fatigue, into the Stone's musing song. *The woof comes from the model,* Estevan used to say. *The warp is strung from the sculptor's soul.* Michael closed his eyes, remembering his excitement the first time he had wakened a Minor under Anya's critical eye. She had been one of the first sculptors—and yes, he was better than she had ever been. That would make her happy, he thought, and felt a pang of loss for her easy humor. She had died long ago, before he'd won the Registry grant. He'd arrived in Taos on a summer afternoon, full of restless energy and grief for Anya's death, a rising star in the hot new art of Stone sculpture.

He had found Estevan drinking beer in the Taos Inn, an empty chair across from him as if he had been waiting for Michael to show up.

Perhaps Estevan *had* been waiting. Their Stones had never been alike, although they had influenced each other. Michael leaned his forehead against the Stone, an alien chunk of asteroid, a Medusa soul thirsty for lust/anger/love. "Tempestuous," the critics had said of Michael's early Stones. "Impassioned." When they talked about Estevan's Majors, they spoke of balance and focus.

Balance. He and Estevan had struck a delicate balance, not quite lovers, more than friends: a blend of love and friendship and rivalry. Then Xia had come along with her river-pool eyes and her midnight hair. At first the balance had shifted to a triad, even though she had been only Michael's lover. The echoes of that time ran through the murmur of the Stones, bright as a vein of gold in the hot, still air. Their muted chords swept him away, the rumble of thunder, the sweet scratch of fingernails on love-heated skin, the scent of rain on dust and freshly washed hair. I remember . . .

The pain in his knees and the glare of sunlight in his eyes finally roused him. Dozing? Michael got stiffly to his feet. Dreaming of Xia? The beginnings of a headache pulsed at the base of his skull, and Michael blinked as the last beams of the setting sun dazzled his eyes. Ah, Xia. The storms had arrived eventually, and finally had come the winter-afternoon finality of the empty studio, the bed neatly made, the absence of her clothes and possessions a shout in the cold twilight.

I never suspected. Michael winced as a rock rolled beneath his foot and pain twinged up his leg. Here, in Old Taos, he should have heard. Everyone must have known about her and Estevan. It had hurt when he'd found out where she had gone. The news had stunned him. *That* news had reached him less than an hour after she had walked through Estevan's door. I never guessed, he thought now, and closed his eyes. Which had hurt more—Xia's betrayal or Estevan's? I never guessed that he and Xia . . . "You're not my daughter," he said aloud. "You can't be."

The next morning Michael went looking for Cecelia Lujan, one of his regular models. He found her in the state-goods store, price-tagging melons that she couldn't possibly afford on her Registry salary and grieving gently.

"Carl again?" he asked her as he fingered the drip-irrigated melons.

"We had a fight, and he didn't come home after the rodeo dance last night."

Carl worked for State Water and pulled extra money as a Registry "local" after hours. He mingled with the tourists, dressed in jeans, shirt, and real-leather boots, his implants and tattoos disguised with makeup.

"I'd forgotten that this was rodeo weekend." Michael sniffed the netted rind of a cantaloupe, then tucked it carefully into his wire cart.

"I wish *I* could forget. The town's bulging at the seams, and I'm putting in double overtime at the hotel and the inn." Cecelia was a full-time Registry employee, Pueblo in face, mostly Basque and Chicano in ancestry. "I don't know when I'm going to have time for Carl, and he's going to think I'm pissed just because he went home with Maria." She pushed black hair back from her broad face, not angry at Carl, just sad at the inevitable misunderstanding.

Cecelia was the most forgiving woman Michael had ever known, and not out of fear or need. She got angry honestly and could deck you while in a rage, but she forgave honestly and completely. Michael put his arm around her, catching a whiff of sweat and woman smell. "Do you have time for a modeling job? It shouldn't take more than an hour. I'll add a bribe to the regular rate," he added as she started to shake her head, and picked the cantaloupe out of his basket.

Cecelia laughed. "I'll take it. Carl loves cants—but I've got to be over at the inn by ten."

"No problem." Michael unloaded his scant groceries—and the melon—onto the checkout conveyor and ran his card through the slot in the register. Not even the Registry could force the state-goods store to go back to human checkers and cash.

Cecelia was waiting for him at the exit. He picked up his plastic bag of groceries in one hand and tucked the melon under his arm. "When are you going to invite Chris to bed?" she asked on the way across the small parking lot. "It must be really tough on her, having the girl show up like that—Xia's kid."

"My *dear*." Michael almost dropped his groceries.

"Oh, stop." Cecelia tossed her head. "This is Old Taos, remember? The letter showed up in the PO's general delivery file, and Maria Torres prints out general delivery. Maria's got the biggest mouth in town. What do you expect?"

What, indeed? "Does everybody in Taos know all of my business? As for Chris, we're friends, and that's all. How can you . . ." He shook his head, a little dazed. "That letter has nothing to do with her at all."

"Maria doesn't pass on *all* your business. Just the parts that matter to your friends. I like Chris." Cecelia's dark eyes considered. "Maybe you ought to look up from your rocks once in a while, huh?"

Chris? No. Well, maybe she did act kind of interested sometimes, but she was so damn *young*.

Well, he'd been sixty when Xia had shown up in town, and she had been in her twenties. Michael shifted the grocery bag to his other hand, uncomfortable suddenly. Yeah, Chris had a thing for him, and he hadn't wanted to know it. What else was he hiding from himself? He wasn't sure he wanted to know that, either. "If you have to be at the inn by ten, we'd better hurry," he said.

Mercifully, the Archenwald-Shen house seemed deserted except for the intangible shadow of Security. Michael left his groceries and Cecelia's melon bribe in the thoroughly modernized kitchenette, feeling sweaty and too tired from their short walk.

He was getting old, in spite of the body shop. Not flesh old. He might be in his eighties, but his body was that of a fifty-year-old. He still felt old. Michael closed his eyes briefly, clearing his mind, readying himself. Cecelia had already settled herself against Tree Stone. She had modeled for him many times, a reliable source of warmth and sex. Eyes closed, head tilted back against the Stone's cool bulk; her breathing had already slowed. He didn't have to put her in a trance anymore. Michael squatted beside her. Some of the new young sculptors used drugs and virtual suggestion on their models, never mind that the chemical fuzz blurred the final resonance. They did it for speed—so that they could produce a mature Major in five years instead of twenty or thirty.

Factories. Michael suppressed the flash of his disdain, calming himself again. Think about Tree Stone . . . listen . . . The touch of his palm roused the Stone, and Michael shivered with the familiar rush of heightened awareness. The scientists talked about synchronized wave patterns and alpha-state harmonics; all Michael knew was that, once awake, a Stone merged with you—alien-asteroid lover, drinker of dreams. Michael closed his eyes, intensely aware of Cecelia, of her fatigue, the small ache of her full bladder, the low murmur of her emotions.

"Tell me about Carl," he whispered. "He was a shit last night. You yelled at each other."

"He was a real bastard, picking a fight because there wasn't any food in the house, when we'd both put in a twenty-hour day already. He was just horny for Maria, he could have said so, but he had to do it his macho way, you know."

She was a little apologetic because she had participated wholeheartedly in the screaming heat of the fight, wasn't angry anymore, was amused/exasperated at Carl's games, forgiving, ready to heal the break . . .

Just what Tree Stone needed.

"I mean, he's such a *kid* sometimes. You know, all pissed off and yelling at me, when he's really mad at himself because he's feeling guilty about wanting Maria. You know the temper I got . . ."

The warp is strung from the sculptor's soul, Estevan had said. *The woof comes from the model.* Tree Stone drank as Michael unraveled Cecelia's emotion thread by thread: the love beneath the fighting, Michael's awareness of that love as the solid base that had kept Carl and Cecelia together in this tight little microcosm of a town for twelve years now, no matter whose beds they had spent time in. Slowly he wove these threads of love, understanding, and forgiveness into the torn fabric of Tree Stone. Gradually the dissonance faded, jagged edges smoothing into harmony. Carl's face filled his mind, too young and grinning, Cecelia's image of her lover. Michael let it soak into the Stone. Not too strong . . . He lifted his palm, felt the electric buzz of separation, felt the Stone sink back into slumber. "Thanks, Cecelia," he said softly.

"That's it?" She shook back her hair, got to her feet, and yawned. "Let me know when you need me again. And thanks for the melon."

Michael listened to the fading sound of her steps, heard the front door close. Tired from the contact, half drowsing, he let the Stone's resonances lift him on a gentle swell of sense and emotion, a slow tidal rhythm of life. Half-seen glimpses of faces, sagebrush, chamisa, and piñon pine flitted through his brain, redolent with gentle memory. He saw a shallow summer river, with watercress among the rocks. The Hondo. They'd picnicked there often, he and Xia. She'd found the polished skull of a goat there one afternoon. Neanderthal goat, she'd called it, and had hung it on the wall of the studio. It still hung there, as smooth and yellowed as old ivory.

With a guilty twitch, Michael realized that he was searching for Xia in Tree Stone, was sifting through resonances as he might sift through a lapful of autumn leaves, searching for that one bit of perfect gold. You didn't *do* this to another sculptor's Stone. Feeling like a voyeur, a Peeping Tom peering through the windows of Estevan's creativity, he started to get up.

And Xia was suddenly *there*, a whisper of presence that made him shiver with the need to reach out and touch her. Feet gathered awkwardly beneath him, Michael crouched, frozen still.

No matter what I do, he shuts me out, Estevan, hides himself in his damned stones. Do I have to throw things? Do I have to kill him to make him realize how much I love him?

"That's not how it was!" Startled by the sound of his own voice, Michael toppled over, banging his knee painfully on the tiled floor. That wasn't it at all. She had been bitter and bitchy because her career as a dancer had been floundering and his star had been rising. She had demanded all his attention, had been spiteful when he had worked on the Stones, hurting him with barbed words, driving him away.

Kneeling on the floor, Michael tried to find her again, but her voice stayed lost, the single note of a moment vanished in a symphony of decades. Shamelessly, Michael hunted through the resonances and found a moment of rich pain when Estevan said, *Yes, yes, you can stay here, but it's going to hurt M'Kile and it will solve nothing. Why must the two of you tear me between you?*

No. Estevan had betrayed him, had betrayed their friendship. This wasn't how it had happened. Michael fled the studio, running down the graveled drive, the years flying about his head like dry leaves. He grasped at them, but they kept slipping between his fingers. *He stole her from me. She betrayed me.* He had turned his back on their betrayal, had poured his hurt and rage into the Stones. "Impassioned," the critics had raved. "Tempestuous."

Xia had left Estevan after a single month, had left Taos. Michael slowed to a stop on the sidewalk, pierced by tourist stares. He ignored them, aware of their curiosity, disapproval, and a sly tweak of amusement because they thought he was drunk, or drugged out, or just crazy. Sweating, head up, he walked back to his studio. Eventually he and Estevan had become friends again—not the same as before but not enemies, either. Estevan had tried to talk about Xia but had finally given up. That silence had grown between them until it had blocked out everything except the empty clatter of trivial words. Sometimes Michael wondered if that silence had finally driven

Estevan to Albuquerque. "It wasn't my fault," Michael whispered. "You hurt *me*."

Hurt. Michael had felt hurt in the Stone's Xia. He had felt Estevan's grief for their broken friendship.

No, no, their doing, their wrong. Not mine. I *remember*.

The Stones remembered, Medusa flesh of frozen souls. Could you lie to a Stone? Could a Stone lie?

But I *remember* . . .

Michael's feet kept wanting to walk faster, to break into a run. As if he could outrun the echoes. By the time he reached his studio, he was breathing in quick, searing gasps. Sweat ran down his face to stick wisps of hair to his neck. Heat hung in the dusty shadow beneath the cottonwood, and the Stones baked silently in his garden. He paused by Small Stone, feeling its shallow youth. It was his youngest Major. He had begun it how long ago—four years?

"Hey." A figure emerged from the cottonwood's shadow. "I was just about to take off."

Michael stared blankly at the youth walking toward him.

"Remember?" Sunlight glinted on his scalp inlays. "You asked me to come by and be a model for one of these." He jerked his head at the Stones.

"Oh. Yes," Michael said thickly.

"Hey, you okay?"

"Yes, yes, I'm fine." Michael turned away from the kid's shop-perfect face and laid his palms on Sun Stone. It felt more than warm beneath his hands, fever hot, and its resonances soaked into him; the sting of sweat salt on lips, the ache of wrists tired from weeding. Xia's garden. Xia's young muscles. He remembered those notes, remembered the afternoon he had wakened Sun Stone to drink her gentle weariness . . .

Sun Stone remembered.

I loved you, Xia. I loved you more than I've ever loved anything. I never hurt you. I didn't deserve what you did to me . . . You and Estevan. Why couldn't he find those resonances in the Stone? They had to be there. He *remembered* . . .

"What do you guys get out of these?" The youth peered into Michael's face. "I mean, you're the ones who do this stuff. What's it like for you right now?"

"What do *I* get out of this?" Michael laughed a single cracked note that made the boy recoil. "Do you really think you remember yesterday? All its pain? Maybe we change everything; maybe our past is all our own construction." The kid was staring at him—maybe he didn't have any pain to not remember. "Here." Michael crossed the garden in four long strides and snatched the goat vest from where it hung on his studio porch. "Come here." He grabbed the kid by the arm and dragged him over to Small Stone, not bothering to be gentle. "Sit." He shoved him down beside the Stone, flinging the goatskin vest into his lap. "Play with it," he breathed. The Stone woke to his hand, responding, absorbing. "Feel it. That's an animal skin—it's as soft and supple as your own. Someone peeled it off that goat's body, fists twisted in hair and slick, bloody membranes, yanking at it, *pulling*." He stared down into the kid's upturned face, breathing fast, his fists clenched. "Muscles twitched as that skin tore away, all red-raw and bloody. Maybe . . . that animal could still feel," he said softly. "Maybe a part of its brain was still aware, screaming, locked in silence."

The boy stared up at him, eyes wide, the goatskin twisted in his clenched fists, lusting for blood and pain, *wanting* it . . .

"You're that goat," Michael whispered. "It's *your* hide peeling back, *your* blood seeping into the sand, legs thrashing as you die trying to run, trying to get away . . . how does it *feel*?"

"Jesus." The pink tip of the kid's tongue slid across his pale lips. "That's . . . gross."

"You want it." Michael picked up a corner of the vest and stroked the kid's cheek with it slowly, sensuously. "You want to feel that pain. You want it . . ."

"Knock it off." The kid jerked away and stumbled to his feet, slapping the vest away, his face slick with sweat. "You're weird, some kind of perv, man." He stumbled backward, shoulders hunched and tight. "Whatever the fuck you want, I don't play."

Michael stared after him as he bolted through the garden and vanished around the side of the studio. Why did I do that? he wondered as he bent to retrieve the fallen vest. His hands were trembling, and he slapped the dust from the skin with sudden rage. What effect had he been trying for? Some note of juvenile S and M blood lust? He hadn't even put the boy into a trance, and this wasn't the kind of note Small Stone needed, anyway.

Or maybe it was. He draped the vest over one shoulder. The critics didn't call his Stones tempestuous anymore. "Measured." That was the word. "Sustained."

Small Stone drowsed in the sun, the cymbal clash of the boy's horror/lust/fear resonating through its muted song. Is this your blood, Estevan? Is that what I've just splashed onto this Stone? What was it like to see that train coming and know that you were going to die? How did it feel? Michael realized he was scrubbing his palms on his pants. As if they were dirty—or stained with blood.

Goat blood or Estevan's?

"Is this a bad time? Am I interrupting?" Archenwald-Shen smirked at him from the shade of the porch. "Ms. Neiman couldn't reach you on your terminal, so I thought I'd drop around. I hope you don't mind." His tone made it a rhetorical question.

How long had he been standing there?

"What do you want?" Michael asked.

"I want to buy one of your Majors. For my office." He looked around the garden, his eyes hungry. "She said that you might be finished with one soon. I'm willing to pay for it in advance."

Sun Stone was finished. Sun Stone hadn't changed appreciably in years. Sun Stone was Xia, before the betrayal, before she left. And he didn't want to let it go. "I'm sorry." Michael looked away, his voice as harsh as a magpie's squawk. "I don't work on commission, and I have no finished Majors to sell."

The little exec's eyes belied his smile. "I'm sorry to hear that. It's been, what . . . six years since your last Major was unveiled?"

It had been longer than that, and Michael wondered suddenly if the little node knew that and had been wrong on purpose. "Majors take time," he said, and heard the defensive note in his tone.

The node heard it, too, and his smile turned creamy and sleek. "Danners's latest Stone was a sensation up on New Tokyo," he purred. "He works in a subsea dome. I understand that he gets some marvelous resonances from dead corals. His latest Major was only seven years old."

No, he wasn't stupid, this flabby little node. He knew how

to hurt. Michael showed his teeth. "Danners drugs his models. He's in a rush."

"The critics love him." Archenwald-Shen smiled at him. " 'A strong new voice,' they called him, if I remember correctly. 'A sculptor for our time.' "

"I'm sorry." Trapped between Sun Stone's Xia song and the raw new notes he'd just woven into Small Stone, Michael struggled for calm. "I'm . . . in the middle of something. You'll have to leave." There was no power behind his anger, only fear.

Archenwald-Shen heard that, too, and smiled gently. "I'll leave you to your work. I'm sorry that I'll have to settle for a Danners." He bowed and walked down the driveway, still smiling, as if he had won a contest. Perhaps he had. Michael turned away, his skin feeling stiff beneath his sweaty clothes, as brittle as sunbaked plastic.

The youth's blood lust and horror clawed at him from Small Stone. Why did I do that? Michael stopped in front of it, not touching it. Because Small Stone was dull. Flat. That horrified note of blood lust had the feel of . . . desperation. *The warp is strung from the sculptor's soul.*

Can a sculptor run out of soul, Estevan? Is it a finite quantity? What happens if we keep the body alive beyond the soul? What is left? Can you tell me?

Why did you die?

Silence. The Stones drowsed, filling the hot air with the echoes of a hundred lives—notes of laughter, weary talk in the cool morning darkness, whispered moments of love and friendship. Fragments of the past drifted on the air like scraps of torn paper. Michael could feel Old Taos drowsing, frozen to unchanging Medusa stone by the Registry, a Brigadoonlike bit of the past. He shuddered, hearing Xia's sigh in Sun Stone's music. She is real, he thought. Here, in this garden, at this moment, Xia—young media dancer, his lover, Xia. This Xia, captured here forever in his garden, had never left him, never abandoned him. She was more real than the daughter who waited for his call in an Albuquerque hotel.

You are my father.

Stumbling a little on the sunbaked dirt, Michael went back to his studio. The goat skull gleamed on the wall above his couch. Michael blinked, his eyes adjusting slowly after the hot glare of sunlight. Hands trembling a little, he touched his terminal's screen and watched it shimmer to life. She couldn't be his, but he owed her this much, this ghost child from a past that wasn't his.

"Albuquerque Hilton." A woman's too-perfect face appeared on the screen, smiling helpfully.

A video construct. Perhaps there were no real people left in the world, just two-dimensional shadows constructed of greed or ordered electrons. "I . . . was trying to reach Ms. Margarita Espinoza. I don't know her room number." Michael's voice cracked, and sweat prickled in his armpits. In a moment her face would appear on the screen: Margarita Espinoza. What would he see? Traces of Xia? Of Estevan?

He would have to ask her—ask her if Xia was alive.

"I'm sorry." The woman's perfect face reflected genuine sorrow. "Ms. Espinoza checked out very early this morning. Is there anything else I can do for you?"

Checked out? Michael felt his blood settle coldly into his stomach. *I will be staying at the Albuquerque Hilton until Sunday. In case you wish to contact me.* This was only Saturday afternoon.

"Sir? Is there anything else that I can do for you?"

"Do you have her address?" Michael croaked. "A personal code?"

"I'm sorry, sir. We cannot divulge that information."

"This is an emergency."

"I'm sorry, sir."

"Damn you . . ."

The construct vanished, and Michael slammed his fist against the screen. Gone? How could she do that, just leave? How could she? I don't even know where the hell she lives, he raged. I don't know if Xia's alive. I don't know anything.

I don't even know if she's my daughter.

He leaned against the terminal, breathing fast. Xia had stayed with Estevan for only a month before she had left Taos. Had she been pregnant on that winter afternoon?

I am afraid. Michael wrapped his arms about himself as if the air had turned suddenly cold. Why am I afraid of this ghost child? He turned his back on the terminal and moved randomly around the studio, picking things up, putting them down again. His hands fumbled, knocking a book from the shelf. He felt numb, as if the nerve endings in his skin had suddenly died. When he bent to retrieve the fallen book, the words of the title had become meaningless lines of ink. He replaced it carefully. The goat skull hung on the wall above the shelf—the Neanderthal goat. He had used the resonances of that picnic afternoon in Sun Stone. It was out there in the garden, sun and love and the smooth old-ivory feel of bone beneath Xia's fingers. It was *there*. Yesterday, not a remembered moment but the real thing. His garden was full of yesterdays.

Hands trembling, Michael took the skull down from its nail.

"Michael?" Chris looked up from her desk with a start. "I was just leaving a message on your terminal. You should have told me that you were sending Sun Stone. I just about fell over when they carried it in. I didn't even have a place for it."

"It was a . . . sudden decision." Michael didn't look at her; he couldn't tear his eyes from Sun Stone. She had set it in front of a bone-white flat and lighted it artfully. "Winter Stone, Dark Stone, and Dawn Stone are ready, too," he said heavily.

"Michael?" Chris came around from behind her desk, worry spiking her tone. "Are you sure? I mean . . . I thought they weren't finished yet."

"They've been finished for years."

"I didn't send Archenwald-Shen out to your studio." Chris laid a hand on his arm. "Please believe me. I was furious when he told me, and I let him know it. Which means he'll probably start dealing with the Crichlow Gallery, but what the hell. I'm so sorry he bothered you . . ." Her eyes strayed to the door, focusing on the carryall he had left there. "What's this?" Her face went pale. "You're going to see her, aren't you? This . . . woman?"

"She left." Michael looked away, trying to shut out Sun Stone's gentle murmur of sun and Xia. "I'm going to find her. I need to meet her, Chris. Because she's *today*, not yesterday. Can you understand?" he asked, and heard the note of pleading in his tone.

"No, I do not understand." Chris's voice had gone soft. "When are you coming back? What exactly are you trying to tell me?"

"I . . . don't know when I'm coming back."

For the space of three heartbeats Chris simply stared at him.

"Xia walked out of your life more than twenty years ago." Her words were soft, sibilant, barely above a whisper. "You don't know that this woman is your daughter. She didn't send you a DNA record. All she did was snap her fingers, and now you're going to go running off on some goddamn wild-goose chase. Michael, this is *stupid*."

Michael blinked at her, Sun Stone's song drowned by the sound of tears in Chris's voice. I shouldn't have let this happen, he thought. I should have stopped this. "It's not just Xia or Margarita Espinoza," he said gently. "I was happy with my ghosts." Old Taos was an egg, perfect and impenetrable. It would never hatch into an ugly duckling, or a vulture, or a peacock. It would never hatch. "I've been here too long." He touched Chris's face, aching for the hurt in her eyes. "I'm sorry."

"Don't be sorry." She slapped his hand away. "You don't have anything to be sorry about. I'm not in love with you, Michael Tryon." She glared at him, lips tight. "Do you think you're going to find your lover of twenty years ago? Do you think she's going to be the same woman, that you're going to just move in, pick up where you left off, and live in some wonderful never-never land?"

Michael shook his head, silenced by her anger and pain.

"Don't go." Chris clutched his hand, her eyes on his face, brown as a summer pool in the Hondo. "Michael, your Minors are the very best. Why are you *doing* this?"

The cities terrified him. Their implanted and tattooed crowds, wired in and inaccessible, choked him, drowned him in silence and noise. They would eat him as they'd eaten Estevan. Michael shivered, then walked over to lay his hand on Sun Stone. The dry heat of sunset enfolded him, spicy with piñon and the promise of twilight coolness. Chris was right about the Minors. He could stay here. She would love him, if he let her. Maybe she already did.

I love you, Xia whispered in Sun Stone's song.

Only the Stones truly remember. Humans are imperfect instruments, and memory is a distorted thing. Who was the Michael Tryon that Xia remembered? *Do I have to throw things . . . ?*

"I've walled myself in with my own past," he said. "I'm afraid to let go." *He* was the egg, a shriveled yolk inside a safe shell. It took Danners only seven years to complete a Stone. The critics loved him. Estevan had found death when he had left Taos. What would Michael find? "Small Stone needs more work," Michael said, hearing the fear in his voice.

Chris heard it, too. "But not yet?"

"Not yet." Maybe not ever. Maybe he would crumble to dust outside the gate, like a mummy when its airtight sarcophagus was opened. Maybe it was too late. "My . . . daughter ran away from me," he said. Was she afraid? Afraid that he wouldn't call, or afraid that he would? Michael slung the carryall over his shoulder, feeling the lumpy prod of the goat skull through the slick fabric. Who are you, Xia, twenty years older? Who have you loved? Who have you hated? You terrify me, Xia. You threw a daughter at me, and my shell cracked. You let in the present.

"Michael—" Chris turned quickly away. "Good luck," she said with her back turned. "Let me know where you are, okay?"

"I will," Michael said gently. "Thanks, Chris." You could find anyone if you looked hard enough. Even yourself? Michael straightened his shoulders, picked up his carryall, and took his fear out into the dusty, timeless egg that was Old Taos. If he hurried, he could catch the three o'clock shuttle to Albuquerque.

Chapter Two

The Albuquerque shuttle left from the plaza in front of the Old Taos Hotel. Michael hurried down the dusty street, avoiding eye contact, hoping he didn't meet Cecelia, or Carl, or anyone else he knew. He had timed it tightly, not wanting to stand around in the plaza with his carryall. This was Old Taos; by now everyone probably knew that he was off to find this daughter of Xia's. Who could be his daughter, too, for all he wanted to deny it.

And why did he want so much to deny it? Michael slowed down, eyeing his reflection in a window full of silver. Because this child—this *woman*—was a symbol? A symbol of love and rejection, both? Why didn't you tell me, Xia? You could have said.

And would it have changed anything? Michael shook his head and glanced anxiously up the street, suddenly afraid that he'd miss the shuttle, that he'd arrive breathless and blown in the plaza to find only a haze of dust and a scattering of curious locals.

If he missed this bus, he wouldn't have the nerve to catch the next one. It was as if a window had opened in the walls around this frozen bit of time, and if he leapt now, he'd escape. If he hesitated, the window would close and he'd be trapped here forever. It was a foolish fancy, but he walked faster, sweating in the sun, brushing past oblivious tourists. Dolores came out of her shop as he passed, waving. Adrenaline leapt in his blood, and Michael hunched his shoulders, pretending that he hadn't seen her. He felt pursued, as if every resident of

Taos were following him, would all converge on the square and drag him back to his studio.

He walked out into the plaza, hearing only the irritable croak of a magpie, seeing no one but a few tourists on their way back to their Albuquerque hotels after an expensive overnight stay in Taos. No mob. Michael slowed his steps, breathing too hard, a little light-headed after his harried flight through the baking streets. The bus was an old city model, dusty and archaic, at least on the outside. Part of the ambience. Michael lined up behind a slender woman dressed in a mauve bodysuit who was climbing the carpeted steps into the bus. At the door the driver held out his hand for Michael's card, flicked it casually through the reader, then handed it back with a slight bow. Boredom glazed his Hispanic features, changing to a flicker of disdain as he picked up Michael's carryall. Its faded nylon didn't go with the sleek luggage stacked neatly in the bus's belly.

Michael wondered if any of those pretty suitcases held a goat's skull. Probably not. He pocketed his card and climbed the steps into the dim recesses of the bus. Jonah swallowed by the whale? He glanced at the arched ceiling above his head, sweat chilling instantly in the conditioned air as he made his way down the aisle. Instead of old-fashioned bus seats, swiveling recliners were scattered across the carpeted floor, flanked by tiny individual tables. Most of the few tourists had clustered near the front; Michael sank into a seat near the back. The crimson velvet upholstery seemed to suck him in, draining the last energy from his body, so that he lay flaccid and without will in its embrace.

Beyond the UV-resistant glass of the windows, the plaza looked tiny and unreal, like a stage set. Which, in a way, it was. I fit in so well, Michael thought as he looked back down the street that led to Chris's gallery. No one was chasing him. No one had run down to the plaza to seize him and stop him from leaving. Perhaps no one had noticed, after all. An unexpected pang stabbed him. Underneath all his noble resolve to leave, he had wanted someone to call him back, and that truth tasted bitter on his tongue. If Chris had run after him, he would have let her persuade him to stay. Because he was afraid.

Of what? he asked himself, but the answer to that one

wouldn't come. Not yet, anyway. Up front, the bus driver swung himself into his seat and the door hissed closed. Michael closed his eyes as the bus shivered to life beneath him. There was no rumble of an internal-combustion engine; the Registry required only a skin-deep conformity to the antique, thank you. The Taos Hotel slid past the window, and for a wrenching instant Michael thought he saw Xia sitting at a table in the courtyard. Then the woman turned her head, and he saw that she looked nothing like Xia, wasn't even Hispanic.

The Hotel vanished, replaced by an unrolling vista of adobe shops, galleries, bed-and-breakfasts. Yesterday they had been part of the landscape. Today, seen through the warping glass of the bus window, they looked absolutely unfamiliar.

"Welcome aboard, Mr. Tryon." A slender youth with shoulder-length blond hair paused beside his chair. "We'll be taking the scenic route over the Rio Grande Canyon this afternoon, including a short stop for refreshments and viewing." He smiled a polished, professional smile. "I'm Antonio, your host for the trip. Can I get you a cold drink? Something chemical to enhance the experience?"

"No, thank you." Michael looked away from Antonio's professionally perfect face. He was the opposite of the tourist kid. This man wasn't so sure of his future. He was willing to buy into it, and the price was posted on his face. Certainty was a pricey luxury in this world. It occurred to Michael that he'd forgotten to give the goat vest back to Dolores. Perhaps that was why she waved at him—to remind him, not to say goodbye or ask him to stay.

Who would really care that he was gone?

Chris. Michael tilted back in the chair, letting it cradle him. He'd e-mail her from Albuquerque and ask her to return the vest to Dolores. And tell her what else? That if she thought she loved him, she was mistaken? She had said she didn't love him. Suddenly, intensely, Michael hoped that was true. The Michael Tryon she knew was an empty shell. He had poured his soul into his Stones, only to reach the final mud at the bottom of the well. He didn't want Chris to love that man.

If there was a spring to fill him up again, it wasn't in Taos. Beyond the window the desert wasteland rolled past, rocky and desolate, patched here and there with the tangled remnants of old fences or weathered gray shacks that were dissolving slowly into the sparse sage. Centuries of irrigation had left vast, perfect circles of white salt on the land. Michael wondered what had grown in those fields, back before the soil had gotten too salty.

The bus was slowing, although the soft hum of the engine didn't change. They were almost at the Rio Grande bridge, and the driver wanted to elicit the greatest effect from the spectacular view down into the canyon. Beside Michael, the woman in the mauve bodysuit sipped at a colorless drink and stared through the window, her face as bored as the driver's. She had a dancer's body, but her eyes were old. Her profile was a shade too dramatic for the day's standard of beauty, with jutting cheekbones and a long sweep of face. Michael guessed that her bone structure was natural in spite of the body-shop skin and muscle tone and found himself watching her as the bus drifted out onto the bridge.

Muted sounds of surprise and delight filled the bus as the other tourists craned their necks or stood to peer down into the spectacular depths of the canyon. The woman tilted her head a fraction of an inch, and her lips tightened almost imperceptibly. Then she averted her gaze and stared calmly up the river gorge.

She was afraid. That carefully controlled fear, refined and hardened to a razor edge, would be a perfect note for Small Stone. It would complement the boy's crude blood lust, refine it. No. No, that was over for now. Michael leaned back in the enfolding chair as the bus pulled into the small picnic area at the end of the bridge.

"We've provided a small buffet tea for your pleasure," Antonio the host announced from the front of the bus. "We'll be spending an hour here, so you'll have plenty of time to sample the goodies our chefs have prepared and take in the view. Remember, please, that there's a small surcharge for visual and tactile recordings . . ."

How much do they charge for memories? Michael wondered sourly. He remained seated as the others got chattering to their feet and crowded off the bus. For a moment he thought that the mauve woman was going to stay behind, too, but she finally stood and followed the crowd out to the cloth-covered table that had been set up in the shade of the ancient picnic shelter. Antonio wandered back through the bus, picking up litter, tweaking a cushion here and there. He grinned at Michael and perched on the arm of the woman's empty seat.

"The caterers can handle the flock for a few minutes. I went to see one of your sculptures once." He tossed his hair back over his shoulders. "It was at the Metropolitan Museum of Art."

"Air Stone," Michael said automatically. This guy had visited it? Michael eyed him warily, half expecting a come-on. "They borrowed it from the owner for a show of contemporary art."

"I don't remember the name. I kind of expected bells and whistles, visions or voices or whatever. Like good drugs, you know." Antonio frowned. "It gave me . . . I don't know. Kind of a stormy feeling, like I wanted to go out and *do* something or break something. Maybe *be* someone. I mean, I liked it, anyway."

Anyway? Even though it wasn't bells and whistles? Take what you can get, old man. Michael sighed. "I'm glad you liked it."

"How do you *do* it? Get that kind of . . . I don't know . . . feeling into a Stone? I mean, how do you pick out what goes and what doesn't?"

"It's a little hard to put a lifetime of skill into twenty-five words or less." Rude words, and they drove him to his feet. "I think I'll get a snack." He retreated down the aisle, yeah, retreated, because he'd felt that flash of hurt. It had been a genuine question. Maybe Antonio had stood in front of Air Stone and it had meant something to him.

Maybe Michael had just destroyed that.

He almost apologized but climbed silently down the steps instead, because he had just been a jerk and there wasn't anything he could say to fix that. The other passengers clustered around the tea table under the watchful eye of the uniformed caterers. Or they wandered at the edge of the canyon, recording the rocky wound in the earth with their expensive cameras. The mauve woman was standing beside the table, not eating, her eyes on some vision that she saw in the hard, dry sky. She didn't acknowledge Michael's presence as he wandered over. He glanced around. How many hours had he spent sitting on the rim of this canyon, listening to the moan of the wind on the rocks? Water had worn this channel, washing away soil, wearing away rock, a teaspoonful or a ton at a time. Now the water was gone, the river dry. Only the damage was left to startle bored tourists and force road builders to call in the engineers. Michael picked up a boneless chicken wing—not real meat, of course, but passably rendered—and wandered over to the bridge.

There was beauty here, too, in the precise angles of iron and the layers of concrete. How many hours of quiet thought and careful calculation had gone into the very conception of this bridge? He had tried to capture some of that quiet frenzy of effort in Silver Stone, blending moments of creation, of fatigue, excitement, and struggle . . .

Who owned Silver Stone now? He didn't know, and wondered why it suddenly mattered when it never had before. *Who do we do this for?* Bending over, he picked up a smooth pebble and tossed it into the canyon. It rebounded from the wall, arcing outward in a long curve, falling in seeming slow motion to the narrow bottom of the gorge. There was so much grace in that brief ballet of stone and gravity. How would it be to dive from this rocky ledge, spread your arms, and fly outward into the clear air, into the welcome arms of lover death? What lay beyond that fragile, impenetrable veil? For a moment the air seemed to waver, as if it were full of heat waves, as if invisible butterflies fluttered in front of Michael's face, stroking his cheeks with transparent wings. The ledge seemed to shift beneath his feet, tilting him forward, and slowly, slowly, he raised his arms.

"Mr. Tryon."

The gentle voice in his ear made him jump. A hand gripped his arm gently, and he stiffened as a tiny pain spiked into the flesh above his right hip.

"I want to talk to you, and, yes, this is a knife blade you feel." The pain grew briefly sharper, then dulled. "I only want to talk, but I'm not going to argue. Shall we go get into my car?" The pain lessened a hair.

This couldn't be happening. Michael turned his head very, very slowly, feeling as if his neck were made of rusty iron joints, half expecting the blade to stab him. He found himself staring into grass-green eyes in an Asian face—the web node's lover. Michael hadn't realized how young he was—Chris's age, he guessed. His surprise must have shown on his face, because the youth smiled. He was enjoying this little scene with a kind of smug, show-off pleasure.

Michael's fear evaporated suddenly and completely. "I'd be happy to talk with you." He returned the youth's smile. "But I think my bus is leaving."

"I'll drop you in Albuquerque." He lifted one shoulder in a lopsided shrug, giving Michael a somewhat theatrical pout. "I had my man put your carryall into my jet. You're not frightened of me. I'm disappointed."

Was that amusement in those green eyes—directed at himself as well as at Michael? "No, you don't frighten me." Michael looked down at the thin killing blade that pricked his shirt, then pushed it gently away. "I was just thinking about jumping into the canyon."

"Why didn't you?" The youth's eyes flickered, a lightning flash that turned his face ice cold for an instant.

"I don't know." Who would that angry lightning strike one day? Archenwald-Shen? "So let's go." Michael turned his back on the blade. "I'm in a hurry."

A little hoverjet was parked near the road. It must have already been there when the bus had arrived, but he hadn't noticed it. Michael walked toward it, trying not to breathe the dust that the departing bus had kicked up. Private license. Of course, Archenwald-Shen could probably afford as many private vehicles as he wanted. A uniformed man with a thick braid of blond hair opened the rear door, turning a blank, mirror-shaded stare on Michael. Hostility was in that stare, never mind the shades. Michael nodded, watched his twin reflections nod back, and slid onto the roomy seat.

Archenwald-Shen's lover climbed in beside him. The blade had vanished, and his long, loose hair fell forward over his shoulders as he touched the door closed. "I'm sorry." Michael leaned back, muscles wanting to tense up as the seat adjusted itself to the contours of his ribs and spine. "I can't remember your name."

"Who can?" He laughed, but the lightning flared in his green eyes again. "I'm Archenwald-Shen's boy, right. What other name do I need?"

Yes, he was young, and slender, clad in one-piece black that made his skin look like antique ivory. Up close, without the distraction of a knife blade in his ribs, Michael noticed the black eye and the bruised cheek. "I'd like to know your name," he said. "Why do you put up with him?"

"Do you really have to ask?" The youth tilted his face to give Michael a clearer view of his bruises. "I thought better of you. I get paid very very well, of course." He smiled. "What did you expect?"

"Just that, I guess." Michael frowned; that flip answer felt a little like a lie and probably wasn't. "I'd still like to know your name."

"Zed." He grinned, slick and hard as diamond. "My name's Zed."

Yeah, Michael thought, there was lightning in those eyes, veiled and tightly controlled. Maybe one day it would burst free, strike Archenwald-Shen, and fry him to a crisp. Or maybe it would short through Zed, shattering him like a tree trunk as it grounded into the earth. "I apologize for my attitude, and I'm sorry if the bruises are my fault."

Zed's face tightened. "I didn't say they were." He jerked his head at the pilot, who was staring impassively through the windscreen.

Without looking back or acknowledging Zed, the man reached for the control panel. The jet shuddered to life, lifting immediately on its vertical jets.

"Actually, you *were* rather responsible." Zed watched the ground recede, his expression thoughtful. "I was blamed for Tree Stone's damage. I usually get the blame. It's in my contract." He snapped slender fingers at the rising jet, the pilot, arching an eyebrow at Michael. "Everything has its price, Mr. Tryon. I'm no prisoner. Like I said, I get paid quite well."

Michael studied Zed, sprawled easily on the custom upholstery. Self-mockery, or simply a desire to shock? They were far above the ground now; the engines swiveled, the wings locked into position, and the jet surged forward. Michael waited for the sudden rush of acceleration to subside, then leaned forward. "What did you want to tell me?" he asked softly. "Just that I earned you a beating?"

"Oh, I didn't plan to tell you that. You asked." Zed arched one eyebrow, grinning. "I fight back, you know. Not enough to really hurt him, just enough to make him feel like he's beaten me, that I'm not just letting him pound on me because he pays me to take it. Does it disgust you, Mr. Tryon? That I'm a whore?"

"Do you want it to?" Michael met his broken-glass stare, feeling full of sadness. What if Anya, his teacher, hadn't been who and what she was? What if she had demanded a similar price to let him touch her Stones? "We all make trades." He drew a slow breath. "It's not my judgment call."

"You're not much fun to needle." Zed looked away at last, frowning at the cloudless sky beyond the window. "Gunner bought Dawn Stone for his place up on the New York Up platform. I picked it out. Gunner pays me to pick out his art investments, among my other duties." He bared his teeth briefly. "I think Dawn Stone is one of your strongest works—not *the* strongest, maybe, but one of them."

This . . . *boy* had passed judgment on his Stones.

"That pisses you, huh?" Zed smiled gently. "I can be a whore, but I can't criticize your art? Or are you pissed because I'm right?"

Michael opened his mouth to retort, then closed it, his anger evaporating suddenly. "Yes, you're right." He laughed, because Zed was so damned accurate. "You're right on both counts. I'm rather small, aren't I?" He gave Zed a wry grin. "Maybe you should try your hand with Stones. And Sun Stone is stronger than Dawn Stone."

"Is it?" Zed gave him a thoughtful look. "I'll check it out and tell you what I think." He lifted one shoulder in a graceful shrug. "You know, a part of me hates you. Because you never had to let some bastard beat on you. But no, you're not small." He touched his pocket lightly. "This little bit of melodrama is actually a present from me to you. You insulted Gunner. You were rude to him. He won't forget that."

"I hope he doesn't." Michael peered through the window, recognizing the Albuquerque towers on the horizon. The little jet was *fast*. "I hope it chokes him," he said, and the rage in his tone surprised him.

"Are you so untouchable, Mr. Tryon?" Amusement and hatred flashed together in Zed's eyes. "I hope so. Because Gunner always gets even—that's how he's gotten to where he is. He can't afford to let you off the hook."

The engines had pivoted, and the little jet was descending, drifting straight down to a public landing pad beyond the dome wall. Michael watched the dusty ground rise to meet them, thinking of his garden baking in the cottonwood shade. It came to him suddenly that he'd never work there again, never waken Small Stone's callow voice. The certainty of it shook him, as if someone had rolled aside the veil of tomorrow and shown him a sure glimpse of the future. "What can he do to me?" he asked with quiet bitterness.

"You might be surprised." Zed's voice was equally quiet.

The jet touched ground with a delicate shudder, and the pilot hopped down to open the rear door for Michael. He climbed out, sucking in his breath at the furnace blast of dry heat. Zed sat in the jet, making no move to get out. "Good-bye," Michael said, taking his carryall from the pilot. "I . . . appreciate your warning. I hope you get what you want."

"Do you really know what I want, Mr. Tryon?" Zed bowed from his seat, expressionless. "I'm sorry you don't take my warning seriously." He turned his face away and let the pilot slam the door.

Michael watched the pilot slide gracefully behind his controls, braid swinging, expression hidden behind the mirror gleam of his shades. He radiated passion every time he looked at Zed. Michael hefted his pack as he turned away, wondering if Zed's lightning would strike *him*, or if perhaps it already had.

He wondered what Gunner would do if he guessed.

And he wondered if the price would ever get too high for Zed. If it did, would Zed be able to admit it? Maybe, after a certain point, you had to stick it out, to prove something to yourself. With a shrug, he slung his carryall over his shoulder. Sweat stuck his shirt to his back and trickled down his sides as he hiked across the public field toward the line of bright little auto-cabs. Beyond the cabs, the jumbled houses of the Skirt lapped at the landing pad, kept back by the black strands of security fence. Years ago this had probably been a suburb of Albuquerque or perhaps an urban residential neighborhood. As water and the climate had worsened, the city had contracted on its center, drawing into itself and retreating into soaring arcologies, leaving the less fortunate to brawl and breed in the Skirt.

Bits of green showed here and there, where families had saved enough rationed water to keep small gardens. Sheets of battered plastic and weathered siding roofed the open-sided sheds that had grown up between the old houses. The streets and tiny yards were empty as residents waited out the midday heat. On the far side of the black fence a toddler lifted the hem of her too-large T-shirt and squatted in the dusty street.

Michael caught a whiff of shit as he popped the door of a bright blue cab. His stomach contracted with nausea or hunger—he remembered suddenly that he hadn't eaten today—and he slid quickly inside, tossing his carryall onto the seat beside him. Then he simply sat there, his debit card in hand. Where to? Until this moment he had simply been running away. He hadn't given a single thought to a destination. Now he had to go *somewhere*. He had to decide.

"Please insert your card in the reader or exit the cab," the cab intoned gently.

Automatically, Michael slid the card through the reader on the padded dash.

"Welcome, Mr. Tryon." The door hissed closed and latched with an electronic click. "Where may I take you?"

"The Albuquerque Hilton." The words popped out on their own; it was the hotel where Margarita Espinoza had stayed.

"The Albuquerque Hilton, sir? Would you like a room? I maintain a reservation link with the Hilton system."

"Yes," Michael said, because he needed somewhere to stay. He didn't know anyone in the city; he had come here only a handful of times since Estevan had died. The little cab pulled smoothly out of line and accelerated toward the city center. The arcologies loomed over him like mountains, and Michael found himself cringing into the cab's seat as if they might fall on him, crush him as Estevan had been crushed. Then the cab locked into a major traffic artery and shot forward into the shadow of the city.

Too late to turn back. The same lethargy that had seized him on the bus took him now. Beyond the cab's windows the glass and ceramic mountains looked as unreal as a painted backdrop. People in the street were moving shadows. He couldn't bring the faces into focus, couldn't recognize a single moment of grief or boredom or anger. It was as if he stood beyond a thick sheet of glass, looking in at the bustling anthill center of this world. He could look, but he couldn't touch.

The Hilton took up one wall of an immense arcology that

overlooked Old Town. The cab zipped into a traffic portal and pulled up in a carpeted lobby. The Hilton was upscale enough to employ human service, so a uniformed bellhop offered Michael his keycard as he climbed out of the cab. His expression didn't alter as he picked up Michael's battered carryall and led him toward the main bank of elevators.

"I'll take it." Michael slung the carryall over his shoulder, realizing with sudden embarrassment that he had no cash in his pockets. He never carried cash because he didn't use it in Taos, didn't have to tip anyone. He felt his face getting red and averted his gaze, pretending not to notice the hot flash of resentment and disdain that crossed the bellhop's face. Nice start. He wondered what other social niceties he'd managed to forget during his decade of retreat behind the walls of static, unchanging Taos.

His room was on the sixth floor, one of the moderately priced levels with a less-than-spectacular view. The elevator was glass-walled so the passengers could look out into the arcology's verdant core. A waterfall tumbled from somewhere above, splashing into a pebbled pool, aerating and cleansing the recycled water. Terraces of flowering and fruiting plants clung to the walls or trailed vining stems out into space. So much greenery made him dizzy. His room opened off the elevator lobby. It was small—a double bed, a table, and two upholstered chairs took up most of the main room—with an angled view of the Old Town plaza. Women in native dress sat in the shadow of the restored buildings, hawking handwoven blankets, jewelry, clothing, strings of dried peppers, pottery, and *kachina* dolls from baskets and spread-out rugs. The Registry owned Old Town, too. It was as if Taos had followed him here. "House, close blinds," Michael said. The hair-fine strands of the blinds unfolded with the static crackle of Mylar tissue and lamps glowed on, filling the room with pools of soft light.

Michael looked around, touched open a drawer in the closet wall, and laughed softly. He was actually looking for some kind of threat from Archenwald-Shen. A dagger in his pillow? A wreath of black roses on the table? Zed's little melodrama had infected him more than he had guessed. Michael sat down on the foot of the bed, eyes on the blank video screen set into the wall. What would Zed's lightning add to Small Stone?

What, indeed? Another thin veneer of directionless emotion,

like layers of silt on the bottom of a stagnant pond? He grabbed the carryall, unzipped it, and took out the goat skull. The weathered bone felt smooth and cool beneath his hands, and he ran his fingers along the ridged curl of the horns before setting it on the table. Its empty eye sockets regarded him solemnly.

"House, send mail," he said.

"Address?" the system prompted him in a gentle neuter voice.

"Christine Neiman. Old Taos Pueblo. Personal, no visuals."

"To Christine Neiman, Old Taos Pueblo. Ready."

"Chris, it's Michael. I forgot to return a vest I'd borrowed from Dolores—could you do it? It should be lying around in my studio somewhere." He paused, and silence fell in on him. Say something. What? Michael licked his lips, groping for words. Should he tell her why he was here, that it wasn't just to look for a ghost daughter whose trail he could have followed from his own terminal in Taos? Tell her that the well was dry, that the Muse had fled and it was *she* he was searching for? "Take care of yourself, Chris." The words came out a croak, like the squawk of a magpie. Cowardly words, hiding from themselves. "I'll talk to you soon. End it."

"Mail sent to Christine Neiman, Old Taos Pueblo. Would you like to send another?"

"No." Michael stood, oppressed suddenly by this sterile, impersonal little room.

He had meant to initiate his search for Margarita Espinoza, but he blanked the screen instead. She had given him a clear message when she'd left early. On the table the goat skull smirked at him. This room could be a metaphor for his soul: a sterile chamber filled with slick, unimaginative furniture. The air seemed to shimmer at the edges of his vision, as if it were full of invisible dancing insects. Now what?

Eat something, a sane voice whispered in the corner of his mind. You haven't eaten all day; no wonder you feel like shit. Michael opened his mouth to call room service, but he couldn't eat in here, in this sarcophagus of a room. He left instead and took the elevator down, dropping past crimson flowers that gleamed among the green leaves like blots of fresh blood. Shops and restaurants filled the ground floor, and the spicy odors drifting from an Indonesian eatery made Michael's stomach growl. Yes, food. That was what he needed most, but he passed the restaurant by and marched through the environmental lock, out into the heat and dust of the street.

It was getting dark. The thick twilight took him by surprise. You could forget the real world, the cycles of night and day, heat and cold, inside one of those towers. Where had Estevan lived? he wondered suddenly. He had never asked for his street address, and Estevan hadn't given it to him. There had been such a gulf of silence beneath their careful friendship. They had tiptoed, afraid they'd break through as one might break through a crust of ice, to fall into the cold, dark uncharted water beneath.

So he had never asked and didn't know.

Michael turned corners at random, ignoring the bright, beckoning holos that decked the street-level faces of the towers. They would all be the same inside, as unreal in their own way as Old Taos. Maybe humanity had evolved beyond physical reality. And had left him behind. Darkness thickened around him as he reached a section of older buildings. Only a few streetlights glowed in this section of town. But light spilled from the doors of bars and crummy virtual parlors, a frenzy of light, as if shopkeepers and residents wanted to spend a whole night's worth of candlepower before the power curfew shut them off. He wasn't hungry anymore. Wandering, letting his feet carry him where they would, Michael reached a small plaza. The rail bounded one side of it. Fires flickered in the dark shadows, and an open-air market spread beneath the concrete pylons of the overhead track.

Jugglers, mimes, and magicians wandered through the crowd. Men and women hawked food, electronics, and black-market drugs from mats and rickety stands. Darkness didn't seem to slow anything down, or maybe the market didn't open until dark. It had been a long time since he'd wandered a city after nightfall. This wasn't tourist country; this was Skirt-town. Michael sidled through the crowd, eliciting only casual glances. In his dusty and rumpled tunic and tights he could belong here. He had belonged once, back before Anya had taken him on. Then he'd known a city's pulse, and language, and rules. A lifetime ago. He was an alien now, an alien anywhere outside the invisible shell of the Taos egg.

In the center of the plaza a man danced in a bodysynth suit.

The dark purple fabric covered him from the neck down, glittering with silver threads like an exotic velvet skin. Those metallic fibers translated each twitch of his body to the music that moaned and throbbed in the cooling air. He was good. Michael paused, leaning against one of the mag-lev pylons, watching the dancer's shoulder-length red hair flare like flames as he spun. He was too good for a Skirt market, and Michael wondered why he wasn't playing the towers. A dozen feet away a withered old woman propped skewers of food over a flickering fire built of scraps. Michael smelled roasting meat, and his stomach growled. Real meat? Out here? He wondered what kind and where it had come from, and an edge of nausea squeezed his hunger. The bodysynth dancer spun in a slow spiral, back arched, arms rising to a crescendo of skirling flutes and rumbling drums. For an instant he poised motionless on one foot while a single flute wove a silver thread of sound against the hiss of an approaching train.

A rough hand grabbed Michael's tunic from behind and yanked.

He staggered backward into the darkness beneath the rail, spinning like the dancer, but gracelessly, his body stiff and full of shock, his cry drowned in the sudden rush of the mag-lev's passage. A fist hit him on the cheek, and pain exploded through him, tumbling him off his feet. As he fell, a single vision imprinted itself on his retina: the old woman reaching for a skewer of meat. Then a boot smashed into his ribs, and the vision shattered into shards of black glass.

Stupid, stupid, stupid, a distant voice shouted at him. Stand in the dark like a foolish tourist, like you know what you're doing . . .

"I don't . . . have anything," Michael gasped, hoping to stop the next kick. "No cash. Please . . ."

It landed, exploding in his belly. Michael doubled over, retching, struggling to suck air into his spasming lungs. Violence—the city darkness was full of violence. The human soul was full of darkness, nothing but darkness, nothing, and he was drowning in it. A hand clenched his tunic, dragging him to his knees. Michael caught a glimpse of a pale face, blond hair. Zed's pilot. He struggled to speak, but a fist came out of nowhere and slammed him spinning to the pavement. Blood trickled warmly down his cheek. *Why?* he wanted to say. Why this? Why now? Tell me. But his tongue wouldn't work, and his mouth was thick with coppery blood.

A swarm of invisible butterflies fluttered in the air about him, fanning him as the blond pilot kicked him again, setting onto his face with the feel of a thousand smothering wings.

Chapter Three

He shuffled across the deserted plaza, a thing of hunger today, all cramped belly and a heavy lethargy that dragged at his legs and bowed his shoulders. An animal part of him that remembered eating around here sent him fumbling through the debris overflowing from a Dumpster. No food. Disappointment squeezed him, and he clung to that brief pain. Pain—hunger, cold, the occasional blow—helped keep back the darkness.

He shivered, afraid to think of it. The darkness. It was full of voices that weren't voices. Like terrible, wonderful singing it sucked at him, would pull him off the solid ground, drag him screaming into space. He shuddered, feeling it just *there*, on the other side of a curtain. That curtain of sun/sweat-sting/hunger/pain got thin sometimes.

Don't. Don't think about it. Think about food. At night there would be food. Eating, belly full, blood running thick with *food*—that drove away the dark dreams. People didn't see him, looked through him. Unless he stole food. Then they chased him, threw rocks. He didn't know why they couldn't see him, although sometimes bright images flickered in his head and he could almost remember . . . But when he groped for those pretty pictures, they fluttered away. Like butterflies. Something orange caught his eye in the litter of trash that had shoaled at the base of a mag-lev pylon. A packet of juice? Full? He veered across the scorching pavement to scoop it up with a feral pounce. Empty. He crumpled it in sudden rage and flung it away.

"Here," someone said from behind him. "I think you need this."

The words struck him like blows, hurting his head. He flinched and ducked, and the sudden movement started the plaza moving with him, rotating gently around his center.

"Yo, take it easy. You better sit down."

Hands on his arm—dark-skinned hands with pale knuckles. He looked up, focusing on white teeth in a dark face, a grin. No anger, just a grin. His knees buckled, and he would have fallen without the hands; he sat down hard enough to hurt as it was. Clammy sweat bathed his face, and brief nausea twisted him. Someone was squatting in front of him, blocking out the glare of sun from the plaza. He trembled, almost yanked his hand away as warmth pressed against his palm. A cup. His fingers closed, clutched.

"Atole," the stranger said. "I bought you a burrito, too. Old Mama Hernandez makes good food. Good for the soul, she says. Maybe it's because she sprinkles everything with holy water. She steals it from St. Michael's, downtown. Oh, well, it doesn't hurt the flavor."

More words, laughing words, not angry as it was when he grabbed food, the laughter aimed at *him*. No, this laughter was *with* him. Like they shared, like they were both laughing. Something stirred inside him, answering that sharing faintly, fluttering against the walls of his skull. *I am . . .*

He lifted the cup to his lips, hunger twisting him, hands shaking a little with hunger's eagerness. The rich soup was just cool enough to drink, and he gulped it. *Like an animal . . .* The thought intruded, coherent, whole. Its clarity thinned the fog in his head, thickening that precious veil between him and the darkness. *I am not . . .* He struggled desperately for more words, terrified that the fog might close in again. *I am not . . . an animal.* The soup seemed to dissolve straight into his bloodstream, sending a dizzy drug-rush pulse of pleasure and energy through him. He emptied the cup, and the plaza settled beneath him, coming into focus at last. "Where . . . am I?" he whispered.

"You feeling better, man?"

Dark skin. Black eyes—bits of night. Michael blinked into a man's face, close to his. Afro-Hispanic? The words came to him, at first just words, but then the meaning seeped through. Jutting nose . . . like Xia's, a little. Xia . . . The thoughts came more coherently now, flowing softly in, like sand rushing into a hole, filling it up.

God. He looked down at his hands, clenched around the cup, seeing old cuts, dirt ground into the folds of skin. "Thanks," he said, and his voice grated like an unused door.

"Here." The man was unwrapping the burrito: an enormous flour tortilla that was barely closed around a filling of fried onions and soymeat cubes. The scent of cumin and cilantro made him dizzy all over again and clenched his stomach into a knot.

"Mama won't use meat—she knows what she'll get for her price—but her stuff's great anyway. She makes the best burritos in town." The man held out the burrito in its crackling wrapper. "It's a dead-flat bribe, man." He smiled, head tilted quizzically. "I just want your name. I'm Andy Rodriguez, and I *know* you from somewhere. It's screwing up my head, jangling the hell out of my day job. And believe me—" He laughed. "—it's a tough enough job without any distractions." He shook the wrapped burrito gently, releasing a fresh cloud of cilantro scent. "One burrito for one name. I'm even trusting you to play square. Hell, if it's a hot name, worth trade to me, I'll up the ante." He grinned outright now, tossing his buzzed head. "I'll buy you a real meal."

"Michael." The name came to him like a thunder clap, gentle as snow falling. "I'm Michael," he said, and began to tremble.

"Uh uh." Andy held the burrito out of reach. "Rings no bells, man. Last name, too."

"Tryon," he whispered. "I'm Michael Tryon. God, what *happened* to me?" He buried his face in his hands. It was like waking up from a crazy nightmare, as if he'd been dreaming all this time. Or trying not to dream.

"It's all right, man. The game's over. Here." Andy tucked the burrito into Michael's slack fingers, his other hand gentle on Michael's shoulder. "Just eat, okay?"

The food smell hooked him, shutting out everything else. With shaking hands, Michael ripped away the paper wrapping and tore off an enormous mouthful of the burrito. The taste filled him, exquisite, more satisfying than sex. Food had never tasted like this, complex and wonderful, a symphony of texture and aroma, like the murmur of one of Estevan's Stones. He swallowed, then took another huge, careful bite.

"Michael Tryon. Shit, I *do* know who you are." Andy whistled. "I met you at some gallery thing a couple of years ago, although you probably didn't notice me." Dry laughter. "I was a little out of my element, was kind of keeping a low profile. For S'Wanna's sake, although she said she didn't care who I was and maybe didn't. She's that together." His voice went thoughtful. "So how the hell did you end up like this?"

"I'm . . . not sure." Michael finally tore his attention from the burrito, looking up to meet Andy's narrowed eyes. "I don't think I know you."

"Like I said." Andy shrugged. "I was playing it low-key. It was in Taos at some big media op. You, S'Wanna, a bunch of other artists. Rarefied. Lots of video cams. And here you are." He ran a hand across his buzzed scalp and gave Michael a wry grin. "So what'd you do to end up on the street? Back some web scam that went blooey?"

"I got . . . beaten up." Michael's fingers crept up to touch the scar on his cheekbone. Memory followed the words: Zed's driver. On Archenwald-Shen's orders? Or Zed's? "I woke up in a fed-med ward." He reached harder, pulled up images, a little scared because the darkness was in there, too. Maybe. "I think . . . I tried to access my account." Yes, that had happened. "It wouldn't recognize me. Someone had diddled with my ID, I guess. So they kicked me out after minimum treatment."

Andy whistled a low, impressed note. "You got an enemy with heavy clout to hire that kind of Net job. You're talking big money. But you gotta know people who can ID you." He tilted his head, curious. "How come you didn't just get it straightened out?"

"I could have." He'd thought about calling Chris. She would have come running to save him, would have gone after the ID tampering like a raging lioness protecting her whelp. It had to be Archenwald-Shen who had done it and maybe ordered the beating, too. Zed's warning had been real, after all. "I didn't want to be protected." Michael started out into the sun glare of the plaza, tasting dust and cilantro on his cracked lips, remembering bitterness and hurt anger. "I—wanted the city to eat me." Because it hadn't been real before. Nothing had been real; he had been living an illusion, and maybe that was the problem. "I wanted the city to digest me and shit me out," he said slowly. "I wanted to know it. Then I could maybe . . . work with it."

"You know, you sound like S'Wanna." Andy rolled his eyes. "I'd say all you Stone artists are crazies, but then . . . I hang out with one of her Stones." He shrugged, giving Michael a crooked grin. "Maybe I understand. And maybe I don't. Seems to me you could've ended up dead just as easily as not. Anyway, you sure got your wish about the shit part, huh?"

"Yeah. In spades." Michael stared down at the remains of his burrito, remembering that thinning veil, the dark on the other side. At some point he had withdrawn into a safe core of animal consciousness to escape it.

Escape *what*? What the hell had *happened* to him?

"Be too bad to lose another Stone sculptor. What would S'Wanna do without competition?" Andy was getting to his feet. "Why don't you come around to my space. Grab a shower—water ought to be hot by now—clean up a little. And this ain't quite charity, either." His crooked grin flashed again. "I can tweak S'Wanna with this. Your name oughta get me some attention, even if my ass is currently out of favor."

S'Wanna—the name finally penetrated the no-food fuzzies. "S'Wanna LeMontagne?" Michael blinked up at the lanky man, registering a worn green shirt hanging outside the loose pants. His skin was lighter than Shen's, and his profile reminded Michael a little of Xia's. "The sculptor?"

"That's the one. Can you make it to your feet on your own?"

S'Wanna LeMontagne had done some genius Minors, and her Majors were coming along. Michael stared at the man's outstretched hand, suddenly aware of his own filthy tunic, his itchy, unwashed skin. He caught a whiff of his sour odor and wrinkled his nose. So this Andy was going to score points with the story of how he'd found Michael Tryon on the street. Michael laughed a single bitter note. Right now a little pride seemed like a good trade for a shower. And besides, he wanted off the street. It scared him that the darkness might come back, send him scurrying into hiding again. He shivered and reached for Andy's hand, a little shocked at just how much he needed it to get up off the ground. The warmth of the man's fingers was an anchor, tethering him to light and sanity. "Thanks," he said fervently, meaning it.

"No prob." Andy's hand under his arm had a professional strength to it. "You okay to walk?"

"I think so."

He was aware of the city around him, as if he had been deaf and blind before, as if he had been living in perennial night and only now had the sun come up. How long had he been scrounging on the street, anyway? He reached up to finger the faint scar on his cheek. Long enough for this to heal without much assistance. He tried to count the days, but they blurred together into one long twilight of hunger and hiding and the nightmare that lurked at the edges of his mind. His thought process, back in that sterile, shabby clinic, had seemed so *clear*. His head felt clear now, but in between . . .

In between lay terrifying darkness. "What day is this?" Michael asked slowly.

"September twenty-sixth." Andy gave him a quizzical look. "Why?"

September 26. He had checked into the hotel at the very end of August—the twenty-ninth or thirtieth, something like that. Michael pressed his lips together against a shiver of fear. A month gone. He remembered the bitter shock in the clinic, accessing his account only to be informed that he wasn't Michael Tryon. He remembered deciding to let it happen, to submerge himself in the city and see what energy he might find there. From then on . . . everything blurred. Michael shivered again. Concussion? Undiagnosed brain damage?

Insanity?

"You okay?"

He had faltered to a stop in front of the rail platform at the end of the plaza. Passengers eddied around them like a stream around a rock, a white-noise babble of fatigue, urgency, small pains and larger ones. Sudden excitement fluttered in his gut. You could catch that in a Stone: what the city *felt* like, that murmur like blood coursing through concrete veins. Andy was doing something, peeling the plastic off a wrapped drug patch.

"Don't." Michael put up a hand to stop him, but Andy seized his wrist and held it with easy strength.

"Relax. It's legal, a stim, nothing you're likely to react to." He pressed the cool disk against Michael's neck and released him. "From your pulse and respiration rate, I figure it's do this or pick you up off the sidewalk in about another minute." He sounded cheerful. "You're too big to carry. If you go anaphylactic, I can deal with it."

"Yeah, sure it's legal. What are you? A doctor?" Shocked by his weakness, Michael gave in to anger.

"Close enough." Andy didn't seem offended. "Licensed technician—same difference in this neighborhood. You steady now?" He nodded at the nearby rail. "You don't want to end up like that other sculptor did. The city'll have to put up another plaque."

Michael stared at the rail platform, chemical strength from the patch already flowing through his veins, raising the small hairs on the back of his neck. "What sculptor?" The words came out a whisper. "What do you mean?"

"Estevan. The Stone sculptor." Andy frowned. "You got to have heard of him, right? You know, I think that's really the reason S'Wanna hangs out in this dried-out corner of the country." He lifted one shoulder in an apologetic shrug. "Don't get bent, she thinks you're hot, but she figured Estevan was a one-of-a-kind genius."

"He was," Michael said softly.

"Uh huh?" Andy gave him a quick look. "Anyway, S'Wanna came out here one afternoon." Andy looked past Michael, frowning at the rail platform. "She just stood in front of the plaque the city put up, and all of a sudden she started crying. When I asked her, she said . . . it was because she couldn't ever be better than him, because he died before he was finished."

He died before he was finished. Maybe that was the worst epitaph an artist could have. Or would it be worse to finish and discover that it didn't matter? Michael turned slowly, following Andy's thoughtful stare. The rail platform looked like any mag-lev stop: white silocrete ramps, fabric roof stretched into taut swells and billows, gates, and card readers. "This is it?" His voice trembled just a hair. "Where he died?"

"Yeah." Andy jerked his head. "The plaque's at the front end. You want to go see it?"

"No!" His exclamation startled them both.

Michael looked away from Andy's surprise. What a strange, bitter coincidence that he had gone crazy or whatever he had done in the shadow of Estevan's death. Or maybe it wasn't such a coincidence; perhaps Estevan's ghost had drawn him here. "Was it a mistake?" he murmured softly. "Should I have stayed in Taos, Estevan? *You* should have stayed." *He died before he was finished.* Michael wondered if, in those last seconds as the train bore down on him, Estevan had regretted all those unfinished Stones.

That would be true hell.

"You knew this guy." Andy wasn't asking.

"Yes." More points to score against S'Wanna? Michael no longer cared. "He was . . . my friend." Before it ended, before Xia destroyed them—or had Michael destroyed them? Whose fault was it? Michael bent his head.

"I'm sorry, man." Andy touched his arm lightly. "Hell of a place to wake up out of a nightmare."

"Amen," Michael said softly. "I'll take you up on your offer of a shower now."

Andy led him to an old office building that had been turned into crummy lofts. The first floor had been converted into protected parking, and inside the barred double doors he led Michael back to a battered ambulance spattered with painted-over scrapes and dings. Inside, it was surprisingly high-tech. Andy had him sit on the edge of the clamped-down gurney, patched electrodes to his scalp and body, and plugged a biochem sampler catheter into a vein.

"A little free service," he said with a grin. "Don't worry. S'Wanna'll cover it."

Whatever he found didn't worry him much. The patch was wearing off already, or maybe Michael was simply running out of resources. Whatever, he made it up the filthy stairs with the last of his strength. The elevator shaft gaped open on Andy's floor, its doors gone, a tangle of dusty cables dangling in a yawning cave of darkness. Five stories down. Michael shivered and kept to the far side of the hall.

"You afraid of heights?"

Not afraid. The dark drop drew him, and Michael remembered standing on the rim of the Rio Grande Canyon, arms spread, so tempted by that clear air. "We're so fascinated with death," he murmured. In art, in religion, in the physical violence of the urban alleys. "Maybe because it's such a mystery."

"You tell me." Andy glanced over his shoulder, busy with

the locks on a mesh-reinforced door. "Just don't jump. Not here on my turf, okay?"

"Okay." Michael shrugged and followed Andy into his room. It faced north and was walled mostly with glass, giving Michael a view of the city towers. A scatter of faded carpets that looked like genuine antiques covered the old linoleum floor, but Andy hadn't bothered to patch the scars where office walls had been torn out to create the vast room. A seemingly random clutter of terminals and hardware clustered around a small holostage, and cables snaked across the floor.

"I do a little freelance Net work." Andy nodded at the equipment. "Don't touch it. The shower's over there. I'm going to catch up on traffic, maybe see if you bought me S'Wanna's ear." He pulled his tunic off over his head, then walked over to his equipment and touched one of the screens. Instantly, color pulsed and swirled above the stage.

A network hacker? Was that how Andy fleshed out his tech's income? Michael wandered over to the shower cabinet in the corner. There wasn't much furniture: a futon on the floor covered with tumbled blankets, a table. A seatless toilet stood beside the shower cabinet and a small utility sink, all open to the rest of the room. A battered cupboard beside the sink held a random assortment of packaged food and a few dishes. No cooking surface. A nearly empty bottle of red wine stood on the table that flanked the kitchen/bathroom. Michael looked at the label—real stuff. Expensive, like the carpets. They jarred with the poverty of the studio. But everyone had different priorities.

Michael pulled off his tunic, grimacing at the stains and dirt. He had lost weight. His ribs pushed against his skin, and the muscles of his thighs looked skinny and distinct beneath his olive skin. He'd need another trip to the body shop soon; age walked harder on his heels every year. Maybe he'd just stop running one of these days and let it catch up.

Images flickered and danced above the small stage, appearing and vanishing in a psychedelic dance as Andy reached, touched, tapped screens. Michael felt comforted by Andy's inattention—secure. Perhaps it was Andy's confidence that kept the ghosts away. He tossed his clothes onto the floor of the shower cabinet and turned on the water. It wasn't quite hot, but the recycled water felt wonderful sluicing across him. Michael washed quickly, scrubbing his skin until it glowed with heat, washing out his tunic and tights as best he could. Finished, he wrung out the clothes. Better wet and clean than filthy. God knew where he'd been.

Andy was still hunched in his electronic lair as Michael stepped out of the shower. He looked around for a towel—there was no warm-air drier in this cheap-model cabinet—and didn't see one. Dripping, he grabbed a frayed blanket from the bed. He wrapped it around himself and hung his wet clothes across the top of the shower cabinet.

The water had washed away the last cobwebs of darkness, and he felt *himself*, clear and whole, as if he'd walked out of the hotel to go look for a restaurant just hours before. Perching himself on the corner of the table, he watched Andy dance through his electronic landscape. His whole body was *focused*, his face glazed with an expression that had the look of rapture or trance. Art, Michael thought suddenly. This is art, too. And he shivered, remembering those moments when it all *worked*, when he wove his soul and the model's into a Stone and felt it come alive beneath his hands, when he knew it was *good*. Maybe that's why we do it, Michael thought with sudden bitterness. Maybe it's for the rush, that fleeting orgasm of *yes*! Maybe we're addicts at heart, chained to that brief surge of brain chemistry. And maybe one day some clever biochemist will isolate that sensation, grow it in a petri dish, and sell it on the street . . .

In the middle of the room Andy's stage grayed to emptiness. He yawned and stretched, muscles bunching on his tawny shoulders.

"Was S'Wanna impressed?" Michael asked.

"She wouldn't answer real-time." Andy sighed. "I left her some juicy little hints in her mail—she can come looking if she wants."

Michael sensed a hint of annoyance behind the easy manner, and worry, too. Andy would add a nice touch of dissonance to a Stone right now. "I'm sorry if I wasn't impressive enough to entice S'Wanna," Michael said gravely.

"You may still be." Andy rolled his eyes. "She might not be home. Maybe she's just got a new lover and hasn't wanted to be up front about it. I don't know, though." He frowned, his manner slipping. "She's been pretty moody for new love."

He was definitely worried. "Maybe she's having trouble with a Stone, or her work in general." Michael knew they were awkward words, an obvious offer of comfort from someone who had no real basis for offering anything.

"Yeah, that could be it." Andy sighed, then grinned. "She'll tell me about it or she won't. Thanks. I'll hang your wet stuff out the window; it'll dry in no time."

"Thank you." Michael handed over his clothes, frowning because something had been bothering him throughout their conversation, scratching like a dog at the back door of his brain. "Down in the plaza." He hesitated, afraid to waken echoes of that darkness. "You said something about losing *another* Stone sculptor."

"Uh huh." Andy opened the window to drape Michael's clothes across the windowsill. "You really were out of things, weren't you?" he said, giving Michael a sideways look that made him wonder just how much of his story Andy had actually believed. "Irene Yojiro suicided last week. It went big-time on the media. No good wars this week, so she got almost as much coverage as a medium-size sports scandal." His tone was ironic, but that glint of worry surfaced briefly in his eyes again. "S'Wanna wouldn't talk to me about that, either. She knew Irene."

"Irene Yojiro is dead?" Michael struggled to make sense of the words.

"She just swam out into the ocean, walked right out her back door one night. They never did find her body."

Michael knew Irene; he had met her twice. The critics called her Stones lyrical. He remembered her warm smile and shivered, goose bumps rising briefly on his skin as if a cold wind had blown through the open window. Life was such a fragile thing. A chance blow could shatter it like crystal. What had shattered it for Irene Yojiro? A sudden urgency seized him. "Andy, I want to ask two favors from you. You've got no reason to do any more for me, and I've got no right to ask, but I'm asking." He licked his lips, hearing a clock ticking silently in his head, ticking away the seconds of his fragile life. "I need to hire a search. I want to start it right now. Can I put it on your account? I'll pay you back when I get this ID thing cleared up."

"Who you searching for?" Andy's face had gone wary. "The dude who diddled your account?"

"Maybe my daughter." He held Andy's stare. "That's why I came here. To find her. The other favor is I'd like to borrow some cash. I want to get my carryall back from the hotel where I was staying, and I'll have to settle my bill first."

"Burritos I'm free with. Cash and Net time are something else." Andy tilted his head. "Your daughter, *maybe*?"

"I don't know yet." Michael had nothing to give this man except honesty. "I don't know if I want her to be my daughter, but I need to know. I'm not sure she wants to know, either." His grin hurt. "She messaged me and then took off. I don't know where she went."

"Why?"

A deadpan question. Michael studied his face. What did this search mean to Andy Rodriguez? "Because if she isn't my daughter, she thinks she is. I—want her to know that I came looking." The words had come to him honestly, without thought, surprising him a little.

Andy was frowning at something only he could see, his eyes veiled by half-closed lids. "That matters." He nodded once, abruptly. "I'm good in the Net, but I know this dude who's better. This is his kind of thing, and he owes me a favor—several favors. He's not real legal, but he could find the devil himself if you wanted to pay. I'll set it up if you want." He frowned. "Bunny's kind of spooky about strangers, you know? What's the lady's name?"

"Espinoza." Michael drew a deep breath. "Margarita. She checked into the Albuquerque Hilton . . ." He paused, trying to count back. "About a week before I did—and that was the twenty-ninth, I think."

"Margarita Espinoza." Andy was nodding. "In the Hilton a week before you showed. She's not hiding from the law, right? That ought to be a cinch for Bunny. I'll pass it on tonight." He flashed Michael a preoccupied grin. "I'll see him later on for sure, and I'll tap him then. Tell you what." He glanced at the watch on his wrist, an antique spring-wound thing with a battered real-leather strap. "I gotta head out. I'm on shift this afternoon, picking up warm bodies for Providence Hospital and a couple of private trauma clinics. I'll have Bunny post the address into general space, put it under the password "Estevan," okay?"

Estevan? Appropriate, Michael thought with a twinge of bitterness. "Thank you," he said softly. "I appreciate it."

"Life's tough enough." Andy's crooked smile came and went. "Sometimes you gotta give a little." He fished a cash card from his pocket, handed it to Michael, and glanced at the windowsill. "This should get your stuff out of hock. I don't think your clothes are dry yet."

Help Andy would give, but he wasn't going to leave a stranger in his apartment with all his expensive equipment. Michael liked him for that pragmatism. And for his watch.

"Thank you," Michael said, but that was all there was to say. He put on his clothes, still damp and wrinkled but clean. Then Andy let him out and locked the multitude of sturdy locks behind them.

Michael followed Andy down the hall to the stairs. He had to find Margarita. If she was Estevan's, he needed to tell her about her father—about the man he was, and the artist. She deserved to know that he had come looking, at least.

And if she was his?

I should call Chris, he thought, and swallowed a pang of guilt. He should get his account cleared and pay Andy back. But he didn't want to—not until he'd talked to Margarita. Not until he knew. This time he walked past the elevator shaft, glancing down into the blackness, daring it to reach for him. It was just space and the absence of light, nothing more.

I'm better, Michael decided as he went slowly down the stairs. Still weak and a little shaky-kneed on the steep stairs, but better.

"I hope you find what you're looking for." Andy lifted a hand in the street, his expression sober.

"Thanks." Michael brushed his palm to Andy's, then turned and started down the street, toward the forest of towers and the Hilton. They were strange parting words from this hacker paramedic. What *am* I looking for? Michael asked himself, and wasn't sure. Margarita? His muse?

Death?

He didn't cut through the plaza where Estevan had died.

* * *

The uniformed doorman at the Hilton stared down his nose in disdain at Michael's rumpled appearance. He would be a good model for a cityscape Stone, Michael decided sourly. The man's disdain turned to absolute disgust when Michael couldn't produce either keycard or ID card for his reader. They were gone, leaving no memory of their theft or loss. Michael discovered that he didn't really care. Scowling, the doorman murmured into a comm link mounted on a silver bracelet.

Security arrived almost immediately, in the human guise of a small angular woman dressed in a gray business suit. "Mr. Tryon." She gave Michael a scant bow, her sharp blue eyes sweeping him once from head to toe. "I'm sorry about the misunderstanding." She ignored the doorman. "We put your carryall into the hotel safe when you didn't return to check out. If you'll come with me, I'll get it for you right away." She stepped aside to usher Michael into the lobby.

Well, the hotel had obviously managed to access his account before the Net pirate had diddled it, anyway; otherwise they wouldn't be acting so civil. And just how could that have happened? Michael hesitated a beat as he preceded the Security woman into the lobby. The Hilton shouldn't have closed his account until sometime the day after he'd been attacked, at the very earliest. So why had the hotel gotten through when his card had been rejected at the clinic the night before? The woman guided him past a tasteful group of real-wood furniture clustered artfully around a stone fireplace. A fire crackled in the stone hearth, radiating a gentle warmth—a holo, and a good one. A hidden door slid open in the papered wall, and Michael stepped through.

"Have a seat, Mr. Tryon." The woman offered one of two chairs that took up most of the space in the small office. Her office? Michael sat down, eyeing the holo stage in front of a comfortable kneeler chair. A Muzak pattern of light and color shimmered above the deck.

"I'll go get your carryall from the safe. Two minutes." She exited through a second door beyond the holo stage.

Why did he think she was a bitch behind that polite face? Michael got up and prowled to the entrance door. He'd never liked cops much, and security guards were worse. They weren't quite legitimate and knew it; they seemed to make up for that lack by being even more pushy and authoritarian than cops. And maybe this was all just leftover prejudice, Michael thought wryly. Echoes from his misspent youth. He pushed on the doorplate. Nothing happened.

Well, maybe it wasn't just prejudice.

The inner door slid open. Another person accompanied the Security woman, tall and dark in a pale blue tunic suit. She could have been someone on the hotel's administrative staff, perhaps. But her face was cold, and two uniformed city cops followed her into the room. "Michael Tryon?" She pulled a small wallet from her tunic pocket, then flipped it open to reveal a gleaming badge. "I'm Lieutenant Ryan of the Albuquerque Municipal Police. I'd like to ask you some questions."

Cops? Oh, great. "What's wrong?" Michael tried to keep his voice steady, but that dark gap in his memory squeezed up inside his head. "What's this all about?"

"If you'll come with me, we'll talk about it," the lieutenant said.

"I don't think I have to go with you." Michael sat on the fear that wanted to seep into his voice. "Not unless you're arresting me."

"I can do that." The lieutenant didn't smile. "If you'd prefer. Or you can cooperate and maybe we can skip some of the red tape."

"What are you talking about?" He wanted to get angry but couldn't do it; he could have done *anything* while he was blacked out. She wasn't going to tell him anything, either—you could read it in her face. He could jump through her hoop or she'd bash him over the head. "All right." He nodded, giving up, letting the fear wash over him. "I'll go with you."

The lieutenant stepped back so that Michael could precede her out the door. As he moved, the two uniformed cops spread out automatically to flank him. They moved like well-trained attack dogs. Yeah, he could create one hell of a Stone: a celebration of the city's dark soul. "What about my carryall?" Michael looked past the cops to the Security woman. "And someone stole my card. I'll need to report that."

"I'll take care of it." She gave him a stiff nod.

"You'll get your property back." The lieutenant sounded impatient. "Let's go."

Their energy pushed him along like an invisible wave,

sweeping him through the lobby and out to the unmarked car waiting beside the curb. Authority, Michael decided. The massive tide of society's agreement on what was right. God help you if you didn't agree—then you got to swim in the surf.

One of the uniformed cops drove, and the other sat beside him. The lieutenant sat in back with Michael, and a thick wall of polyglass separated them from the cops up front. "Where are we going?" Michael asked without much hope that she'd answer him.

She ignored him.

In Taos he would have lost his temper, told her to arrest him or get off his back. When he had left Taos, he had left something behind—his identity, perhaps. He wasn't Michael Tryon out here, wasn't sure who the hell he was.

The car, which had been threading its way insolently through the pedestrians and the scatter of private-license vehicles, was now slowing, pulling over to the curb. The towers leaned over them, one per landscaped block. The door locks popped, and the rear door swung up. Michael climbed out slowly, shading his eyes against the level beams of the setting sun. They'd parked in front of another older building. This one looked more upscale than Andy's studio, but it huddled between two soaring towers like an ignored little sister. Michael wondered how it had survived as its neighbors had gone down to make way for the towers.

Gravel and boulders landscaped the ground between sidewalk and entry. The concrete facade was clean, and an ornate metal grille guarded the first-floor windows and the entryway. But the lieutenant stuck a card into a reader beside the entry gate, and with a squeak of hinges, the grille folded open. Wall-mounted security cameras tracked them as they proceeded up the walk and into the lobby. Michael wondered if they shouldn't all march in step.

The entire first floor had been opened up. Thick white pillars supported the ceiling, and concealed fixtures sprayed light across a lush indoor garden. Michael took a slow breath, smelling moist earth and flowers. Water trickled and splashed somewhere. "I need to piss," Michael said.

The lieutenant gave him an annoyed glance. "Fine, wonderful, this way." She jerked her head toward a carefully trimmed hedge full of white flowers.

It didn't conceal a bathroom, but it did hide a bank of three elevators. The four of them crowded into a car. Too bad he'd showered, Michael thought sourly. He was getting tired of the lieutenant's game. The elevator stopped on the top floor, letting them out into a small carpeted lobby. The carpeting was new and clean, and one wall was a holowindow, offering a view of San Francisco Bay and the Golden Gate, still standing in its prequake glory. Some artist had touched up a modern recording to give it a historic flavor, Michael decided.

"This way." The lieutenant put her hand on Michael's elbow.

He shook her off. She was excited, although she was keeping it under close rein. Hair prickling on the back of his neck, Michael walked through the door she had just opened.

The color hit him first. The walls rioted with a painted veldt, harsh with sun, dotted with grazing herds of zebra and wildebeest. An enormous tiger crouched in the middle of the room, and, seeing it, Michael froze, realizing a heartbeat later that it was a holo. Thorny shrubs bloomed in every corner—holos—so that the kaleidoscopic walls seemed to merge into the living space. A zebra skin covered the long sofa beside the tiger. Michael touched it, realized with a start that it was *real*, not synthetic, and then jerked his hand away. He hadn't noticed the woman. She lay on the sofa, covered with the zebra's soft hide, face pillowed on one arm, the other arm trailing to the floor. She had an African face, and her skin was darker than Andy's, as dark as the polished wood of the table that stood in front of the sofa. It was so dark that you didn't see the blood unless you looked for it. It wasn't red anymore; it had dried to a dull reddish-brown that barely showed on her dark skin. You could see it on the floor beneath her trailing hand, making a brownish puddle on the straw-colored carpet.

Michael recoiled. She looked so *peaceful*. He could see the hole that something—a bullet?—had made just above her left eye. That was where the blood had come from. And her nose. He recognized her suddenly, remembered polite chatter, hot Taos sun, boredom . . . S'Wanna LeMontagne. His stomach heaved suddenly, and he turned away, struggling not to vomit.

The lieutenant was watching him. So were the two uniformed cops. "I always like to watch a suspect's face when he visits the scene of the crime." The lieutenant nodded, smiling as if Michael had done something clever. "Michael Tryon, I'm arresting you for the murder of S'Wanna LeMontagne."

"What?" Michael stared at the lieutenant, feeling as if the room had suddenly imploded. "I—I met this woman *once*. Two years ago in Taos." He shook his head, trying to understand. "Why would I kill her?"

"Where were you last night?" She was still smiling a little.

"I was down in . . . a plaza. South of the towers. Below the—the rail platform where Estevan died. Someone must have seen me." He was babbling, shocked by the proximity of death and the unfurling wings of darkness in his head. Anything could happen here; there were no rules anymore, none at all. Maybe he *had* done it. Michael felt his face going pale. Why not? What did he remember? Why couldn't S'Wanna LeMontagne have drawn him to her the way Estevan's death site seemed to have drawn him?

No, no, *no*! he wanted to shout, but the words wouldn't come. The lieutenant was staring at him with an expectant expression, like a predator contemplating its prey. Then she must have given some kind of signal, because one of the uniformed cops grabbed his wrist, twisted his arms behind him, and cuffed him. The cop had sagging skin that a cheap body shop could fix and old, sour eyes.

"Let's go, shop meat," he said.

"Why?" Michael's tongue felt as thick as felt in his mouth, but he managed to push the words out. "I want you to tell me . . . why you think I did it."

The lieutenant turned her back on him. "You left something behind," she said over her shoulder.

"I said go." The cop with the old skin planted a hand between his shoulder blades and shoved.

Michael stumbled forward, struggling for balance. The last of his energy was draining away, leaving him hollow and trembling. I am crazy, he thought as the cops herded him into the elevator. I am a murderer.

Only he wasn't. A part of him *knew* it, and he clung to that fragile certainty. Maybe he had embraced that darkness, maybe he had hidden from everything for a while, but he hadn't killed anyone. No, he hadn't done that. Warmth flooded him, and he straightened his shoulders. He was sure.

The aging cop scowled at him. Jealous? Hating Michael because Michael could afford the body shops and he, on his city salary, couldn't? Or wouldn't. Michael felt a rush of sympathy for him, doomed to soften and age and hate it. The shops can't renew your soul, he wanted to tell the man, but he wouldn't understand. They had reached the lobby, and Michael negotiated the steps down from the entry carefully, unsteady with his hands locked behind him.

The lieutenant was watching him, frowning a little. Displeased, Michael thought, and wondered what he had done to piss her off. Maybe she'd wanted him to fall down and confess in a frenzy of repentance. He ducked his head, narrowly missing the door frame as the sullen cop shoved him less than gently into the backseat. He didn't get in front; neither did the other cop. Instead, they stood and talked with the lieutenant for a few moments, then went back up the walk. The lieutenant got into the driver's seat by herself and started the engine.

They pulled away from the curb with a jerk that snapped Michael's head back against the seat. Yeah, the lieutenant was pissed. Or nervous. It came to Michael that if he was considering her for a Stone, he'd be reading anxiety, not anger. Why was she anxious? It was a puzzle. He pondered for a moment, wondering if it mattered, why he bothered to give a damn what this cog in the legal machine might be thinking. It was taking them a long time to reach whatever den of legal machinery they were headed for. He would have to call Chris. Michael let his breath out in a slow sigh, already cringing inside. No way around it—time to yell for help.

Chris would bring him back to Taos; he wouldn't be able to say no. And he'd never have the strength to leave again. The car rolled gently to a stop, and Michael frowned through the window. Crumbling concrete buildings lined the street. Trash littered the cracked and buckled sidewalks, forming drifts against the boarded-up truck bays of a sagging warehouse. Leaving the engine running, the lieutenant got out and slammed the door. Michael eyed her as she opened the rear door and slid onto the seat beside him.

"You're in a lot of shit, honey." She crossed her arms on her chest and sighed. "Do you have any idea exactly how deep you're in?"

"I didn't kill her."

"Spare me." She sighed and stretched, grimacing. "Actually,

I believe you. I don't think you're that good an actor, and I don't think you knew what the hell was coming down up there."

"So why'd you arrest me?" Michael controlled his voice with an effort.

"Because we have enough evidence that you were there to convict you, I'm guessing." She looked at him sideways. "Who wants to see you go to prison?"

Archenwald-Shen. Michael shook his head, numb inside. Zed had warned him, but *this*? For what? A little rudeness?

"I'm into justice." The lieutenant stared through the thick poly shield into the empty front seat. "Sometimes I hate this job. I think I need to go piss." She shoved the door open, got out, and walked away from the car.

Michael stared at the small black disk that lay on the worn upholstery of the seat. The electronic key for the cuffs. Not daring to believe, not able to do anything else, he twisted sideways, his fingers groping frantically, brushing the cool plastic of the disk, losing it, finding it again . . . It was awkward as hell trying to maneuver the key against the lock of the cuffs. Sweat beaded his face, prickling, and stung his eyes. In a minute she'd come back, she'd *have* to come back. This was his one chance, so come on, *do* it . . .

The cuffs released so suddenly that he nearly lost his balance even though he was sitting down. With a gasp of relief, Michael twisted his hands free and tossed the cuffs onto the floor. He scrambled out of the car, then bolted across the street. Don't run! a tiny voice yelled in his head, but he was past listening. His pituitary was pulling the strings now, sending a fight-or-flight wash of adrenaline through his muscles, overlaying coherent thought with the urge to escape. In front of him, the sheet of plasticboard that had covered a door had been crowbarred off, and the door had been hammered open. Michael wrenched it out of his way and squeezed through the crack into darkness.

Panting, he looked around. Light filtered in through dusty skylights, filling the vast space with dim twilight. Gray concrete pillars supported the ceiling, covered with scrawled gang signs. A forlorn stack of fiberboard crates filled one corner. Some of the crates had been broken open, and foam packing beads mounded the stack like a drift of old snow. Michael's heart was slowing back to normal as he peered through the crack in the door. The lieutenant's car was gone; she had let him go.

For the sake of justice? Because Archenwald-Shen had set him up? So she had said. Michael turned away from the crack, uneasiness gnawing at his gut. Something didn't quite feel right. Something nagged at him. A sense of falseness? But the harder he tried to grasp at it, the more elusive the tickle became. He let his breath out in a gusty rush, his footsteps echoing too loudly on the cracked gray floor. It was possible that he had just committed the most stupid act of his entire life.

Make that *likely*, not possible.

A bird fluttered past his head, disappearing through a broken skylight. The thick twilight and the pillars gave the empty warehouse an almost cathedral air. A church to what god? Michael wondered as he picked his way through the scattered debris. The black and red scrawls of gang signs twined around a bright caricature of a skateboarder left by some tagger. The adrenaline was ebbing from Michael's veins, leaving a tremble in his muscles. He needed food; he needed to go somewhere and sort this last month out, to figure out what the hell was going on.

What he needed to do was wake up and discover it was all a dream.

He laughed, a single cracked note that echoed too loudly through the warehouse. Call Chris? Sure, and she'd risk her gallery if she helped him. Michael shook his head and sighed. No. He shoved his hand into the pocket of his tunic and felt the small hardness of the cash card Andy had given him. Andy was going to feel really good when he heard that Michael was wanted for his lover's murder. Yeah. Nice repayment for his Good Samaritan rescue. He headed for a shaft of sunlight that must be falling through another door or maybe a busted-in window.

It was a door, a monster truck bay that had run on an overhead track. It looked as if a tank had smashed into it, peeling one side of the door off its track, curling back the edge like tin. Michael stumbled to a halt, skin crawling between his shoulder blades. In the shadows beyond the seeping light a huddled shape lay against the wall. A man. Michael caught a glimpse of a stubbled cheek just visible above the filthy quilt that wrapped him. Breathing? Yes, the quilt moved slightly with each slow breath. Michael tiptoed by, catching a glimpse of the side of the man's skinny neck. Red blotches marred it like eczema or sunburn, and the flesh-colored disk of a drug patch clung like a leech to the carotid groove of his neck.

He knew the god who lived here now. Michael wriggled through the peeled-back bay, out into the harsh afternoon sun. He knew it too damn well. Blinking in the sunshine, Michael wondered what dark notes the derelict's drugged, dreaming mind would lend to a Stone.

A couple of small shops occupied the block across the street from the warehouse. The top floors were crusted with crude balconies and catwalks cobbled together from scraps of plasterboard, old plumbing, and whatever. Pots and boxes of plants crowded some of them, watered with someone's precious welfare ration and probably protected with some heavy weaponry. An old woman squatted outside one of the shops, offering fried vegetables wrapped in handmade tortillas. Her dark face was so wrinkled and folded that Michael couldn't begin to guess her ethnic origin. She grinned at him as she rolled him a tortilla, revealing plastic fedmed teeth, then snatched at his cash card with withered, long-fingered hands like pale spiders.

The vegetables were spiced with curry and peppery enough to make Michael's eyes water. He ducked into a boarded-up doorway to eat, trying to think as he wiped his face on his sleeve. How much time did he have before the cops started looking hard for him? He needed to leave Albuquerque fast, and he had only the cash Andy had given him. Which limited his options a whole lot. He fingered the small card, wondering how much he actually had. Enough to pay his hotel bill, Andy had said.

The media would have a field day with this murder thing—it was sensational enough to make them plenty of access points, and they'd use it hard. He thought of Chris but pushed the image aside. Margarita Espinoza would hear, too. As he swallowed the last bite of vegetables, he was no longer uncertain. He knew where he had to go—to see her. He just hoped he had enough money to get there. Wherever "there" turned out to be.

Wiping his fingers on his thigh, he scanned the street for any sign of cops, then headed down the block, searching for the bright shell of a public terminal.

Chapter Four

The gallery was enormous, an entire city block that had been gutted to the outside walls, then stabilized with a free-form tracery of alloy girders. They arched and intersected through the spotlit space like the mad creation of a steel-weaving spider, a webwork of Escheresque scaffolding. Balconies interjected here and there, splashed with dramatic light, like stages in a vast theater in the round.

They *were* stages. Margarita tilted her head back, letting her gaze wander. Metallic sculpture on this balcony, silver and somehow threatening; color compositions on that one—complex canvases layered with shattered bits of stained glass; a twisting helix of chrome there . . . A small flower of excitement unfolded in her chest. The Yamada boasted that they featured the cutting edge, but they didn't risk space on anyone who hadn't already gained a sturdy foothold in the art world.

Margarita's lips twitched. Her foothold was seriously less than sturdy.

They had offered her a showing, anyway. Because she was truly a rising star? She ran a hand through her thick mop of black hair, her doubts overlaid for once with a heady sense of making it. Yeah, rising, or Yamada wouldn't take her. Yes.

Maybe the doubts would stay away this time.

Urgency seized her, and she shook the hair back from her face. She had until tomorrow evening to get this baby up and running; the Yamada Gallery was on the First Tuesday promenade. The art scene would come to her this time.

And *Crystalline* wasn't perfect. Not yet.

Margarita bent over the holostage console again, shoving

back the sleeves of her too-large tunic, chewing on her lower lip as her hands flew over the keys. *Fracture: Crystalline*, she had titled this piece, third in the *Fracture* sequence that had earned her this show. It was a winter song of the soul, a crystalline desolation that wrung the heart with beauty and despair, a perfection so far beyond the crude and fervent energy of spring that it could only return there. A song of what humanity had put aside as it turned its face to the world of the Net, body shops, and insulated, environmentally self-contained living.

Was it enough—what she was after? Desolation, perfection, the soul? Doubting again . . . Margarita let her breath out in a rush, trying to feel it, what she wanted. She grabbed the console pad, flipped the harness over her head, and stepped up onto the stage as color and shape swirled to life. Cold. She shivered as the first breath of frigid air touched her bare arms. Snow covered the ground, pierced by birch trees whose black-scarred trunks pointed crooked fingers at the sky. Here and there bare ground showed where snow had melted and refrozen to a satiny glaze.

Make that my skin, make its chill mine . . . It still didn't feel quite right, but there wasn't time. She chewed her lip. More rocks? She touched keys, brought the rock menu up onto her tiny screen, selected for glacial moraine, scrolled through samplers. That one, but add erosion; the moraine would have washed it a long way to end up in those birches. Multiply, vary the size over one-point-five, and randomize to modify the shape. She began to place them, sinking them into the hard, frozen soil. One by one they blinked to life onstage.

Margarita frowned as a fist-sized stone popped into slow-motion existence at her feet. Hurry up. Touching her console, she selected the rock, fractured it, a memento of the sun-and-ice cycle, its sharp edge a threat, a resonance, *yes*. She hit *continue*. Music swelled almost imperceptibly—the cool gossip of chimes that became the auditory presence of the cold breeze tickling her. A single *doumbek* tapped in the background, almost beneath the threshold of hearing. And an Andean flute skirled softly, dry as frozen snow.

Margarita breathed through her nose, smelling winter. No. She hit *pause* again. Lip caught between her teeth, she brought up the scent menu. Arrow had told her, back when she was just a raw student, that scent was the toughest part. The nose was connected directly to memory. Get it right, and they'd cry; screw it up, and they'd laugh for the wrong reasons. Maybe a touch of resin, but not enough to make people look for forests or think of Christmas . . .

Shit. She let her breath out in a disgusted rush. Okay, Arrow. What am I doing wrong? He had been so sure of himself. Sometimes she thought he had been that sure of her. Other times she didn't know . . . Margarita drew in a quick breath, her fingers flying. I'll get it, Arrow. Just stop looking over my damn shoulder. I can make this work.

But he wasn't looking over her shoulder. He was dead.

Better to use real recorded effects. No time. Try this. Closing her mind to Arrow and doubt, she breathed memory, childhood, winter. Yes. *Yes:* cuff of a wool shirt drawn unconsciously across the nose, the mouth. Wool stiff and cold, the sudden indrawn breath capturing scent *and* taste, resin and sweat, woods and ice, friend or lover or child. She chewed her lip again, thinking of all the things the cuff of a wool shirt could touch on a chilly day. Wood smoke, soap, saliva together . . . yeah, *forlorn* . . .

Play. Pause. Edit. Play. Pause. Play.

And now the words—the lex. She'd used Katrina's voice, only slightly altered. It was . . . an apology. Because Katrina had asked to see this piece in progress and Margarita had said no. No, she had snapped that "no," wanting to hurt because the piece was hurting *her*. Stifling a pang of guilt, she wondered suddenly if Katrina would recognize her own voice, if she would understand.

In the foothills of the mountain, amid wintry autumn before winter begins, you visit me, come in heavy clothes that carry no spare warmth.

They yielded to sharp lines, languid lines:

Again I hold you with my winter's color,
With the white sum of hues
Soon worn by the year's darkness.
Remember me without regret.
You think I'm gone, abstract, dead,
But your body knows that I am now the broken stones
Gentle beneath these first snows.

The flute's voice rose in pitch without becoming louder. Piercing yet chaste, Margarita thought. Katrina, why do you want to watch me work? I don't go to your dance rehearsals . . .

We walked here once when we both wore the same kind of life. Your hand was cold until I held it with my cold hand; one palm, five fingers; two palms, ten; warm pieces now part of single recollection. My body has gone to another flesh, to time and seasons without need to be numbered.
Your hand, alone now: if you hold it in your other hand, they are both only more alone.
I did not mean this pain, elemental, lost to the elements just as I am.

So I come to tell you the birches are pointing,
Waving and dancing in their raven dreams.
And the fat raven dreams, full of the fall.
The glacier dreams of a snowy fatness still to come.

This was for Katrina, Margarita told herself, but she hadn't yet affixed a dedication. She'd do it in a minute, when she got the last details polished and perfect. Margarita closed her eyes, fingers lax and still on the console as Katrina's altered, strange, but so-familiar voice whispered on:

Again and again I will arrive in winter's color to hold you without warmth, but in brightness; to hold your fingers with my birch fingers; to touch your heart with my granite heart; to show you the cold that can break the ground more easily than heat.

Beautiful words. Yeah, no shit. Then how come it hurts? Why did she feel she was *missing* something . . . ?

"Mar, that's wonderful."

Margarita jumped slightly, then thumbed *pause*. "Trina?" She peered into the twilight beyond the holo stage. "What're you doing here?"

"It's late, girl." Katrina leapt lightly onto the stage, landing in a holoed snowdrift. "Time to quit."

"It's not finished." Margarita tapped the console, wanting to feel triumph, wanting those words, that sensory poetry to sweep her away as it had swept her away as she had first roughed *Crystalline* out. All she felt was tired. "Yeah, I guess it's time to quit." She wouldn't meet Katrina's eyes. Small and slender, Trina might be some golden-haired winter sprite come to tempt sleeping spring. *To show you the cold that can break the ground more easily than heat* . . . Margarita shook her head to banish the echoes. "It's just another *Fracture* piece. The people who liked the other two will like this." The words came out flat. "Big deal."

"Yes, it *is* a big deal. Maybe you'll sell all three to some hot web node. You didn't eat anything today; that's your problem." Katrina grabbed the console, snapping it free of its harness with a deft twist. "You got it all saved, girl?"

"Yeah, okay, shut it down." Margarita turned her back as the snow blurred into opalescent haze and vanished. The scent lingered for a moment longer before dissolving on the air currents. Still too much resin? Speak to me, Arrow, she thought. If you're going to lean over my goddamn shoulder and disapprove, at least tell me if I got the scent mix wrong.

That was unfair. He had never disapproved, had never leaned over her shoulder. He had let her play, explore, crash and burn sometimes . . .

She shook her head so that her hair whipped her face. "I've got to come back here tonight. Trina, why can't I make it *work*?"

"It does work." Katrina brushed a wisp of hair back from Margarita's face and slid an arm around her. "Like dynamite. You've got First Tuesday jitters is all."

"Bullshit." Margarita shrugged off her hand and reached for the console. "It's got nothing to do with the damn opening. Trina, if it was so good, people would pay attention. It would *reach* them. What if . . ." What if nobody even looks at it tomorrow? She couldn't speak the words out loud, couldn't give them that much power. "What does it *do*?" she whispered.

"It makes me . . . sad," Katrina said softly. "It makes me look at myself, at you . . ."

But Trina had listened to Margarita talk about it, and she just wanted Margarita to feel better, to smile and be fun instead of down. "Thanks." Margarita twisted from beneath her arm. "Let's go, if you're so anxious."

Katrina sighed.

That sigh was so damn tolerant. Like Tía Elena when one of the boys got in trouble at school or with the local cops—that soft exhalation of breath that meant resignation, because it wasn't ever going to get any better and she had to get up at four to get to her job on the cleaning crew, so why waste energy being pissed? It was a sigh that said, *It doesn't really concern me . . .* Margarita hunched her shoulders, because it *didn't* concern Katrina. Katrina was already a star—she made it into the media at least three or four times a year.

Margarita jumped off the stage and slammed the console into its rest. "So I'm taking a break. Are you happy now?" She shook hair out of her eyes, wanting Katrina to get pissed, daring her to. "Maybe I'll just quit and to hell with it all."

"You need some dinner." Katrina sighed again and put her hands on Margarita's shoulders. "Come on home and I'll give you a massage. You can come back later." She stroked Margarita's back gently. "Girl, it's okay. *Crystalline* is great."

Great . . . Margarita's throat closed on a knot of wanting. Wanting to believe her, wanting to cry, to hold her and be held, to *know* that it was great.

It wasn't.

Katrina knew it, too. The shadow lurked in those clear blue eyes. Margarita shivered inside the circle of Katrina's arms, wanting to bury her face against Katrina's shoulder and weep. Which wouldn't help; she'd learned that before she could walk. Margarita drew a slow breath, smelling the musky odor of Katrina's skin overlaid with the tang of healthy sweat and something unpleasantly perfumy. "How come you're here so early? I thought Argent was going to work your butts until midnight at least?"

"He quit early." Katrina hugged her, her dancer's muscles going hard. "He's squabbling with Li again." Reluctantly, she let Margarita go. "Sooner or later Li's going to walk or he's going to throw her out. Which won't be any big deal." Katrina shrugged. "That solo's too much for her, and she knows it. So does Argent. He'd be better off if he wasn't so willing to give new dancers a chance." She sighed theatrically. "We all know he's going to have to let Li walk. Even *Li* knows it, and to be perfectly honest, I think she'll be relieved. She's a good enough dancer to know that he's giving her stuff she can't handle. Question is, Will he wake up before our first gig or not? The bet's running five to three that she'll still be doing the solo at Danjo's." She rolled her eyes. "Pia could step into that role tomorrow and do better than Li. She's working on it, I know, but she won't say. That's Pia for you."

Margarita frowned because Katrina was chattering, and she didn't chatter; she said what she had to say and shut up. "Something's wrong." Margarita looked back at Katrina. "It's *us*, right?"

"No. This certainly isn't the time to discuss anything serious with you, anyway." Katrina's smile was wary. "Let's go. I'm hungry, and you'll be much more rational after you eat."

Why that wariness? I'm tired, Margarita thought. Maybe that's all it is. And I'm a bitch, and I deserve it if Katrina's pissed. She picked her jacket up from the floor where she'd dropped it. "So, all right, let's go eat. I'm glad you got off early." She swept an arm around Katrina's shoulders, trying to smooth over the last splintered half hour. "You want Thai? That little place around the corner has a new cook. Killer peanut sauce."

"You wait till tomorrow." Katrina leaned against her. "You're going to be a sensation."

"Yeah. Sure." Doubts crowded after her like ghosts. What if the crowd *did* love her? *Crystalline* still didn't work. She would know if it did, damn it. "Lustik's got his new Stone down on the main level," she said tightly. "You watch. The browsers are gonna walk straight back to it, drink their wine, and then move on."

"No way." Katrina gripped her arm, fingers pinching. "You're hopeless. I'm going to give you such *shit* while they're lining up to get into *Crystalline*. Honey, you're on the second level. Pity the poor suckers up above the timberline." She tossed her head and laughed.

Katrina was so damn *sure*.

Margarita had never been sure of anything. Perhaps because there were no certainties, growing up in the barrio. Not if you planned to get out. The only certainties came with acceptance: poverty, violence, and ultimately death. Margarita paused at the edge of her balcony. Narrow metal mesh platforms rose from the ground level through the balconies on endless loops of chain. Katrina hopped onto one of the descending platforms, holding casually to one of the chains as she sank through the floor. Suppressing a shudder, Margarita stepped onto the next platform, clutching the supporting chains with both hands. The platform swayed with her weight, rattling and vibrating from enormous toothed cogwheels at top and bottom. Dangerous as hell. Don't look down.

She swallowed hard and looked up instead, to where the stairs vanished into the next balcony up from hers, her eyes following the shadows outward and upward, up into the dim shadows at the very top of the huge gallery, where a half dozen stair loops hung from their clanking masses of gears and motor. Dizzy suddenly, Margarita clutched the chains, her stomach turning over, her fingers threatening to cramp. The floor was rising to meet her. In a spurt of terror—that she'd miss it, sink down into the darkness beneath the main floor, and be ground to bloody hamburger by the fanged wheels—Margarita leapt off. The step swung backward in response, banging against the opening in the floor, chains clashing with the sound of metal on metal.

"Easy, girl." Katrina steadied her. "They even scare *me*. A shrink could do a temporary suppression on the height thing—just until the show's over."

"No way. Nobody fucks with my head." Bitchy again, wanting to just *stop* it, but unable to, Margarita turned her back on Katrina. "You know, you'd be better off going over to Argent's, maybe sleeping there." Her voice quavered just a hair. "I'm just going to keep snarling at you all night."

"You can snarl."

Still angry and ashamed of that anger, Margarita paused in front of Lustik's new Stone. It had half the floor to itself, tastefully lighted and mounted, the star of the opening. Even here, a meter from its polished wood pedestal, the resonance enfolded her: lightness, a sudden sense of *newness*, as if she were looking at the world for the first time . . .

"I don't know why everyone's so hot over these things." Katrina came up behind her and sniffed. "So what? Your stuff has as much impact."

"No, it doesn't." Margarita stretched out a hand, brushing the Stone's surface. Stones didn't feel like stone and didn't feel like flesh. They felt like something in between. "I wonder what they *are*." She trailed her fingertips across the flesh-stone, eyes blurring with a sudden vision of dawn breaking over a horizon of low hills, a sense of anticipation. "I went to the Museum of Modern Art when I was in New York last spring. They've got one of Michael Tryon's Stones. I . . . listened to it."

"You didn't tell me that," Katrina said quietly. Hurt?

"Why should I have told you?" Margarita said, then pressed her lips together because, yeah, she should have mentioned it and she hadn't. "I—didn't know how I felt about him yet. It was right after Xia told me."

"You still don't know how you feel about him."

"Yeah, I do." Margarita stepped away from the Stone, its bright dawn fading from her mind. "It doesn't matter one way or the other." She looked away. "Trina, I'm . . . sorry. That I'm such a bitch tonight."

"You sure are." Katrina took her hand, smoothing Margarita's fingers around hers. "You're a bitch and a basket case, and I want peanut sauce. You're coming out the front door with me *right now*."

"Yes, ma'am." Margarita let herself be marched toward the door. Katrina could be so *fierce*. And sometimes she could be so nurturing.

That warmth scared Margarita sometimes. She didn't have a clue as to why. "I'll behave." She held Katrina's hand tightly, telling herself that the shadows between them were opening jitters, nothing more. "I promise. Trina, I need some more memory." She circled the rattling stairway chains warily. "And a better processor chip. It took me forever to get my rock file up tonight."

"Already?" Katrina blew out a breath that stirred the fine hair on her forehead. "Girl, you just expanded, remember? We got rent due next week."

"I know." She shrugged.

"Put some of it into the Net. The trivial stuff, you know." Katrina frowned. "Stuff nobody wants to steal."

"Yeah, and give 'em an access straight into my hard memory? No way. Look what happened to New Moon. That hacker dude had her entire piece sold on the market before she ever got a gallery offer. No *way* she can prove he stole it."

"You'll have to suffer." Katrina didn't look at her as they neared the main door. "We can't do it right now."

"I've *got* to—"

"Rita? Heading out?"

Ari Yiassis, Yamada's manager. She hated being called Rita, and he knew it. Swallowing exasperation, Margarita halted in front of the door. "I thought you went home."

"I came back." He emerged from the shadows, tall and body-shop fit, smiling. "Hi, Trina, when did you get here?" He tugged at her loose braid.

He never could take his eyes off Katrina, but the intimacy of this gesture widened Margarita's eyes. *Mistake*, boy. She smiled, waiting for Katrina to unsheath that razor tongue of hers.

"Hi, Ari." Katrina merely moved a half step sideways, out of his reach. "Mar's piece is great, isn't it?"

"It's not bad." He smiled at her and edged closer. "I hope it does well tomorrow night."

"Come on." Margarita slipped her arm around Katrina, making the gesture as possessive and openly sexual as possible. "Let's go home." She got a whiff of his musky perfume and wrinkled her nose. "I'm coming back later, so don't lock me out."

"I won't." His grin mocked her. "Good night to you both."

"Good night, *Mister* Yiassis." Katrina leaned into Margarita's embrace, propelling her through the open door. "Horny little bastard." She blew out an exasperated breath and rolled her eyes at Margarita. "How can you stand him?"

"I'll kick his knee out from under him if he touches you." Margarita ducked her head against the cold, dusty wind that blew down the street.

"No, you won't. You'll be very polite, girl, or I'll take your damn head off." She stopped so fast that Margarita walked into her. "You *need* that gallery slot, and that creep offered it to you. So you don't throw it away like that, do you hear me? I can say no loud enough without your help."

"Hey, relax. I'm not brain-dead." Margarita backed away a step, their brief, easy moment shattered now. "I know which side my ass is covered on. Give me a break, okay? I won't lose us our rent."

"Yeah, okay, I apologize." Katrina forced a laugh. "*I'll* deal with Ari; don't worry. You concentrate on *Crystalline*, okay? And don't forget to smile for all those nice, rich inside art fanciers who are going to be panting to commission you after tomorrow night."

"Yeah, sure." They'd reached the end of the block. Margarita started left, toward the restaurant, but Katrina pulled her back. "Tell you what." Her face looked ivory-pale in the rainbowed glow from a VR parlor's fancy holo display. "If we stay out of the fancy eateries around here, you can buy that memory you need and we can still make the rent."

"Great." Margarita blinked, surprised. "I really *do* need the memory. Are you sure we can swing it?"

"We can squeak by." Katrina's eyes evaded hers. "Look, we've got peanut butter in the cupboard, and rice noodles. *I'll* do the killer peanut sauce tonight."

"With that fake junk?"

"When I get through with it, you'll think I grew the peanuts myself." Katrina laughed. "Let's go." She tugged at Margarita. "I'm getting dust in my eyes from this shitty wind."

"All right, all right!" Margarita let Katrina pull her into a wild run down the sidewalk, laughing for no reason at all, friends again, drawing wary eye-corner stares from the couples out doing the entertainment in this district. But underneath the laughter a small doubt gnawed at her. Something felt . . . wrong. Maybe the relationship was simply ending. *No,* a part of her cried. But in the depth of her soul she wondered if she wouldn't be . . . relieved.

That hurt most of all. "Hey, wait up," she cried as Katrina let go of her hand and darted ahead.

Katrina leapt onto a sidewalk sculpture of a bear slapping salmon from a stream. "Girl, you're *slow*." She balanced on one foot on the bear's back, bounced up onto his composite brow, then vaulted into a somersault that landed her lightly on her feet. A couple of leathered punks down the block whistled and whooped mockingly. She swept them a deep bow, laughed, and tossed her head. "Catch me if you can," she said, and danced down the sidewalk.

"Are you ever gonna grow up?" Margarita yelled after her. Panting, laughing, she ran after Katrina, telling herself that everything was all right, that she loved Katrina and it would *never* end between them.

Katrina let her catch up two blocks later. The streetlights ran out, along with the lighted restaurants, the plush VR parlors, the bars, and the bored men and women with enough money to buy their excitement there. Night filled those streets. Light seeped from beneath doors and around the cracks in shuttered windows. It was two hours yet until the power curfew, but the bars, dives, and sleazy parlors didn't let much light escape into the street. It was as if light were precious, had to be hoarded behind closed doors. What light did escape drizzled away into the darkness like spilled wine.

Margarita caught up to walk beside Katrina, not touching, paying attention to the other shadows on the sidewalk. If you paid attention, the predators figured you weren't worth the effort and went looking for something easier. Mostly. She slid her hand into her pocket, fingertips making contact with the smooth plastic handle of the blade she carried there. Just in case.

"The flea market should be over on Oak tonight, under the rail track. Damn, I *hate* wearing my hair up." Katrina unpinned her thick braid and combed her fingers through her long hair. "Want to swing over to Oak and buy a couple of green onions for the noodles?"

Margarita shook her head. "Let's just get home." She was regretting this meal break. Too much resin, that had to be the problem. She'd have people singing "Jingle Bells."

Katrina sighed, but Margarita ignored her. They'd reached their building, an old hotel not too far from the rail. Someone had made a halfhearted attempt to fix it up years before but hadn't gotten farther than upgrading the wiring to allow reasonable Net access and remodeling the uppermost floors. They lived on the fourth floor—far enough from the street to be safe, not far enough up to pay for the view or the old remodel job.

At least it had a working elevator, and it wasn't a bunch of flimsy steps hung from chains. They took it up to their floor, and Margarita wrinkled her nose at the musty odor of the worn carpeting in the hall. Smells were bugging her tonight. Maybe the resin just needed something to balance it. A hint of wet wool? Or maybe horse barn, with just enough ammonia tang to harmonize with the resin . . .

She was groping, pretending. *Crystalline* wasn't lacking some trivial tech note. It just didn't do what she wanted it to do—if she even knew what that was anymore. It was slipping farther away with every passing moment.

"I might as well have left you there." Katrina pushed her through the open door. "Or do you *want* to stand out in the hall staring at the wallpaper?"

"Sorry." Margarita tossed her jacket onto the pile of cushions against the wall, seeing her reflection in the mirror-tiled wall toss an identical jacket. She glanced sideways at Katrina and picked it up. "I guess I can't shut it off tonight."

"No kidding." Katrina whisked the jacket out of her hand, shed her own, and flung them both into the closet. "So go curl up and space out while I cook." She kissed Margarita lightly on the cheek. "If I didn't know how bitchy *I'm* going to get next week when we open, I'd be pissed. God help us if we both end up with an opening scheduled for the same week. We'll kill each other for sure. *Sit!*"

"Yes, ma'am," Margarita said, but Katrina had already vanished into the tiny kitchen. So, okay, don't fight it, she told herself. Pulling the cushions into a comfortable nest, she settled herself into the middle of them, her feet propped on the low, lacquered table she'd bought for Katrina's last birthday. It was a Japanese antique, authentic, and had cost her more than she'd been able to afford.

She'd bought it anyway. Last fall Trina had turned twenty-nine. As a dancer, she was getting old. Eventually she could start her own troupe, as Argent had. Hell, half the troupe would desert him and go with her if she left tomorrow . . . but that wasn't why she danced.

In the kitchen Katrina was singing something low and lilting in that clear midrange voice of hers. Poetry, Margarita thought, and leaned her head back on the piled cushions. She writes poetry with her body, and it takes an audience to make it whole. Margarita closed her eyes, shaken by a sudden rush of love for this fierce, demanding, loving *dancer*.

Then why am I afraid of her?

Afraid? Her eyes snapped open. Where had *that* come from? The terminal chimed the three-note e-mail signal. Someone wanted a real-time reply. Margarita sat up straight, relieved at the distraction. "Okay, I'm here." She tapped the screen. "House, who is it?"

"Argent." Katrina had given their House system a soft androgynous voice.

He never called after a rehearsal. Margarita glanced toward the kitchen, where Katrina was still singing. Maybe it wasn't just Argent feuding with Li tonight. "I'll talk to him."

"Hi." Argent's long, worried face materialized on-screen. "How's Kat?"

He *always* looked worried. "Katrina's fine. What's up?"

"Fine? She better not be too fine." Argent's pale eyes sparked. "She leaves a hole the size of a missile crater when she's gone, and a couple of people fall right into it. I might as well have canceled the whole damn rehearsal. How's her stomach?"

Margarita stared at him for an instant, groping for some missed beginning to this strange conversation. "Uh, I guess it's better. I . . . just got home." What was going on here? "Was she . . . pretty sick?"

"She looked pretty pale when she left at noon. I told her to go to a clinic if it got bad." Argent's face, if possible, got longer. "You get food poisoning from some of the dives that pass as restaurants in this town, you could die. We got some schedule for the next three months, and she's gotta be there when we open at the center. Or it all goes smash. You sure she's okay?"

"Yeah, yeah, I'm sure." Like *hell*. "Don't worry, Argent. She'll show tomorrow." Margarita forced a smile. "She was even talking about working a little tonight."

"Forget it. Tell her to stay in bed." Argent sighed. "I got enough trouble. See you." His face vanished.

Margarita stared at the opalescent screen.

"Mar?" Katrina wandered into the main room. "The noodles are ready, and the sauce is *great*. If I do say so myself." She grinned, working her fingers through a tangle in her golden mane. "Who was on the phone?" Full of static, her loose hair framed her face like a cloud of spun gold.

"It was Argent." Margarita blurted out the words. "Worrying about you."

"Because I told him I was sick." She made a face and yanked at the knot. "Do this for me, will you? I can't see, and *you're* the one who nags me to keep it long. I had to give him some kind of reason for skipping out." She folded her legs under herself, dropping gracefully onto the cushion in front of Margarita. "God, I can't *stand* it when he gets after Li."

Yeah, of course. Margarita knelt beside her, working at the tangle, Katrina's hair sliding like cool silk between her hands. "Got it." She combed her fingers through Katrina's long hair. The braid had crimped it into soft waves, and it crackled, tickling her fingers with tiny sparks of electricity. Something nagged at her, an elusive thought that refused to be pinned down. Margarita leaned forward against Katrina's back, her breasts pushing against the muscled hardness of Katrina's shoulders. Katrina sighed, eyes closed, face tilted to the ceiling. The line of her slender neck was so *perfect*. Margarita ran one fingertip along her jaw and down the long curve of her neck, throat tightening with that perfection. She had captured it in the clean crisp line of snow against sky in *Crystalline* . . .

"I love you, you know." She buried her face in Katrina's hair, breathing her scent. That too-sweet musky smell tickled her nose—the one she'd noticed earlier.

It connected suddenly.

"You smell like Ari." She straightened. "Jeeze, what did that bastard do? Back you into a corner and paw you?"

"Will you just knock it *off*?" Katrina bolted to her feet, throwing back her hair. "What is *with* you tonight? You were right there. Did you see Yiassis back me into any corners?"

"No." Margarita stared up at her, stunned by this sudden anger. "Hey, I'm sorry, okay?"

"Sure." Katrina rubbed both hands across her face. "No problem. Just accuse me of anything you want. Just shut me out of your life. Your precious art is none of my business. I get to deal with the angst when it isn't working, but I don't get to comfort you—oh, no, not that."

"You comfort me."

"You tolerate it," Katrina snapped. "Look, just go back to the damned gallery. I'm going to work on my solo, because *good* matters to me, too. Then I'll *really* stink."

"Hey, that's not true." Margarita stared up at her. "None of it's true."

"Isn't it?" Katrina turned away, her shoulders slumping. "Maybe it isn't. Look, just go get to work. *Crystalline*'s important to you."

And Katrina wasn't? And if Margarita did leave, go back to

the gallery, would it be over between them? Was that what Katrina was saying? "Trina?" Margarita scrambled to her feet, full of jagged, scattered emotion. "Listen, Trina, let's cut this out. We're going to mess it up, two years together. It's me, *my* jitters." Was it? She shook her head. "I love you. I really do. Let's both remember that, okay?"

"Yeah." Katrina's shoulders slumped, and she wouldn't meet Margarita's eyes. "I guess you really do, and maybe I just want too much. I don't know. Let's put it all on hold until after tomorrow night." She tried a feeble laugh. "Want to try that killer peanut sauce?"

"Yeah. I'm starved." Margarita stared moodily after her as Katrina vanished through the kitchen door. It's ending, she thought. I thought it was forever. I wanted it to be forever. I did, she told herself. Goddammit, I *did*!

Someone knocked on the door.

"Who is it?" Margarita scowled at the door-mounted security screen. Someone from the troupe, come to look in on the supposedly sick Katrina?

A man's face blinked into focus, and Margarita swallowed, her throat suddenly dry. He had gray hair braided into a thin tail down his back, and his gray eyes seemed to fix on her face. Which was just because he'd spotted the video pickup above the door and was staring straight at it.

"I'm looking for Margarita Espinoza," he said. "I . . . it's important."

"Who's that?" Katrina paused in the kitchen doorway, a bowl of steaming noodles in each hand. "I don't know him."

"I do." Heat and cold rippled across Margarita's skin in waves. "I know him." She'd pulled a holo from some media story on the Net, but he'd looked younger. "That's Michael Tryon."

"What?" Katrina's eyes widened. "How did he end up *here*? I thought you changed your mind about seeing him. What now? Mar?" She sounded hesitant. "Do you want me to chase him off?"

"No," Margarita said numbly. "You're spilling the peanut sauce."

Katrina glowered down at the tan splatters on the wooden floor and sighed. "This is just what we need. Let me get a sponge." She spun on her heel and vanished into the kitchen with the dripping bowls.

She sounded upset. On-screen, Michael Tryon looked over his shoulder, then back at the pickup. "Is anybody home?"

Sudden anger unfroze Margarita's muscles. "Come in," she said, and squashed a fleeting instant of terror as the lock clicked.

He came in quickly and closed the door behind him. And then he stopped. It was a rigid kind of stop, as if he had turned to stone just inside her doorway. His eyes were fixed on her face, and he seemed to turn a shade paler beneath his dark tan.

"Margarita."

It wasn't a question. Margarita lifted her chin, wondering what the hell he saw in her face to make him so damn sure. Maybe it was just because she looked Hispanic. Maybe that was as far as he wanted to look. Screw polite games. The anger warmed her like brandy, blunting the jagged edges of her fight with Katrina. "Mr. Tryon. How come you're here? How did you find out where I lived?"

He blinked and recoiled half a step. "I . . . got someone to dig your address out of the Net. I'm sorry. But I needed to find you. There are some things . . . I need to tell you. And I needed to—see you. Meet you. To see if you were . . . mine. Or Estevan's. I'm not saying this right, am I?"

"Mar, *catch* him." Katrina lunged past her to seize the sculptor by the arm as he swayed. "Sit down, already. Here."

Margarita stood frozen as they half fell onto the cushions in a tangle of arms and legs.

"Call medical on the terminal." Katrina glared up at Margarita. "Move it."

"No, don't." Tryon struggled to sit up straight, ashen-faced now. "I'm sorry. I don't think I've had anything to eat since yesterday. I just got . . . dizzy. I'll be all right in a minute."

Katrina growled something that Margarita couldn't quite catch. "Bring him a glass of orange juice, Mar. There's a little left in the fridge." She disentangled herself and rocked back on her heels. "Come on." Her voice prodded. "Hurry up."

Still numb, Margarita went into the kitchen. Clumsily she poured bright juice into a green and white striped glass and brought it back into the main room. "Here." She held it out to Tryon. "I'm sorry you're not feeling well." She realized suddenly how thin he was. His hands trembled as he took the glass, slopping a little juice over the rim. His collapse had betrayed her anger, and without it she felt adrift, groping for words that refused to come to her. "What was it you wanted to tell me?" Those weren't the right words, but they were all she could get hold of.

"Mar, give him a minute."

"No." Tryon shook his head. "That's all right. I tried to reach you at the Hilton, you know." He looked up at her, hands clasped around the glass as if to hide their weakness. "You were already gone. You haven't . . . heard about me on the news, have you? I thought everybody would know by now," he said bitterly. "I didn't think you'd let me in."

"What are you talking about?" Katrina pried the empty glass gently from his hand. "I'll get you some more."

"Thank you." He waited until she reappeared from the kitchen with more juice, then emptied the glass in four long swallows. "That does help, thank you." He smiled at Katrina, a warm smile, full of life. "Margarita, I need to be honest with you." His eyes, pale gray, the color of a cloudy sky, sought hers. "If Xia was pregnant when she left me, I didn't know. When I got your letter, I thought maybe you were Estevan's daughter. I never had a clue that you existed. Xia never got in touch with me. I needed to tell you this. I need you to know that I loved Xia." His voice trembled just a hair. "I loved her more than I let myself know. By the time I understood how much, it was too late." He looked away. "It was way too late."

"You never tried to contact her?" Katrina peered into the empty glass as if there were something fascinating in the bottom. "What's this about the news?"

"I never tried to find Xia. I told myself that she walked out on me, that it was her choice. I think maybe . . . I was wrong." Tryon bent his head. "There's a warrant out for my arrest," he said softly. "For the murder of another sculptor."

"Shit." The word escaped before Margarita could close her lips against it. Thanks a lot, she wanted to yell at him. I didn't ask you here. Why did you bring *this* to dump on my doorstep?

"Mr. Tryon, I have to call the police." Katrina stood up, her face full of real regret. "You can't do this to Margarita."

"It's all right." He raised his head and met Margarita's stare.

"I didn't kill her," he said softly. "That's the truth. I was framed. I think the police are still looking for me in New Mexico. Or maybe by now they've traced me to San Francisco. Anyway, I didn't come here to make trouble for you." He got to his feet and nodded at Katrina, poised in front of the screen. "I'll leave. Actually, I was planning on turning myself in after I saw you, anyway. I'm not too good at playing fugitive."

"No." Margarita sucked in a breath, wondering why the air seemed so thin. "Stay here. For tonight, anyway." She looked an apology at Katrina.

Who wasn't buying it. "Are you crazy?" Fists planted on her hips, Katrina glared. "If he's innocent, let him turn himself in and get this over with. You want to go to prison as an accessory or something? Girl, you'll blow your gallery opening in spades."

"It's my choice." Margarita returned Katrina's glower, not sure why she wanted this but sure that she did. "If you don't want to risk it, you could go crash with Jeannette or Pia until he's gone. Tell 'em I'm too bitchy to take right now."

"Which is sure as hell the truth," Katrina said between clenched teeth. "Oh, Mar—" Her voice broke suddenly, and she turned away. "All right, all right. This is your show. You handle it any way you want." Her voice faltered. "I just hope we don't both regret it." She set the glass onto the low table very gently and went into the bedroom. The soft click of the closing door made them both jump.

Tears again? Margarita took a step toward the bedroom door and stopped, torn between that closed door and Michael Tryon's silent presence.

"I'm sorry." He was on his feet, still pale but not swaying, anyway. "She said . . . something about a gallery opening. I . . ." He paused, shaking his head. "Are you an artist?"

What was she seeing in his face? "Yeah, I am." Margarita looked away. "Nothing as hot as Stones." She didn't try to keep the bitterness out of her voice. "I do holoture—words, music, sensory stuff. When I can afford the hardware."

"I didn't know." The words came out in a harsh, breathy rush. "Before I go, is Xia still alive?" His eyes fastened themselves on her face. "Can you tell me where she is?"

"I . . . don't know where she is," Margarita said. Was there anguish in his pale eyes? "She shows up here every year or so.

We don't get along." In spades. "Sit down already." She avoided his eyes. "I said you could stay. As long as I've pissed off Katrina anyway, you might as well take me up on the invitation. This isn't exactly your upscale neighborhood. You're damn lucky some punk didn't strip you naked on your way here." She drew a deep breath, light-headed again. "If the law comes busting in, we'll all just pretend you didn't tell us about any murder, okay? I'm not all that hot on honesty." And hopefully he wasn't going to bring a bunch of cops down on her head. She didn't do well with cops.

"Thank you." His eyes caught hers, held them. "Don't knock honesty. Sometimes it's the only thing that can save you."

For a moment those eyes became windows into a landscape of endless shadows. *In the foothills of the mountain, amid wintry autumn before winter begins, you visit me,* Katrina's altered stranger's voice echoed in her head. . . . *come in heavy clothes that carry no spare warmth.* Then his face contracted into focus again, and Margarita shivered. Low blood sugar, she told herself. That's all. He's just an old man, and I'm just hungry.

"You need something to eat, and so do I." She blinked, her eyes suddenly full of burning, unexpected tears. "We've got noodles. With this killer peanut sauce." She wiped her face roughly on her shoulder as she went to get him a plate of noodles, wondering who she was crying for.

She had a feeling that she was going to find out, and too damn soon.

Chapter Five

He dissolved into darkness, expanding forever, so that Earth's sun contracted to a pinpoint of light, infinitely small. He *was* forever, made up of a billion souls, a billion sighs, pleasures, loves, hates, fears. All he had to do was let go and he would be . . .

. . . complete.

A woman's face, dark-haired, eyes full of reproach.

Xia?

He struggled upright, dazzled by light and shape without meaning, still aching for that forever darkness. The dark-haired woman crouched beside him, no dream, her wide-eyed face framed by tangled hair.

"Xia!" He raised a faltering hand to her face.

"Wake up." She jerked her head away. "It's a dream."

Not Xia. Memory rushed in like a breaking wave, bringing the room into focus, and the texture of the cushions beneath him.

Margarita. His daughter. He'd spent the night here on her floor. Michael drew a shuddering breath, pressing his palms into his eyes to banish the last black shadows. *His daughter.* Have I made up my mind? he asked himself, and found no answer.

"Are you all right?" She was eyeing him warily. "You want some coffee or some tea or something? That sounded like you were having a bad dream."

"I'll take coffee if you have it." He stood, finding more strength in his body than he'd expected. "I'm sorry if I woke you."

"I was up." She retreated to the kitchen.

Yes, retreated. He could use her to add a fine, sharp edge of tension to a Stone. Michael looked around the small room, trying to banish the dark echo of his nightmare. No, not a nightmare. He had felt no fear; rather, he'd been full of a vast excitement.

Which maybe scared him more than if he'd been scared shitless. He stretched gingerly. Where did these dreams come from—a leftover resonance of his blackout? Something struggling up from the pit of his subconscious? No doubt. A set of free weights lay scattered in the corner beside the bedroom door. Margarita's, he guessed, remembering her broad shoulders and the sculptured muscles in her arms.

He leaned down, hefted the barbell, and set it down quickly. Heavy. The scattered cushions, the table, and the weights were the room's only furnishings. Few as they were, those items had the feel of clutter, as if an empty floor was the natural state of the room. The windowless inner wall was solid mirror. In it, Michael watched himself straighten and look at the kitchen door. He looked like shit. Frowning, he tugged at his stained and rumpled tunic, aware of the door yawning like a cave mouth.

She had retreated, yeah. Michael tugged on his braid, making a face. And he was afraid to follow her. Tossing his braid back over his shoulder, he marched into the kitchen. It was about the size of a closet; it had probably been a closet once. Margarita leaned one hip against the narrow counter, staring moodily at the humming microwave.

"Water's almost boiling." She jerked her head at two mugs set out on the counter. "It's instant. That's all we have."

"Who can afford the real stuff? Not me." Michael picked up one of the mugs and turned it over. Hand-thrown pottery, glazed with layers of opalescent blue. He wondered if her roommate was a potter.

Margarita didn't look like Xia. They had the same coloring, but her face was longer. Her prominent cheekbones deepened her eyes, shaping her face into almost harsh planes. She was taller than Xia, a hair taller than himself, taut, her weight lifter's muscles unsoftened by fat. Did he see himself in her flesh? Maybe, and maybe he was seeing what he wanted to see. Michael set the mug carefully down, wondering why he was so sure all of a sudden. Because she was an artist? He gave a jerky shrug, suddenly aware of the silence that filled the kitchen like cotton, pressing against him, muffling words.

"I hope your roommate isn't too pissed at you." Awkward words. He winced. "I didn't catch her name last night."

"Katrina." Margarita gave him a quick sideways glance. "She's pissed, but we'll get by." The microwave chimed, and she popped the door open. "We always do."

There was a lot of depth to those three words. They were a couple, then. He watched Margarita pour boiling water from a glass pot into the mugs. She spooned in dark coffee crystals and handed him one of the mugs.

The coffee was too strong and bitter. Cheap synthetic. He sipped at it but didn't make a face. "Did Katrina make these?" He touched the satiny curve of the mug.

"No." Margarita sipped at her own coffee, not meeting his eyes. "One of her friends did. Trina's the principal in a local dance troupe. They do the upscale music bars and sometimes make the media."

He sensed intense pride in those words, and pain as well. "Xia was an incredible dancer." Michael looked into the black pool of his coffee, seeing Xia on stage, translating sound into motion. "The band did mixed-media—instruments, holos, and dance. Xia was their soul." He looked up to find Margarita staring at him. Coffee dripped slowly from the bottom of her mug as if her hand had jerked and slopped coffee over the rim.

"I didn't know Xia danced." She looked down at the brown stains that spotted the front of her shirt. "She never said."

Something had hit home here; he wondered what. "I . . . I don't even know how you lived. You and she." Xia's name had filled the air between them with tension. "I don't know where you lived."

"I never lived with Xia." Margarita set her cup down abruptly. "She left me with her sister in LA. She came by to see me once a year or so. Tía Elena was always a little pissed at her. I don't think she really wanted another kid. She had two already, and a couple of jobs. Xia was supposed to give her money. To pay for me. She didn't always bring it." She reached for her mug, concentrating on drinking.

So Margarita had grown up as the family burden. It came through in her voice, even if she wasn't going to say. Michael sighed, giving her credit for that bit of silence. "Is that why your last name is Espinoza?"

"Tía Elena had to adopt me to get a child-support subsidy." Margarita moved restlessly. "Xia never would tell her who my father was. I used to hear them arguing about it after us kids were supposed to be asleep. I guess Tía wanted her to get money from him—from you." She looked suddenly disconcerted. "I don't know . . . why she told me. I didn't ask her to," she said sullenly.

Tough transition from that ephemeral "him," to "you." What kind of father had she imagined as a kid? Which stars or celebrities had she cast into that role? A video voice murmured from the other room; Katrina must be up.

Margarita heard it, too. "I've got to get to the gallery." She looked at the microwave clock with an almost panicked expression. "Shit, it's late. It's going to take the whole damn morning to get that resin toned down. You're taking off, right?" Her eyes challenged him.

Was she expecting him to walk out or needing him to leave? "Yeah." Michael met her eyes, realizing suddenly that they were Xia's. "Yeah, I'm taking off." He swallowed an unexpected thickness in his throat. "Thank you for taking me in last night. If you ever need anything . . . If you ever want to get in touch . . ." She wasn't helping, wasn't giving him any signals. "You can contact the Neiman Gallery in Taos, New Mexico," he concluded lamely. "Chris will give you my current address." If he told her. And if this wary, independent woman ever wanted to see him again.

She shrugged, her eyes avoiding his, and brushed past him, careful not to touch. Maybe it had been a mistake to come here, but he'd needed to say the things he'd said. For better or worse. Maybe it hadn't made any difference at all. Michael grimaced, sighed, and followed Margarita into the main room. Katrina stood in front of the terminal, her face full of worry as she stared at the screen.

"You made the media, Mr. Tryon."

"Call me Michael, please." He eyed the screen. She'd brought in some popular-news program, and a sexy young commentator was overlaid against a still shot of Michael's profile. "And the police are still searching for renowned Stone sculptor Michael Tryon in connection with the suicide of sculptor S'Wanna LeMontagne." The commentator leaned forward with a conspiratorial nod. "According to our sources, he's also wanted for questioning in connection with the death of the sculptor Andre Lustik last night. Currently, our sources report that Lustik's death is also listed as a suicide."

"Lustik?" Margarita started. "He's got a Stone at the gallery."

"Lustik suicided?" Michael stared at the screen, his thoughts in chaos. He *knew* Andre; they talked on the Net. The previous summer he had come to Taos to stay with Michael for a week. He was quiet, like his Stones. Gentle. A little too gentle, perhaps. The critics called his Stones passive, and they weren't. "That makes three," he said softly.

"They're calling S'Wanna LeMontagne's death a suicide." Katrina eyed him, her expression enigmatic. "They don't think you killed her, I guess."

"Three Stone sculptors have died. Suicided." On-screen, they were showing stock takes of S'Wanna's empty apartment; the vid jockey was focusing on the bloodstained zebra hide. "First Irene Yojiro, then S'Wanna LeMontagne, and now Andre. What the hell is going on?"

Margarita was looking at him with a cornered expression in her eyes. "I've got to get out of here. I've got a fucking *opening* tonight." She bolted into the bedroom and slammed the door.

"I think maybe you shouldn't have come here." Katrina's expression was sad. "Margarita had dealt with you, I think. Now . . . I don't know." She turned her face aside, but not before Michael saw her grief. "I don't know what's hurting her. But I think you're part of it. I hope she gets through it."

Love, pain—did they always have to go together? Michael touched her arm. "You love her," he said.

"I love her." Katrina's face was full of sadness and understanding. "I'm not sure that makes much difference. I think you should go."

"You think that's the right thing to do?" He was asking her, and she heard it, acknowledging his sincerity with a bare dip of her blond head.

"I'm not sure what the right thing is." She spoke slowly, almost hesitantly, only the twitch of muscle at the corner of her mouth giving her away. "But yes, I think you should go."

"I will." Michael sighed, tired suddenly, his newfound energy draining away. "Like I said last night, I needed to find her, to say . . . the things I said. And I did that." He met Katrina's golden eyes. "You love her. I'm glad. And I'm sorry for disrupting things."

Someone tapped on the door.

Katrina made a small sound of exasperation and turned. "House, who *is* it?"

"Uh . . . hello." The man outside the door hadn't spotted the pickups; he was focusing on the door-mounted speaker. "I'm . . . looking for a Michael Tryon. I'm a friend of his."

Andy Rodriguez. Michael stared at the red-haired musician, his stomach contracting into a cold lump. S'Wanna's lover. *Here.*

Why? And how?

"Wait," Michael cried, but Katrina had already opened the door. Michael stood frozen, staring across the scant two meters of clear air that separated him from Andy. "I didn't kill her," he said thickly.

"I know, man." Andy tilted his head, a strange expression on his face. "I never thought you did. I need to talk to you." He walked past the startled Katrina and closed the door.

"Who the hell are you?" Margarita stood in the bedroom doorway, dressed in a faded green tunic and gold tights. "What's all this about?"

"Andy Rodriguez." He shrugged a carryall off his shoulder, dropped it at his feet, and grinned at her. "I drive an ambulance most of the time. You must be Margarita Espinoza, right?"

"Yeah." She eyed him warily. "So how come you're here?"

"A buddy of mine cracked your address out of the Net. I figured maybe Michael'd turn up here. He seemed awfully hot to see you." He raised his eyebrows as Margarita scowled, then turned to face Michael. "You know, you may be some hot artist, but you're stupid." He wasn't laughing. "*I* know you didn't kill S'Wanna. How come you bolted?"

"I—" Michael looked away, his cheeks getting hot. "They had some kind of evidence that I'd—been at her apartment. It had to be some kind of frame, and . . . I guess I panicked."

Andy made a disgusted noise in his throat. "What hole did you crawl out of, anyway? The science wizards call the shots, not the cops. You can't *fake* evidence. Not enough to matter, anyway." He snorted. "By the time the lab crew gets done working over S'Wanna's room, they'll know every person who's been there for the last month, and they'll know exactly who killed her. Which means you'd be off the hook if you were sitting peacefully in jail."

"Great." Anger flared in Michael's chest because he'd just spent three hellish days running, seeing recognition and judgment in every pair of eyes that looked in his direction. "So I'm stupid, all right? If it wasn't me, who was it?"

"She killed herself," Andy said flatly. "I was afraid it was going to happen. I thought maybe I could help, but she wouldn't let me. She wouldn't even talk to me."

Oh. "I'm sorry." Michael almost reached to put a hand on his shoulder but didn't. "Pretty worthless words." He sighed.

"I'm sorry, too, for what it's worth." Andy's voice was rough. "Two sculptors suiciding within a week." Bitterness tinged his voice. "You guys aren't too stable, are you?"

"Three." Michael stared at the wall, searching for visions in its flat whiteness. "*Three* sculptors have suicided. Andre Lustik killed himself last night."

"Three?" Andy narrowed his eyes. "That strains the bounds a bit. You sure?"

"Coincidence." Katrina frowned, not looking at all certain.

"It's not coincidence." Michael looked from one to the other. "I don't think they're suicides."

"Why not?" Andy's gentle tone raised the hairs on the back of Michael's neck. This man was very capable of violence.

Michael met his eyes. "I *know* Andre. He didn't suicide. Irene Yojiro wasn't the type, either. What about S'Wanna?"

Andy's face hardened. "Two months ago I would've laughed if you'd told me S'Wanna might kill herself. I mean, man, she was so *hot.* Doing what she wanted and happy doing it. *We* were happy." He opened one hand, then closed it very gently into a fist. "Then all of a sudden she started getting . . . dark. Moody." He stared at the white gleam of his knuckles. "Who killed them?"

"I don't know." Michael turned away. "But I know Hawk Danners." He frowned; he and Danners had never gotten along very well. "He lives here. And he's still alive. I think I want to go talk to him. Maybe he knows something."

"This guy's right about the lab being able to clear your ass." Margarita opened the closet door and grabbed a jacket from the floor. "Go turn yourself in and get it straightened out."

"I can't." Michael frowned, feeling their eyes on him like prodding fingers. "I *did* play fugitive. There'll be a mess of red tape to untangle, and I don't think anyone is going to do me any favors by hurrying it along." At that Andy made a rude noise. "Somebody is killing sculptors," he said softly. "I'm not going to sit in a cell, counting the hours and waiting for them to come to me."

"This Danners might be the place to start." Andy looked thoughtful. "If you're right about any of this at all."

"Thanks," Michael said wryly.

"I'm going to go with you to see Danners." Andy's face had turned to a mask of carved wood. "If you're right about this . . . *if.*" He paused and drew a slow breath. "Then someone owes for S'Wanna. They owe big."

"You're welcome to come," Michael said softly. He turned to Margarita. "Thanks again for letting me stay here and . . . hearing me." Such bland, sterile, final words. He clenched his teeth, wanting to grab her suddenly, shake her, kiss her.

"Yeah. I mean . . . I'm glad I met you." Her eyes slid away from his. "I'm outa here." She slung the jacket over her shoulder and yanked the door open. "See you."

"Good-bye." So *final.*

"Michael?" She paused, palm braced high on the door frame, sinews taut in her neck as she looked back over her shoulder. "I believed you last night. When you said you didn't do it."

And then she was gone, the sound of her boots muffled by the carpet in the hall. Michael sighed, his shoulders drooping. You couldn't go back and fix the past, no matter how much you wanted to. "We're leaving." He bowed to Katrina, who stood still and silent, sorrow like a shadow on her face. Sorrow for whom? he almost asked. "I apologize for intruding."

"Maybe you didn't intrude enough." Katrina's eyes were troubled. "You can come back if you want. I think she'll still be here."

Such resignation in that sentence. And understanding. Michael bowed to her, turned on his heel, and left. Andy was waiting in the corridor. "So what did I interrupt?" He jerked his head at the door as it banged shut.

"I don't know." Why had Michael thought that there could be anything between himself and Margarita? *I believed you,* she had said. Michael let his breath out in a gusty sigh.

"So." Andy slung his carryall over his shoulder and shook his hair back from his face. "Let's go call this Danners."

"Uh huh." Michael started down the hall. "I need a public terminal."

"I've got a hotel room." Andy palmed the elevator door. "I'll access Bunny, and he can route you through to Danners. Unless you'd rather hit the local police station and straighten all this out?" He raised his eyebrows at Michael. "She gave you some good advice."

"No." Michael leaned against the wall as the elevator plastered his stomach against his diaphragm. No breakfast, and he was still a little shaky. He swallowed a mouthful of saliva as he followed Andy out into the shabby lobby. "No cops yet." They would hold him for some kind of hearing and . . . he would die. His certainty on that score almost scared him, as if death itself had whispered the future in his ear. "How come you showed up here today? How come you're willing to help me?"

Andy stopped short, then slowly turned to face him. "I showed up here because for a while the news said you'd killed S'Wanna. You told me you'd been blacking out. I figured you might think you'd really done it, even after they'd changed the verdict to suicide." His face gave nothing away. "S'Wanna wouldn't want you to think you had her blood on your hands."

"Thank you."

"Oh, I get something in trade." Andy didn't smile. "I'm going to be there if somebody shows up to off you or this Danners. The hotel where I'm staying is just a few blocks north." He slung his carryall over his shoulder, giving Michael a thin smile. "In a better neighborhood."

Michael followed him, glad Andy wasn't his enemy.

On-screen, Bunny the Net operator was a large white cartoon rabbit with pink eyes. He bent one floppy ear down to tap his cheek thoughtfully. "You want this Danners dude, and you don't want anybody tracking you back here, right?"

"You got it." Andy nodded. "ASAP, okay? I owe you."

"You could do this yourself, so yeah, you do. We're even." Bunny wiggled his whiskers. "Deal?"

"Deal, I guess." Andy rolled his eyes. "You're coming out on top on this one. How soon can you have us in?"

Bunny's ears tied themselves into a bow. "Let's see . . ." His image froze for a long moment, then his ears untied themselves. "Piece of cake." He wriggled his nose and sniffed. "He's got a nice private access, but he doesn't know shit about security. Waste of your credit, sweetheart." He waved a three-fingered hand. "You're in."

Michael looked over Andy's shoulder. The hotel screen was entertainment-sized and took up most of the wall opposite the bed. Only the really upscale hotels had a holo stage. On the huge screen Bunny was dissolving, flowing like melting ice cream to the bottom of the screen. The resolution was good enough that Michael half expected white goo to start dripping down the wall beneath the screen. "Handy pal to have," he said.

"Yeah, but he's smart enough to cost when he figures he can pull it off. This was a pricey deal, but he's into brain shots." Andy shrugged. "He'll owe me again, soon enough."

Brain shots? Michael looked sideways at Andy. Illegal neurotransmitters infused directly onto the cortex via implanted ports could do a lot of damage. Andy was staring at him, the corner of his lip curled into a crooked smile.

"I don't peddle, if that's what you're thinking. I just pull him out when he goes too far in." He nodded at the screen. "This is your show. I don't know this dude."

No apologies from this guy. Michael looked up to find himself facing a coral reef. A school of yellow and black fish darted by, veering in eerie unison, then vanishing in a cloud of silver bubbles. A scarlet octopus crawled slowly and fluidly across an outcrop of gray-green coral, and a silver-gray shark lazed by, heavy head swinging from side to side. Rows of pointed teeth gleamed in the dim light, and Michael shivered.

"Who is it?" Hawk Danners appeared suddenly, standing on a ledge of coral. "Turn on your damn video or get out."

Nice overlay. "House, visuals." Michael hoped Bunny had given him visual access. Apparently he had, because Danners nodded his shaggy-maned head.

He reminded Michael of a bear, with his thick hair and beard and his heavy shoulders. His hips were narrow above crooked legs that looked too short and skinny for his massive torso. Rumor was that the body had come from a shop, that he'd selected it on purpose. "Hello, Hawk."

"Mike, I swear." Danners bared crooked yellow teeth in a grin. "I hear the cops want your ass. What happened? S'Wanna steal a commission? Or did she cheat on you?"

"I didn't murder her. Which you know perfectly well if you've had the news on lately." Michael held on tightly to his temper. "Did you hear about Irene Yojiro and Andre?"

"Yeah, so what?" Danners shrugged. "Lustik was always a wimp."

Michael counted to ten, wondering if he should bother. Let the jerk find out for himself, and to hell with him.

But Danners lived right here in San Francisco—or offshore, anyway—and no other sculptor was within such easy reach. Except himself. And Danners wasn't likely to turn him in, either. It would tickle his bad-boy self-image, keeping this secret. Michael sighed and dangled the hook. "I know something you don't, Hawk. About these supposed suicides. Invite me down there and I'll tell you."

"What? You want me to break the law and deal with a fugitive?" Danners's eyebrows rose into twin furry arches. "I am shocked."

Reading the curiosity behind Danners's manner, Michael smiled. "That's fine. I'll go talk to Jeranna."

"She'll sell your ass in a minute." Danners threw his head back and scratched in the nest of his beard. "Yeah, I might let you drop in. For a laugh. I'm almost between projects right now, so I can spare you some time."

Don't do me any favors, Michael didn't say. "Fine." He kept his tone unimpressed. If Danners thought he was anxious to do this, he'd put the damn visit off for a month. "If we get time. How do I ring your doorbell?"

"I'll send my boat over to the Bayside Marina in the morning." He yawned pointedly. "I'm not home right now, but I'll be free by then. Ask for the Danners boat at the gatehouse if you decide to come."

The screen went blank.

"So that's the infamous Hawk Danners?" Andy stood in

front of the single big window, hands clasped behind his back. "S'Wanna said his soul was too small for his body."

"I hadn't put it quite that way. I'm not so generous." As Andy chuckled, Michael stretched, wincing as the vertebrae in his neck crackled. "Just don't let him prod you into a fight. Those muscles are bioenhanced, from what I've heard."

Andy grunted and threw himself down on the bed. "So now what?"

"We wait until tomorrow." Michael wondered if Danners was really gone or if he was just jumping them through hoops for his private enjoyment. "Then we go see Mr. Danners of the too-small soul." Michael wandered over to the small table in front of the window. It was plasticboard grained to look like wood. Andy had left a small pile of wrapped sandwiches and pouches of juice on it. "Can I have one?"

Eyes closed, Andy nodded. "That's why I got 'em. You know, that last fight S'Wanna and I had was so trivial. Like an excuse. She'd been getting darker, more into herself, but she wouldn't tell me why. I'm not sure she knew."

And if Andy had still been there, would she have died? Michael picked up one of the sandwiches and broke the irradiation seal. He had a feeling the man was asking himself that very question and could ask it for the rest of his life.

"You never told me who you pissed off so bad that they went to the trouble to try and frame you." Andy rolled onto his side, propping himself up on one elbow. "That's a pricey bit of nastiness. Cops don't buy cheap."

"He's an inside node in the Worldweb." Michael peeled back the plastic and took a bite of the sandwich—salami that probably didn't have a gram of meat in it and tasted mostly like pepper. Tired lettuce and tomato. It tasted as if it had been on some shelf for at least a year. Michael swallowed quickly. "His name is Gunner Archenwald-Shen."

Andy whistled and sat up. "Archenwald-Shen, huh? You don't do things in a small way, do you? How did you piss *him* off?"

"You know him?" Michael said around a mouthful of sandwich. "I think he's a jerk, and I guess I let him know it." He swallowed, reaching for a packet of juice. "Bad move, I guess." He punched a straw into the juice packet and emptied it.

"I don't know him, but I've heard of him." Andy crossed his arms on his raised knees, frowning. "If you're in the Net, you've heard of him. He goes into hard-up little countries and dangles fat manufacturing contracts in front of desperate governments. He gets all kinds of concessions for land use and dumping and that sort of stuff, and cheap labor, too. Soon as the market's saturated, he pulls out. No capital investment, everything's rented. Sometimes the country in question does well by the deal, and sometimes it doesn't. Rumor is, he sets up some of those shaky conditions himself." Andy shook his head. "You need a keeper."

"He was obnoxious, and I was rude. What was I supposed to do?" Michael crumpled the sandwich wrapper and juice packet into a ball. "Grovel? Lick his shoes?"

"It might not have been such a bad idea." Andy sounded serious.

Michael shoved the trash into the recycle chute. "If he showed up and wanted to buy you, would you do it? Grovel?"

"If it was worth it." Andy shrugged. "If I had to. Does it bother you? Selling your stuff to some stranger? Sometimes it bothered S'Wanna."

"It didn't." Then why hadn't he sold Sun Stone? Michael stared through the window, down into the street below. It was lunch hour, and pedestrians cluttered the wide sidewalks, all of them in a hurry. Bright sunbrellas clustered around food vendors like small, mobile gardens. "I guess that's not quite true. All of a sudden I started asking questions. Why was I doing Stones? Who was I doing them for? Some rich asshole like Archenwald-Shen? So he can put it in a spotless room somewhere, listen to it when he's bored? I don't know." And Sun Stone had been a fragment of yesterday—Xia and love and summer. He'd kept it and let the present move on without him. Michael sighed, then nodded at the screen. "Do you think your friend Bunny left that protected access open for us?"

"Try it and see. Access rabbit first."

"House, access rabbit." Michael held his breath, not sure whether he wanted the access to happen or not. The screen flickered, then cleared, blank except for a tiny white pair of rabbit ears in the lower left-hand corner.

"You're in," Andy said.

Time to do it. "Access Christine Neiman Gallery, Taos, New

Mexico, personal to Chris," Michael said in a single breath. If she wasn't there, he could leave her a message.

The screen shimmered, and Chris stared out at him. "My God, *Michael*. Where have you been, and where the hell *are* you? Are you all right? What's going on?"

She looked so worried. "Chris, take it easy." His fingers twitched with the desire to reach through the screen, put his arms around her, and comfort her. "I'm fine. Really."

"You don't look fine." Her face enlarged, as if she'd leaned forward. "Michael, what's all this insanity about murder? The police were here, looking for you. I know you didn't do it. You couldn't have."

"I didn't. Chris . . . I'm up to my ears in a mess."

"You're telling me." She was angry now, her lips tight. "For God's sake, get back here. Ted's a business lawyer, but he knows some good criminal people. We can deal with this, Michael."

Did he see tears in spite of the anger? Ah, Chris, did you really fall in love with me? How could this have happened? She was Margarita's age. "It's more complicated than just the murder charge," he told her gently. "Chris, I can't turn myself in, and I can't explain right now. It's too complicated." And he had no solid basis for his certainties about those deaths, and she'd point it out in an instant. "I'll tell you everything as soon as I can. I promise. Don't worry about me, okay?"

"Don't *worry* about you?" Chris's voice soared upward half an octave. "Yeah, sure, I'll just go dust the sculpture and put you right out of my head." Her voice shook. "Jesus, Michael. You self-centered *bastard*."

The screen went blank.

"You have this strange effect on women," Andy drawled from the bed. "Must be a little tough to find a date."

"Ha, ha." Michael turned his back on the screen, leaning his forehead against the window. I didn't ask you to care about me, he told her silently. I didn't know. I wasn't really living in the present. The sun glare dazzled him, making the street below shimmer as if the air were full of invisible butterflies.

Michael rubbed his eyes until red webbed the blackness, struck with the sudden sense that if he *reached*, he'd thrust his hand through an invisible veil, that he'd touch . . .

"Hey? You okay?"

"Yeah—yes, I guess so." Michael straightened and shivered, strange images flickering at the edge of vision. "I've been having some strange dreams lately. Nightmares." He let his breath out slowly, not wanting to see the surmise in Andy's face. "Maybe I'm really going crazy." He tried to laugh, but it came out weak and fragile. "Maybe that blackout was only the beginning."

"Do you feel like you're going crazy?" Andy swung his legs over the side of the bed, his eyes on Michael's face.

"No." Michael shrugged. "But if you know you're crazy, you're not, right? Isn't that the cliché?"

"You tell me." Andy got up to prowl restlessly across the room. "You should maybe listen to your lady friends. They've given you some good advice."

"I thought you were so hot to find S'Wanna's murderer."

"I am." His stare was measured, doubting. "If there is one."

Michael rubbed his eyes again, unable to blame him. "I'm going to see Danners tomorrow. You can come or not—it's up to you."

"Oh, I'll tag along." Andy rolled over on the bed and bu
his face in the pillow. "Just in case you're not crazy."

"Thanks." Michael sat down beside the table, leaning back in the chair. He was so *tired*. In the blackness behind his eyelids, those dark butterflies danced. What would happen if he let them in, accepted that eternal darkness? His eyes
open. "I think I'll watch a movie."

Andy's only answer was a soft

Chapter Six

The First Tuesday crowd circulated through the gallery like bright, exotic fish in a tank. From the shadows at the edge of the floor Margarita watched a bone-thin woman climb up onto *Crystalline*'s stage. She had an intricate fiberlight inlay: a green and scarlet gecko that curled from above her left breast, up her neck, and onto her cheek. She looked back at her companion. "It's cold. I should have brought a jacket."

He brushed a speck of dust from his gray silk tunic suit and shrugged. "Nice, technically, but bland. Have you seen Chianini's new composition yet?"

"Well, I think it's pretty." She stepped down from the stage, sipping at the glass of wine in her hand. "I'm a sucker for snow. All right, I'll come look at the Chianini with you." She tucked her arm into the gray-suited man's, and they strolled away together.

Margarita leaned back against the wall, a headache pulsing at the back of her brain. The dry-snow skirl of the Andean flute tickled her ear. *Again I hold you with my winter's color,* the almost-Trina voice whispered. She'd caught herself keeping count of how many people actually stayed on the stage for the entire piece—not many. Margarita closed her eyes. She'd finally made herself stop, but she had a sneaking suspicion that the number was in there anyway, stored back in the hindbrain. Sometime in the middle of the night it would come popping out, reeking of failure.

The gecko woman and her gray companion sank past Margarita, riding the chains down from an upper balcony, through with the Chianini. They'd move on to the next gallery on the circuit, drink some more wine, point and judge, and maybe yawn when nobody was looking. Or maybe yawn when the right person *was* looking.

Had she felt *anything*, gecko woman? Had she even *listened*? Margarita looked down at the empty wineglass in her hand, wanting to smash it on the metal-mesh floor. I didn't do this for you, she thought sullenly. And then: Who the hell *did* I do this for?

Herself? Then why exhibit, why *try* so hard? Maybe not for gecko woman; maybe she hadn't sweated, wept, struggled over *Crystalline* for her.

She had wanted to reach . . . someone.

She had *said* something. Maybe. Or maybe not. Maybe it was all posture and politics—nothing but another kind of power game, not so much different from the games her cousins played in the barrio. The delicate stem of the wineglass snapped between her fingers. With a hiss of indrawn breath, Margarita stooped down and tucked it into a pool of shadow cast by a supporting girder. Blood dripped from a gash in her finger, and she sucked at it, her mouth filling with the coppery taste of blood.

There had been something there when she had conceived of *Crystalline*. It had had meaning.

A man had climbed onto the stage and was turning slowly, his head canted as if he were lost in thought. He stayed there, not moving, until the last flute note died.

What did you see? Margarita clenched her fists. What does it *mean* to you? Did I show you loneliness? Did I touch you? Stroll up to him, she told herself in Katrina's voice. Go talk. Smile. Be charming, because he might be thinking of a piece for his office or his ski cabin or his bedroom.

She didn't give a shit if he needed a piece for his office. She stood still and safe in the darkness as he looked around and consulted the small electronic catalog in his hand. He left, and she stared at the endlessly moving chains, waiting for the next bored body to rise or descend. She shouldn't have come; she should leave, go home and take a shower, or get drunk. But the thought of clinging to the chains while a dozen bored art patrons watched her flight closed her chest with panic.

Once more she looked down through the mesh, scanning the floor below for a small bright-haired figure. Katrina had said she'd come by even if Argent wanted to work late. Margarita swallowed a knot of worry. First Tuesday was almost over; the crowd was thinning out. The worry sat like a small stone in her belly, making Margarita nauseous. Argent was a prick tonight, she told herself. That was all. He'd found out that Katrina had ducked rehearsal yesterday, and he had raised hell. Yeah, sure. But a part of her whispered, *What if she's pissed at you, what if she leaves* . . . and a sudden chasm opened up inside her, full of darkness and aching emptiness.

And then, suddenly, Katrina was there, stepping off the chains as if she'd materialized just beneath the balcony, looking around, her brow creased in a frown. She didn't see Margarita back in the shadow. Margarita held herself very still as Katrina climbed onto *Crystalline*'s stage. She hadn't been in the finished piece yet; Margarita hadn't let her in. The flute skirled, and wind teased the snow into white sprays of ice crystals. A stray breath of cold tickled Margarita's skin, and she realized she was holding her breath, her eyes on Katrina's face. She let her breath out slowly, rubbing her goosefleshed arms. On the stage Katrina turned in a slow-motion pirouette, her head tilted back, her golden hair caught in a loose knot below the nape of her neck. Her eyes fixed on some vision in the snow, and her face was dreamy, soft.

To show you the cold that can break the ground more easily than heat . . . The last flute note trembled and died. Katrina's shoulders moved slightly, as if she'd sighed, and she bent her head, hair falling forward to curtain her expression.

Margarita stepped softly from her shadow.

"Mar?" Katrina turned.

There were tears on her face. Because the piece was good or because she knew what Margarita wanted to do and saw what was missing? Katrina was so damn *honest*. Margarita looked away, afraid to meet her eyes as she stepped down from the stage.

"Hey, love, easy." Katrina stroked the tight muscles along Margarita's spine, her hand gentle and full of comfort. "Mar, it's . . . wonderful. It really is." Her voice was bright. Too bright? She pushed Margarita away slightly and cupped her face, tilting it until she could look into Margarita's eyes. "Mar, was it that bad tonight?"

"Yes, it was that bad." Margarita twisted away, eyes on the

sparkle of broken glass at the back edge of the balcony. "They don't give a shit. They don't *care*. They don't even try to hear what's there. They think it's *pretty*." Her voice cracked like the glass stem, shattering into razor-edged pieces. "That's not what I'm *doing*."

"Isn't it?"

Margarita's head jerked up.

"You got to start somewhere. Get some attention. Some recognition." Katrina put her hands on Margarita's shoulders, her face full of compassion. "*Crystalline* works. People will pay attention to you. They'll hear what you want to say."

"Yeah?" Margarita turned away. "Or they'll look elsewhere, because I won't give them what they want. Maybe . . . I just can't do it." And maybe that was what had bothered Arrow at the end. He'd believed in her talent, and . . . he'd been wrong. Was that where the pain came from? She tilted her head back, wanting to scream the words into the vault. Did you leave me to figure it out for myself? That I can't do it?

Katrina grabbed Margarita's hand, winning the brief tug-of-war as Margarita tried to pull free. "Whatever you're thinking, it's not true." She hissed softly between her teeth. "What did you do to your hand? For crying out loud—"

"I just cut it."

"Yeah, you did." Katrina's face was full of worry. "Are you ready to leave? I don't think you're adding much to *Crystalline* right now."

"Yeah, I'm ready. It doesn't matter if I'm here or not." Margarita pulled her hand free and shoved it into her pocket, getting blood on her tunic. So what? What did *anything* matter?

"You're a mess." Katrina touched her face, ignoring her angry flinch. "Suffer the stairway one more time, and we'll stop at the store on the way home. We're going to split a bottle of red wine. Real vineyard stuff, and if we both have a hangover tomorrow, too bad."

"We can't afford real stuff. We're broke, remember?" Margarita winced at the anger in her tone but couldn't help herself. Why was she angry at Katrina? *She* didn't deserve it, of all people. "Tank wine is fine." The anger twisted stubbornly in her gut.

"Tank wine is crap, and we're going to buy good stuff, whether we can afford it or not." Katrina stepped onto the elevator and sank through the floor. "We're celebrating. So hurry up."

And maybe that anger came out of that chasm, that awful gulf of emptiness that had threatened to swallow her back there in the shadows. Need was a dangerous thing. Need made you weak. And for a minute she had needed Katrina. "I'm coming." Margarita grabbed the chains and swung out onto a step, swaying, clutching the metal links, and, for once, not giving a damn if she fell.

The main level was almost deserted now. Most of the browsers had moved on to other galleries or had gone home. Lustik's Stone glowed on its pedestal, washed in soft-focused light. Its sculptor had killed himself. Margarita hesitated, then walked slowly over to it. Lustik was dead, and the Stone was here, singing his memories, his moments of dawn and love and hope. Was art nothing more than fear of mortality translated into light, or stone, or color? She touched the Stone and shivered, deluged with the soft scents and bright textures of sunrise. The Tryon Stone in New York had been a storm. It had seized her, sucked her into a whirlwind of pure hot emotions: anger, triumph, and determination, touched with a grace note of fear. It had filled her with a sense of awesome power, until she had stretched out her hands, fingers spread, half expecting lightning to crackle from their tips. For a few moments she hadn't been Margarita Espinoza; she had been part of the Stone, the spiral center of that emotional whirlwind.

It hadn't felt like death fear. And what about *Crystalline*? Margarita let her hand fall, then stepped back from Lustik's Stone. "He's better," she said.

"Who's better?" Katrina looked over her shoulder.

"Michael Tryon." She couldn't say "my father" and didn't want to. "His Stone was better than this one. I wonder if I'm really his kid."

"You could find out." Katrina put a tentative hand on her arm. "Does it matter, after all?"

"I . . . don't know."

Katrina sighed, a distracted sound. "Have you seen Yiassis tonight?"

"No, I haven't seen him, thank God. I figured he'd be breathing down my neck all night." She gave Katrina a sideways look. "How come?"

"I . . . I just wondered if he was being a prick." Katrina wrinkled her nose as the main doors opened for them. "I thought that might be why you were a little down."

Margarita wondered how much of the hesitation in Trina's manner was because of her bitchiness and swallowed a twinge of guilt. "He wasn't here tonight. Miracle of miracles. Look, I'm sorry. About my mood."

"Hey, you're allowed. Keep your hands out of your hair." Katrina slapped Margarita's hand aside, then smoothed her bangs. "Or I'll shave it off and you can get a tattoo job. You look like a sheepdog."

Her motherly tone was covering something. Filled with sudden remorse and a wrenching flood of love, Margarita flung her arms around Katrina. "I want that wine." She kissed her and twined her fingers in Katrina's, wanting to make up to her. For the temper. For the mood. "So, how was rehearsal tonight?"

"Not bad." Katrina made a face. "Better than last night."

Something was bothering her. Tomorrow, Margarita told herself. Ask her about it in the morning. Get drunk tonight, play, forget *Crystalline*'s weakness, the bored patrons, Arrow's ghost—everything. Tonight they'd just *be*. She and Katrina.

They stopped at a wine shop just far enough from the fancy towers to be cheap but close enough to carry a good stock. Katrina rolled her eyes when Margarita plunked a bottle of cheap tank wine down on the counter beside the California zinfandel she'd picked out. But she didn't say anything. One bottle wouldn't be enough. Not tonight.

Their apartment was dark. Margarita stood for a moment on the threshold, listening to the echoes of Michael Tryon's visit. Why had he come? she asked herself. Just to tell her that he'd loved Xia but had never looked for her? Just to say that he hadn't known she existed? And how did you feel about him, Xia? Margarita breathed softly through her mouth, listening to the silence. Xia hadn't told her anything, had just said it was a long time ago. Had she loved him? Margarita couldn't do it—couldn't put Xia and Michael together.

"Yo, girl. Wake up." Katrina pushed past her. "House, lights."

Margarita blinked as the darkness vanished. Cushions, table, weights: the familiar objects banished Michael Tryon's presence, sent it back into the past where it belonged. Margarita closed the door and kicked off her boots. The past was the dead-letter office of time, she thought, and sighed. "I wonder why she kept it secret. Who my father was, I mean."

"We're talking Xia?" Katrina gave her a wary look. "Maybe she figured your aunt would lean on her to hit him up for child support. Maybe she thought he'd try and take you away from her. Ask her next time she turns up." She threw herself onto the piled cushions. "This is not celebratory conversation." She crossed her arms and pinned Margarita with a ferocious glare. "As penalty, you go open the wine. The good stuff, please, and I want my glass *full*."

"Yes, ma'am." A bottle under each arm, Margarita headed for the kitchen.

"There're some breadsticks in the cupboard. Bring those, too, okay?"

"Okay."

The corkscrew wasn't in the usual drawer. She found it finally in the crack between the counter and the wall. Along with a lot of dust and crumbs. Yech. She fished it out and screwed it into the synthetic cork. The wine smelled good, complex and oaky, with a bright hint of acid. Tank wine never did taste like real stuff, no matter how hard the chemists tried to duplicate all those complicated little molecules. The dirty dishes from yesterday were still stacked in the sink, but Margarita ignored them, reached down their two wineglasses from the shelf, and tucked the sack of skinny breadsticks under her arm.

To hell with the bored, brain-dead sheep who'd grazed their way through the gallery tonight. *Crystalline* was good, and she would do better.

I *will* do it, Arrow. Wait and see.

Silence answered her, broken only by the hum of the refrigerator. For an instant she could feel his ghost, standing right behind her, wanting to tell her something.

But why was he sad? Margarita grabbed the wine bottle and fled. The terminal screen was just darkening. "I didn't hear the chime," she said. Too busy listening for ghosts. "Who was it?"

"Argent, of course." Katrina looked flushed and angry. "I

guess he and Li got into it good after I left." She got to her feet. "Damn them, anyway. I'm going to have to fix things."

"No way." Margarita stepped back, glasses clinking. "Not tonight. I thought Pia was all set to step into the role."

"Yeah, yeah, but it's such a *mess*." Katrina brushed past Margarita and disappeared into the bedroom.

"Trina?" Margarita set the glasses down on the lacquer table. "What's going on?" The breadsticks fell out from under her arm, scattering across the floor. "Damn." She banged the bottle down beside the glasses and raked the breadsticks together with both hands, hurt because they had been going to celebrate, be happy together for a little while, forget that she'd been a bitch. "*You* dragged me away from the gallery to celebrate." Angry again; oh, shit, couldn't she just *stop*? "I want to spend some time with just you."

"What happened to my amber pendant?" Katrina yelled from the bedroom. "The one I got last winter?"

"*I* don't know." Margarita dumped the breadsticks onto the table. "Do you have to play mother to the damn *world*?" Anger won, cracking her voice. "It was in that bowl on the dresser. With your hair clips and stuff."

"It's not there." Katrina appeared in the doorway, hands braced against the frame. "Damn it, Mar, where *is* it?"

"I said I don't know." Margarita's anger faltered because Katrina was upset—really upset. "What's it got to do with Argent and Li?"

"Nothing, never mind. It's a long story." Katrina swept her loosened hair out of her face. "I've got to go—over to the studio. And straighten this out." She was already heading for the door. "It won't take long."

"Trina, *wait*." But the door slammed as Margarita scrambled to her feet. Trina was *scared*. That was what she'd heard in her voice—fear. The last of her anger gone, she yanked the door open and ran out into the hall barefoot. *"Trina!"* It was empty, and the elevator was rattling slowly streetward. Damn. Margarita went back inside and slammed the door.

Forget this Argent and Li story. Something was wrong. Margarita leaned on a corner of the table and began to pull on her boots. Something had been wrong for a while now. Little incidents began to surface in her mind like oil rising from a sunken wreck—unexplained absences, bursts of uncharacteristic temper. Monday night Argent had said that Trina had gone home sick at noon. But she hadn't shown up at the gallery until late. She always told Margarita where she'd been and what she'd done, no matter how trivial the errand. Sometimes it drove Margarita nuts.

She hadn't said a word about going anywhere Monday night. I should have noticed, Margarita thought bitterly. I should have paid attention. But she had been too busy with *Crystalline*. The lights blinked; five minutes until the power curfew. As she scrambled to her feet, her leg bumped the wine bottle. It tipped over, and she grabbed for it. Wine splashed the cushions, puddling on the floor. Margarita snatched up the bottle and set it back on the table. The wine on the floor looked like blood. Fresh blood. Margarita shivered. I should have paid *attention*, she told herself, but she hadn't. She'd been buried in *Crystalline*, lost in a filthy sea of doubts. No—a sea of self-pity.

The lights blinked out. Swallowing a curse, Margarita fumbled her way into the kitchen to yank the flash from the drawer beside the sink. The yellow pool of light splashed wall and ceiling as she opened the front door and slammed it behind her. In the hall, the night-lights shed small pools of weak yellow light on the faded carpet, timid islands in a sea of darkness. Too late for the elevator. She took the stairs, clattering down the five flights, swinging crack-the-whip around the corners.

No sign of Katrina in the lobby, of course. Out on the street the wind had picked up. It gusted down the street canyons, whipping dust and trash along the sidewalks, filling the air with stinging grit. In this block, postcurfew didn't make much difference. Margarita blinked watering eyes, searching the dark street for Katrina's slight figure. She'd had more than enough time to turn the corner. Margarita shoved her fists into the pockets of her tunic and started down the sidewalk, not quite running. Go to the studio, she told herself. If this had anything to do with Argent at all, she'd be there. He lived up above the studio in a crappy little two-room apartment.

If this had anything to do with Argent. She wasn't sure anymore that it did. Beneath the anger, fear tickled at her. Margarita shivered and ducked her head against the wind. It was cold, winter cold, as if this were December instead of barely

October. The wind pried beneath the neck of her tunic, sliding cold fingers down between her breasts. Margarita clenched her teeth to keep them from chattering. The gallery was in the next block. It was still lighted; they must have paid for an all-night curfew exemption for the opening. The Arnsten helices that covered the front of the building twisted Möbius-like back on themselves in brilliant strands of humming neon. By now it would be locked, but maybe Ari had come in to do his possessive late-night check, touching and gloating as if the pieces on the balconies belonged to him, were part of his private collection.

She could call the studio from inside. If Argent was there, he'd answer her code. He could tell her if Katrina had shown up. And if she hadn't . . . She would worry about that when it happened. Hugging herself, hunched against the wind, Margarita ran across the empty street. The main doors ignored her palm on the lock plate. She hissed between her teeth, then ducked around the corner to the service entrance. That door responded, opening for her silently. So Ari *was* there. Margarita closed the door and thumbed off her flash. The lights were mostly off, although Lustik's Stone still glowed at the focus of its soft floods. *Crystalline*'s stage was barely visible in the gloom, its shape only hinted at by the orange glow of the console lights.

The chains were still running, rattling through their endless loops. They sounded louder now, filling the vast space with a clattering like metal teeth clashing in the darkness. Margarita realized she was tiptoeing, looking over her shoulder. She shook her head, wanting to laugh at herself. The public terminal was in the hall outside Ari's office. She started for it but froze as footsteps slapped the floor. Running footsteps? A figure coalesced from the darkness and burst toward her.

Margarita flung up an arm as a body slammed into her. The figure screamed a shrill, wild note as Margarita staggered, then twisted violently away, hair glinting gold in the stray gleam of light from Lustik's Stone.

"Trina!" Margarita grabbed her arm. "Trina, it's *me*!"

For an instant Katrina strained against her grasp, muscles rigid and trembling beneath Margarita's hands. Then she fell against her, trembling, arms going around her tightly enough to crack her ribs.

"Trina, my God, what's wrong?" Margarita held her, thinking *Ari*, and for this she would kill him, never mind the show. "Trina?" She kissed her forehead, stroked her hair back from her face, scared because she'd never seen Katrina like this. "It's okay," she whispered. "I'm here."

"It's not okay." Katrina pushed her away suddenly. "He's dead. Ari. There's blood everywhere."

Oh, shit. "What did he do, Trina?" The words came out a whisper, because the night was cracking like glass, showering down in deadly bits. "Tell me."

"*I* didn't kill him." Katrina recoiled. "My *God*, Mar, what are you *thinking*?"

"I—I'm not thinking anything." Margarita reached for her hand again. "Trina, *tell me what happened*."

Without a word Katrina yanked her hand out of reach, spun on her heel, and started for the rear of the gallery. Margarita followed her slowly, seeing the stiffness, the clumsiness in Katrina's walk. Katrina never made a clumsy move; she flowed like water through the present. Now she moved as if something were . . . broken. Margarita ran to grab her hand and wouldn't let Katrina pull away. They'd reached one of the looping chains, and Trina stopped suddenly, a meter from the opening in the floor through which the chains vanished to wind around their wheel and rise again.

"I already looked," she whispered. "He's dead."

Margarita sucked in a silent breath because she saw it now: blood on the rattling chains in dark streaks and spots, barely visible in the light from the Stone's floods. Blood spotted some of the steps, too. She moved closer to the hole in the floor, one step at a time, her legs as stiff as carved wooden posts. There was a safety grid down there. If someone fell onto it, the machinery shut down instantaneously. Ari had given her all the specs the first time she'd ridden the damn steps, as if it made a difference. You could fall three stories; what the hell difference did it make if they kept you from falling into the damn machinery?

It had made a difference to Ari. Reflected light spilled into the basement space, as if someone had intentionally focused it on him, as if this were nothing more than another piece: a gruesome exhibit of human fragility and death. He lay down beneath the cogged wheel, below the safety grid, sprawled out on the concrete floor. Twisted, changed. Damaged. The eye was a camera, and in a nanosecond the image was imprinted, too fast for the brain to say no and not see. Margarita stepped quickly back, focusing on outlines, not wanting to know how the chain and wheel had killed him. It was there, though, stored in her brain. Sooner or later she'd see it.

"Oh, shit." She closed her eyes. "What the hell *happened*? Did you call the cops?"

"No." Katrina looked around with a dazed expression on her face. "I should have, shouldn't I? I'm sorry."

"Damn it, Security should be watching this." Margarita glared up at the closest video eye. "What the hell's wrong here?" Something. "Come on, Trina." She put her arm around Katrina's shoulders. "We've got to go call someone."

They had been alone in there, in a private universe of shadow and blood and shock. Now the flat, shiny reality of the terminal screen in the wall brought the real world crashing in. "Public access, emergency, police," Margarita snapped.

"Public access." The screen brightened to solid blue. "Police."

"This is Margarita Espinoza at the Yamada Gallery. There's been an accident, and a man is dead."

"Please insert your ID card for identification confirmation."

Margarita fumbled her card out of her pocket and slid it through the reader.

"Thank you, Ms. Espinoza. An emergency team is on the way."

Reality had them in its claws, hard and inescapable. Margarita took a deep breath, wanting to cover her ears, block out the questions that flooded her brain. "Did you find him?" she asked breathlessly. "They're going to want to know, the cops and all. Trina?" Urgency clenched her fingers on Katrina's arms as she tried to pull away. "What's going *on*? That was Ari who called, wasn't it? Not Argent. How come you came down here?" She shook Katrina, one hard short jerk that snapped her head forward. "*Why*, Trina?"

"Stop it." Katrina grabbed Margarita's wrists and broke her grip. "Yes, he was dead when I found him. Did you really think I killed him, Mar?"

The bitterness in her tone made Margarita wince. "No." She

let her hands fall to her sides. "I didn't. I don't. But what were you *doing* here? Please—" Her voice caught. "Tell me, Trina?"

Katrina looked away. "He asked me to keep something for him. That necklace. Only it wasn't just a necklace—there was a hard memory sphere hidden in it. I don't know what was on it." She shivered, and her head drooped. "He called tonight, you're right. He wanted it back, and he—was upset. He wanted me to bring it down here. When I . . . couldn't find it, I came down here to tell him. You were there, so I couldn't call. The door wasn't locked, and I couldn't find him. I was looking at the Stone when I—when I noticed the chains. The blood, I mean. That's all." She didn't lift her head, didn't look at Margarita.

"Why?" Margarita whispered. "What was on that sphere? Some kind of blackmail thing? Why did you do this for him?"

And then it came together. Suddenly, like a fist closing, squeezing her ribs until they shattered, buckled, pierced her heart. "You were his lover, weren't you?" Her voice was hushed. "That's why I smelled his cologne in your hair; that's why I didn't see you come in Tuesday night. You were there already, weren't you? Down in his office? Trina, why?" She turned her face away, struggling to catch her breath. "Why the fuck didn't you just *say* something?"

"Oh, sure." Katrina's voice was low and bitter. "And you would have said, 'Fine, go ahead and have fun,' right?"

"I don't know. I just don't *know*." Margarita spun away from her and leaned her forehead against the cool hardness of the wall. Ari? My God, *Ari*? What *would* she have said if Katrina had asked her? Two years they'd been together, ever since that day when Katrina had stopped to watch her work on a piece of simple holo sculpture in the seedy mall where she'd set up her portable stage.

Katrina had sat on the ground watching her, saying nothing. Usually that kind of gawking pissed the hell out of Margarita, but this small, muscular woman had watched with a focused attention that had spurred her into a burst of creation. When she had finally quit for the day, exhausted and halfway satisfied, Katrina had asked her to come and have dinner, had helped her carry the bulky stage back to her apartment. They had eaten real cheese and stale bread on the cushions on the floor, and they had talked about art and life, exploring unexpected and wonderful connections between holos and poetry and dance until the early hours of the morning. She had spent the night there in Katrina's bed. Two weeks later, when rent had come due on her crummy basement room, Margarita had moved in.

Two years wasn't much time, really. It had felt like the first part of forever. Margarita squeezed her eyes shut, willing the tears not to happen.

The main doors whispered open. "Police," a male voice called. "Anyone here?"

The tears didn't happen. Eyes dry and aching, Margarita straightened. "We're here," she called.

The two uniformed officers standing just inside the doors looked their way, and one of them walked warily over. "Someone reported an accident."

Cops always sounded so damn hostile. Margarita wondered if they got that way by being cops or if you got to be a cop only if you were like that to begin with. "He's over here," she said, and led him back toward the beacon of Lustik's Stone and the bloodstained chains. She didn't once look at Katrina.

The police were polite in an officially suspicious sort of way. More of them showed up, along with medical people and people who looked sort of medical and were probably lab types. Margarita sat cross-legged on the floor with her back against the wall, watching their controlled chaos, recording images, sounds, and smells like a camera but not processing any of it. The cops had questioned her first; they were questioning Katrina now. They had kept them separate. They always separated you, always figured you were going to agree on some kind of story or alibi. They were untrusting but politely untrusting this time, because in this here and now she was *someone*, not just another grimy barrio kid.

She hated cops.

She'd told them exactly what happened, each detail coming back to her with surreal clarity, sharp-focused in her brain. She hadn't said anything about the pendant or the memory sphere. She hadn't lied, didn't know if there was anything to lie about, but she hadn't said anything. She didn't *know* anything. Except that Katrina had been Ari's lover.

Why?

An answer kept wanting to occur to her. Margarita leaned her head back against the wall, letting the bustle around the hole in the floor record itself in her short-term memory somewhere. If she filled up her mind with images, she didn't have to think. A blond-haired cop who seemed to be in charge nodded to a pair of medics. They had sealed Ari's body in a plastic bag and were hauling it up from the basement. It bumped the turned-off chains, making them swing and clash together. With a grunt, they heaved the bag onto a stretcher, handling it like a sack of dirty laundry. So much for life, for hopes and doubts and the future . . . The medics strapped the bag down securely, their faces bland and bored, and the stretcher rose between its wheels as they walked away, trundling itself obediently after them.

Why, Katrina? Because . . . Don't think about because, just *don't*.

"Margarita Espinoza?" The blond cop was standing in front of her, looking down at her with a curious expression on his face. "You can go if you'd like." He offered a hand to help her to her feet but didn't seem offended when she ignored it. "We may have some more questions in the future, but for now we're finished."

He'd told her his name, but she couldn't remember it. "It was an accident?" Why *shouldn't* it be?

"We'll let the laboratory tell us that." His pleasant smile might have been cast from plastic. "However, you're free to go."

"What about Katrina?" It was hard to say her name out loud.

"She's free to go, too." He glanced toward Ari's office. "I think she already left."

Good, she thought, but the clench in her chest denied her words. "Thank you." Margarita closed her eyes briefly. The Stone tickled her with a hint of the sun rising, of hope welling up in a young heart . . . She moved a step farther from its pedestal. "There's nothing else, then?"

"No." The cop was frowning a little. "Are you sure you're all right? Do you need a ride home, Ms. Espinoza?"

"No, no thank you." She turned away quickly. "I'm fine, thank you." Ari's little assistant, Delia, had shown up and was bustling here and there, looking over everyone's shoulder.

Margarita avoided her, keeping to the shadows as she crossed the main floor. The cops had left all the chain stairs on except the one that had killed Ari; she grabbed the set that led to *Crystalline*'s balcony and rose, eyes fixed on the wall as the stairway carried her upward. Down below, nobody seemed to have noticed her ascent. Or they didn't care.

"Fracture, power on. Run." She stepped up onto the stage as winter shimmered to life around her. *In the foothills of the mountain, amid wintry autumn before winter begins, you visit me* . . . the voice that wasn't quite Katrina's whispered.

I am good. Margarita closed her eyes and drew a slow breath, tasting wet wool from a winter's walk, sweat, and wood smoke, and ice. A winter's walk, a brief communion with loss and love and the winter's fractured soul so like our own. A portrait of loneliness and the icy shell that can fracture beneath the right touch . . .

"I am good," she whispered. I am, Arrow, aren't I? You never told me.

"Mar?"

Katrina's voice. Margarita jumped, her eyes snapping open. "He said you left." She climbed down off the stage, awkward where Katrina was always so sure. "The cop. I didn't hear you."

"You can't hear anything over those chains." Her tone was light, but her face was drawn, almost gaunt. She stood beside the chains as if she'd just stepped off the stairway.

"Get away from the edge," Margarita snapped, seeing that body bag again, its flaccid slump. "Why Ari?" She hadn't meant to ask, and it was too late now to stop the words, but her hands twitched as if they could catch it in flight, snatch it like a bird out of the air.

"I liked him." Katrina looked away.

Lying. She was too damned honest to lie for shit.

"Look, I know it hurt you." Katrina looked down at her clasped hands. "Mar, it was just this passing thing. I don't know. Some kind of whim or something. Maybe I was . . . doubting myself or something. I'm not sure, but it was already over. I *love* you, damn it." She raised her head at last. "Someone killed him, Mar. Because of that pendant, and I'm *scared*. Mar, I want to heal this. Somehow. Please?"

She really was scared, but she was lying about Ari. Margarita closed her eyes, wanting to hug her and tell her it would be all right, wanting to slap her. Because Margarita had believed in it—their love. She had *believed.*

And . . . she had needed Katrina. She writhed, unable to deny the truth.

"Ari offered me this show," Margarita said softly. "I was doing pieces in ninth-rate galleries." She opened her eyes, cold settling into her, freezing her heart. "Yamada doesn't pick up artists from the basement. They can skim from the top."

Katrina's head jerked almost imperceptibly, as if she wanted to look away and had stopped herself.

"Did Ari . . . give me this show so that you'd take him to bed?"

"No! You're here because you're good, Mar."

Katrina couldn't lie, and her face gave her away in an eye blink of revelation. *No,* Margarita wanted to scream at her. *Tell me you're lying. Tell me I'm wrong.* "You bitch." Her voice trembled. "Oh, yeah, I'm good, just like you keep telling me. Good enough for the Yamada, right? Sure, as long as you pay my way on your back. Good thing I've got a pretty dancer for a lover, huh?"

"Mar?" Katrina took a half step forward. "Will you *listen* to me?"

"Listen to *what*?" Margarita spun, slamming both fists down on *Crystalline*'s stage. "Listen to what? Another lie? Like the one about how good I am? Like how much you love me? Get *out* of here. You *whore*!"

Katrina's face had gone white. For one long moment she stood still; then she turned, grabbed the clattering chains, and vanished slowly through the floor.

Margarita closed her eyes and sank to her knees on the metal mesh.

Your hand, alone now, Katrina's almost-voice whispered to the wandering sigh of an Andean flute. *If you hold it in your other hand, they are both only more alone.*

"Shut up. Fracture, power off." A lingering breath of snow and wet wool caressed her cheek as the stage shut down. Margarita buried her face in her arms, silent above the cops and the shadows and the Stone.

Chapter Seven

Margarita woke up suddenly, blinking in dim light, her throat aching with dream tears. For a moment Katrina's face overlaid the shadows, but it faded almost instantly. Head aching with those blocked tears, Margarita struggled to place herself among the unfamiliar shadows that surrounded her. Fabric . . . a sofa beneath her. Oh, yeah. The shadows coalesced into familiar shapes. She was on Delia's sofa; she had coaxed the assistant manager to let her stay there tonight. Because she couldn't go home. Margarita sat up, stiff because the sofa wasn't quite long enough for her and she had slept curled up.

And she had dreamed of Katrina. The lumpy ache in her throat came back, refusing to give way to anger. She couldn't remember the dream itself but was left with a crushing sense of loss, of being left behind.

Katrina, how could you *do* this?

For love. Last night's rage had turned to ashes in her chest, cold and reeking. I would have made it on my own, Margarita told herself, but the shadows mocked her. Katrina hadn't thought that she would. "Office, light!" She bounded to her feet, blinking in the glare. "Office, time?"

"Five-forty-five," Delia's office intoned.

The words turned her knees shaky with too little sleep. Margarita sat back down on the sofa and rested her face in her hands. Last night Delia had found her sitting beside *Crystalline*'s lightless stage when she had locked up the gallery. Delia had made her an unwanted cup of hot chocolate and had offered drugs and a back rub that Margarita had very quickly declined. She had been full of a sly knowledge that had made

Margarita want to yell at her and a bright, hopeful anticipation that had shut her up. She had slept here, and if Delia thought that meant something, she was wrong.

Margarita paced across the room, not touching anything, caged by the early hour, by the distant apartment and Katrina, who would be sprawled across the bed, stretched out from corner to corner as she always was when she went to sleep before Margarita.

She sat down again and leaned her head in her hands, shoulders slumping. Love was such a bloody *pain*, she told herself bleakly. Delia had hung out over the cops' shoulders last night, sucking up every dropped word; then she had trotted out her collected gems for Margarita. Security hadn't recorded any intruder because Ari—or someone—had disabled it from inside. He had been badly mangled, and an expert would have to discover why the safety grid hadn't shut down the wheel the instant he fell.

Delia didn't think that the cops thought it was an accident. Margarita didn't think so, either.

The dream ache came back to her, and she shivered suddenly, although the room was warm enough to be almost uncomfortable. Ari had asked Katrina to keep a hard-memory sphere. Someone wanted it and had killed him when he hadn't produced it. What if that someone found out that Katrina had it? Or didn't have it? And where the hell was it, anyway? Down behind their dresser? Lost on the rug?

It wasn't. Katrina always found the little things that Margarita lost around the apartment—she knew how to look for things. If it was there, she would have found it. Margarita closed her eyes, trying to remember when she'd seen the damn pendant last. She remembered the day Katrina had brought it home; she'd noticed it because it was big and garish and Katrina never wore jewelry. A gift, Katrina had told her. From Argent. She had made a joke about how it was a good thing he wouldn't expect her to wear it while she was dancing.

Yeah, a gift. Margarita sighed, remembering that Katrina's tone had been too bright, a little nervous, then wondering if she really remembered that or if she was just looking back on the episode with 20/20 hindsight. It had been late last spring, only a couple of weeks before Xia had shown up.

Xia. Margarita's eyes blinked open. Katrina had gone to

work out in the studio because she wouldn't work out in front of visitors. So Margarita and Xia had been alone in the apartment, and Margarita had been shut into herself, struggling with twitchy anger because she had just started *Crystalline* and wanted to be working on it. Because Xia had told her that Michael Tryon was her father. Xia had prowled the apartment, touching everything, prying, as she always did, as if she could fill in the months-long gap since her last visit by handling every physical bit of Margarita's life. She had found the pendant in Katrina's bowl.

Michael gave me an amber necklace, she had said, holding Katrina's pendant up to catch the light. *Some friend of his made it—tiny droplets of petrified tree sap strung together, each one lumpy and unique. It was ugly and wonderful, and the center pendant was a chip from one of his Stones. I lost it.* Her weathered, aging face had smoothed into something eerily like youth. *Some things come and go in our lives, and we really have no control, no matter how much we may think we do. I loved that necklace. It was an accidental fragment of his soul, perhaps the only fragment that Michael was able to give away.*

It jarred Margarita to remember that. Back then Michael Tryon had been a name only, a twisted knot of surprise and anger. *An accidental fragment of his soul . . .* Margarita shook her head, dismissing Michael. What if Xia had taken the pendant? Margarita stared at Delia's desk, not really seeing it. Xia had done that sometimes—taken things from the apartment. They had always been Margarita's things: a bottle of wine once, and one of her shirts. She'd gotten really pissed about the shirt. *I think it's her way of taking a little bit of you with her,* Katrina had soothed. *You don't give her much of yourself.*

Damn right. And didn't owe her anything, either. Margarita hunched her shoulders. What if Xia had taken the pendant and sold it? What if she had lost it? What if the person who had thrown Ari Yiassis down into the grinding jaws of the machinery knew that Ari had given it to Katrina? Margarita bolted to her feet, afraid suddenly, terrified for Katrina. What if someone had been waiting in their apartment for her? Breathless, she rushed around the desk and slapped Delia's terminal to life. "Access Katrina Luoma, personal emergency."

"Accessing," the terminal told her in a woman's husky

southern drawl. "There's no answer, honey. Do you want to leave a message?"

"No—yes, yes I do." Margarita drew a quick breath, wondering what had happened to the air in this room. "Trina, just stay till I get there, please? End it." She had the door open before the screen had gone completely dark, and she ran through the shadowed gallery, her footsteps echoing in the vast silence.

Someone had it least turned off the damn chains. Lustik's Stone was unlighted. As Margarita slapped the door open, she caught the faintest whisper of his dawn hopefulness. Hope for what, artist? she thought angrily. You gave up on hope, remember? She dashed through the opening door, out onto lightless streets grayed with approaching dawn. The blocks between the gallery and the apartment blurred past, featureless, empty or not, she didn't notice, didn't care. She fumbled her card into the slot beside the apartment building's main door, hissing between her teeth as the old, cranky reader rejected her fumbling. Finally it acknowledged her and clicked the door open. Margarita burst in, heading for the stairs, although curfew had ended by now. She raced up all the flights, her footsteps rolling like thunder up and down the stairwell. In the featureless glow of the strip lighting, it could be night or day. Margarita hauled herself upward, dizzy with the sudden notion that she had stepped back into yesterday, that she might meet herself racing down these stairs to catch Katrina.

If that happened, would there be time to turn the clock back? Or had she already lost Trina before she ever set foot on the stairs? Grief filled her as she staggered onto her landing. The fire door refused her card, too, as if the building were trying to hold her back, discourage her. Panting, hair stuck to her sweaty forehead, Margarita jammed it in again, shoving the heavy door open as the lock finally clicked. A few meters to their door . . . she caught herself on the frame, staggering, then unlocked it and burst through, her heart a pounding drumbeat in her chest.

Red stained the floor. Not blood—the spilled wine from last night. Gasping for breath, Margarita leaned against the wall. The half-full wine bottle caught the first stray beam of morning sun, turning it to sparks of emerald fire in its sleek depths. The untouched glasses stood on the table where she'd left them, beside the pile of breadsticks. Had it only been last night? Margarita looked around slowly, feeling disoriented, as if the room had subtly changed. Or maybe she had changed. "Trina?" Her name came out thin and hesitant. "Trina?" The bedroom door stood ajar, and Margarita pushed it open.

The worn quilt had been pulled up neatly over the pillows. There was no clutter, no sign that anyone had been here, either Katrina or a thief searching for amber. Numb, Margarita pulled open a dresser drawer, a new terror taking shape in her chest—that Katrina had never made it home last night.

Well, hell, neither had she. Thin comfort.

Margarita stared into Katrina's drawer, struggling to inventory the neat pile of underpants, the folded shirts, and the rolled-up tights. Some things were missing: the green shirt and her black tights—the heavy ones. Her terror lessening, Margarita hurried into the bathroom. Katrina's toothbrush was gone, too. Yes. Margarita went back into the main room and perched on a corner of the table. She had come home, then, and had gone somewhere else.

She was all right.

But where? She leaned forward and tapped the terminal screen to life. "House, access Argent Zeladio, personal and urgent."

"Accessing."

The terminal screen shimmered and cleared slowly, revealing Argent's dark, mournful face. He looked rumpled, as if he'd just woken up or had never made it to bed. "Margarita," he said without enthusiasm.

As if he'd anticipated her call. "Is she there?" Margarita's heart leapt. "Did she call you?"

"Yes, she's here." He sighed, looking more tired and mournful by the moment. "I'm not going to let you talk to her."

"Fuck that." Margarita clenched both fists. "Put her on, Argent."

He sighed. "If you throw a temper tantrum, I'll exit. Decide, sweetheart."

Fuck you, too. But she didn't say it out loud and got control with an effort. "You don't really understand this situation, okay?" She kept her tone level, even tried for a wry smile. And failed. "I need to talk to her. Right now."

"Sorry." Argent shook his head. "You can exit now or you

can listen to me. I think you should listen, but that's your option."

Margarita closed her eyes, then opened them. "Trina's in danger. I'm not kidding, and I don't want to talk about it on an open access, okay? I need to come over there." She'd expected raised eyebrows and skepticism but got a pained nod instead.

"She told me." Argent wasn't smiling. "She told me the whole story."

The story she hadn't told Margarita? Margarita bit back a retort, swallowing the hot words with difficulty.

"The police are dealing with it." Argent sighed again. "She's not a suspect, but Ari was murdered. Margarita?" Argent hesitated, lips pursed. "You hurt her a lot last night."

"Me?" Margarita sucked in a ragged breath. "*I* hurt *her*? Oh, yeah, I guess I did, I guess *I* should apologize for—" She bit off the rest of the sentence because she'd said it all last night and it had felt like shit then and felt more like shit now.

"I didn't say she didn't hurt you, too. I think the two of you need a little space. I think you both need to decide what you mean to each other, and what got damaged last night, and whether you can fix it. Then you should talk. Not now."

"Thank you, Doctor Zeladio." Margarita loaded her tone with sarcasm but couldn't quite hide the tremor in her voice. Katrina had told Argent, had gone to him for comfort.

You called her a whore. Margarita struggled to keep her expression neutral so that Argent wouldn't see. You said it. You can't ever take the words back. Of course she went to Argent . . .

It would have been easier to take if he'd been snotty to her. "Look, you tell her—" What? That everything was okay? Sure, you bought me a gallery slot with your ass. Because you didn't believe in me? Katrina, I thought you believed. Maybe nobody else—but *you*, at least . . . "If she wants to come back to the apartment, I'm going to be gone for a while. So I won't get in her way." She flung the words at the screen, hard as stones, not sure who she was aiming at—Argent or Katrina, who was presumably listening. "I'll see you."

"Wait." Argent glared at her. "I hate being in the middle of this crap. I'm doing this because Katrina means a lot to me, as a friend and as a damn good dancer. And I see the two of you breaking up when it doesn't have to happen. I don't want it to happen, but if you don't sort yourselves out, it's going to. If that matters to you, *work* on it."

And the screen went blank. Margarita stared at the afterimage of Argent's angry face overlaid on the apartment walls. She'd never seen Argent get angry outside the studio. There, his anger was a tool, a finely controlled scalpel that he used to carve a dancer's performance into perfection.

His anger hadn't been very controlled just now. And he was wrong. There was no going back to yesterday, not by any path that she could see. Margarita found herself staring down at the table, at her distorted reflection in the depths of the glossy lacquer. Motherly, loving dancer Katrina. Margarita let her breath out in a slow sigh. Xia must have mentioned that she'd danced, maybe back when Margarita was little. Or Tía Elena had said something. Surely. And she had forgotten, had filed it away with those bits of information that you heard when you were a kid but that didn't really mean anything.

And then, years later, she'd fallen in love with a dancer, a loving, mothering woman who was the antithesis of Xia Quejaches. Was that why? Margarita stared at the warped reflection of her face. Was that why she had ended up in Katrina's bed two years ago? She had been almost twenty, so sure of herself and her talent.

What did you need, Margarita Espinoza? A lover? Or a mother?

Margarita lifted her head, body aching with the sourceless twinges of fatigue and stress. She needed to find Xia. She might still have the pendant that would maybe keep Katrina safe. No matter how smugly sure Argent was about the cops, Margarita didn't share his faith.

And she needed to look into her mother's eyes and see if Katrina looked out at her. And if she did? Margarita shook her head until her hair whipped her cheeks. How the hell was she going to find Xia—where could she *start*? Xia just showed up, brought tales of a new city, a new round of flea markets and malls, wandering, doing the fortune-telling that was more a mix of performance art and scam than magic. Xia the gypsy. Xia the ghost. Might as well whistle for the damn wind.

Michael Tryon had found *her*. Margarita went very still. Yeah, but she wasn't so hard to find. *He* was going to look for Xia. She was willing to bet on it—*was* betting on it.

Betting Katrina's life, maybe.

She didn't want to have anything more to do with Michael Tryon. His presence in the apartment had been like an earthquake, shaking things loose that she'd thought were rock solid. And maybe she wouldn't be able to find him any more easily than Xia. Maybe his friend would know where he'd gone. What was his name? Frowning, Margarita picked up a breadstick. Andy something . . . Andy . . . Rodriguez? Yeah, that sounded right. *He* didn't have any reason to hide; she'd look for him first. The stale bread cracked between her teeth, shattering into sharp-edged crumbs. She ate it, made herself a cup of instant coffee, and ate two more breadsticks as she accessed local hotels.

Rodriguez was easy to find—he was in a hotel no more than a few blocks from the apartment. As if they'd been waiting for her to come looking. Margarita grimaced, blanked the screen, and went to pack a few items into her carryall. Then she swept crumbs from the table, cleaned up the wine stain, washed the dishes, and put them away. So that Katrina wouldn't have to. Standing in the doorway, she gave the apartment one last glance.

It looked flat and unreal, like a photo from an old album. A memento of yesterday. Could she turn back a corner of this picture and find cardboard and glue underneath? Margarita turned on her heel and left, locking the door behind her.

Time to see if Michael Tryon was home. As soon as she ran one important errand. This time she waited for the elevator instead of taking the stairs.

"You there? Yo!"

Michael started. "Sorry, Andy." He turned away from the window, the whisper of a headache pulsing at the base of his skull. "What did you say?"

"I was thinking we might wander down to the marina." Andy lifted one eyebrow. "One more hour here and we get charged for another day. Me, I'd rather not pay. You all right?" He narrowed his eyes. "You're acting a little strange."

"I know." Michael stared through the window again, down at the sun-bright street. "There's this . . . curtain in my head. Or maybe it's not in my head, but it's there. There's something on the other side. I could reach out, pull it aside, and *see*. Only

I'm scared to." Because it might be endless night and nothing more? Or because it might be . . . everything?

He looked at Andy and flushed. "Yeah, I'm probably going nuts."

"Seems like a possibility," Andy drawled. "I won't rule it out."

"Well, you're honest, at least." Michael gave him a crooked smile but let it fade. "Sometimes I don't think it's *me* on the other side of that curtain—my insanity, I mean. I think it's . . . someone else. Does that make any kind of sense?"

"Nope."

"It doesn't to me, either." Michael stifled a sigh because he was just about convinced of that explanation himself. Except for that hint of *otherness*. If it were me, I'd know it, he told himself. Or would he? Maybe that's what insanity was all about, becoming truly alien to yourself. He lifted his shoulders jerkily, let them drop. "Let's go visit Mr. Hawk Danners. Maybe he can shed some light on all this."

"Maybe." Andy didn't sound confident.

The terminal chimed, and a phone logo appeared on-screen in red—a real-time access. Michael frowned and moved out of video range as Andy touched the screen. The cops? He squashed a surge of anxiety. Why should the cops expect him to be hanging out with S'Wanna's lover? He narrowed his eyes as a woman's face shimmered into focus on-screen. Margarita.

"Mr. Rodriguez, I'm looking for . . . Michael Tryon. Do you know where he is?"

"Uh . . ." Andy flicked an inquiring glance in Michael's direction. "Why don't you come up here?" he said at Michael's nod.

Margarita's face tightened into a mask of wariness, and Michael almost stepped into video range to reassure her. But he didn't, because he needed to talk to Danners and the cops just might be monitoring Andy. Maybe. So he stood still and held his breath.

"All right." On-screen, Margarita gave a single curt nod. "What room?"

"Eight-oh-four. Turn right when you get off the elevator." Andy gave her a smile and a mock salute. "See you in a couple of minutes." He rolled his eyes at the blank screen and grinned at Michael. "You passed on some very nice DNA. But she's safe from *me*, with those shoulders. Unless she says hello and welcome."

Why had she tracked him down? Michael found himself watching the door and made himself look away.

"You know, she doesn't look a whole lot like you." Andy lifted one eyebrow. "The nose? Maybe the jaw. She's a lot better looking."

Distracted, Michael grunted just as someone tapped on the door.

Margarita's face appeared on-screen. She was staring at the door, her face profiled by the wall-mounted video pickup. She looked tense. Well, that was about how he felt. Michael drew a slow breath as Andy unlocked the door.

She walked into the room, her attention on Andy, not seeing him yet. She looked bad. Shadows smudged her eyes as if she hadn't slept, and her face looked gaunt. "Margarita?"

She started at the sound of his voice, her head snapping around, eyes widening. "I didn't—know you were here."

"I'm still keeping a low profile." He studied her face, thinking that he could use her to add a dark note of angry grief to a Stone. "Even if the cops only want me for questioning, they're going to give me a lot of shit about ducking out like I did. Margarita?" He reached for her, moved by the pain in her face. "What happened?" She flinched as he touched her, and Michael took his hand away. "What's wrong?" he asked gently.

"Nothing. I mean—" A spasm twisted her face, and her expression hardened. "It's a long story, okay? I wanted to find you to ask, Have you found Xia yet? Do you know where she is?"

Yes, something was wrong. *Very* wrong. "I don't. I'm sorry. I haven't even started looking."

"Shit." She bent her head, her cropped hair swinging forward to shadow her expression.

Andy cleared his throat. "I hate to break this up, but we were just about to check out. You could finish this down in the lounge or something, okay?"

"Where are you going?" Margarita's head jerked up, eyes narrow and dark.

Maybe she didn't believe him about Xia. "I'm going to go see the Stone sculptor Hawk Danners," Michael said. "About

. . . these suicides. And then I'm going to start looking for Xia." Margarita's eyes flickered at the mention of her name. "Why don't you come along?" he asked quickly. Suddenly he was afraid to lose sight of her. If he did, he thought with brief, terrible certainty, she would disappear as Xia had disappeared. "I don't think Danners will mind," he added, although that wasn't a sure thing at all. He held his breath, expecting her to bristle and refuse, but to his surprise she was nodding.

"Why not?" she said, and the bitterness in her tone made even Andy raise his eyebrows.

"You'd better call Katrina." He remembered her name this time. "Hawk is . . . rather reclusive. There's no guarantee that we'll have outside access from his dome."

"I don't need to call." She didn't look at him. "Don't worry about it."

He recognized the feel of her now; he had added it to how many Stones? Loss and love— they were such a part of everyone. As if no one could have one without the other . . . We don't love well, Michael thought, and sadness pierced him. Maybe that was the next step in human evolution: the ability to love and receive love. "I'll be glad to have your company," he said gently, and this time he didn't try to touch her.

"You're welcome to it." Her lips twitched, and she walked quickly past him, out into the hall.

Andy mimed a heavy sigh and slid his card through the reader beside the screen to pay for the room. He could agree with that sigh, Michael decided as he followed him out into the hallway. Margarita was waiting for them, arms crossed, leaning against the wall. She straightened, eyes on Michael's face, and held out a paper envelope.

"I picked this up on the way over here. I thought I'd better clear things up for us both."

Puzzled, Michael took it. The flap bore a laboratory certification seal. He slid his thumb beneath it, glue crackling, paper fraying as he opened it. The folded hardcopy it held was also stamped and notarized—a human DNA analysis. For Margarita Theresa Espinoza. "You didn't have this done this morning," he said, because words were balling up inside him and these were the only ones that would shake loose. And then, "Xia told me once that her mother's name was Theresa. She said it was an ugly name."

"Tía Elena gave me my middle name." Those dark eyes challenged him. "When she adopted me. I had the report done last summer. I brought it with me to Albuquerque because I figured you'd want it. And then . . ." She shrugged. "I changed my mind."

Chris had wanted him to ask for this. Michael folded the flimsy paper very carefully and tucked it into his tunic pocket. "Why did you change your mind?" he asked softly.

Andy had called up the elevator and was waiting for them impatiently, holding the doors.

Margarita shrugged and stepped inside. "I decided it didn't matter," she said over her shoulder. "You contributed a bunch of DNA, that's all. If you even did that. Whatever was between you and Xia, it never had anything to do with me. Why should I pick on you?"

She wasn't being hostile, for once. She was genuinely puzzled. That hurt. Michael followed her onto the elevator, a clench of pain in his chest. She was right. What did it mean that she had resulted from a moment of unknowing passion? What rights did that give him? Any? None? Why *should* she pick on him? Andy was whistling softly between his teeth, staring up at the mirrored ceiling as the elevator dropped. Margarita kept her eyes fixed on the doors, her body stiff, held tightly to herself. I've been thinking of her as *mine*, Michael thought, and winced. She wasn't his. Not unless she chose to be. And she hadn't chosen—not yet. Maybe never. She had just told him so.

He wanted her to chose. He wanted her to be his. Disturbed by this sudden revelation, Michael turned his hand slowly over, examining the lines engraved across his palm. They represented a lot of years, those lines, never mind the youthful skin that the body-shop drugs and treatments had given him. Was mortality what was bugging him? The whisper of death's footsteps creeping up behind him—was that what waited on the far side of the veil?

Our children have always carried the burden of our mortality, Michael thought. He bent his head as the elevator slowed and touched lightly down. Sometimes it was an unfair burden. Maybe most of the time. Maybe always. With a sigh, he walked through the opening doors, out into the cheerful artificial light of the carpeted lobby. It wasn't his burden to lay on her, he told himself as they left the hotel. Not even if she would accept it.

Outside, Andy flagged a cab. They piled in, and Michael found himself pressed against Margarita. She was still tense, her muscles rigid and unyielding as the cab zigzagged through traffic. What do I represent to you? he wanted to ask her. Abandonment? Was I the focus for your anger all these years? Andy stared out the window. He was giving them space, Michael guessed, if they wanted to talk. He had nothing to say, or everything, but the cab enforced their silence. It settled around them like stagnant water, until the only sound was the air-conditioning's tuneless hum.

"Bayside Marina." The small, aged cabbie braked to a halt beside a steel-mesh gate set into a graceful stone wall. Head tilted to the side, he watched them curiously.

His skinny neck and beaklike nose made Michael think of a bird, a robin, maybe, listening for the sound of a worm beneath the grass. His skin was as dark as old leather, as if he'd spent most of his life out in the sun and wind. Do you have any kids? Michael found himself wanting to ask. What do they mean to you? What do you see in them? *Your* immortality? He closed the car door and turned away. "Sometimes I think we're only vehicles for our DNA," he said thoughtfully. "Culture, art, love, war—it's all secondary, an accident that doesn't really matter much."

Andy eyed him. "You might have something there, you know?" A thin irony edged his voice. "Which is a damn depressing thought."

Margarita gave Michael a swift, rather surprised look as she followed them away from the cab. What had those words meant to her? he wondered. He stopped square in front of the screen set into the wall beside the ugly gate. The stones weren't real; they were high-quality fakes made from silocrete. Late-morning sun glittered on shards of broken glass and metal that jutted up like fangs from the top of the wall, and a fine black wire ran along the inside edge. Electrified? So if you didn't slash yourself to pieces on the glass, you'd fry?

"Life's cheap," Margarita murmured. She had come to stand beside him and was following the direction of his stare. "Compared to the cost of a boat, I guess." She met his eyes but looked quickly away. "So how come we're here?"

Michael winced at the edge of bitterness beneath her words. "Hawk Danners promised to send his boat over for us. He works in a subsea dome in the bay beyond Alcatraz." He reached up to touch the dull face of the screen.

It brightened instantly, and a blond youth smiled out at them, too perfect to be real. "Welcome to the Bayside Marina," he said cheerfully. "This is a private facility. Please insert your card for access."

"This is Michael Tryon, guest of Hawk Danners."

The youth's electronic smile froze for the space of two heartbeats while the computer searched its database. Had Danners been jerking them around? Michael wondered. Playing some little game of his own?

"Please come in." The steel gate began to rattle open. "Mr. Danners's boat is in slip number thirty-seven-A, on Dock C. If you need anything, just touch any screen. I hope you enjoy your visit." The face winked out.

The marina was huge, upscale, landscaped in Japanese pebble-garden style. The paths were laid in natural stone, and bleaching driftwood had been artfully scattered here and there between them. Signs led them to Dock C; slip 37A was out near the end of the floating walkway. Michael walked slowly, unsteady on the rise and fall of the dock. He breathed slowly, tasting dank mudflat burnished with bright overtones of fuel, fresh paint, and the distant smell of frying onions. An alvin was tied up in Danners's slip; a small woman lounged on the submersible's humped back, wearing only a pair of faded green bikini bottoms. She sat up as they approached, casually oblivious to her naked breasts and the choppy buck of the alvin beneath her. Taking her time, she swept each of them with a searching head-to-toe stare. "You Tryon?" she asked Michael at last.

"Yes." Michael nodded, legs spread against the dock's motion. She looked Caucasian, but her skin was Afro-dark from the sun. Her bleached-white hair had been braided into hundreds of beaded strands that clicked and rattled as she hopped to her feet. "You'll get melanoma from this sun." He nodded skyward.

"Who asked you?" She shrugged and snagged a shirt from behind the alvin's hatch. "All aboard. Watch your heads getting in—this ain't no bay tour." She stepped into the hatch and vanished down into the belly of the boat.

Andy gave Michael an amused glance and a mocking half salute, then scrambled up the ladder that was bolted to the alvin's side. Michael frowned after him, bothered and not sure why. He gave a jerky shrug and stepped back to let Margarita climb ahead of him. She went up slowly, knuckles gleaming white as she clutched the metal rungs, face impassive as she swung her leg very carefully over the lip of the hatch. Michael climbed after her, his stomach knotting as the alvin dipped and rose beneath him. Great. He sucked in a quick breath, his skin going clammy. Clutching the hatch rim, he scrambled quickly down the inside ladder, trying not to notice the rise and fall of the horizon.

Andy steadied him as he stepped backward onto the deck. "Pretty cramped." He jerked his head at the twin recliners that filled most of the passenger space. "I don't think he throws too many parties down here."

Michael looked forward, squeezed by necessity. "I think I'm going to be seasick."

The tanned pilot, seated in front of her console, threw him a quick, annoyed glance. "Not in here you don't." She fumbled in a tiny cupboard. "Do this *now*, sit down, and hold it in." She threw something at him and began to pull on a pair of elbow-length virtual gloves. "Soon as we go under, it's still."

Michael caught the small object she'd tossed—a plastic-wrapped drug patch. He peeled the plastic back gratefully, nose wrinkling at the sharp smell of the carrier. The patch tingled briefly as he smoothed it over his carotid groove, then warmed.

Margarita touched his arm. "Are you going to be okay?"

"I think so." Already the drug had taken the worst edge off his nausea. Andy, seated in one of the recliners, was staring thoughtfully at their pilot.

"Go ahead and sit." Michael nodded at the vacant seat. "I think I'll take the floor." He sat down awkwardly, leaning back against the hull as the pilot kicked in the alvin's engines. They hummed through the hull, soaking through his flesh and into his bones, softening the discomfort in his belly. The pilot spread her gloved hands, and the alvin edged away from the dock, then sank as she lowered them. A snap of her fingers turned on hull-mounted floods, spraying yellow light through the darkening water. She tilted one hand sideways, and the alvin turned smoothly.

She was playing the alvin like an instrument, dancing with the sub. And she'd been right about the motion. Michael looked over her shoulder, letting out a slow sigh of relief as the tossing of the waves ended. A school of silver fish scattered in panic as the alvin drove through them, and the gray flicker at the edge of the light might have been a shark.

The enormous butt of a pier drifted past, thickly crusted with brown mussels near the surface. Tube worms waved feathery orange tufts among the mussels, and an orange starfish the size of a dinner plate raised one arm as if to beckon the alvin on. But it was Margarita's face that held Michael's eyes. She leaned forward on her seat, breathing slowly, her face rapt. What was she seeing? Michael crossed his arms on his raised knees and leaned his chin on his forearm. What meaning were those tube worms taking on? What visions was she filtering out of the light-struck strands of kelp and the frightened dart of the fish out there?

"We're alien down here. A hull's thickness away from death." He closed his eyes briefly, smelling his fear sweat, sensing Andy's subtle tension and the pilot's boredom. Margarita? He opened himself as if she were a Stone, sensed . . . excitement? He remembered how it was, back when he was working on Summer Stone or Air Stone. The sense of power? Was that it? He shook his head, groping for that feeling, trying to resurrect it. It kept slipping away from him, as the fish slipped away from the alvin's light beam, leaving the eye nothing but the flash of silvery fins and an afterimage that suggested fish. Once upon a time it worked for me like this, Michael thought. Before it became work.

Before I ran out of soul, Estevan?

"What do you see?" He spoke to Margarita, to her alone. "What does it mean to you?"

She turned, eyes bright, lips parted.

Then her eyelids dropped, and wariness descended like a mask over her face. "It's . . . different. I've never been underwater before."

Evasive words. She had been going to tell him. Michael stifled a clench of pain. I needed you to tell me what it feels like, to remind me, he said silently. I don't know if I feel that way anymore.

What if these deaths were suicides? Michael shivered. Did you fall in front of that mag-lev, Estevan? Was it really an accident? He rested his forehead lightly on his arms, visions crawling across the red-webbed darkness behind his eyelids. What if the soul was a finite quantity? What was left when you poured out the last dregs of your soul?

Darkness?

A touch on his shoulder scattered his thoughts. He lifted his head to find himself looking up into Margarita's face.

"Are you okay?" Vision still shimmered in her eyes.

Vision she wouldn't share and maybe . . . something he couldn't comprehend anymore. "I think so." He rubbed his bare arms, feeling his skin lumpy with gooseflesh. "But I'm not sure."

"You don't mean the seasickness, do you?" Her eyes refused to release him. "Are you sick? Are you dying? Is that why you came looking for me and for Xia?"

Am I? He frowned, hearing challenge in her tone, but beneath that challenge another note—like a child's thin, distant voice. "We're all dying, aren't we? No, that's no answer." He gave her a crooked smile. "I don't think I'm dying any faster than anyone else." He pushed the memory of his dark nightmares to the back of his mind. Insanity was a different type of death. "I'm not sure why I came looking for you," he said slowly. "I think it was because you made me see that I was . . . petrifying. I was becoming just another Stone." He looked away from her silence, staring out at constellations of glittering motes dancing in the floodlight's beam. "I had let the world go on without me. I was hiding in my garden, clutching my polished, careful memories to me like a scared kid." He let his breath out in a rush. "You scare me," he said. "You cracked my nice, safe walls when you sent me that letter. You let in the sun." He nodded at the viewport, where filtered blue-green light had replaced the harsh glare of the floods. "I think we're here."

The alvin surfaced in a wash of silvery bubbles and fractured light. Through the viewport, Michael caught a glimpse of waving kelp stems and a plastic-mesh walkway. He got slowly to his feet, grabbing for the ladder as a rush of dizziness tilted the deck beneath his feet.

"Those patches get you sometimes." The pilot glanced at him, then went back to stripping off her gloves. "Better than barfing your guts out."

"Can you climb the ladder?" Margarita took his arm, holding it above the elbow, leaning her weight into him.

"I think so." He shook his head, which only turned the inside of the alvin wavery and strange. He climbed up carefully, making sure of his grip before he shifted his hands, aware of Margarita close behind him.

The alvin bumped gently against the walkway he'd seen through the pilot's port. He climbed down onto it, relieved that it was stable, never mind that the patch had erased his nausea. They had surfaced in a small domed chamber with just enough room for the alvin. The air was cool, dense with the scent of the sea and the sound of water. The walls were transparent, the twilight of the shallow water outside glossed with mirror reflections of the alvin and themselves. Margarita leapt lightly down to the walkway, and Michael took her offered hand, grateful for her stability, a little surprised by these overtures. Andy was climbing down behind them, his carryall over his shoulder, his expression closed and introspective.

"So you came, after all," Hawk Danners's voice boomed out from behind them.

They all turned, startled by the volume. Michael gawked at the empty walkway for an instant, then turned quickly back, just in time to catch Danners stepping through a door farther along the wall.

"Sorry, I can't resist games." Grinning, he strolled toward them, moving with a clumsy sideways gait that fit his misshapen body. "I didn't say you could bring baggage. Who's the dude?" He jerked his head at Andy as if he were a dog on a leash.

"Andy Rodriguez, meet Hawk Danners," Michael said smoothly. He remembered Danners's games. "Andy's part of the story I was thinking about sharing with you." And fuck you too, Hawk. Michael kept a smile on his face. If Danners got you pissed, he won and you lost.

"You don't have to explain about *her*." Ignoring Andy, Danners took a quick step forward and cupped Margarita's chin in his hand. "How can you stand an old goat like him, sweetheart? Even when he was young, you could've done better."

Michael tensed, half expecting her to kick him in the nuts, pissed at himself because he hadn't had the brains to warn her about Danners. But she didn't recoil, didn't say a word. She simply stared at him with an expression of mild disgust, as if she'd turned over a rock to expose a cluster of pale fat grubs. Nice, although Danners was probably sensitive enough to pick up the anger underneath her act. "Hawk, meet my daughter, Margarita Espinoza." *My daughter*—he hadn't said it out loud before.

"Your daughter, huh?" Danners let go of her. "She sure didn't get her looks from you." If he was disappointed or annoyed by her lack of response, he didn't show it. "Actually, I was working. You can make yourselves at home." He finally acknowledged Andy with a curt nod. "I'll show you the guest room. I didn't figure you were bringing guests, and this isn't a hotel." He gave Michael a quick, sour glance. "You can fight over the bed."

"That's fine." Michael nodded.

"You can sit in on the session. Who knows, you might pick up something new." Danners grinned in challenge. It was an invisible gauntlet tossed down on the floor.

"I'd like that." Michael returned his grin. Two can play at this game, Hawk.

"Great." Hawk Danners's thick fingers closed around Michael's upper arm, gentle but hard as steel bands. "You two, you get to the house through that door there." He jerked his chin. "Go fuck, or find yourself something to eat, or whatever. Just don't bother us. We'll catch you later." He turned a crooked, ferocious grin on Michael. "My studio's down at the bottom. Let's go."

Chapter Eight

Danners's subsea studio was made up of a cluster of polyglass spheres anchored just off the Alcatraz reef. That reef, built by the mutated, fast-growing corals that plagued the West Coast, had begun to clog the bay. Through the transparent wall, a squat fish stared at Michael from less than a meter away, its long jaw opening and closing rhythmically, revealing hundreds of fine white teeth. As Michael followed Danners through a short, accordion-walled tube that connected the alvin's bay with the next bubble room, he found himself having to remember to breathe, as if his body had been fooled into believing that he was in the water.

"What if a wall cracks?" Michael forced himself to take a deep breath, fighting the tightness in his chest.

"You'd get air pockets above the level of the crack." Danners shrugged. "And there are plenty of hatches. We're not very deep—even you would probably make it to the surface. With a little luck. Are you so scared of dying?" He gave Michael a sideways look and grinned. "It's getting to you, isn't it? All that *sea*. We don't belong down here, and your flesh knows it, even if your head knows it's safe." He stepped through into his studio, waving Michael in after him with an expansive gesture. "Welcome to the whisper of corals."

The studio was larger than the alvin port, and the transparent walls curved down to meet a floor carpeted in soft tones of blue-green, gray, and brown. It blended in so well with the reef colors that it seemed to disappear.

"I use the bottom of each sphere for storage," Danners said. "Food, water, the storage batteries—they make good ballast. A computer pumps seawater in and out of temporary cells to keep the place at a null buoyancy."

Michael walked past Danners, barely hearing his words. Coral rose up around the sphere in twisting towers, as if it were growing over the bubble and would someday entomb it here in a calciferous shroud. There was no artificial light on in the studio, just the soft twilight that filtered down from the distant silvery ceiling where air and water met. A school of fish swam by, turning in perfect unison to dart away in a precisely straight line. An orange sea slug the size of his hand undulated slowly along the invisible curve of wall, its tongue flattening and contracting within the small circle of its mouth as it rasped algae from the sphere. Delicate, feathery fronds trailed from its back like strange seaweed, edged in crimson. Beyond the corals, kelp stems undulated in unfelt currents and a larger shadow moved. A shark? A rare orca? Michael squinted, but the furtive movement had vanished. Pale anemones blossomed in fleshy bouquets, and a delicate spider-legged shrimp climbed slowly up a spire of dead coral. Its body was clear as crystal, banded with dark red, and it waved long feelers at Michael's face as if in surprise. Then the squat fish he'd seen earlier darted down to bite the shrimp in half with a terrier shake of its blunt head. It swallowed and swam away with a snap of its powerful tail.

Michael stared after it, stunned by this tiny moment of violence, feeling it all around him: a hundred deaths, a thousand tiny dramas playing themselves out in shadows and small cataclysms of shock and pain, dulled and darkened by the smooth swell of hunger satisfied. On the far side of the glass a tiny coral died within its stony cup. A million tiny tragedies, a million triumphs. They merged, energy feeding on energy, coming full circle to close on itself. And the worm eating its own tail, the circle, the sum of all these lives and deaths was . . . eternity. So big. So much bigger than anything we can imagine, and all . . . linked. In touch. We are so *lonely.* Michael swallowed with the sudden clench of that isolation. Dear God, so cut off . . .

He turned slowly, goose bumps tightening his skin even though the room was warm enough. That was where these feelings came from: the Stone stood in the center of the floor, set up on a pedestal of silvered driftwood. His fingers twitched, moving on their own as if to reach out and touch its gray and silver surface. It sang life and death. It sang eternity and loneliness, and the strength of that song almost brought him to his knees. "I . . . haven't experienced any of your recent Stones." Michael licked his dry lips.

"I do them all down here." Danners leaned against the wall, hands clasped behind his back. "People react to the sea." He stared at his Stone, brow furrowed. "I bring the models down here at night, sedated, put them to bed while it's dark. Then I sit with the Stone, and we wait for them to wake up in the light." He looked up and touched the curve of the wall between them.

A hairline crack ran across it like a bolt of crooked lightning. At Danners's touch, beads of seawater began to swell along its length. Slowly they grew, combining one by one until a single drop trickled down the curve of the wall, leaving a glistening path like the track of a tear. Michael shivered, and Danners smiled.

"Yeah," he said. "Bring the sea in here, just a drop, and it's *real*. Those walls don't mean shit anymore. They're cracked. They can't protect you, and all of a sudden you're face to face with our mother. You can't hide from how you feel." He stroked the curve of the Stone gently, sensuously, as he might stroke a lover's thigh. "That's the first thing I lay onto a Stone." He wiped his hand across the weeping crack, and the water stopped instantly.

"I'm . . . impressed." Michael looked away, letting that gray-green horizonless distance absorb his gaze. Spirituality, he thought. That's what he felt beyond the circular song of eternity. A deep, vast sense of . . . godhead? The realization jolted him, hard to reconcile with Danners's rudeness, the rumors about his personal habits, and his intentionally ugly body. With an effort he forced his gaze back to Danners's face. "You're very good."

"Coming from you, that's very flattering." Danners didn't smile. "Honesty's an expensive luxury, no?"

"How about modesty?" Michael's lips tightened.

"Why should I be modest with you?" Danners shrugged, one hand still caressing the Stone. "Once upon a time you were better than me; I've never quite been able to get the power and complexity you put into your early pieces. Maybe you'll get a second wind and be better than me again one of these days. I don't care. I'll still make enough to pay for new Stones." His teeth flashed in the unruly nest of his beard. "You're pissed. I don't waste much energy on tact, either."

"No, you don't." Michael turned away from the Stone. *Once upon a time* . . . Was it a second wind that he needed? Was that a possible thing at all?

"So what was all the mystery about these suicides? And, yeah, the cops are officially calling S'Wanna's death a suicide. Just in case you haven't been paying attention." He grinned at Michael. "You could tell me how you got yourself mixed up in that one, too. I never figured you were S'Wanna's type."

"Andy was her lover." Michael didn't look at Danners. "You might want to lay off around him—he might be willing and able to take you on. Those deaths weren't suicides, by the way."

"If he wants to try, he's welcome," Danners said absently. "So what were they? Accidents?"

It wasn't his usual mocking tone. Michael turned around to find him frowning at his Stone. "Murders, I think. And I don't have a single shred of evidence."

Danners grunted, shoved his thick fists into the pockets of his tunic, and stalked across the carpeted floor to stare into the murk. "I could say it was so much shit, paranoia, one of those coincidences that doesn't fit the statistical norm until you look at about a three-thousand-year sample." He frowned, thick brows drawing in over his jutting nose, his eyes narrowing. "I don't know. For the last week, I've felt as if something's out there. Not like a shark. It's more like—all of a sudden I'm not looking out into the bay. I stare into that murk, and I get this weird feeling that Berkeley's not out there. There's no Embarcadero. It's like . . . I'm looking into *forever*. And, shit, man, sometimes I just want to swim out there and . . . drown in it." He laughed a short, barking note. "Which I'd say is just the wrong combination of party drugs, except for those damn deaths." He whirled suddenly, his eyes pinning Michael's. "What else do you know?"

"Nothing." Michael looked away. Eternity? Yeah, the darkness in his head had that feel. "I've been having nightmares lately. Strange ones. They're pretty bad."

"So what? Dreams don't kill you." Danners made a chop-

ping motion with his hand. "So you came down here to pick my brain, huh?" He raised one eyebrow. "Or did you plan on waiting around to see if someone showed up to murder me?"
"Something like that." Michael nodded.

"Well, hell. You can do that. I may toss your little entourage into the bay if they piss me off. Daughter and all—if she *is* your daughter." He leered at Michael. "Which I rather doubt. You don't like me much, do you?"

"Is that a concern?" Michael bared his teeth in a smile.

"What do you think?" Danners laughed. "Do you know how much this body cost?" He thumped his chest. "But it goes with the attitude, don't you think?"

"How come you use drugs on your models?" Michael circled the Stone once more, shivering at the depth of its resonance, wanting to touch it, wake it.

"It's a shortcut. Hey, it works." He shrugged. "Maybe my stuff would be better if I took fifteen years instead of six or seven to layer it in, but hell, it's good enough."

"Drugs blur your models' emotional state."

"I use the sea a lot." Danners's voice had gone cold. "You see any clarity out there, Mike? Go ahead and take your time. Feel free. Me, I'm always looking down the road to the next Stone."

There was a restless note in his voice, a hunger. Was he looking for something? Something he might never find? How many Stones had he completed? This one was good. No, it was more than good. Michael sighed, noticing the draped form of another Stone near the door. Beyond it, beyond the wall, an eel thrust its head from a cave of darkness, fanged jaws gaping. That darkness drew him, plucking at his soul like fleshless fingers. Michael spread his hands against the cool polyglass, seized by a fierce urge to dive deep into that darkness, burrow like a maggot for its beating heart, sate himself in it, fill himself until he burst. This was what Danners had meant. Michael shook his head, reaching for the fabric that covered the Stone. This was where it came from.

"Don't touch!"

Michael yanked his hand away. The woven drape slid to the floor, pooling around the slender, oblate Stone. It was shot with threads of silver, and hints of green and amber seemed to brighten and dim in its rough surface. Michael closed his hands into fists and shoved them into his pockets, that dark note humming through him, singing a siren song in his blood.

"This is a virgin Stone." Danners brushed past him and picked up the drape. "I've got a model coming in tomorrow night, and I don't want Michael Tryon's handprints on it, thank you very much." He grinned ferociously and tossed the drape over the Stone.

Michael shook his head, feeling numb and a little dazed, as if he'd just woken up. The dark note had come from the finished Stone, then? Had he been mistaken? Perhaps the new Stone had picked up one thread of its resonance and had amplified it in a fluke of proximity. He looked sideways at Danners's blunt, ugly face. He'd worked one hell of a dark note into that finished Stone; he must have buried it so that it would leap out at unsuspecting listeners and really nail them.

That bit of trickery was out of keeping with the magnitude of what he'd felt, and it diminished his respect for Danners a little. "I think I'll go find Andy and Margarita," he said.

"Do that." Danners was staring moodily at his finished Stone. "I'm still polishing here. Anything you want, find it. Don't bug me."

"Sure." Michael turned away. That buried darkness was uncalled for, the crude kind of trick an apprentice might try. He ducked to enter the connecting tube, stabbed by a pang of disappointment. The Stone was so *good.* Except for that.

"Pretty Spartan for somebody who can afford to build this place." Fists on her hips, Margarita eyed the room bubble they'd just entered.

This one had a carpeted floor, although the dense carpeting had been colored to blend into the mottled gray-green landscape of coral. The small holostage that must have been Danners's Net access shared the space with one recliner and a scatter of sea-colored cushions. Yeah, she could just see it. Margarita grimaced. Danners the king on his throne, with his admiring court at his feet. Fuck that. She kicked one of the cushions. I'll stand. Above her head, a school of small yellow fish drifted slowly past. In a rush of motion, something gray and big arrowed into their center. They scattered, exploding like shrapnel, vanishing into the murk. If the gray thing had scored, it had happened too fast for her to see. Excitement stirred in Margarita's belly, a whisper of blood lust, as if it were she up there, slashing into that defenseless school, teeth bared, reaching . . .

With an effort, she tore her eyes away from the blue-green distance and wandered over to the compact kitchen wall. Microwave, dishwasher, a hot and cold drink bar; no alcohol, just juice and water. Expensive tastes in food. She scrolled the freezer inventory across the tiny inset door screen. All real stuff, the fruits and veggies? She'd bet he didn't stock anything grown in a tank or made out of flavored paste. No meat, either. Or fish. Huh. She flicked her fingertips against the screen and blanked it. She had imagined Hawk Danners tearing into a big slab of meat, bloody juice dripping from his ugly chin.

"That looks like our bedroom down here." Andy was peering warily down another clear-walled accordioned tunnel. "You know, I was going to make a suggestion sort of in keeping with that of our ugly host." He shrugged and laughed wryly. "Only this place is giving me the serious willies. Too bad."

"If you're asking for a quick lay, fuck off." Margarita lost herself in the watery spaces beyond the dome. What she would *give* to live here.

"Michael said something about that—how we're just a hull's width away from death down here." Andy swallowed. "I really feel it here." He gave a strained half laugh. "I never figured me for a phobic."

He was really scared. Margarita gave him a startled look as the corridor tube undulated gently beneath her weight. His knuckles were white, and he was breathing hard, as if he'd been running. "Hey, relax. If anything was going to blow, it would have already happened. Besides—" She nodded towards the top of the tube. "—you can *see* the surface. Can't you swim?"

"No. I don't think it would matter." Andy took one cautious step into the corridor and went pale as it gave beneath his weight. "Damn it, this is as bad as your dad's seasick trip."

He edged past Margarita, walking as if he were on a tightrope above the Grand Canyon, hands splayed against the walls on either side. Scared shitless. Margarita tried for sympathy but couldn't quite make it real. How could you be scared down here? Spires of coral grew on either side of the corridor, swarming with small fish. She knelt, peering at the dull orange fringe of an anemone only inches from her face. The fleshy tentacles waved slowly in the water, groping for unwary swimmers, waiting to sting and capture and eat. Margarita smiled as a tiny crab scuttled across the coral, striped in bright copper and white. The walls of the corridor comforted her, enfolding her. She drew a slow breath, feeling currents of seawater in her lungs, flowing in and out as the water flowed around the anemone's hunger.

"I think I'm bowing out." Andy's voice jolted Margarita.

With a scowl, she looked up. He was sitting on the king-sized bed in the room at the end of the tube, his face pale and almost greenish in the sea light.

"I'll give my adrenals a rest. Maybe I'll feel better when I wake up. When you can't beat the biochemistry, use it." Andy fumbled in his carryall. "Tell Michael I'm ready to go whenever he is. I'll wake up if you shake me hard enough." He pulled his hand out of his carryall and began to strip white plastic from a drug patch. "Good night." He smoothed the patch onto his carotid groove, tossed his carryall onto the floor, and threw himself facedown onto the bed.

He sounded more pissed at himself than scared. Margarita left him to his escape and went back into the main room. It was too big, with too much furniture. It interfered with the sea. A nagging itch like desire tickled her, and she prowled across the room. Three more corridors opened into this sphere. She chose one at random, a frisson of chill climbing her spine as the sea enclosed her. It didn't squeeze her the way it probably squeezed Andy. The pressure flowed through her, compressing the atoms of her body, compressing, perhaps, her self, until she and the sea and the shadowy twilight became one, the colors a language, the sea surge ebbing and flowing with every beat of her heart.

The corridor opened into a small sphere cradled in stony coral fingers. This one was unfurnished, unlighted. Instead of a carpet, cushions and thick featherbeds were piled on the floor, so that she had to pick her way carefully across the uneven surface as if she were walking across the reef itself. End of the line? She sank to her knees in the feathery softness, tempted to curl up there but still nagged by that restlessness. An opening caught her eye—another corridor? This one was small, half-hidden by a tossed pile of cushions. She would have to crawl on hands and knees.

She shoved cushions aside and stuck her head in. Was it a service tunnel of some kind? The thought of machinery made her pause briefly, thinking of chains and Ari's mangled body. But she would see it, and she could always back out. She crawled into the tunnel, a sourceless excitement building inside her. Was it darker? Yes, she was crawling down, and the corridor was getting narrower. The cool plastic brushed her shoulders and back now, seeming to press against her, pushing her along in some enormous metaphor for birth. Breathing faster, Margarita sank onto her belly, skin thickening with the sea's cold caress. The blue twilight seeped into her, filling her lungs like water until she was swimming, breathing water, sinking down into the corals, where she would emerge to spread fins and swim away . . .

The twilight thickened to near darkness. Above her head, coral arched and nearly met, enclosing her in its stony, living fist. But I am a fish, and you can't crush me. Margarita slithered forward, the air dank and water-thick, making her dizzy. Am I dying? she wondered. Shapes moved in the darkness, welcoming her, keeping her company. Dying *toward* something, toward life? Yes, life into death, into life forever, twisting back on itself, a worm devouring its own tail. The water squeezed her, comforting her with its pressure as the pressure of Katrina's arms had comforted her, without need, without censure. And suddenly, terribly, Margarita missed her. I want you to be here, she thought. I need to *tell* you about this.

Turquoise light broke through the leaden shadows, and suddenly she was climbing *up*. Up into spring? Margarita paused, twisting awkwardly in the widening tunnel, panting a little in the thick chill. Katrina was still down there, left behind in the shadows. And it was too late to go back. She could never go back, only forward into tomorrow. And are you there waiting for me, Katrina? Somewhere in some tomorrow? Swallowing the stony thickness in her throat, she crawled on. Blue light brightened, and she was able to get to her feet as the tunnel enlarged.

It ended at another door. A song whispered suddenly in Margarita's head, a sea voice, siren voice, singing a note that made her tremble. Hooked, snagged by that song, she broke into a run, stumbling a little on the undulating floor, the song filling her head, swelling like a chorus that was one voice and a million, filling her up to spill over in bright waves of vision.

She burst through the doorway into another sphere and gasped as a hand yanked her to a halt. A knife blade touched her throat with cold promise. "Chill," a voice hissed in her ear.

Stones filled the sphere, singing a dozen soft counterpoints. Cold steel at her throat, Stone song in her soul, Margarita absorbed it in a single overwhelming instant. They stood on intricate pedestals of silvered driftwood and what looked like old bone. There was no light except what filtered through the deep water and the soft glow from bioluminescent sponges that crusted the wall of the sphere in an open and strangely ordered lacework. Were these Danners's Stones? Danners's private gallery, hidden away here in the sea's dark embrace? Margarita drew a slow breath and tore her attention from the Stones, letting her gaze slide sideways along the arm that held the knife against her throat.

It belonged to a man with black hair and green eyes. He was part Asian, her age, maybe younger, and he was laughing at her. Sneering. It was an *act*, this blade—a game—and it didn't belong here. And he didn't know blades; she could tell. The Stone song lifted her, mixing with the hot flood of her anger, amplifying it, singing it into her bones. She shrank back a hair as if in fright; he grinned, paying satisfied attention to the look of fear on her face.

The edge of her hand slammed his arm aside, knocking the blade away from her throat. She grabbed his wrist as he recovered, twisting it. The blade clattered on the floor, and he yelled, going down hard on one knee to keep his wrist from breaking. Spinning sideways, she twisted his arm up behind his back and slammed him facedown onto the wood-planked floor. Try *this*, baby. She knelt beside him, pinning him by his twisted arm, then bent it gently toward her chest.

"Oh, *shit*." He lunged up against her hold, gasped, and went limp. "Don't break it!" he said to the floor, his voice muffled and ragged with pain.

"Oh, dear. You startled me." She didn't relax the tension on his arm.

"So you startled *me*, bitch. Hey, all *right*." He gasped again as she tightened her hold a tiny bit. "So I'm sorry."

"Are you sure?"

"Yeah. *Yes*, okay? Get *off*."

She laid his arm gently down but didn't let go, ran her fingertips down his lean back. "Nice muscles, bad attitude." She patted his butt lightly, released his wrist, and got to her feet, balanced and ready as he reached for his dropped knife and scrambled up. Macho to have left him his blade, she chided herself. Her cousins would have beaten her for it, but hell, sometimes you had to make a statement.

He glared at her a moment, then sheathed the blade and slid it out of sight beneath his tunic. Quality fabric, that—flashy and custom-cut to flatter his lithe, tawny body. "You know, you're shitty with a blade." She let her lip curl, her anger still singing harmony to the Stones' song. "That's a dangerous game, baby. Better get some lessons before somebody cuts your nuts off."

"Fuck you, bitch."

She slapped him hard across the face.

His eyes glazed, then blazed with green fire. Margarita's muscles went loose and ready on their own, reading attack. But instead of throwing himself at her, he looked away and laughed. "That's what I get for playing out of my league." He gave her an ironic bow. "You're *still* a bitch. And keep your hands off." He grinned at her. "Unless you really want to deal with Archenwald-Shen."

Archenwald-Shen? "You're too young." Not even the best body shop could give you back real youth.

"Yeah, I'm young." His grin was cold. "Gunner likes them young."

He was Archenwald-Shen's boy? Margarita looked away. Two days ago she might have sneered. Now . . . I didn't even pay my own bill, she thought bitterly. She had played her game of being above it all, of pretending that the rules didn't apply to her. So Katrina had paid for her.

Who got to sneer at whom here?

"Truce? No more rough stuff?" He'd won, and he knew it. The smirk didn't show on his face, but it was there. Margarita eyed the hand he was holding out, wanting to put him on the floor again, wanting to break his wrist this time. Who are you really mad at, girl, she wondered. What's the truth here, huh?

"So we got a truce." She ignored his hand, which only widened his grin.

"My name's Zed." He tilted his head so that his long dark hair fell forward over one shoulder. "You're tougher than you look. Where'd you learn your stuff, anyway? And how did you end up in Danners's private little kingdom? You're definitely not his type, although I'd kind of like to watch him try."

"Damn right I'm not his type." She looked beyond him at the austere Stones, caressed by them, unable to resist them. Danners had done these. She shook her head, unable to put that into any kind of perspective. "I grew up in LA. My cousins were tough. You lose points if you let other members of your family get kicked around, so they made damn sure I didn't lose them any points. I'm here with Michael Tryon."

"Him? How'd *he* snag a she-stud like you?" Zed skipped back a step, grinning.

"He didn't snag me." She shrugged, letting him know he wasn't worth the effort. "I'm his daughter." Not *He's my father* but *I'm his daughter.* Was there a difference, and why?

Zed's eyebrows rose into sleek arches. "Small world, indeed. Too bad he's not tougher than he looks, too."

"As compared to looking tougher than you are?" She bared her teeth at him.

"Back off." He kept a wary eye on her. "I'm trying to be nice, okay?" He gave her a mocking bow. "Not many folks get invited down here, although I guess you snuck in the back way. Nice trick, by the way. I can't take the squeeze. Me, I like solid land." He grimaced and patted the nearest Stone gently. "Come on, I'll show you the rest of the inner sanctum. Since you're here." He patted the Stone again and turned away.

His casual possessiveness reminded her of Ari's in the gallery, as if he owned these Stones. And if he wanted to own them, maybe he could. If he really did belong to Archenwald-Shen. She followed him into another corridor, watching him move. Yeah, Zed belonged to him, with his carefully beautiful body, full of aristocracy and shame. And the knife was an affectation; there were a dozen better weapons to carry, from stunners to thread guns. Steel macho? she wondered. A challenge to death, or maybe an invitation. She frowned, remembering the fire in his eyes when she'd slapped him.

Maybe we all belong to somebody, whether we admit it or

not. And maybe part of us wants to belong to someone, whether we admit it or not. A spasm of pain clutched her. Katrina, I didn't want you to pay my way.

"What are *you* doing here?" she asked.

"Picking up a commission. So Tryon's here, too?" Zed had reached the end of the corridor and stopped to look back at her, smiling with studied innocence. "How interesting. Too bad he doesn't have any Stones to sell. Danners is hot, but he doesn't have a clue when it comes to hurting. Not like your dad."

Your dad. Margarita flinched, but Zed didn't seem to notice. He was rubbing his shoulders against the corridor wall like a cat.

"He reads people awfully well, your dad. I guess he has to, to do the things he does with his Stones."

This—this punk admired him. Michael. Margarita turned away, not ready to call him Dad, anger knotting in her gut, mixed up with too damn many emotions to sort out. Was hurting what he put into his Stones? Margarita looked out into blue water and the gray shadows of distant coral, remembering the soft whisper of that Stone in New York. Yeah, she'd felt *hurting,* layered in human love, and in hope, despair, and . . . compassion. Acceptance? Was that what it had been about? Acceptance of pain, because it was part of everyone, as much a part of life as love? She shook her head. "They've all got to read people," she said. "That's what it takes to sculpt a Stone."

"Danners doesn't read people." Zed shrugged. "He just sort of uses them. I think he's reading himself. Your dad touches something real. You know, it's not worth doing if you can't make it real, even if the results sell."

"You've decided all this, have you?" Her hackles were rising again, and she made an effort to hold on to her temper. "You're quite the authority."

"I'm not." He shrugged, frowning, as if he regretted what he'd just said. "Tryon needs to be a little more careful about pissing people off. The wrong people, anyway. You might tell him that."

Something flitted across his face, gone too fast for her to identify it. "Who did he piss off?" Margarita asked absently.

"Gunner really wanted one of your dad's Stones." Zed gave her an oblique look. "Your dad wasn't too polite about saying no. Hey, check this out." He turned his back on her and ducked through the door.

Margarita followed him slowly, eyeing the irising portals that would probably close tight if one of the corridors ruptured. Then she looked into the room and stopped still, sucking in a quick breath. A holostage took up the center of the otherwise empty sphere, adrift in dim green light, its console powered down and lifeless.

"You play?" Zed was eyeing her.

"Play, do visuals, write . . ." Suleman image generators, Nilsson remote stims. Her stage wasn't half this good, and she'd sweated blood for it.

"Danners goofs around in here." He grinned, sly now. "I watched last night. Sex and flesh and beach sand. Gritty." He rolled his eyes. "What's your angle? Not that, I bet."

She walked toward the stage, setting one foot down in front of the other carefully, as if the polyglass were thin crystal ready to shatter beneath a careless step. Her eyes scanned the evolution programming modules—the latest versions—and a Prendergast synthesizer. For an instant she hated Danners because he had this to screw around on, to *play* with. At the same time she loved him—because he knew the best and had it all. Holding her breath, she touched the console. It powered on instantly, filling her teeth and bones with that indefinable hum that Katrina claimed she couldn't feel.

If Katrina could only *see* this.

She snatched the console from its rest, not caring if Danners busted in and threw her out of the nearest lock, and patched the throat mike onto her skin. She seemed to levitate to the stage, then bent down to check the gain and bring up the inventory on the Suleman. Marine categories, mostly—what a surprise. Net interfaces. She grimaced. Well, hell, it was a *toy*; what did he have to lose to a cracker? She swept her hand across the keypad, bringing up corals in shades of maroon and dark blue-green. Enough coral already. She vanished them, coaxed darkness from the pad: nighttime darkness with a hint of wave motion to set glowing motes of tiny life rocking in an unseen swell. Sea scent, salty wind, but muted, overlaid with a hint of decay, of something dead on the beach, waiting for the tide to seize it. A touch, a bare hint of myrrh for nuance . . .

"Hey, I'll come back."

Zed sounded . . . sad? "You can stick around," she mumbled. Not myrrh, try jasmine. "It's not mine or anything."

No answer. Blinking, she raised her head and looked around. He was gone. Alone, released, she closed her eyes. Darkness. She remembered her scramble through the narrow tube beneath the coral, the squeezing sense of birth or death. And Katrina's face, overlaid on the darkness. Her cheeks were wet. I'm crying, Margarita thought, and opened her eyes. For Katrina? The answer was *here* somewhere; she only had to find it. She touched up a lex file and bit her lip. Lex was the hard part, the struggle. It took time, soul, inspiration, and a lot of sweat to do words that fit. Later. Frowning, she brought in audio, the slow, unstoppable march of the waves done in oboes and the soft deep throb of a drum.

The ocean lends me gills and fins,
but the warmest waves have chilled . . .

No way. Nice lines, but they didn't work in this dark sea. Chewing her lip, she caught a flicker of movement beyond the stage. Zed? She squinted. Or Danners come to toss her butt out of here?

"You just composed this?" Michael Tryon emerged from the shadows to lean his elbows on the edge of the stage.

Oh, shit, don't let him be good at *this*, too. "Yeah." Margarita stared down into his upturned face. "It's all canned stuff. I'm just playing around."

"It's good," he said softly. "Do you mind if I watch?"

Yes. She didn't say it, struggling instead with the sudden rush of her feelings. What did she see in his face, anyway? Curiosity? Wariness?

Pride? She flushed and looked away. "Come up and play." She jerked her head at the auxiliary console, hearing challenge in her tone. "I don't work in front of an audience."

Michael heard that challenge, and nodded slowly. "I will." He climbed awkwardly up onto the stage. "I've never been very good with this." He touched his console pad to life, putting it into duet mode. "You have the last word."

She thumbed her own pad over to duet and sucked in a quick breath as the scene shifted. Didn't take him long to jump right in. She swallowed a quick twinge of annoyance as the swell increased to storm-wave intensity, tumbling plankton in murky clouds that glowed with bioluminescence. She could restore her slow swell. Margarita's fingers hovered over the keypad, but then she shrugged, ducking involuntarily as two big waves collided overhead and clouds of glowing plankton spilled down around them. Okay, not bad. She could go with this. She killed the jasmine and went to the scent of wet sand tinged with the barest hint of sulfur.

Michael nodded and touched his keypad.

The ocean lends me gills and fins . . .

His voice, but younger, slightly higher and more androgynous. Now what? Margarita bit her lip hard:

But the warmest waves have chilled,
for the sea is more a time than a place . . .

"Nice," Michael said softly. "Cold. I like that."

"Not cold." Margarita shook her head. "Too much like *Crystalline*, the piece I just finished."

"Deep?"

"Yeah!" Deep; that was it, that was what she was after with her darkness. Not night, not cold—depth. Her fingers raced across the keypad—there were a dozen files to choose from—and they sank. Green grayed out, then darkened to deep twilight and became blackness, the utter black of the abyss. A low wandering note followed them down, the drums a whisper of presence. Michael's audio. Not bad, if a little too spare. Now what? She starred the black void with a constellation of pale squid, trailing clouds of luminous ink. A school of tiny glowing fish twirled past her like a galaxy in motion, and Michael smiled.

She grinned back and spotted the darkness with jellyfish, their cups a rich scarlet cloaked in transparent flesh above coils of opalescent tendrils. She sent one of the jellies to hover above his head and laughed as he ducked the trailing filaments. He grinned and perched a scarlet crustacean on her shoulder.

Yes, this *worked*: depth and crushing pressure, a place where life glowed with its own living light. She touched her keypad.

Adjusting her own voice down a notch, she replayed his spoken lines, speaking along in duet;

The ocean lends me gills and fins,
but the warmest waves have chilled,
for the sea is more a time than a place

A place of yesterdays, like glowing jellyfish in the abyss—a place of a lover's touch, of a man's lost youth? Yesterday was gone, like Katrina, walled away behind time and fear and . . . Damn it! She stalled.

And Michael's voice took over, hesitant at first.

Among the currents like clock springs undone,
I sink toward the past and a child's myth,
its lines threaded in sediment now stone.

He paused.

Having mistaken ascent for achievement,
I fall toward my first self,
swift as air's life, no pressure but my own blood.

Silenced, Margarita let her hands rest on the keypad. *Having mistaken ascent for achievement . . .* So he was looking at himself, too? Michael Tryon, legend among sculptors? *I fall toward my first self . . .* Margarita swallowed. Who were you looking for, Michael Tryon, when you knocked on my door? You? Me? Or something that is both of us, or neither of us, and maybe doesn't exist? The tears wanted to come again, and she seized control of the input, angry, wanting to leave him behind, outrun him. Needing anger, she coaxed it from her pad, building the audio through the octaves, traveling impossible distances at the edge of hearing; she added sea scent, a tinge of pheromone, desires aroused and sated in turn. Her anger modulated, tinging the abyss with violet and indigo, an overlay of loneliness and unspeakable pain. Slivers of the entire spectrum appeared, exploding minutely and returning in the blink of an eye to the blackness of yesterdays, forever gone.

The words came to her at last.

These depths write fear in new bone,
darkness teaches the flesh luminescence—
the touch of the high seas black and subtle—
here the senses are perfect beyond time,
and vision rests in the eye, not in light.

For one heartbeat, silence. Two. Three. She bent slowly to lay the keypad down as the abyss faded.

"Margarita," Michael whispered. He held out a hand, his eyes shining in the dim subsea light. "You are very good."

She raised her own hand, reaching across the meter of space that separated them. Their fingers brushed, palm sliding across palm.

"You *are* good."

Zed's voice broke them apart in a simultaneous start. He was leaning against the transparent wall, hands clasped behind his back. "It looked like you were having fun." He smirked. "Sorry if I intruded."

But in spite of his smirk and his needling tone, he looked wistful.

"Zed?" Fists clenched at his sides, Michael stared at him. "What are you doing here?"

"Picking up a commission." He lifted his shoulders in a graceful shrug. "The boss bought from Danners, since you wouldn't sell. They're dreck compared to yours." His grin vanished. "I warned you, Tryon. Gunner's going to find out that you were here, and he's going to expect me to tell him why. He's not done with you yet, and he's going to take it out on you. Or on me." His grin bared his teeth. "I guess he's spoiled. Me, too. Enough so I give Gunner what he wants. Like I told you back in Taos." He straightened, shoving his hands into his tunic pockets. "So be careful, Mr. Tryon." For an instant he turned his bleak eyes on Margarita, then he turned his back on both of them and almost ran out of the room.

Margarita had the unsettling feeling that he had watched their entire improvisation. And that he had been crying.

"I didn't know you knew Zed," Michael said softly.

"I just met him here." She looked sideways. Michael's shoulders were hunched, his fists still clenched at his sides. Angry? Maybe he was big and safe enough that he could be angry. Maybe. "Gunner Archenwald-Shen makes the world go round. Or he thinks he does. Hell, maybe he really does." She couldn't keep the bitterness out of her voice. "If you want the cops off your back, be nice to Mr. Gunner and he'll buy them off for you."

"Bend over, you mean?" His face told her nothing.

"Yeah." She jumped off the stage and racked the keypad. "That's what I mean." Why not you, too? Why should it just be Katrina? "Oh, *shit*," she said very softly.

Michael touched her shoulder. "I'm sorry about you and Katrina."

"What do you know about that?" She whirled, slapping his hand aside. "You don't know *anything*."

"I know you're hurting." He sighed. "I know what that feels like."

"Do you?" She wanted to be scathing but merely sounded sad. "You mean Xia?"

"Not just Xia."

She met his eyes, seeing pain beneath the compassion, seeing years like layers of old leaves on a forest floor. So many years. So much laughter, so many tears. *Hurting*, Zed had said of Michael's Stones. Do you hurt, Michael Tryon? "Who are you?" she said softly. " 'My father.' What does that mean?"

"I don't know what it means." His eyes held hers. "I guess that's what I'm trying to figure out. I meant it that you're very good. I'm—proud." He grimaced, not quite a smile, but almost. "That sounds patronizing, doesn't it? I could say that I'm impressed, but that's not it. I'm . . . proud."

He sounded so unsure of himself, almost puzzled. You're not the Michael Tryon, legendary sculptor, that I imagined, she thought and did not say. So, was the real man greater or less than that imagining?

"Andy was asleep when I looked in on him," Michael said. "I wanted to talk to him. We're supposed to leave Danners alone until he's through in his studio."

"Andy did a couple of patches. I don't think you should wake him up for a while." She sighed. "I'm hungry."

"Don't sound so surprised. It's late, and I don't recall that we got offered lunch."

It *was* late. Margarita realized that she was squinting to make out Michael's face. It must be getting dark up top. Down here the twilight was thickening rapidly to darkness. Margarita looked through the polyglass wall into dark water and shivered. "I think I need some dinner."

"Maybe Danners will be finished. Maybe Andy will be up." Michael's fingers twitched as if he wanted to touch her, but he stilled the impulse.

"Thanks for the help with the lex. I . . . I always have trouble with the words." She reached out and took his hand. "I think I took the long road to get here." She smiled at him, feeling suddenly, incredibly shy. "Do you know a better way back?"

"Yeah." He returned the smile. "I do."

Chapter Nine

Michael led her back to the main sphere through wide, easy corridors. The sea had gone night-dark, but embedded fibers in the corridor walls filled the space with soft light. Margarita wondered if the tunnel beneath the corals was lighted. She had indeed taken a back road, and she wondered why Danners had put it there. He would have a tough time squeezing his bulk through it. Zed had said he couldn't take it, that birth canal trip through the darkness and coral. She looked sideways at Michael, wondering what he would make of it.

He was frowning a little, his eyes glazed with an inward stare. Neither of them had said anything since they'd left the holo chamber, but the silence that stretched between them had a strangely comfortable feeling, a connection instead of a wall. Margarita explored its texture in her mind. There were a lot of unspoken words between them—twenty-two years worth. Some of those words they might actually utter one day; others would remain forever stillborn, children of a past that had never happened. She sighed, and he looked at her at last, smiling a little, his eyes still shadowed with whatever vision he'd been seeing.

"I'm not very good company," he said. "Thank you for letting me share the holoture with you."

"I enjoyed it," she said. Which was the truth. It had been fun. "When did you learn your way around a stage?"

"I knew this woman who did holoture." He smiled as he remembered. "Tarot liked to jam with a partner, and she didn't put up with a klutz on the keypad. I missed her when she left Taos."

An old lover? "Tarot?"

"Tarot Delgadio. She exhibits sometimes. She's good, too."

"*Yes*, she's good." Margarita stumbled over one of the gentle ribs in the corridor floor. Tarot Delgadio was the *best*—the top galleries, the cutting edge in equipment. And her style . . . She shook her head, a little dazed. *She's good, too.* "Too," as in "also." Michael had just compared her to Tarot, casually and without thought. Which was ridiculous, and he had said it only because he didn't really know holoture.

But it warmed her anyway. More than she could have expected it to. "Thanks," she said softly.

"You're welcome." He sounded a little uncertain, as if he wasn't sure what she was thanking him for.

Margarita looked over her shoulder, back toward the gallery with its siren chorus of Stones. "He's such a jerk." She ran a hand through her hair, shoving back her bangs. "How can such a jerk be so good?"

"I had the same reaction." Michael smiled wryly. "I haven't paid much attention to his Stones in the last few years. He uses drugs to cut his time, and I dismissed him because of that. I was feeling a little righteous, I guess." A hint of self-mockery tinged his smile. "I'm not anymore."

"Zed said something up in the gallery. He said Danners used people, was only putting himself into the Stones. He said you *read* people, that Danners didn't understand—" She stopped abruptly, noticing the stiffness in his posture. Oops. Wrong person to quote? So much for trying to repay his praise. Margarita winced. "Andy's awake," she said, glad to change the subject. They had reached the main room, and he was sitting in the recliner.

"I thought maybe you drowned." Andy eyed them, his face still glazed with drugs and sleep. "It's not so bad down here now that it's dark. Think you could wrap this business up and get us out of here by morning?" He grimaced. "My pride is suffering."

"I'm sorry you're having a tough time down here." Michael walked into the room and hesitated, his shoulders tensing almost imperceptibly. "Hello, Zed. Has Hawk been in here?"

"No." Zed, busy in the kitchen area, tossed them a preoccupied over-the-shoulder look. "He works all night sometimes. I'm playing chef. Or the microwave is, I guess."

"I'm glad someone knows where the food is." Andy cocked his head, giving Zed a quick up and down. "You do know your way around here, don't you? Come here often, or are you just bold?"

"Yeah, I come here often. Got a problem with that?" Zed half turned, his hand sliding into his pocket. His eyes flickered from Andy's face to Margarita's, and he took his hand out again. He grinned and shrugged. "Hey, I go where I'm sent. I'm a good little errand boy," he said as he turned his back on them.

"Me, I'm starving." Margarita flopped down on a cushion and gave Andy a too-sweet smile. Zed won that round, bucko. "I'm glad *somebody* figured out where the food was."

Zed didn't say anything, but he gave her a quick sideways wink.

Andy grunted and looked up at Michael. "So what about it? Did you get what you came for?"

"I need to stay for a while." Michael sat down on another cushion, his knees hurting. "Hawk thinks someone's stalking him. Or maybe he's just paranoid." He sighed, feeling his age today. "You better go back if the space is bothering you."

"I might have to." Andy frowned, then gave Zed a quick skewering glance. "Much as it offends my pride to give in to brain chemistry."

Zed smirked but didn't say a word.

"But I don't think I should." Andy met Michael's eyes. "You sculptors don't have much of a track record if somebody's picking you off. And if S'Wanna's killer shows up, I want to be here."

His tone was almost flip. But the flicker in his eyes worried Michael. It had a dark feel to it, an obsession that was growing, filling him with shadow. An obsession with revenge? Or was it death itself? Michael closed his eyes briefly, the invisible butterflies fluttering in his head, luring him, promising eternity . . .

He could almost hear the darkness like a low, throbbing note below the range of the human ear. Like the dark song that threaded Danners's Stone. Such power. He flexed his hands, remembering how much he had wanted to break that glass, swim into that murk and find its dark heart.

He had never captured that much power in his own Stones, no matter what Hawk said.

"It's ready." Zed turned away from the counter, a loaded tray in his hands. "Actually, it's cheese and fruit. And bread." He set it down on a low table near the wall, just out of Andy's reach.

Andy reached deliberately, helping himself to a wedge of pale cheese and some yellow grapes.

"You keeping score?" Zed winked at Margarita.

"Tie." She met his mocking stare, poised between laughter and annoyance at this posturing.

Michael reached for fruit and a chunk of crusty bread. "Did you send your pilot to beat me up?" He looked up at Zed.

"What are you talking about?" Zed's eyes narrowed, but not before Michael caught the flicker in their depths.

"I think you know, or you just guessed."

"Raoul was a hothead." Zed made a show of turning away, putting down a plate of dumplings. "That's why I fired him. No, I didn't give him any orders." His shoulders twitched. "Raoul blamed you for that . . . episode over the Estevan. I told him it wasn't your fault. I'm sorry if you got hurt."

"I got hurt." Drowned, not just hurt. Only maybe that dark cellar he'd fallen into had had nothing to do with Raoul's fists. Maybe they had just opened the door. Michael sighed, aware of Margarita's sudden, intent stare, seeing the shadows in Zed's eyes.

"I fired him right after I dropped you off." Zed was looking into a dimension Michael couldn't see. "He—he didn't take it very well. But he was a good guy. You don't fuck around with Gunner."

Yeah, Michael had seen what he thought he'd seen. You could pay one hell of a price for your security. What price was I paying? Michael wondered bitterly. My creativity? Is that what it cost to do good Minors and stay on in nice, safe Taos? Was that what had called the darkness?

No. He lifted his head, hearing that dark note, feeling its tug. That darkness came from outside him. He was sure of it—almost. Ice tickled the back of Michael's neck. It was the same song that had seized him in Danners's studio that afternoon. The ice spread through him, raising goose bumps on his skin. Not *similar*—the same. What if it wasn't Danners's power? No

Stone should have that kind of range. Where had that dark note come from?

"Michael?"

He realized he had gotten to his feet. Margarita was staring at him, a crease of worry between her eyes.

"I've got to talk to Hawk. I'll be right back."

"If he said for us to keep out, he means it." Zed leaned one hip against the counter, frowning at him. "What's eating you, man?"

"Michael?" Andy was staring at him, eyes narrowed. "You look a little like you did that afternoon I met you. Michael, are you all right?"

He wished they would all stop staring at him. "I think Hawk knows who we're looking for, after all."

Andy stood up. "So let's go ask him."

"It's a long swim to shore," Zed said to no one in particular.

"Something's wrong." Margarita got to her feet, her eyes on Michael's face. "What?"

"Nothing." He started for the corridor that led to Danners's studio. "I need to ask him for a name."

A name, a label for that terrible darkness. Someone had left it like a fingerprint on that Stone, strong enough to affect them all. And what did that have to do with S'Wanna, or Yojiro, or Andre Lustik, anyway?

Unless it had drowned them as it had drowned him. What if Andy hadn't fished him out?

This was crazy. Nobody could *do* something like that . . .

Michael wanted to run through the corridor but forced himself to walk. The floor bounced beneath his feet, jarring his steps. He looked over his shoulder and found that they had all followed him, even Zed. Great. Danners would love this, for sure. He paused in front of the studio doorway. It was closed, barred with a sphincter of transparent plastic. Beyond it the studio was dark, lighted only by the ghostly glow of bioluminescent sponges that crusted the sphere here and there. Michael stared at the door, seeing nothing that resembled a lock or controls.

"Open sesame," Zed said from behind him.

The door opened slowly, retracting into the walls. An intentional metaphor or just casual tech? Michael stepped through into the studio and froze, heart pounding in his ears.

The dark song engulfed him, stroking his face with ghostly fingers, singing of oblivion, of death, of space beyond death, space one reached only by dying. Beyond death . . . life . . . immortality. The song curled like invisible fingers across his face, slid into his head through eyes, nostrils, mouth, ears, dug long nails into the soft gray matter of his brain. Slowly it drew him forward, past the Stone that cried with Danners's voice—how could he have thought that this power emanated from that damaged ruin? Michael stumbled to a halt. Hawk had preceded him. His slack, empty flesh lay on the floor, sprawled facedown. His head was turned toward the far wall, and blood spread out in a dark pool on the floor, floating like a glossy oil slick on the black sea. Michael stepped over him, bumping one cold, stiff leg with his toe.

Beyond him stood the virgin Stone. The drape lay crumpled at its feet. Green and silver shimmered in its depths, pulsing like a beating heart. It reached out to him with dark, taloned fingers of yearning, love, and agony and caressed him.

"Michael?" Margarita stepped through the doorway right behind him, but he didn't seem to hear her. She halted, her skin ridging with gooseflesh. Such a tense feel in here—like a storm brewing, heavy as the dirt on a grave. She drew a gasping breath, suffocating, squeezed by the sensation, diminished by it. Her fingers curved, twitching with the desire to claw her way surfaceward, to escape.

"Margarita?" Zed's hand closed on her arm hard enough to hurt. "Snap out of it."

She blinked and shuddered, her eyes focusing on the shadowy bulk of a Stone. No, the ugly darkness didn't come from that one. Andy had pushed past her and was a pale shape of movement in the eerie light.

He stopped abruptly, then knelt. "It's Danners. Dead."

"Shit." Zed tensed, head swinging, searching the darkness.

Beyond Andy, Michael stood in front of another Stone. Margarita took a single step forward, her insides turning to water.

"Don't," Zed said hoarsely. "Don't touch it."

Yes. That was it. The source. The dark song beat at her, beyond hearing, setting her teeth on edge, twisting her bones inside her flesh until she wanted to scream. Michael lifted his hands, moving slowly as if he were walking in his sleep. It almost seemed to her that the Stone grew larger, reaching out to him with a million shadowy arms. "No!" The word tore itself out of her throat. "Michael, *don't*!" She stumbled toward him, but the darkness wrapped around her, holding her back.

Zed darted past, knocking her roughly aside. He leapt across Danners's sprawled body, past Andy's upturned face, to slam hard into Michael. They stumbled sideways together and crashed into the wall hard enough to make the sphere shiver. "Light!" Zed yelled. "Damn it, *light*!"

The walls of the sphere glowed to opalescent life, turning the sea opaque, washing away the shadows in a flood of soft light. Zed and Michael lay in a tangle against the wall. Suddenly released from the spell that held her, Margarita ran to them. Blood streaked Zed's face and Michael's tunic; she gasped, then realized a second later that it had come from the floor, from a thick pool that had spread from beneath Danners's slashed throat.

"My God." Her voice shook as she dropped to her knees beside Zed. "What happened? Is he dead?" She touched Michael's throat, then drew in a quick breath of relief at the steady pulse of blood beneath her fingertips. "He's alive."

"I think he passed out." Zed disentangled himself and squatted against the wall. "When I hit him. Did you *feel* it?"

He looked dazed, and Margarita wondered what her own face showed. "I felt it. Michael?" She touched his face, patted his cheek lightly. No response. In a rush of anxiety she lifted one eyelid, caught a gleam of white. "Maybe he hit his head. Did he touch the Stone?" She clutched Zed's arm in a spasm of fear.

"No." Zed shook his head, eyeing the Stone warily. "It's fading now."

"It was the Stone," she whispered, and looked up as Andy knelt beside her.

"Danners is dead." His face had taken on a professional distance. "It looks like he cut his own throat. At least, he's got a knife in his hand." His eyes shifted to Zed.

Zed's lips tightened. He slid his hand beneath his tunic and whipped the blade out with a practiced snap of his wrist. "My blade is right here." He tilted the point delicately toward Andy's left eye. "Nice and clean."

"I wasn't implying anything, actually." Andy's tone was mild. "You just look a little pale. Are you feeling all right?"

"Just fine," Zed snarled.

He did look pale. Beyond him, Danners lay in his own blood. Margarita had seen it before in the barrio: that awkward, inelegant sprawl of death. It always jarred her—there was such a thin line between life and death. Margarita slapped Zed's blade aside, glaring at Andy. "Help me get Michael out of here. Did you bring any of your medical stuff with you?"

"I'm on vacation." Deadpan, Andy squatted beside Michael, grabbed his arm, and heaved him over his shoulder. With a grunt, he staggered to his feet, then started for the door.

Andy was strong despite his slight build. Margarita followed, circling the Stone warily. The dark music had faded. Zed was right. She looked back to see him staring at the Stone, a blind, glazed expression on his face. "Come on." She grabbed his wrist. "I don't think any of us should stay in here."

"Don't worry, it's over," he said in a thick voice. He blinked, his eyes focusing suddenly on her face. "I think we ought to wake your dad up. Now. He didn't hit his head."

"Yeah, sure, but *why*?" She was relieved when they reached the corridor and Zed closed the door behind them. "What happened in there?" she asked breathlessly.

"You tell me." Zed pushed her down the corridor. "Some kind of booby trap?" He shrugged. "Something that hit Danners hard enough that he killed himself to stop it?"

And Michael? Margarita hurried down the corridor and through the main room into the bedroom module. Michael lay on the bedroom water bed, his tunic bunched beneath his armpits. Andy was sticking small monitor disks to his neck and chest.

"Everything looks pretty normal." He stared at the monitor in his hand. "And, yes, I take this with me everywhere. None of the blood is his, far as I can tell. If he knocked himself out on the wall, I don't see any bruises." He began to peel the disks from Michael's skin, grimacing at the bloodstains on his hands and clothes. "I'm going to go wash up. I think I'll rinse out my tunic, unless you do laundry, too." He raised an eyebrow at Zed.

"Fuck yourself." Zed stalked past him, still pale. "How is he?" he asked Margarita.

"I don't know." Fear was growing in her, swelling like a balloon. She sat down on the frame of the water bed. Her motion sent waves undulating across the mattress, lifting Michael gently. It made her think of a body she'd once seen out on the streets with her cousins one night—a man floating in LA Harbor, rocking gently in the scum of trash beneath a pier. "Michael?" She clutched his shoulder. "Michael, wake up!"

She was afraid for him. It had been only a handful of days since he had knocked on her door and walked in to fall down on their cushions. She had been angry. Resentful. And now . . . she was afraid. She didn't want to be afraid, didn't want him to matter. "Michael?" She slapped his cheek lightly, telling herself he didn't matter, didn't have anything to do with her. A lie. "Come back," she said, and slapped him more sharply. "Come *back*!"

Come back . . .

The words floated endlessly down through the darkness that buried Michael, drifting, turning, settling like fallen leaves to the tiny corner where he had taken refuge. *Come back . . .* Margarita's voice? Calling him? Go away, he wanted to tell her, but there was no room for words down here, there was room only for *him.*

Michael . . .?

Her voice snagged him, dragging at him, drawing him upward into that dangerous darkness. He resisted because *there* was . . .

. . . knowledge.

. . . understanding.

. . . *comprehension.*

Writhing, he struggled to tune her out, to burrow and hide once more, because he didn't want to know.

"Damn it, wake up!"

Tears? For him? Not for him. She shouldn't cry for *him.* His lips shaped the words, and their movement yanked him out of his safety, hauling him up from the depths like one of the glowing creatures with which they'd populated the holostage. And somehow . . . he bypassed the darkness. Anchored by her voice, he escaped it. With a sigh, he opened his eyes.

Her face was inches from his own. She looked so much like Xia. Tears rose in a sudden rush, filling his chest, rising like a tide to block his throat. *I wish* . . . The half-formed words fluttered away. "It's . . . all right," he whispered.

"No, it isn't. You scared the shit out of me." She straightened, seizing his hand, clutching it. "Are you all right?" She shook her head and let out a quick, angry breath. "Michael, what *happened* down there?"

What was he picking up from beneath her angry surface? *I wish* . . . What had he wished for? Michael closed his eyes, too tired to figure it out. Yesterday was long out of reach, twenty-two years out of reach. He was empty, hollow, nothing but a sack of flaccid skin, sucked dry and flung aside.

"Michael?" Her hand tightened on his, nails digging in so that he winced.

"I'm here." He opened his eyes, amazed at the weight of his eyelids.

"What *happened* down there?" She didn't let go of his hand. "Danners is dead. He killed himself."

Dead. Oh, yeah, dead. He'd have to be.

"It was the Stone." Zed leaned over Margarita's shoulder, his face strained and pale. "That's what killed him."

"Yes," Michael whispered. He recognized the shadows in Zed's eyes, traces of that darkness. "You, too?" he whispered.

"I think we all felt it." Margarita frowned briefly up at Zed. "What was it? It—it scared me."

That had the sound of a tough admission. Michael sighed. "Yes, it was the Stone." He shuddered, remembering how that dark song had reached out to seize him. What if it was still there inside him, way down deep, lying in wait? "I don't know what it is." His voice shook, and he sat up, struggling against the yielding water bed, his stomach tightening. "Some kind of . . . resonance. I thought it was from a model, but it isn't. Nobody is . . . like that."

"Could it have been a drug on the Stone's surface?" Andy walked into the room, bare-chested and frowning. "A fast-acting poison that absorbed through the skin and sent Danners into some kind of hallucination or suicidal frenzy?"

Zed made a rude noise. "Margarita and I *heard* it. It wasn't any poison."

"I didn't hear anything."

"It's not something physical. *You* heard it?" Michael looked up at Margarita, frightened with a new fear.

" 'Heard' isn't quite the word. I felt it the same way I . . . feel a Stone." She glanced sideways at Zed. "It was . . . powerful. But it faded right away."

Thank God, Michael thought. "It was something in the new Stone—the one Hawk hadn't started working on yet. I felt it this afternoon." He shuddered, cold suddenly. "When I touch a Stone, I waken it. Not all the way, but it responds. I can't keep it from happening; I'm so tuned to them that it's automatic. So Hawk didn't want me to touch his new one. I think he wakened it. And whatever resonance was planted in it . . ." He faltered, ran out of words. "I can't remember." He looked beyond himself, seeing their reflections in the polyglass, looking beyond into the dark sea and feeling the remnant of that song inside him like puddled blood. Waiting for him. "I almost knew what it was—what made him kill himself. I almost had it," he whispered. "I can't remember. I think . . . if you wakened a Stone that carried the full resonance, you'd kill yourself. You'd have to." The air shimmered as if invisible butterflies fluttered above the bed, hovering over his face. He squeezed Margarita's hand, concentrating on the warm feel of her flesh, banishing that terrible shimmer. "I don't know what it is," he whispered. "It's not . . . from any human model."

Zed made a soft sound in his throat, but when Michael looked at him, his face was turned away.

"You're talking touch, which makes some chemical a likely candidate in my book. Small-chain peptides can really mess with your mind." Arms crossed on his chest, Andy leaned against the wall. "Or how about some kind of electronic frequency, tuned just right to drive someone nuts?"

"You didn't feel it." Margarita was frowning—not skeptical, just thinking hard. "But Zed and I did. So it's something not everyone can feel."

She had felt it because she was his daughter. And Zed? Michael looked at him. Yeah, that darkness had hit Zed hard, maybe harder than it had hit Margarita. "Zed, what do you feel when you stand beside a Stone?"

Zed frowned, his eyes sliding away from Michael's. "I'm a sensitive, if that's what you're asking. I keep my hands off the Stones I buy for Gunner."

Michael sighed, remembering the first time he'd gotten close to a Stone. He had sneaked into the protected service dock behind Anya's studio, nineteen years old, a punk, doing nothing with his life. She had been shipping a finished Stone to some gallery or other, and it was out on the dock, half-crated, its gray surface gleaming with a thousand elusive colors in the hazy morning light. He'd had no interest in the Stone; he'd been hoping for something small and valuable he could lift and sell in the flea market.

The Stone had reached out and snared him. A thousand soft voices had sung to him, beckoning him until he walked over and laid his hands on that smooth/rough surface that had felt like stone and flesh beneath his palms. It had sucked him in then, and he had dissolved into a thousand moments of peace, and pain, and love, drowning in a kaleidoscope of summer evenings and pale winter mornings, trapped in a thousand human murmurs, unable to run as Anya came out to discover him, not caring that he was trespassing, not caring about anything, lost in the rich wonderful song of the Stone.

She had peeled him off of it, then had brought him dazed and helpless into her studio to eat freshly baked muffins and drink tea. Then she had called the cops and had him arrested. And after the brief electronic trial and his three-year community service sentence, she'd filed a bid on his contract and bought him from the state. *You distorted that Stone,* she had told him on the day the van had delivered him to her door with the contract collar locked around his neck. *You owe me for that.* For the next three years she had taught him how to sculpt Stones. And he had worked his ass off keeping house for her and running errands. When the collar had finally been disarmed and they could take it off, she had hacked it to bits with a kitchen cleaver and had washed the pieces down the drain in a burst of rage.

He had never understood that rage, and she would never explain it.

If he had died today, would Anya have been disappointed?

Michael sighed, missing her suddenly and intensely. "You could have been a sculptor," he said to Zed. Why "could have been"? Zed heard that automatic past tense, and his lips tightened.

"You're going to have to be careful," Michael whispered. "You, too, Margarita."

"I'm always careful." Zed flung his hair back over his shoulder. "I'm going to make some tea." He left quickly, his shoulders still hunched.

Angry. Michael looked after him, wondering why.

"S'Wanna always said you could do one hell of a scary Stone if you wanted to work with a bunch of crazies." Andy drew a deep breath, his face naked for an instant, revealing grief. "You're sure it's not that, huh? Look, if this . . . resonance isn't electronic and it's not somebody's pet psycho embedded in a Stone, then what *are* you guys picking up? You got a guess?"

"Not yet," Michael said softly. He swung his legs over the edge of the bed, briefly dizzy. "Andy?" He hesitated. "Had S'Wanna bought any new Stones recently?"

"She'd ordered one." His eyes narrowed. "Just before we had that fight and she kicked me out. I don't know if they delivered it before she died or not."

What about Lustik? And Irene Yojiro? Michael got to his feet, paced over to the slick curve of the wall, and leaned his head against the cool polyglass. He had no way to find out short of turning himself in and asking the cops.

They'd bought new Stones—he would bet on it. Maybe he *was* betting on it. And the stakes might be his life . . . and not just his. "What if they're *all* booby-trapped?" He stared out into the dark water, catching distant gleams of moving light. "A half dozen companies retail them. Who the hell's going to *believe* this?" He clenched his fist and slammed it against the wall. Danners's Stone was so damn *good*. And now he was dead. S'Wanna might have become one of the best. "Damn them," he whispered. "Whoever is behind this, damn them to hell."

"Amen," Margarita said in a soft, cold voice.

"The Stones all come from one place." Zed stood in the doorway, a glass teapot in one hand, mugs in the other. "They get sold to retailers, but only one firm mines them. It's a very well protected monopoly." His teeth flashed as he set the pot down on the bedside stand.

"So, okay feed us the punch line." Andy picked up a cup and poured amber tea. "Who is it?"

"It could have happened at the retail level." Zed ignored him, focusing on Michael.

He shook his head. "Stones are hefty things to move around. And you don't want too many people handling them—in case you run into a sensitive on some loading dock somewhere." He nodded at Zed. "Yojiro worked in a Manhattan arcology. Lustik was down in Antarctica in some protected preserve. They would have gotten their Stones from different places." And retailers screened their employees for any trace of sensitivity that might accidentally wake a virgin stone, so the dark resonance would have gone undetected. "It happened at the source," he said softly.

"Vildorn BeltMining." Zed's eyes had gone flat and hard. "It's supposed to be the same little independent firm that's always held the rights to the part of the belt where the Stones got found, but it's a front for the real owner."

"Who's the real owner?" Michael met Zed's opaque stare and guessed the answer even before he spoke.

"Gunner Archenwald-Shen."

"Why am I not surprised?" Andy grimaced. "Nice little bit of circularity you've got going here, Tryon. Everywhere you turn, there's Archenwald-Shen grinning at you. So what are you going to do? Go knock on his door and tell him someone's contaminating his Stones? Think he'll listen?"

"You don't believe me, do you?" Michael asked slowly.

"Believe you about what?" Andy looked down at the cup in his hands. "S'Wanna didn't kill herself because she touched some contaminated Stone. She was having some bad downs even before she ordered the Stone. And it hadn't been delivered yet when she booted me." He set his tea down abruptly. "I thought maybe you had something about somebody being behind this. I'm not so sure anymore." He let his breath out in a slow sigh. "So, no, I guess I don't believe you. Hell." He laughed shortly. "I don't even know what you're getting at. I'm not sure you do, either."

"He said the resonance wasn't human," Zed announced to the ceiling. "He didn't say some jerk didn't put it there, whatever it is."

"I'm *not* sure," Michael said before Andy could say anything. He rubbed his eyes, a headache beginning to pulse inside his skull. "I could be wrong about all of this." But he *wasn't*. He had damned near drowned in that darkness in Albuquerque, and it was the same note, the same torturing voice that he'd felt in Danners's studio. "I wonder if I can visit Vildorn BeltMining without attracting too much attention."

"Not a chance." Zed's head shake swung his hair across his face. "They don't give a shit up on the platforms if the Earthside cops want your ass, but you got zero privacy. The platforms are Gunner's home turf. Anything he wants to know, he'll hear. He'll know you're there within a day if he doesn't expect you. If he does expect you, he'll know in about ten minutes."

"I hope he's not expecting me."

"You don't get it." Zed spoke patiently, as if he were talking to a slow child. "You can't get out to the Vildorn operation in one day. A week, maybe, if you stumble over the right connections. The miners pack the Stones into freight modules, drop them down the well into the freight orbits. The sling shoots the modules down into the ocean for pickup. The platforms don't figure in at all."

"How do you know all this?"

Zed's face went cold. "Gunner hired me to run his core concerns and ride herd on his more peripheral connections. I am good at it, believe it or not." He didn't look at Andy. "He keeps very close track of the Stone mining. It's a solid moneymaker, and its acquisition was a . . . personal triumph."

Michael felt himself blushing. It was so easy to make assumptions, drop a mask over someone's face and stop looking for the real person underneath. He'd thought he was above that. "I apologize," he said softly.

"I could get you out to the Vildorn operation. I could get you there well within a day. I'm Archenwald-Shen's boy, remember?" Bitterness razored Zed's tone. "I can go anywhere I damn well please, as fast as I need to get there. I'm offering."

"Why?" Michael met his eyes, feeling as if he were looking over the edge of a cliff, down into a bottomless green sea. "You'll blow it all, won't you?"

"Will I?" Zed struck a pose, tossing his hair back with a twist of his head. "Maybe you underestimate my charms."

Andy made a disgusted sound in his throat. "Right now we need to pay a little attention to the fact that we've got a dead sculptor on our hands," he growled. "Anyone want to come up with a *sane* suggestion for where we go from here?"

"Yeah." Margarita stared at the teapot. Danners lay a few dozen meters away, dead in his own blood. She didn't reach for a cup. "I think it's reality-check time. And I hope one of you smart guys has it all figured out, because I don't have a clue, damn it. Let me know when you figure something out." She picked up her cup and stalked out of the room.

Something was bothering her. Michael looked after her, wanting to call her back, but hesitated. Maybe she just didn't want to be involved and was struggling to find the words to tell him. Andy made another disgusted noise and went after Margarita. To make plans? Michael hoped so. He was too damn tired to even try. With a sigh, he sat down on the carpeted floor, leaning his back against the glassed-out ocean.

"Here." Zed handed him a cup of tepid tea. "You look as if you could use this."

"Thanks." Goose bumps rose on his arms as the sea's slow chill seeped through the polyglass wall. You could lose yourself in what he'd felt. Or find yourself, maybe. Find . . . something.

"It calls you, doesn't it?" Zed spoke so softly that Michael almost missed the words. "That darkness—it's inside us, too, not just in the Stone. It's hidden away down in some deep pit that we're all scared to look into, but we *want* to. Oh, yeah, we want to look down there so bad, maybe drop a couple of pebbles in, listen for them to hit bottom, straining our eyes in case something *moves* down there. But we don't dare touch it. We're afraid to connect." He snapped his fingers twice, turning off the room lights, letting in the sea's night darkness. Constellations of living light spangled the void, filling the room with a faint eerie glow. "It's calling from down there, that voice." His whisper came from everywhere and nowhere. "Maybe it was down there all the time and we just didn't hear it. I hear it now. You hear it, too, don't you? You want to touch it, too."

"Yes," Michael breathed. That's why we're going up to Vildorn, he thought, and realized that he couldn't do anything else, and maybe Zed couldn't, either. Because it was calling them, and, yeah, he wanted to touch it. *Needed* to touch it. "You could have been a hell of a sculptor," he said softly. *Could have been.* That past tense again, unconscious and undeniable. "Zed?" Silence. Michael strained his ears but heard nothing except the soft whisper of air from the ventilation system.

Slowly he levered himself to his feet, weighed down by a heaviness that felt like grief. Grief for whom? For Danners, dead in his studio, who would never sculpt another Stone?

Or for Zed, who would never sculpt one at all?

A school of squid jetted along the wall, speckled with luminous dots. Michael straightened, surrounded by the sea's living night. Time to make real-world plans, to decide where to go next and with whom or how. He didn't have to hurry. Slowly, he made his way along the invisible wall to the door.

That dark voice would wait for him.

Chapter Ten

Margarita curled up in one of Danners's recliners, chilled in spite of the dome's mid spring temperature. Blood spotted her tunic, already going brown. There'd been so much blood in her life already. She had tried to leave it behind when she had left the barrio, but maybe it was universal. Violence. Death. Part of the human psyche. She closed her eyes, and *Crystalline* unfolded in her head. Nice, but maybe too subtle. Maybe she had to hit people between the eyes with it: look inside, man, stare down into that well. Hey, lady, somewhere in there you're squatting with a bone, waiting to kill something. Look yourself in the face and see that blood lust, that hunger for pain and blood. Her fingers twitched, tapping out console commands on her thigh. Yeah, scent of copper, like blood, touched with old meat. Brazen sun, stark shadows. Shadows you look at, realize they're holes.

We are the darkness. We stare into that well in horror, to find our own face grinning up at us . . .

Zed walked into the room, carrying the teapot and dirty mugs.

"You know, I think we'd better have a little talk," Andy drawled. "We have this body in the other room."

Margarita watched Zed silently stack the dishes in the cleaner. "Call the cops," she said.

"Well, yeah." Andy gave her a thoughtful sideways look. "Sooner or later we'd better get around to that."

"Don't give me 'sooner or later.' " She glowered at Andy. "What else can we do, anyway?"

"Tryon and I are out of here, first." Zed threw himself onto a pile of cushions and closed his eyes. "Then you guys do whatever you want."

"No way." Margarita shifted her glare to him. "Michael's in enough trouble as it is. He didn't kill Danners. Why the hell should he take off and run?"

"Are you sure he didn't kill Danners?" Andy's voice was soft and utterly cold.

With a shiver, she met his eyes. Cold eyes. Demanding eyes.

"Yes." The word came out on its own.

"Good." He looked away, his expression troubled. "I think Danners really did suicide. Like S'Wanna."

"So this time the lab can clear him, and he can settle all this crap about running from the cops." My God, Margarita thought, and stifled a broken laugh. Here I am, suggesting the *cops*. Her cousins really would beat her for this one. "I'm going to go find a terminal." She got to her feet.

"Better not." Zed didn't open his eyes.

Margarita stared at him, waiting. He didn't look at her; he might have been sound asleep. Punk. "Why not?" She bit off the words.

"Because Gunner bought and paid for your dad's nasty little dance with law and order last time. I told him that Gunner's not through with him. He'll end up in jail pending lab results, no bail, because he ducked out once already. And then if Gunner's in a bad mood, your dad's right there to get squeezed." Zed winked, flashing a wolfish grin. "Gunner can get rough."

"How do you know?" Margarita snapped.

He smiled. "I set it up. I told you. I take care of all his core concerns."

"You know, I *should* have broken your wrist."

"Probably." Zed's grin widened. "But you didn't, and you know better now."

"Zed and I do need to leave before the cops show up." Michael stood in the doorway, looking pale and very tired.

"Michael, you can't *do* this." Margarita bounced to her feet. "Didn't you hear what he said?" She glared at Zed, who was still grinning at her. "He did it; *he* set you up for that arrest you were running from when you busted into our apartment." Not "our" apartment, not anymore. That sudden, bitter realization wrung her, choked off her words.

"Don't get angry at me, Margarita." Michael was staring at

her, an enigmatic expression on his face. "If I don't follow this to some kind of source, I'm going to end up like Hawk. It almost happened this time. Every time I start a new Stone, it'll be a risk."

So quit. She opened her mouth to say the words, then closed it silently. *So quit.* What if Katrina had said that to her during one of the really bad times? She never had. If she'd even thought it, she'd hidden it too well to show.

"I'm . . . sorry." Michael looked away. "I wanted to spend more time with you."

He thought he was going to end up like Danners, anyway.

"You can come along." Zed tilted his head at Margarita. "The more, the merrier."

Oh, yeah, sure. Margarita turned her back on them both. "Do whatever you're going to do. I don't care." Andy looked as if he were going to say something, and she didn't want to hear it. She ducked into the corridor that led to the gallery, light running ahead of her as the system sensed her presence and powered on. Damn Michael Tryon. Damn him for busting into her life in the first place. She'd had it all settled—that it didn't matter, that one lucky sperm cell didn't make any difference to what or who she was. She wanted to tell herself that it still didn't matter, but something had happened on that holostage.

If she went with him on whatever crazy quest he was planning, she'd leave Katrina behind. *Forever,* a voice whispered in her head.

But how could you know forever? Forever was a word without meaning, a casual promise to be tossed out on a date. Katrina had never promised her forever.

And hadn't asked for it, either.

Something had changed. Between herself and Michael. Between herself and Katrina? Margarita veered left, down a Y in the corridor, and came to the small cushioned room where she'd found the tunnel mouth that led down into the coral.

It yawned beyond the cushions, a round "oh" of surprise opening on a throat of darkness. "You're asking me to choose," Margarita whispered. "And I can't." And, really, there was no choice. She bent her head, tears a hot pressure behind her eyelids. Nothing really mattered except that dance of light, and sound, and scent. No one. Let them go, both of them, open your arms to your art, because that's really all that matters, and maybe that's all there is. All there *can* be. Maybe the well, the source, is loneliness . . .

Someone touched her shoulder, and she choked back a cry.

"I didn't mean to scare you." Michael's hand was gentle on her shoulder. "You can't hear footsteps on these cushions. I'm not asking you to make any kind of choice."

He sounded so damned sad. She wanted to be angry at him for that, to be pissed because he was levering her with his pain, but the anger wouldn't happen. He wasn't levering her. He was hurting, too. She closed her eyes, remembering his words on the holostage, their voices in duet, a close harmony in tone and content. Modulated by the same genes? And what the hell did that *mean*? Are you alone, too? she almost asked him. Is that where your Stones come from? Is that the price for all this?

She drew a shuddering breath, looking for traces of herself in his face. But if they were there, she couldn't let herself see them. "I think I'd go with you. I really would, but Katrina's in trouble." She swallowed, remembering splashes of drying blood on the bright metal chains. "I don't know what I can do. I don't know if there's anything I can do, damn it, but I can't just go off. Katrina and I—" She looked into his face, suddenly seeing a stranger there, a man she didn't really know.

"You're lovers." He said it gently, a given. "You love her. What kind of trouble is she in?"

"I . . ." The tears took her by surprise, burning her eyes, spilling over as she tried fiercely to hold them back. He put his arms around her, and she resisted for a moment, fists clenched, body rigid. "I don't *know*." The words tore their way out of her. "But a man already died, and—" And Katrina hadn't believed in her enough to let her make it on her own. Desolation came with that admission, terrible and absolute. Maybe the only people who could really hurt you were the ones you loved. The first sob tore its way out of her, racking her with pain.

She had no energy to push Michael away, so she buried her face against his shoulder, a stranger's shoulder, more than stranger and less. Crying hurt. The sobs bruised her, hard and rough-edged as stones. Maybe you knew what counted only when you'd smashed it. The racking sobs softened after a while, fading slowly to hiccups and a trembling weakness that wanted to buckle her knees. Margarita finally drew a shuddering breath. She was leaning against Michael, face against his shoulder, his arms still around her, warm and comforting. She made an abortive movement to push him away.

"I'm so sorry." He didn't let go; his cheek was against her hair, his whisper gentle in her ear. "I wish it had been different. I wish Xia had told me. I wish she hadn't left." His soft laugh cracked with pain. "I don't know. It might not have worked, anyway. It seems so easy to fix yesterday, looking back at it. Maybe Xia was right." He stroked her back gently. "Maybe I would have been a shitty father. Maybe I would have scared you away from art forever. I was pretty self-centered back then." He laughed that cracked note again. "I guess I still was until a few weeks ago. I think it took Estevan's ghost to wake me up."

"Did you love her?" Margarita whispered. "Xia? Was it real?"

The sound of whistling came from the corridor. Michael didn't answer but kept his arm around Margarita as Zed appeared. He'd moved so silently in the shadows beyond the holostage. That whistle had an artificial sound, and it struck Margarita suddenly that he had perhaps been standing in the corridor while she wept and had tiptoed away to return noisily. Anger stirred, withered, and died. What did it matter?

Zed's face lacked its usual smirk. "Andy's on the terminal, calling the cops." He glanced at Margarita and then shifted his gaze to Michael. "Time for us to go."

"Yeah." Michael's arm tightened briefly around her. "I guess so." His eyes were tortured as he turned to face her. "I want to stay. I have to go, Margarita."

"I know." There was nothing else to say.

"What gallery are you with?" He held her hand as they followed Zed down the corridor. "In case I want to find you."

"Yamada." The name tasted bitter on her tongue. "For now, anyway."

"Gunner owns Yamada." Zed looked over his shoulder at her, his face thoughtful. "It's another of his core concerns."

"Archenwald-Shen owns everything, doesn't he?" Michael grimaced.

"Yeah, just about." Zed snapped his fingers. "Espinoza.

Crystalline: Fracture." He gave her a quick, enigmatic glance. "I should've connected."

Maybe he *did* handle all of Archenwald-Shen's affairs. She gave him a quick look. He had a good memory, anyway. "Ari Yiassis brought me in." The bitterness had soaked into her words. "So I don't know how much longer I'll be there."

"I liked *Crystalline*. I should've recognized your style on the stage." He jerked his head, shrugged. "I guess it was the two of you together—it was different."

He had walked into *Crystalline*? She stared at the black river of his hair, his slender shoulders, not sure how she felt about this at all. Her assessment of this *punk* was cracking like so much glass.

"I was thinking about showing it to Gunner," Zed went on. "He might be interested."

"What's the price," she asked, and felt Michael's hand tighten on hers.

"If there was a price, I'd tell you up front. And it would be a very steep one, lady. Some things I charge for, and some things I don't." He looked back at her, angry and full of pride. "Gunner isn't all that impressed by holoture, even good holoture."

Margarita flushed, suddenly and unutterably ashamed. "I apologize, Zed."

He stopped so quickly that she nearly ran into him, then faced her, hair swinging, his expression unreadable. "Thank you." He turned his back on her again and resumed his quick stride. "Ari wasn't a big loss, to my way of thinking. I never liked most of the stuff he brought in, but it sold."

A cold epitaph for the man, even though he'd been a jerk. "Who killed him?" Margarita realized that a part of her expected Zed to know, and she shivered. No, this man wasn't quite what she'd thought he was—up for sale to the highest bidder. He might sell parts of himself, but he chose what to sell. And what to keep.

Zed seemed unoffended by her question, as if it had been quite reasonable. "I don't know who killed him. I think Gunner would like to find out. It shouldn't be hard." That wolf grin flashed again. "The dude did such a *bad* job."

"Zed . . ." She paused, aware of Michael's attention, swallowing a rush of hope that threatened to choke her. "Whoever killed Ari Yiassis might come looking for my friend, Katrina Luoma. Because she held some kind of file for him. She didn't know that it was important; she was doing him a favor." A favor that had been part of the price for that first-level balcony, because her ass hadn't been enough. Margarita drew a quick, hard breath. "If Archenwald-Shen sent someone to . . . keep track of her, he could catch Ari's killer."

"Keep track of her, huh? What kind of file?" Zed slowed as they reached the end of the corridor.

"I don't know. I don't think Katrina does, either. Maybe nobody does except the killer." They had reached the alvin bay. Sea smell wrapped them damply as they stepped out onto the mesh floor. The pilot was sitting on the alvin's closed hatch, a palm-top reader on her lap. "The file was hidden in a necklace that got . . . stolen." No need to mention Xia's name to him. "It's gone, but who'll believe that?"

"Good question." Zed's enigmatic glance shifted between Margarita and Michael. "You ready?" he called to the pilot.

She nodded a sharp affirmative and stood, balancing lightly on the alvin's back. "You again." She jerked her chin at Michael.

He caught the drug patch she tossed him.

She didn't seem to have a clue that anything was wrong and acted ready to take Zed's orders. "Zed?" Margarita waited for him to look at her. "Will you tell Shen what I told you? About Katrina Luoma?"

"Are you *asking* me?" He took a long step toward her. "Me?" he repeated softly.

"Yes." She held his stare, fighting the urge to look away. Green light smoldered in the depths of his eyes, and she could feel heat radiating from his skin, as if a furnace burned inside him somewhere. "I'm asking you."

"This is quite a turnaround." His voice had gone silky. "I'm a bit surprised."

She could see a faint bruise on his cheek where she had slapped him. No, it was an old bruise, and there were others, faded to yellow, nearly invisible on his tawny skin. "Do you want to hit me back?" she asked softly. "Your turn? Or do you want me to get down on my knees and beg?" She swallowed. "I will." She owed Katrina that much. She owed more than that.

"Zed?" Michael put a hand on his arm.

Ignoring Michael, he didn't take his eyes from Margarita's face. "I'm tempted." He smiled a slow, soft smile that vanished abruptly. "Sorry, I'm not going to ask him to save your lover. Yeah, there could be a price tag on this one, but it would be out of your range." The smile came back, hard this time, like the smile on a carved mask. "Tell you what. You can ask him yourself. I'll get you five minutes with him—and that is one hell of a free gift."

His smile had vanished, and his face had gone utterly cold. Margarita looked away and shivered, suddenly wondering just how much she had underestimated Zed. "I'll take it." She lifted her head, met his eyes. "Thank you."

"You're welcome." He grinned. "Bitch." He turned to Michael. "Let's go. We do need to get out of here."

"What about Andy?" Michael hung back, frowning. "The cops are going to come down hard on his head."

"His choice. He's clean." He grinned at Michael. "He said to tell you that you owe him. I don't know what you owe him. Maybe your firstborn." He smirked at Margarita. "Now let's go before the cops get here."

They hurried over to the alvin. The pilot was already at her console, and the engines hummed as they climbed onboard. Apparently Zed had given her orders, because she locked the hatch as soon as they cleared it and dropped the alvin down into the dark water. Beyond the yellow cone of the floods the water was as black as ink. Michael leaned back against the padded seat beside Margarita, holding her hand. His face was smooth, with a look of resigned peace that made her want to shake him, yell at him, do something to shatter that porcelain calm.

Zed sat across from them, smiling his sly smile, watching them. Margarita looked away, tight-lipped, and said nothing. She wondered if Michael knew where they were going exactly and decided she was damned if she'd ask Zed. Would it help Katrina, this wild-goose chase? Or would Katrina end up getting hurt or killed anyway? And Margarita wouldn't be there. Her fists clenched slowly, nails digging into her palms. Good choice or bad? No way to know; just roll the dice and pray. But who do I pray to? she asked herself bitterly. She stared at the back of the pilot's blond head, watching Katrina dance across the stage of her mind. Katrina became part of the music, a summation of its soul created in curves and planes of muscle and bone. You didn't *hear* the music; you watched Katrina dance, and the music was part of you both . . .

I love you, she cried, trapped in silence and pain. When had she said those words to Katrina last?

She couldn't remember.

Michael squeezed her hand gently, his face full of compassion. Oh, yeah, he was a sculptor. He could sense her pain. Margarita let her breath out slowly, remembering their duet on the holostage. She would use that dark sea one day, would add Zed's slick edge to it, and the twisted note from the Stone, and she would find the words to harmonize.

For you, Katrina, because I love you and I'm afraid. Afraid of what? She reached for that fear, for its source, but it eluded her.

"You look tired." Michael slid his arm around her. "Put your head on my shoulder and see if you can sleep."

She couldn't, but she leaned against him because he wanted her to, waiting for this ride to end, for the next stage of this crazy, maybe-useless journey to begin, counting the seconds ticking by because Zed's presence silenced her and there wasn't anything else to do. Beyond the viewscreen, the floods illuminated blue water and drifting jellyfish that gleamed like small moons.

It took them nearly three hours to reach their destination. Margarita drowsed finally, rousing to the subtle shift in engine vibration as the alvin slowed. Michael's head leaned against hers; he was asleep, his face smooth and peaceful in the dim light. Curled on his seat like a cat, Zed was awake.

"We're here." His teeth flashed as he grinned. "Since you won't let yourself ask where *here* is, I'll be nice and tell you: we're catching a ride to New York Up. Law and order will check for us on public flights, because cops don't think." His lip curled slightly. "By the time they start checking private lifts—if they bother—we'll be up on the platform. There's this little bit of friction between downsiders and upsiders." Zed grinned again. "Upsiders don't help downside cops too much. Which is why Gunner keeps a place up there. He likes the platforms."

"What do you like?"

"Honesty." He smirked, raising his shoulder in a lopsided shrug. "Mostly I like what Gunner wants me to like," he said lightly. "That's what I get paid for."

He was doing the boy act again. Maybe it wasn't completely an act. She looked at him from beneath lowered lashes, catching a flicker in those eyes, that buried flame.

The alvin surfaced, water washing down across the viewscreen in a cascade of bubbles and giving way to yellow light. The floor began to rock gently beneath their feet.

"End of the line," the pilot announced—the first words she'd spoken during the entire trip.

Michael jerked suddenly awake, eyes stretched wide, face clammy with sweat.

"Are you all right?" Margarita touched his arm.

"A dream." He blinked at her as if he'd forgotten who she was. "It was a dream," he said thickly. His eyes cleared suddenly, and he shook his head. "They're the same as the Stone, the dreams. The same . . . voice."

He wasn't speaking to her, was frowning instead into some middle distance.

"Maybe you're just remembering it." Zed was on his feet, scowling. "Dreaming about finding Danners."

"No." Michael shook his head slowly, a haunted look in his eyes. "It started weeks ago, in Albuquerque, right after I left Taos." He let his breath out in a rush and got unsteadily to his feet.

"So what is it?" Margarita reached for his hand, wondering if Andy had been right, if Michael was chasing ghosts. His fingers were cold as ice. "If it's more than just Danners's Stone."

"I think it's a voice." He looked at Zed as if for confirmation. "Someone—something—is trying to tell me something, maybe tell anyone who can hear."

"Why?" Margarita pushed an image of Andy's face from her mind. "Forget it." The pilot had the hatch open, and she grabbed for the ladder rungs. "I know what I felt in that studio. If that's communication, it's news to me."

Michael didn't have any answer for that one. Neither did Zed; he hadn't said a word. Margarita stuck her head up out of the hatch and blinked in a yellow flood of light. They were in some kind of hangar. More alvins bobbed in their slips, and scuba equipment was racked along the walls. Enormous cables dangled from overhead tracks. She stepped off the bottom rung of the ladder onto a plastic mesh walkway and held out a hand to Michael, who was clutching the ladder awkwardly. He grabbed for her, hand closing around her wrist with anxious strength, and stepped gingerly onto the walkway. Margarita watched Zed climb gracefully down, noticing the pilot. She hadn't said anything to him, but there was deference in her movements.

He leapt lightly onto the walkway. "This is the retrieval unit for a freight service." He gestured around the vast bay. "The tugs collect the dropped modules and bring them in here." Beckoning, he started for the far side of the hangar at a brisk walk. "We've got a ride on a personnel shuttle that leaves in two hours."

Archenwald-Shen's name opened all doors and greased all wheels. That was what Zed bought with his boy act: power. She yawned, suddenly aware of the grainy feel of her eyelids, the fatigue ache in her muscles. Michael was falling behind, and she slowed down to keep him company.

He gave her a sympathetic smile. "It's been a long night." Shadows stained the skin beneath his eyes, and he looked gray in the harsh light. "I'm just tired," he went on, as if he'd felt her worry. "I'm too old for all-nighters."

"How old—" She caught herself, blushing.

"Am I?" he finished for her. "Eighty-one. Body shops do a good job of preserving the flesh." His smile turned sad as he looked down at the alvins bobbing in their slips. "Sometimes I wonder if that's all that wears out—our flesh. I've been sculpting Stones for sixty-three years." He let his breath out slowly. "I wonder if I've outlived my talent."

Arrow had been 136 when he had died. "The Stone in New York—the one I went to see—it was fantastic. It was like—" Margarita struggled for the words she wanted. "It was like you'd given me a glimpse into the soul of everyone on the planet, all at once, all at the same time, and I *understood*." She'd stopped still in the middle of the walkway. "How can you talk about outliving that?"

"I finished Silver Stone ten years ago." He waited for her to catch up, then walked on beside her, head down, eyes on the mesh beneath his feet. "When you came looking for me, I hadn't finished anything since Silver Stone." He grimaced.

"Oh, actually I had, but I didn't want to admit that they were finished. I was afraid to let go of them." He lifted his hand at last. "I was afraid that there wouldn't be anything to take their place."

Had Arrow ever felt this fear? That he might run out of talent? If he had, he hadn't shared it with Margarita. Maybe he would have if she had let him. Maybe he had needed to share it. I didn't want him to doubt, Margarita thought, and pain clutched at her. I wanted him to be God so he could judge me. "Is there anything there?" Margarita whispered.

"Yes and no." Something like pain glazed Michael's face. "Those Stones were done, but only because I couldn't add anything more to them—not what they needed, anyway. They weren't *finished*."

They had reached the end of the walkway. Only a few lights were on at the end of the building. Margarita looked up and down the walkway that ran along the wall, where helmeted scuba suits hung like shed skins from hooks. There was no sign of Zed. She eyed a small gray door beside the suits, wondering if he had gone through it.

"When Xia told me . . . I was angry." She touched the thick orange fabric of the nearest dive suit. "I was jealous." The helmet clunked softly against the wall as she took her hand away. "You had it all. You were the best—a name. You didn't have to *work* anymore. And I—" She jerked her head sideways, groping for the words. "I started out doing visuals and words on a portable stage in the malls. The stuff I'm doing I can't do in a mall. It's got to be in a gallery, where I have space for the hardware and the armature. You don't get into a gallery unless people like your stuff. I'm *good*." It came out a whisper. "I *know* I'm good." But was she good enough to do what she wanted and keep her spot? Good enough to stop playing it safe?

Katrina hadn't thought so.

Margarita closed her eyes, squeezing them together until red light webbed her eyelids. I *am* good," she whispered.

"You are. For what my opinion's worth." Michael stroked her hair back from her face. "Such a bitter irony; newcomers can't afford to take too many risks, and once you're established, you can get scared. Hang on to your belief, Margarita."

His voice faltered. "Sometimes it's all we have, and it seems so damn thin. But when you've lost that, you've lost it all."

"Did you ever doubt?" She couldn't keep the bitterness out of her voice. "I mean really *doubt*, like you weren't going to make it, that your Stones would be so much shit and nobody would give a damn? The stuff I found when I started looking sure made it sound as if you took off straight to the top from the first time you laid a hand on a Stone."

"Gallery PR. And the media filled in any gaps the galleries left. I wonder where Zed took off to." Michael sighed and leaned back against one of the orange suits, making the hardware clang softly like off-key bells. "I was lucky. One of the original Stone sculptors took me in as an apprentice. She believed in me." His smile remembered. "That didn't mean she didn't work my butt off and flay me when she figured I was getting sloppy or trying to take shortcuts." His smile faded, filling his eyes with shadows. "The doubts didn't come until much later."

"Arrow believed in me." Margarita bent her head. He hadn't particularly wanted to take on another apprentice, but he'd finally agreed. He'd taught her how to blend her visuals with scent, music, and words to create a single poem. "He's dead." He had taken her to the edge of good, and then he had died. It had seemed like a betrayal, a violation of some unspoken promise between them, never mind that Arrow had been old, that he hadn't had any intention of dying. He had wanted something from her. You never told me what it was, she raged silently. You never *said*.

Maybe because she hadn't wanted him to say it, had been afraid to hear him. As if she hadn't wanted to see his doubts. Perhaps Arrow had read that and had been willing to give her what she had asked for.

Michael reminded her of Arrow. It hit Margarita suddenly, deeply enough to make her shiver. Not looks; that wasn't it. The similarity came from something else: body language or attitude. Something.

"What's wrong?"

"Nothing." She didn't want to see Arrow in Michael, didn't want him to mean that much to her. "I'm just wondering where Zed took off to." She looked around the vast, shadowy space. "I don't trust him."

"I do." Michael nodded. "I think it's calling him, too—whatever's calling me. He's a wide-open sensitive. No wonder the Estevan Stone distorted," he said softly. "He probably wakened it accidentally."

Margarita shook her head, exasperated. "*What's* calling you? You were talking about resonances in that Stone, some kind of contamination. That's what I felt, or I thought I did, at least."

"I don't want to try and explain." He spread his fingers and stared down at his palm. "This isn't your burden. It's mine."

"Oh, so *noble*." Margarita clenched her fists, suddenly furious. "Tell me I'm your daughter, tell me you wish you'd been around to play father, and then just tell me to fuck off. Sure, Michael Tryon. Keep your secrets. I'll just trot along at your heels, nice and quiet. And when some monster leaps out of the shadows and swallows you whole, I'll just go home and start a new holo. Fuck *you*, Michael Tryon."

"You're yelling," he said.

The shocked look on his face made her want to giggle. She choked it back, hearing the echoes of hysteria behind it.

"I'm sorry." He looked abashed now. "I wasn't trying to shut you out; I'm just not really sure . . . about anything anymore. I just don't want this to touch you, too."

"This *what*?"

"God? The devil? Aliens? Ghosts?" His shoulders drooped. "I thought it was ghosts for a while. Maybe Estevan's ghost. Maybe it's the devil, after all." He looked at her, gave her a wan smile. "Or maybe I'm just insane and Zed's sharing in it for some reason. I don't know, Margarita. I really don't."

"I shared it, too. That darkness." She turned her face away. "You're going to go looking until you find it, right? Alone, because you don't need any help." She grabbed the old-fashioned handle, kicked the locked door.

"Do you ever ask anyone for help, Margarita?"

"Yes." She let her hands fall to her sides. "In the alvin bay."

"You asked Zed to help Katrina." His tone was implacable. "You didn't ask for yourself."

"What is this ghost hunt? This is absolution, isn't it? For your doubts about your own work? Or is it just suicide dressed up as duty?"

He flinched as if she'd hit him. Margarita turned her back on him, her anger fading suddenly, leaving sticky shame in its wake. She'd drawn blood, but only because he'd handed her the knife. "Look, forget it, I'm sorry." She drew a shallow breath, feeling as if her ribs were closing around her lungs, squeezing all the air out of them. "I'm tired, and Zed was right; I'm a bitch." She swallowed, still not looking at him. "I think that little hustler ran out on us."

The door unlocked. They both stiffened as it swung open. A small coveralled man with a broad African face and purple hair looked in. A fiberlight tattoo gleamed on his left cheek: a bright purple eye that seemed to stare at Margarita. "Shuttle's this way," he drawled, sounding like Texas. "You all want to follow me?"

The words were polite, but it was a command, not a question. She nodded, Michael nodded—because what else was there to do?—and they followed the man through the door. Cold wrapped them, and Margarita shivered in the predawn breeze. Overhead, stars spangled the sky like chips of diamond. It looks so far away, that sky, so big and open and distant after the immediacy of the subsea universe. Their guide walked quickly, forcing them to hurry to keep up. Ahead, floods lit the long, low shape of a shuttle crouched on its pad. More coveralled figures bustled around the shuttle's open bay, slipping in and out between crawling cargo movers in a choreography of controlled chaos.

This was just a freight launch, so a simple set of stairs led to the passenger hatch. Zed stood at the bottom, talking to a uniformed man with a gleaming pilot's patch on his sleeve. Margarita watched him nod at something Zed was saying. The man's shoulders were rigid, and his spine rod-straight. He didn't like what Zed was telling him. Or maybe he didn't like it that it was Zed who was doing the telling.

Zed turned and waved to them. "You're slow." He grinned as they reached the stair. "I didn't feel like waiting. The other passengers ought to be showing up soon, and then we'll take off. I got us cleared for an earlier launch."

So that was why the pilot was pissed?

Zed ushered them into the shuttle, almost dancing, his body tight, crackling with energy. What got him so high? Margarita wondered sourly. His eyes glittered as if he had a fever. Stifling a sigh, wondering if she was making the biggest, most costly mistake of her life, she followed him through the door.

The interior was Spartan—this was a working cargo carrier, no luxury cruiser. Four seats across, two on each side of the aisle, cramped quarters designed to move a maximum number of people while sacrificing minimum cargo space. There weren't any windows in the hull, and Margarita said a small thanks for that. She chose a seat against the wall, not entirely surprised when Michael didn't sit down beside her. He and Zed had their heads together across the aisle. Piss on them and their damn crusade. She moved over to the aisle seat.

"What do we do when we get there?" She leaned across the narrow space. "And what happens then?"

"I find us a ride out to Vildorn." Zed rolled one eye in her direction, not really including her in the conversation.

"What about my five minutes with your boss?" She glared at him, daring him to look away.

"Later." His tone dismissed her.

Margarita clenched her teeth against the words she wanted to pitch at him. He was still paying her back for that toss back in Danners's gallery. How much more did she owe here, anyway? Probably a lot. Margarita looked at the door, wanting to walk off this damn shuttle and to hell with his promises that were probably worth so much shit.

But they might not be worth shit. *Honesty,* he had said when she'd asked him what he liked. There had been a feel of naked admission to that word. His promise might possibly save Katrina. So she'd pay Zed's bill. Margarita leaned back and closed her eyes. It wasn't just Katrina; it was Michael, too. She had said she couldn't choose, but maybe she was doing just that. Is this the right thing? she wondered silently. Or am I running away from you, Trina, using the illusion of a father as an excuse?

"Do you want some breakfast?"

The new voice snapped her eyes open. A lanky man in coveralls stood in the aisle, a thermal carafe in one hand, a plastic tray in the other. Wrapped Danish were piled on the tray, along with stacked cups and some shrink-wrapped apples.

"I brought this over from the cafeteria." He offered it with a smile.

"Thanks." She reached for a Danish, and her stomach growled, reminding her sharply of its condition. She took a second one and coffee. The coffee was weak enough to look like strong tea in the cup and tepid. She sipped at it, grimaced, and began to unwrap her Danish.

"The coffee's cold." Zed put his cup down on the tray. "Bring some fresh."

He said it with casual and intentional rudeness: *You are beneath me. I don't need to notice you or waste any energy on you at all.* The man flushed. "I'll see what I can do."

"Quickly, please." Zed didn't even bother to look at him as he carried the carafe down the aisle.

Margarita caught the hostile glare he gave Zed from the doorway. Zed had the power, so that look had to be a careful one. She glanced at Zed, pretty sure that he'd seen it, and caught a gleam of what might have been satisfaction in his eyes. He liked this little demonstration of power. The guy with the tray might dream about dumping that coffee on Zed's lap, but he wouldn't do it because he'd lose his job. Straight-line reasoning.

Only it wasn't really power. She moved back to her wall seat, leaned against the shuttle's hull. Gunner Archenwald-Shen held the power. It was Shen—his invisible presence—who had sent that crew member scurrying off to the cafeteria for more coffee. Zed drove that power like a borrowed car. She looked sideways at the clean planes of his perfect profile. Zed knew the score. He was smart enough that he couldn't help but know it and know what his own status would be if Shen dumped him. And maybe that knowledge ate at him, so that he stuck his verbal dagger into everyone who played the game.

And even Shen's power—what was it but the ability to control, or manipulate, or destroy? Maybe the only real power was the power to create. And maybe Zed knew this, too. But Shen's power you could buy. You could trade for it.

Zed turned suddenly, as if she'd spoken out loud. For an instant his eyes met hers; then he looked away and began to unwrap the Danish in his hands.

Margarita felt a sudden and unexpected pang of pity for him. His power was an illusion, and he knew it. And what about her own? She leaned back, her pastry untouched on the seat beside her, and closed her eyes. Did she create? Or did she play a game of self-delusion, telling herself that she was good, hiding her nakedness under a cloak labeled artist?

Which made her no better than Zed.

She kept her eyes closed, pretending to sleep, as the surly crewman brought Zed fresh coffee and other passengers began to trickle onboard. She pretended during the squeezing discomfort of the launch, face turned to the wall. Finally, once she was released from the crushing fist of acceleration, pretense faded into real sleep.

Chapter Eleven

The shuttle trip to New York Up was one long, weary misery. Margarita woke up all too soon, disturbed by her stomach. Trying to ignore the faint nausea, she huddled in her seat, waiting for it to end. Across the aisle, Zed postured, needling the shuttle's crew until their hostility filled the cabin atmosphere like the reek of burning insulation.

The other passengers, a handful of employees on their way back from vacation, kept to themselves. Zed's attitude isolated the three of them about as well as a case of resistant hep. Maybe Zed was the reason for her nausea. The crew probably had drugs that would help, but by now all three of them were getting the same cold treatment from the crew, so she could forget it.

"We'll be docking in about a half hour." The lanky young crewman wandered down the aisle, his smile frozen on his face.

"Thanks." She watched that smile relax as he paused to banter with one of the returning employees.

"Hello." Michael sat down beside her. "I wasn't trying to ignore you. I was trying to get a sense of what Zed's picking up, and then you were asleep . . ." His words trailed away, and he shrugged. "I—I'm glad you came along." He moved uneasily in the padded seat. "I just want you to know that. And I want you to know that your business with Archenwald-Shen comes first, no matter what Zed's priorities are." He took her hand, his movements awkward and full of hesitation. "Katrina's important. To me, too, because you love her. We'll get this settled first, before we go off on any crazy jaunts. I promise."

He was thinking about dying again. Margarita looked down at her hand in his. "I don't know who's important to me anymore. Maybe no one." She pulled her hand free. "Maybe nobody *can* be important to me. Maybe that's how it works." Is it? She wanted to ask. Is that the price of doing what we do—loneliness? Did you love Xia? Did you love anyone? *Could* you love anyone? "If I get to talk to Shen, that's really all I can do." The words came out so cold, and she didn't really mean them to be cold. Or maybe she did. "Thanks for caring about Katrina," she said awkwardly, and looked away. If there was love in his eyes, she didn't want to see it. Or was she afraid that she wouldn't see it? Why should she, and why should she even *care*? She was more of a stranger to him than Andy.

Any love he felt would be his own illusion. "You don't need to worry about me," she said. "I do fine on my own."

"Well, if there's anything . . ." He let the words trail away.

"Excuse me." The lanky crewman marched briskly down the aisle. "You'll have to strap in. We're about to dock." His words were polite but edged with hostility.

"Of course." Michael sighed. "Maybe we can talk later." He touched her arm lightly and went back to his seat.

She had hurt him. How? Margarita yanked the webbing straps snug. She hadn't meant to hurt him.

Or maybe she had. Because he wanted to die.

I fall toward my first self, swift as air's life . . .

She clenched her teeth against the remembered magic of their shared holo. He was falling toward death, not life. Pain that felt like grief stabbed her. His choice. Margarita jerked her harness savagely tight. His alone.

Outside, something clunked against the hull.

"We have arrived," a man's voice announced from the rear of the shuttle. "Home sweet home."

Somebody clapped.

Customs was an education. At first brush the officials—upsiders all—were cool bordering hard on rude. Margarita looked around the barren little room where they'd been herded, a heavy sense of familiarity settling into her belly. The walls and ceiling had been painted an unappealing pastel green, like the local juvenile center of her childhood. No carpet covered the slightly grimy floor. Functional chairs. She hunched her shoulders, tired, surly. Oh, yeah, she knew this place—knew the snotty, smug dudes in the uniforms. Old mannerisms were surfacing, barrio reactions to uniforms and authority. Not appropriate, she told herself, but she was too tired to fight it. She leaned against the wall—a silent commentary on the crappy chairs—knowing what would happen. They didn't like downsiders up here. So the uniforms would make them wait and wait, and finally somebody would come in to sneer and ask questions that weren't questions so much as rude commentaries on their clothes, sexual habits, whatever. And she'd get pissed and mouth off the way she had as a kid when the patrols picked her up for being out after curfew or outside the perimeter without a work card. And she'd get herself, maybe all of them, in trouble.

Which was an incredibly stupid thing to do, but she was too tired to keep it from happening, and she didn't really give a damn, anyway. It would serve Michael right, she thought bitterly. You want to know who I am, huh? Maybe you're gonna find out in a few minutes. She lowered her head, glowering at the door as a small, wiry agent with very white hair stepped into the room.

To her surprise, he smiled and flicked his fingers in a quick fanning motion. "You're cleared. Do you need transport?"

Australian drawl, or was it upside local? Margarita swallowed surprise, her hostility crumbling into confusion. So, she'd gotten it all wrong?

"I don't know about transport." Michael looked sideways at Zed. "Uh, can you recommend a good place to stay for a few days?"

Zed was standing a little apart, staying out of the conversation. It struck Margarita suddenly that the customs agent was being very, very careful not to look at him. As if he were invisible.

By choice? The agent was ushering them out of the room, rattling off hotel names to Michael, and his manner was obsequious. That was not the way uniforms usually behaved. At least not for her—probably not for a bunch of bedraggled downsiders with no luggage and no obvious reason for being up there. Margarita lounged along in the rear, watching the agent not see Zed. It took a lot of power to become invisible. That borrowed car of Zed's was pretty damn impressive.

And how expensive?

Margarita thought she could make a guess. She shrugged, following Michael and the invisible Zed through the automatic doors into the main port. It was about as austere and uninviting as the customs waiting room had been. Cheap rigid-form chairs formed islands in an echoing space, bright with the harsh glare of strip lights. Voices, footsteps, and machinery noise echoed back from the high ceiling. Catwalks made of expanded mesh crisscrossed the overhead space, reminding her of the gallery. Low-slung cargo beds trundled across the floor or overhead, stacked with shipping crates or bundled merchandise. People came and went, dressed mostly in shorts and singlets. The colors shouted in the dim light: neon orange, fuchsia, lime green, silver. Margarita blinked as a woman strode briskly by. Her hair was buzzed, revealing a tracery of light fibers embedded in her scalp. She wore a teal halter above brilliant yellow shorts and looked right through Margarita and Michael. Zed, however, got a tiny lift of her chin.

Margarita watched Zed return that tiny chin lift. Yeah, he carried himself differently. So did the rest of the people, at least the ones in native dress. She didn't really know anything about the platforms, only that they were clusters of modules, strung together somehow, full of strange people and upscale industry. And they didn't go in much for downsider art. Margarita sidestepped a man in hot pink who seemed willing to run her down. Yeah, fuck you, too, baby. She wondered what would happen if she elbowed one of those jerks off his feet. None of them looked really muscular. They were mostly shorter than she, too.

Zed was leading them down a wide street. People crowded the space, walking, driving the slow little cargo movers that carried crates, plastic drums, or benches full of people. More bright colors. Margarita blinked, half expecting to see spots in front of her eyes. Was this taste for loud colors some kind of reaction to living in this artificial environment? Houses lined the street, tiny, edged with about two feet of yard space. The buildings looked like bad reproductions from a Mediterranean travelogue: white stucco walls, blue painted widow frames, red geraniums in rickety window boxes. Margarita looked at the arch of wall that took the place of sky and hunched her shoulders, thinking of meteors, holes, and the hard, hard vacuum beyond that fragile skin.

Yeah, think of that. This place was more alien than the sea; it was only the illusion of air and sun and earth painted on eggshell walls. Illusion contained in a glass bubble, death denied in a riot of color . . . Margarita stared at a door marked with a bright turquoise splash. This corridor was lined with doors—a world of doors that opened into private spaces. You'd have to hide from so much up here. Your fears, your comprehension of how close to death you lived. And we see it, we downsiders, she thought. See you hide from us behind a language we don't speak, behind doors with no names.

"Lost?" Zed grinned back at her. "That glyph means public bathhouse. That green triangle is a public access node for the Net. We don't go out of our way to make things easier for you downsiders."

"We?" She lifted one eyebrow, made it scathing.

"I fit in wherever I am." His smile was silky. "Call me a chameleon."

She didn't answer. He was enjoying her uneasiness, and that pissed her off. She didn't know the rules here, and that bothered her, too. *Always know the rules*—survival skill numero uno. And she didn't know them here, which meant she was dependent on Zed, and she didn't like to be dependent on *anybody*. "How far is that hostel?" she snapped.

"Pretty close. Next plaza." He winked at her, then walked ahead to catch up with Michael.

Who looked totally calm. Margarita lagged farther behind, angry at them both because they were so sure of what they were doing. She wasn't. Up here she wasn't sure of anything at all. Ahead, the corridor emptied into a street. Blue sky shimmered overhead, dotted with puffy clouds, blessed by a late-afternoon sun. After the claustrophobic corridors of the port, Margarita could almost believe that she'd stepped back onto Earth again. She halted, her face turning up to feel warmth. A breeze lifted her hair, soft with the scent of warm earth and grass. Daffodils and tulips bloomed in weedless beds bordered by neat gravel pathways. From the back of an old-fashioned park bench a squirrel flicked its tail at her, paws busy with a peanut. In the distance kids chased each other across green grass on their bicycles.

Couldn't be . . .

And, of course, wasn't.

Margarita bent to brush her hand across the daffodils. Her fingers passed through the bright petals, although the gravel beneath her feet was real enough. The bench was real, but the squirrel scampering away wasn't. She could tint a breeze with spring, too. No sweat. Not a bad job, this park. She sat down on the bench, eyeing the mix of holo and reality. The bikes-in-the-park scene looked a bit flat; too much of the wall projection and not enough dimension. But the flowers were good. Nice random detail work. And the scent mix of the wind was first-rate.

She breathed deeply feeling her heart lift slightly. Just a touch of pheromone along with the flower and warm-earth blend? To *really* make it feel like spring? She grinned and got up. Yeah, whoever did the craft here was talented with scent.

Michael and Zed had disappeared. Hands on her hips, Margarita searched the plaza. Lots of strolling couples, a small group eating lunch together on another bench . . . Damn. As she turned, squinting in the fake spring sunshine, movement caught her eye. A woman. Margarita shaded her eyes. Hispanic, old, and it was the *walk* that looked familiar. Margarita studied her back, which was covered by a sky-blue tunic above magenta tights. Gray hair in a knotted braid . . . Recognition hit her an instant before the woman turned her head.

Xia! Up *here*? On a platform? Well, why not? Why not *here* any less than Paris or São Paulo? "Xia!" Margarita hurried after her, breaking into a run as Xia turned the corner. "Xia, *wait*!" People stared at her, affronted, and glared as she ran past. Margarita skidded around the corner into another street. Where . . .?

Xia had vanished. Damn, damn, *damn*. Panting, Margarita slowed to a walk, ignoring the looks she was getting. She had to be here somewhere. Shops lined this corridor: clothes, fancy food items, and fresh flowers were displayed behind small windows. Margarita peered through the glass at a display of tiny, perfect heads of lettuce mounded between perfect tomatoes and finger-sized purple eggplants. She couldn't see into the shop.

"Gods, Rita. Don't you know better than to run in a platform corridor? And it's bad manners to press your nose against a shop window like a starving street kid. Or it should be, if it isn't."

Margarita started convulsively and whirled. "Xia!"

"Why the surprise?" Her mother planted her fists on her narrow hips, a carryall slung over one shoulder. "You *were* running after me, weren't you?"

"What are you *doing* up here?"

"I was on my way home. In a moment I will once again be on my way home." She tilted her head and looked up at Margarita, amusement glinting in her eyes. "Coming?"

"I—" Margarita glanced back toward the park. Michael would be looking for her.

But she didn't need Zed's intro to Archenwalk-Shen if Xia had the pendant. She could just get it and take it back to Katrina on the next shuttle flight. She turned back to discover that Xia was a dozen meters down the street, walking casually, not looking back.

Damn her.

"Wait!" Margarita started to run, then jerked herself up short and began to walk. Fast. "Just hold it a minute." She grabbed Xia's arm. "You stole Katrina's pendant."

Xia spun, her forearm slamming Margarita's hand aside and flinging her backward. "Don't ever grab me again." Her eyes flashed. "What pendant are you talking about?"

The controlled rage in her eyes was like the white-hot flare of a cutting torch. Margarita took a deep breath, sitting hard on her own anger. "It's amber. You took it last time you visited."

"Did I?" She sounded thoughtful, not angry. "I might have, although I think I would have asked if it was Katrina's. Well, come on if you want to talk to me." She arched one eyebrow at Margarita and started walking again. "Sorrel is cooking tonight, and I don't plan to be late. He's a better cook than he is a lover, but I don't tell him that." She gave Margarita a twinkling glance from the corners of her eyes. "So you're up here and your dancer isn't?"

Oh, the layers beneath those simple words. "Yes." And how had she guessed? Margarita flushed. "I need that pendant." What if Xia *hadn't* taken it? What if someone else had, or it was really lost, or Xia had sold it? What then? Margarita had just lost Zed, her entry to Archenwald-Shen.

"Oh, I took it." Xia swung her carryall to her other shoulder and sighed. "I thought it was yours, not Katrina's. It wasn't her style. You should know better than to let me run around loose in your space—I'm completely irresponsible. Just ask Sorrel." She gave Margarita a quick sideways look. "You're not showing your holos up here. Don't tell me you came all the way upside just to ask for the pendant?"

"I . . ." Margarita paused, damned if she was going to tell Xia anything more about this. She glowered at a shop-window display of bright tank tops. "I came up here with Michael Tryon." She slapped the name down between them like a gauntlet. "You remember him, Xia? My father?"

"Michael? Up *here*?" Xia stopped and stared at her daughter. "You mean somebody managed to pry that man loose from his damn Stones? Gods, whoever she is—or is it a he?—*I'm* impressed." She laughed, head tilted back, a strand of gray hair uncoiling over one shoulder.

It was a happy sound. No, not quite that. Not bitter, anyway. Not angry.

Had she been angry when she'd told Margarita that Michael was her father? Margarita tried to remember but could recall only her own stunned silence, the sudden tumble of a name, an identity, into the dark vacuum inside her.

Your father's name is Michael Tryon.

A name: a focus for feelings that had blown through her childhood like a restless wind. He had been a stranger, but not quite. His face could be found in the media. And his biography. But he was still a stranger. And now? Margarita blinked, realizing that Xia was watching her face, one eyebrow lifted, a faint smile on her lips. She flushed.

"Sorrel's not the patient type." Xia tossed her head. "If he gets pissed, he won't cook." She shrugged the carryall higher onto her shoulder. "Bitch at me about Michael Tryon later. And tell me who managed to get between him and his Stones. *That* story I want to hear." She turned her back to Margarita and walked briskly up the corridor.

As if she didn't care whether Margarita followed or not. Which she probably didn't. Why should anything have changed between them? Margarita wondered bitterly. She glanced back once but saw no sign of either Michael or Zed. She shrugged, uneasy, angry, just wanting to get this over with and get back to Katrina. In the distance Xia turned a corner and vanished. "Shit," Margarita said out loud, and ran after her, ignoring the nice, sedate hostile upsiders.

Michael shaded his eyes from the noontime glare of the artificial sun. No sign of Margarita. Kids rode bicycles across a field of freshly mowed grass while a little girl struggled to get an orange kite into the air. Holos? Michael touched the slatted back of a park bench and was reassured by its solidity. Not *all* holo. He swept the plaza again, searching the strolling lunchtime crowd.

"See her?" Zed edged up beside him.

"No. She must have ducked down another corridor. She was right behind us." And he'd been giving her a little room because she'd seemed so upset. Michael struggled with growing concern. "How could she just get *lost*?" Violent crime wasn't supposed to happen up here. So had she just walked away?

"Look, I want to get to the hostel." Zed glowered at a woman dressed in neon yellow with matching hair who was smiling at him. She lifted one shoulder and mimed a kiss. "If Margarita wants to sightsee, let her. We don't have time to go looking for her." He turned his head away from the yellow woman with a sideways jerk of his chin. "Let's go."

Time. Yeah, time *was* precious. Michael felt it in the tension knot between his shoulder blades. Urgency. A sense of hurry that danced in the air like heat waves.

Heat waves. Invisible butterflies. "Zed." Michael clutched his arm. "What do you see?"

"Where?" Zed shook him off. "See what?"

The air was just air, soft with the scent of spring, full of sunshine and soft music drifting on the breeze. What have I been seeing? Michael asked himself. Perhaps nothing, but he had had the feeling that an invisible finger had stirred time itself, could wrinkle it suddenly, crumple up yesterday, today, and tomorrow into a wad so that everything touched. Crazy image. He shook his head and sighed. Maybe he *was* crazy and the suicides were simply suicides—a stress reaction in artists dealing with a medium no one really understood.

But he could still *hear* it—something was calling him, a

voice, music, darkness. Michael looked sideways at Zed, his profile carved like stone. Yeah, he heard it, too. So it was there. Not insanity; *something*.

Maybe it was a good thing they'd lost Margarita. "Let's go." Michael sighed. "How soon do you think we can take off for the Stone-mining site?"

"I don't know." Zed glanced around, his shoulders hunching again. "Right now I just want to get off the street. You never know who's looking."

"Like your boss?"

"Yeah." Zed's face was closed. "We've got a day, maybe a little longer. We'll see."

"Why *are* you doing this?" Michael scanned the plaza but still saw no sign of Margarita. "Why risk everything?"

"Maybe I'm tired of it." Zed's glance scorched him. "Maybe I'm bored with the pretty perks. Maybe I just feel like pushing a few boundaries, just to see how far I really *can* go."

"Is that it?" Michael asked softly.

"In Danners's studio . . . I don't know." Zed stared down the street, frowning. "That voice, or song, or whatever you want to call it—it was so big. I think . . . it's part of everything. I got the feeling that if I . . . found a way in . . . I'd be part of everything, too. Part of you, the rocks, dear sweet Andy . . ." He laughed. "He'd love it, wouldn't he? You know, I think I want that."

"Godhead," Michael said softly. "Only I don't think that's it. Maybe that's the name we've had to give it." Had Danners wanted it, too? And found the door only in death? "Be careful."

"You said that already. I think I'm tired of being careful." Zed turned abruptly aside. "This is the place."

White-painted shutters made the front of the hostel country-cottage cute. Red and white striped tulips waved gently from behind a low picket fence, interspersed with clumps of blue flowers on long stalks—holos. The fence was real, though. Michael's lip curled. Margarita's work made this garden look like clip art from a network advertisement.

He followed Zed up the fake-stone steps into the hostel's small lobby. The country theme was carried out in here in claustrophobic profusion: gingham tableclothes, ruffled upholstery, and white china ducks. Holoed flames crackled in a fake-brick fireplace. The dim light and the clutter gave Michael an instant headache. He gave Zed a sour sideways look as Zed dealt with a touch screen set into the antique-look desk.

"Self-service." Zed raised his eyebrows at Michael's expression and shrugged. "Discreet. Room service'll have lunch waiting for us. Go smile in the mirror so that Security can recognize you for the room lock. And stop looking like you're going to puke." He bared his teeth. "I hate this country crap, but it's private, as in *very* private. And you get your own bath here. One of the only places in New York Up with private baths. I don't share bath space with *anybody*."

"I'm rather glad this isn't your idea of elegance." Michael matched Zed's grin, then went to peer into the ornate gold-framed mirror above a dark, heavy sideboard. A china pitcher and bowl stood on the polished wood. Molded designs fluted the edge of the bowl, and a film of dust showed on the white curve of the handle. He examined his face in the mirror, grimacing a little at the dark circles beneath his eyes, the gaunt edge of his face, as if the bones were eroding through the flesh. Yes, tired. And old.

"Let's go." Zed fidgeted beside a wooden door with beveled glass panes. "Private starts in the room, not in the lobby."

He was edgy—scared of his boss? Michael wondered how much he was underestimating Archenwald-Shen. Frowning, Michael pushed the door open and followed Zed down a carpeted corridor to another door, white, this time. The walls were covered with flowered paper. One more bit of country cute, Michael decided as he looked up at the impassive video eye above the door, and he *would* throw up.

The lock clicked, and Zed pushed the door open. Cool. Scent of food. Chicken? Michael sniffed, sudden hunger squeezing his stomach. That Danish suddenly seemed like a long time ago. The room held two quilt-covered beds, more overdone wallpaper, another fake fireplace, a closet, and another door that must lead to Zed's private bath. The table redeemed the room: covered with a white cloth, it was cluttered wonderfully with a whole roast chicken on a platter—Real? Could it be?—a plate of fruit, a basket of bread, and bottled beer in a plastic ice bucket. Folded napkins filled another basket, crisp and white. Silver. China plates. He stepped into the room, bumping into Zed, who had gone rigid.

"What's wrong?" Behind Michael, the door closed on its own, locked.

"That's not what I ordered."

"So the kitchen made a mistake." Michael edged past him, wanting food and no more complications, thank you. "Zed? We're both reacting to whatever it is we're picking up. You're getting paranoid."

"Actually, he's not at all paranoid." The voice, a slightly nasal tenor, brought back the scent of dust and summer heat. Gunner Archenwald-Shen walked out of the bathroom, naked except for the towel wrapped around his hips. "Hello, Michael." He beamed, his soft jowls quivering with the breadth of his smile. "How nice of you to come visit me up here." He turned his smile on Zed. "You did your usual flawless job of arranging things. You truly earn your salary, you know. Do I praise you enough, Zed?" The corners of his smile turned downward into an aggrieved frown. "Sometimes I worry that I don't."

"You praise me enough, Gunner." Zed spoke in a flat tone.

Betrayal? Michael turned slowly. Zed looked relaxed, his posture attentive, his expression pleasant, with a hint of a smile at the corners of his mouth. A setup? Michael wondered bitterly. Had this all been one long series of hoops held up by Zed—the flight from the dome, the promise of a trip to Vildorn—so that Gunner could sit back and watch him jump through them?

Above his smile, Zed's eyes glittered like bits of broken glass.

Michael looked away quickly. Maybe Zed hadn't been following orders. Who had betrayed whom here? Michael was willing to bet that Zed would be too intense for any Stone right now, never mind his smile. Michael met the node's smiling eyes. "Did you engineer my arrest? Did you bribe someone to plant evidence that I was in S'Wanna's apartment?"

"I would never do such a thing." Archenwald-Shen didn't waste much energy dissembling. "Have a seat, Michael." He waved at one of the upholstered chairs. "Have some chicken. The apples are dirt-grown and imported, none of this local hydroponic stuff grown in processed human shit. There's juice as well as beer, although you're a beer drinker, as I recall." He dropped his towel very deliberately and wandered back into the bathroom. His voice drifted out into the room. "Serve Michael a plate, Zed. And have something yourself."

Zed began to carve the chicken with a long silver knife. Face impassive, he lifted a pale curl of breast meat and deposited it on a plate.

"Stop it." Michael frowned.

Zed picked up a roll, placed it neatly beside the chicken, and reached for a slice of some yellow fruit.

"Zed?" Michael grabbed his wrist. Muscles so tight that they ought to be humming, face so smooth that it was scary. "Knock it *off*," he said softly. "How much trouble are we in?"

A muscle in Zed's face twisted. *"We?"* He removed his wrist gently from Michael's grip, then forked the slice of fruit onto the plate and offered it to Michael. "Would you like beer or water?"

"Oh, Zed's not in any trouble." Archenwald-Shen reappeared from the bathroom, dressed in an elegantly simple jumpsuit. "He anticipates my every slightest need, even when he thinks he's acting independently. And I *don't* praise you enough." He put a casual arm around Zed.

Who reacted not at all. Archenwald-Shen smiled gently as Zed opened a beer. But violence trembled beneath the surface of his pose, setting Michael's teeth on edge, making him want to shout or throw his plate—anything to shatter the tension. Dominance. A little demonstration that he could own anyone, or what it meant to be owned. Wondering just how much revenge Archenwald-Shen would want for his rudeness, Michael took the bottle Zed was offering him. It was the brand of beer he'd drunk in Taos. The first sip wrung him, dragging him back across the weeks to that wooden table in the Taos Hotel, to Chris's worried face across from him. *How's the Sun Stone coming?* she had asked him. And he had told her it was coming along.

And now she knew the truth. Michael bent his head, peering down the brown neck of the bottle into creamy foam. Sun Stone was finished. Not done but finished. And the others. You have all of them, he thought bitterly. And I'm finished, too. I didn't realize it until now, but I am. He tilted the bottle and drank.

You *can* run out of soul.

"This is really a pretty little place. Not quite your style, though, Zed." Archenwald-Shen helped himself to a slice of chicken and picked at it delicately. "Your driver, Raoul, used to stay here. A bit expensive for his salary, but everyone has their own little frivolities." He held out his hand for the bottle of sparkling water that Zed had opened for him. "Too bad you fired him. I thought he was very good, myself. And what is *your* pet frivolity, Zed?" He smiled, bright-eyed, his round belly pushing against the fabric of his expensive tunic-suit. "I've never asked you."

"I'm not the frivolous type, Gunner." Zed smiled, searching the room as if for a place to hide. "You should know that by now."

"I do know." For the briefest flicker of time Archenwald-Shen's smiling mask drooped, revealing a ruthless face stark with emotion. The mask slipped back into place too quickly for Michael to identify it and Archenwald-Shen reached casually for a slice of apple.

"Unless you're very set on staying here, I'd like to invite you to stay with me." He beamed at Michael. "I just bought two of your Majors, you know." He popped the apple slice into his mouth and chewed. "Even though you were so unkind about accepting my commission. You *are* better than Danners. His Stones are stronger, perhaps, but they lack your depth of complexity. Your subtlety." He reached for another apple slice. "Dawn Stone is exceptionally fine. It's full of an earthy energy."

Michael looked away, frowning. The little exec's evaluation of his Stones and Danners's had been . . . thoughtful. It occurred to Michael that perhaps Zed was not the only person he had misjudged lately. "Danners is dead," he said, feeling rather than seeing Zed's twitch of reaction. "He cut his own throat."

Archenwald-Shen's expression didn't change, but the rhythm of his chewing faltered just slightly.

The silence stretched on, tugging at Michael. The node popped another apple slice into his mouth, his eyes on Michael's face. Waiting for him to speak. The pressure was effective. Michael suppressed a desire to squirm, aware of Zed's silent amusement.

"I don't think it was suicide." The words sounded too loud in the small, cluttered room. "I think . . . I'm sure . . . the Stone killed him. I think S'Wanna LeMontagne, Irene Yojiro, and Andre Lustik all suicided because they were working on new Stones. Something has been layered into them. Some kind of . . . compulsion, perhaps." Not insanity, or not just *mine*. Michael licked his lips, struggling against the node's silence, struggling to put the darkness he'd felt into words. Godhead, he'd told Zed. But he couldn't use the word to this man's face. "I've . . . felt something."

"Have you?" Words at last, flat and without shading. Archenwald-Shen's eyes slid toward Zed, rested briefly there, slid away, and considered. "What does that have to do with me?"

"Vildorn BeltMining. I think the contamination is happening at this end. That's why I came up here. To find out." Was it his imagination, or had Zed flinched? Michael looked his way, but Zed's smooth face might have been molded from porcelain.

Archenwald-Shen leaned forward, hands clasped on his knees, his face pleasant. "You're such an altruist, Michael Tryon. Coming all the way up here to protect innocent sculptors? You know, I wouldn't have thought it of you."

Michael flushed. "I'm not an altruist. I never have been, and since you probably have access to every detail of my life, you're aware of that. I could just go about my business, maybe make a media fuss for a day or two. 'Poisoned Stones Kill Sculptors' " He grimaced. "Most people would probably assume that it was the temper tantrum of a past-prime sculptor or that I *had* murdered S'Wanna and was trying to cover for it. But I already feel it—whatever's planted in the Stones. Sooner or later I'm going to kill myself." He met Archenwald-Shen's cold, depthless eyes, aware of the breath sliding in and out of his lungs, the beat of his pulse, the tickle of cloth against his skin. Life was such a precious thing. But that darkness sang in his blood, too, in his muscles, resonating through his bones. Calling him, and maybe there was no way to avoid that ending no matter what he did. "I want to know *why*," he whispered.

Archenwald-Shen raised his head to rest his thick chin on his steepled fingers. "To know why you die." His eyes peered into a faraway vision in the air. "To know that there is a reason . . . I can understand that." He nodded slowly. "It fits with what I get from Dawn Stone, I think."

Unexpected words. Unexpectedly deep. Michael met the node's pale eyes, then looked away. "Will you let me check the Stones that are being mined? I should be able to tell where and when the . . . resonance . . . is being introduced."

"Perhaps." Archenwald-Shen tilted his head, his smile firming. "And perhaps not. Perhaps I will turn you over to the downside consul for deportation. Perhaps the police would like to talk to you about Danners's death?"

The node didn't believe him. He could respect a desire to face one's killer, but he'd dismissed Michael's theory about the Stones. Maybe he was right. Michael's heart sank as Archenwald-Shen's smile turned creamy. He was going to finish punishing Michael for that bit of rudeness back in Taos. He was going to dangle access to the Stones over his head and see how high Michael was willing to jump for it.

How high *are* you willing to jump, Michael Tryon?

"Unless you're . . . ah . . . very set on this particular ambience—" Archenwald-Shen flicked his fingers at the overdressed room. "—I would rather you accepted my hospitality. I maintain a rather nice little enclave up here, if I do say so myself. I would enjoy your company."

And if he didn't accept, the consul would have his name and location inside an hour? Move number one in this little game. Michael read the subtext and sighed, his weariness coming back like a breaking wave. "Sure." He shrugged, wondering how long and complicated the game was going to be. "I'd be delighted."

"You're so polite," Shen murmured. His glance moved to Zed, resting on him gently. "This move suits you? I'm not . . . ah . . . interrupting anything?"

"Of course not." Zed reached for Michael's untouched plate and set it on the cart. "We can leave any time."

Archenwald-Shen nodded and levered himself to his feet. "I'm glad you're back." He nodded at Zed. "Your assistant isn't nearly so glib with numbers. Two or three affairs need your immediate attention. A cab is waiting for us." He turned his attention back to Michael. "I took the liberty." He paused on the way to the door, clucking his tongue gently. "You know, Zed, you should try sculpting Stones. I think you'd be quite good."

For an instant Zed went pale. In another instant he had recovered and was smiling a slow, lazy smile that was betrayed only by a very faint flush. "It just wasn't my style." He glanced into the bathroom, shrugged, and started for the door. "I'll go fetch the cab, shall I?" He sidestepped Archenwald-Shen.

As he went through the door, he gave Michael one brief, splintered look.

"He's a moody boy." Archenwald-Shen put his thick-fingered hand on Michael's arm. "But very, very good at what he does. Quite worth the investment in his education. Shall we go? I'm looking forward to having your undivided attention for a day or two." He beamed, becoming in a moment the slightly gauche, social-climbing, airheaded node he had seemed in Taos.

It occurred to Michael that Archenwald-Shen might have been playing with him deliberately even then. Feeling his face go hot, he looked away. He could see through the open door into the bathroom. It was a mess: sodden towels piled the floor and hung from the shower cabinet. Black hairs peppered the white sink, and the bowl was full of soapy water.

Michael looked after Zed, but the hallway was empty. As he preceded the node to the cab, he wondered if his quest was worth this. Maybe it would be better just to turn himself over to the downside consul, get himself sent back to untangle the fearful mess of red tape that had to be waiting for him. Let it happen. Let the darkness take him, and who gave a damn who was behind it? He'd be dead or insane, and he wouldn't care. Nothing would matter after that, right?

Margarita mattered. Her memory of him mattered.

Besides, he told himself as they exited into sunlight, he might be able to do something for her lover. It was remotely possible. So he would play the game.

Zed opened the cab door for them, then got into the front seat without saying a single word. Not once did he catch Michael's eyes. Michael leaned back against the foam upholstery as the little automatic glided away, wondering wearily what he had done to piss off Zed, wondering what Gunner Archenwald-Shen was going to want in exchange for a ticket to Vildorn.

A lot, probably.

Chapter Twelve

Sorrel was a bit of a surprise. He was small and downsider-wiry, a mix of Polynesian and maybe Amerind with some Caucasian in there somewhere, and his face reminded Margarita sharply of Arrow. Similar genetic mix, anyway. His sleepy eyes and slow speech didn't impress her much. His skin was darker than hers, making his light eyes look almost shockingly bright above his high cheekbones. A nice pet, she decided: good cook, okay in bed, and not smart enough to cause trouble. Curled on a floor cushion in his tiny apartment, she watched him toss slivered vegetables in an electric wok. Beyond him the apartment wall was the wall of the platform module, transparent, fragile skin between her and vacuum. A million stars glittered in the blackness. It wasn't like the night sky on Earth; Earth's sky had a texture. Up here you realized there was *nothing* between you and those points of light. That nothing went on forever. Margarita swallowed and closed her eyes against a sudden dizziness. When she opened them, the wall had gone comfortably pastel blue.

"That view's a little much for newbies." Sorrel reached for a handful of something bright red and vegetable, tossing the fine slivers into his wok. "I like wall space, myself. They drop the rocks down from the belt, and you can see 'em come in. Fun to watch when the tugs go out to catch 'em. But not much action tonight." More red slivers sizzled into the hot pan.

"It's even more fun to watch when they miss." Sprawled on another cushion, Xia yawned. "I hope you're almost done." She stretched one leg to prod Sorrel's thigh with her bare toes. "I'm hungry."

"You're always hungry." Sorrel leaned a little backward against the pressure of her foot. "Distract me and you get scorched 'fry."

Xia laughed and took her foot away. "So, Rita. You did the reunion thing with Michael, after all." She lifted her small glass of local brandy in a silent toast, then watched Margarita over the rim as she sipped. "I'm surprised."

"I didn't do it." Margarita sniffed at her own untouched drink, wrinkling her nose at the harsh smell. "He came looking for me." Almost true, anyway. "Why didn't you tell him?"

"Why should I have?" Xia raised one eyebrow. "His contribution was accidental. We both thought my implant worked." She laughed softly. "You should see your face, Rita. If looks could kill . . . Be glad I didn't get an abortion."

"Yeah, thanks a whole lot. Instead, you just dumped me on Tía Elena's doorstep." Her hand was trembling. Margarita set the glass down before it spilled, crowded by the words that pressed against the back of her throat. "Why *didn't* you get an abortion?" she asked softly. "Why the fuck did you have me?"

"Are you so unhappy that you'd rather not exist?" Xia's face was hard as agate. "Life is cheap, and maybe none of us really need to be in this shitty world. And I knew I'd never be any good as a mother. Oh, I thought about it, dear." She raised one eyebrow. "I think I had you because you were Michael's daughter. I guess a crazy part of me really wanted to hang on to some part of him. He wouldn't give anything away, so I took something."

Margarita blinked, groping for words, for anger, but finding only silence.

"Oh, yeah, I loved him." Xia tossed her head, her eyes full of shadows. "If he had let me, I would have stayed with him. Forever, I told myself, because 'forever' had some kind of meaning back then. But he couldn't love me, couldn't love anything but those rocks of his. And eventually I would have gotten restless, anyway." She laughed softly. "I'm not a forever person. I don't stay anywhere very long, or with anyone, and I would have hurt him. But it would have been nice for a while." She looked at Margarita at last, half smiling. "So who did it? Who does he love more than his Stones?"

"I . . . don't know." The anger had gone, and it wouldn't come back to save her. "I don't know who he loves; I don't know if he gives a shit about anybody. He's sort of like you that way, isn't he?" Margarita got stiffly to her feet, fists clenched. "Just give me the pendant, okay? I'll get out of your hair. I think we've about had all we can take of each other."

"You're always so *angry* at me." Xia laughed. "Every time I visit you, you spend the hours tiptoeing around your anger like it's a big sleeping dog, like it's going to jump up and bite you. I keep waiting for you to kick the son of a bitch, just to see something happen, but no, you just keep tiptoeing. So I leave, because it's boring." She shrugged, a short sharp lift of her shoulders. "*Be* angry, Rita. Hate me if you want, but *do* something with it. No, never mind; you're not listening." Xia sighed, tilted her head, and drained her glass. "Just because I have the uterus to get pregnant doesn't mean I should raise the kid. At least I know *my* limitations." She licked her lips, eyeing her empty glass regretfully. "Elena's a good mom, and blood matters to my baby sister. I knew she'd treat you like her own."

"Oh, yeah." Margarita bent and picked up her glass, not trembling anymore, her knuckles white as she clutched it.

"You think it would have been better with me?"

Xia's quiet, utterly cold tone stopped her. Margarita looked sideways into her mother's eyes, looked away from the old shadows there. Dark shadows, some of them ugly. "All right." She drew a slow breath. "So you had a tough life and I had a tough life, and so maybe that's just the way it is for most people, okay? So we're both grown-ups and what else is there to say?"

"*You* were saying." Xia was unperturbed. "Not me."

No victories here. Just more of Xia's clever words, as always. Margarita let her breath out in a rush, glowered into her glass, then swallowed a mouthful of burning, pungent brandy. And choked.

Coughing, eyes streaming, she doubled over, her chest on fire. She felt someone take the glass from her fingers and pat her on the back. Gently. Comfortingly.

"Here. Water helps."

Sorrel's voice. Sorrel's comfort. Blindly, Margarita closed her fingers around the mug he pushed into her hand and swallowed cool water. It did help. Slowly the spasms subsided, and she straightened up, wiping her face on her sleeve.

"That brandy's strong stuff." Sorrel set the wok on the small table. "You need to go easy, first time."

Do tell. Margarita looked around, but Xia had vanished.

"She went down to the bakery, next street over. They do good chapatis." Sorrel gave the bright red and green contents of the wok one last thoughtful stir, then turned to her. "And I think maybe she needed a walk because you got under her skin, and that's something, because I've been trying to do it for years, and I haven't found any cracks yet." Sorrel laughed softly. "She wasn't kidding about the restlessness, you know. I've known her for a long time. When she's around, it always feels like forever, but it isn't. It never is. But she comes back." He got plates down from a cupboard and collected silverware.

"She dumped me," Margarita rasped. "I met her for the first time when I was five. *Five*."

"Long time for a kid." Sorrel set a plastic wine bottle down beside the wok and eyed the table critically. "She's like a moth, I think. She's chasing this fire, only I'm not sure she knows what it looks like." He sighed. "When she finds it, she's going to burn up, and it'll be so bright." He turned the bottle a hair so that the label showed. "Yeah, it's gonna light up the night," he said softly. "It's gonna be some blaze."

He loved her. Margarita looked away from the sadness in his face just as Xia came through the door.

"Chapatis." She held up a plastic bag. "They taste like they're made from real ground-up wheat seeds and not tank-grown cells. Don't know how they do it, but they do it well. So let's not keep your creation waiting, Sorrel."

"It's ready." Sorrel kissed her lightly on the cheek as he took the bag from her.

Margarita saw the tenderness in that kiss, overlaid with resignation. Because Xia would move on again, and that was just the way it was. How did Katrina feel about *her*, about *them*? Something like terror gripped Margarita. She didn't really know.

Hadn't wanted to know.

The stir-fried bits of vegetable were good, laced with cubes of some kind of vegetable protein, seasoned gently with curry and subtle, sweet spices that Margarita couldn't identify. She was hungry, and Sorrel watched her eat with open approval. If he liked to cook, he liked to see people eat his cooking. Xia ate with abandon, scooping up vegetables with pieces of bread, licking the juice from her fingers, and occasionally feeding Sorrel a choice bit.

It was a little too much abandon for Margarita's taste, and she had the uncomfortable feeling that Xia knew it and was enjoying the effect. "This was wonderful," she told Sorrel, carrying her plate to the kitchenwall. "I was starving."

Sorrel nodded, took the plate from her, and stuck it into the cleaner. "I think I'm going to mosey off to the Earthlight and drink beer." He stuck the rest of the dishes into the rack. "I'll see you later." He winked at Xia and wandered out of the apartment.

He was giving them a little privacy and was comfortable enough to let it show. Margarita nodded as the door closed behind him, liking him for that. "Nice guy," she said without looking at Xia.

"Yeah, he is." Xia picked a last tidbit from the wok. "So, tell me about this wonderful pendant that's so valuable you had to come all the way up here to get it back."

Uh oh. "I told you—"

"Yeah, yeah, you just thought you'd ask, as long as you were here anyway, playing tourist with Michael." Xia curled herself onto her cushion again, chin propped on one hand. "You don't lie for shit, Rita. I wouldn't ever count on fooling anyone with that up-front, angry face of yours." She laughed. "At least not until you take some lessons in body language. So." She sat up, tucking her feet into the lotus position. "What kind of data is in it, anyway? Some nice salable bit of information for the Worldweb market, or is it blackmail?" She pursed her lips and winked. "I had your gorgeous dancer pegged as rock-solid honest, myself. Or is this *your* little treasure?"

"Data?" Margarita closed her mouth with an effort, face heating. "What are you talking about?" But she knew from Xia's expression that she'd already blown it. "Oh, shit." She banged her fist down on the tabletop. "Will you stop playing cute games with me? Just for once? *Damn* it." She pressed her lips together tightly, shocked by the tears that threatened. No way. Not in front of Xia.

"What else could it be but data? Clever place for a microsphere. The fractures in the amber would hide the insertion; you'd have to scan it to find anything." Xia sighed. "*I* don't play games, Rita. Not with you, anyway. Maybe one day you'll realize that. And maybe you won't. So it *is* your dancer who's in trouble, right?" She nodded, her tone brisk. "I think you should tell me about it. I think I have more experience with this type of thing than you do."

Again darkness glimmered and vanished in her eyes. Margarita bit her lip, staring at the pastel wall that hid the endless outside emptiness. I don't trust her, she thought. And who *did* she trust? Katrina, yes. And who else? Margarita let her breath out in a slow sigh, empty inside and out. "I don't know what's on the sphere." She swallowed, her heart beating faster, dizzy with the sense of standing on a brink. Of what? A cliff? One more step and she would maybe find out, maybe find herself falling. "The manager of my gallery got Katrina to keep it for him. A little later somebody killed him. Shit, I don't even know if the damn pendant's part of it or not, but I'm—" She faltered, then shook her head. "I'm scared." The words came out in a whisper. "For Katrina." She buried her face in her hands, overwhelmed by the incredible magnitude of that fear, wondering where she had kept it, how she could have hidden from it. "I need to call her." She drew a shuddering breath. "I need to know she's okay." Oh, yes, oh, please, dear God. "Right now."

"I can take you to a public terminal." Xia shrugged. "That's no problem." She tapped her lips with one long finger and combed a strand of hair back over her shoulder. "There is only one way to find out the value of your little prize. You'll have to access it, of course."

"How?" Margarita asked dully. "It'll be protected, won't it?"

Xia snorted. "Security is only as good as you can afford. And I can afford the best." She grinned, baring the tips of her teeth. "Or one of the best, anyway. We'll hope your mystery installer couldn't afford better." She nodded, still smiling. "I think we should join Sorrel at the Earthlight. Liza hangs out there in the evening."

"Liza?"

"She's good with code. We'll turn her loose on your little puzzle." She reached into her pocket and held out a golden teardrop on a fine chain.

Margarita reached for it.

"Not so fast." Xia pulled it away. "I think I should carry this." Her smile was amused. "You know, you're right not to trust me. I don't fault you for that."

Margarita almost grabbed for it but stopped herself. "Whatever you say." She pressed her lips together and tried to put nonchalance into her shrug. Bitch. "You're the one with the cracker contact, not me."

"That's right." Xia winked and tossed her braid back over her shoulder. "Nice recovery, by the way. You might learn to do a poker face yet. Maybe." She laughed and pocketed the pendant. "Let's go find Liza before she finds some gorgeous body to take home with her."

"You *are* a bitch."

"Did I ever say I wasn't?" Xia laughed again and walked out into the corridor.

The Earthlight was a popular if small hangout. It was roofed by a transparent blister of hull, and cushions and low tables crowded the floor. Most were occupied by lounging couples or small groups talking, drinking, or doing recreationals. Holos shimmered above a couple of small stages: porn in one corner, something that was probably wrestling and looked about as sexual as the porn in another. Neither was very well attended.

Margarita looked away from the groaning bodies on the porn stage. Beyond the invisible boundary between air and vacuum, Earth hung in the starred darkness. Huge, blue and white, it seemed to shrink everything. Margarita took a step back, her throat swelling, filled suddenly with a terrible yearning. I want to go home, she thought. What home? Even Tía Elena's house had felt like a temporary thing—a place to stay because she didn't belong anywhere else.

Tearing her eyes from the blue-white vista, she scanned the crowded room. Sorrel was sitting at a round table near the wall. Margarita followed Xia over to his table, wading through the almost palpable sea of music and conversation. Couples danced on a polished floor, writhing to a driving monotone beat that pounded its way through the noise. Behind her on the porn stage the woman came with shrill, gasping cries. Someone clapped.

"Glad you came by." Sorrel slid over to make room for

Margarita. "Rock just dropped down. Made the tugs scramble."

"Liza around?" Xia folded herself onto a cushion.

"Dancing." Sorrel jerked his head at the floor. "Cruising."

"Doing any better with the moves?" Xia tilted her head.

"Some. You're a good teacher, but I think she's hit her limit." Sorrel unfolded himself, stretched, and picked up his empty glass. "Want a brandy?"

Xia nodded and raised an eyebrow at Margarita, who shook her head. "Liza's got a great body, but she moves like a teenager." Xia sounded condescending, but her grin mocked her tone. "She still does okay for company."

Margarita searched the dance floor, suddenly restless, filled with urgency. She wanted to get this over with, just read the damned sphere and go home. To Katrina, who was maybe as much of a home as she was ever going to have. I didn't understand, Margarita thought. And maybe she still didn't. She sighed, then looked up as Xia waved. A tall, lanky woman with cropped blond hair was heading toward them, brushing through the crowd with edged grace. A knife fighter, Margarita thought. She had the same moves, anyway, the same come-on expression.

"Yo, Zee." The woman dropped onto a cushion, legs folded so that she could get up fast. "You should've been around. This downsider got up to dance a while ago. Thought he was hot stuff. You woulda blown him off the floor." She considered, one side of her mouth lifting. "He thinks he's hot stuff in bed, too. We'll see."

Xia rolled her eyes. "Before you get too busy, I got a job for you. Interested?"

"Maybe." She flicked Margarita with a quick, hard glance. "Got a price tag?"

Xia put a thoughtful expression onto her face. "Well, I won't call it even, but the debt is seriously reduced."

Liza grunted.

"Take it or leave it." Xia smiled up at Sorrel as he returned, taking the glass he handed her.

"What is it?" Liza propped her elbows on the table, glowering. "I had other plans tonight."

"No rush. Next week or whenever." Xia ignored Margarita's twitch of protest. "I want to know what's on a sphere."

"That's all?" Liza raised a contemptuous eyebrow.

"Ask me that after you crack the code." Xia took a complacent sip of brandy. "If you can."

"Fuck *that*." The glower was turned on Margarita. "Nobody's good enough to keep me out."

Xia sipped more brandy.

"So give me the damn sphere." Liza shoved her hand out, palm up. "I got nothing really important to do tonight."

Without a word, Xia dropped the amber pendant onto her palm. Margarita started to say something but shut up at the hard look Xia flashed her. Okay, this was Xia's turf. And on somebody else's turf when you didn't know the rules, you followed their lead. For a while, anyway. Until you *did* know the rules. And she needed to know what was on that sphere. Margarita pasted a neutral smile onto her face and sat still as Liza casually pocketed the pendant.

"There's the hot boy." Liza jerked her head at a pale, red-haired man making his way out onto the dance floor. "I'll give five to Dino to play Synchotron, and you can show him how to do it." She rose smoothly to her feet and winked. "I bet he's just as lousy in bed. We'll see."

Xia looked out at the floor, head tilted, smiling as the music changed. Then she got to her feet, her body already picking up the beat. Yeah, Xia was a dancer. Like Katrina. Margarita watched her thread her way between the tables. She'd put on a smooth, controlled body language: a rhythm and tension that flaunted, dared you to look, challenged you. A few eyes followed her, drawing others.

She did a lot with a short walk through a crowded room, Margarita thought grudgingly. Maybe more than Katrina, even, who didn't put on her dancer persona until she stepped out onto the floor. Slowly Margarita got to her feet, aware of Sorrel's eyes on her, and began to work her way closer to the dance floor. She could hear the music better now, a complicated syncopation that would be hell to work with—Liza's little trick on the red-haired guy, she figured. The few dancers on the floor were retreating to their tables, waiting out the unforgiving music. Not the dude. He was out there in the middle, keeping up with the rhythm, more or less.

Margarita circled over to the wall and leaned against its smooth coolness. On the floor, Xia raised her arms, body picking up the bass beat, making it her pulse, her heartbeat. Katrina did that, as if she'd opened her veins and let the music flow through her flesh like blood. She got a glazed look in her eyes, as if she were seeing God or the music. Xia had that look in her eyes now, as she began to dance. She took the heartbeat of the bass, wove brightness around it, made a counterpoint of flesh and movement, line and shape and motion. Until music and flesh were one and no one watching could imagine the music without the dance or the dance in silence.

Katrina would do it like that. Xia almost did. Almost. You could see the small falters, the tiny lapses where muscle and bone couldn't quite make the reach, where the music went beyond the flesh and shouldn't have.

Xia was old. Good, incredibly good, but old. For a dancer. Margarita looked away, her throat tight. Once, maybe, she had been better than Katrina. Now she was almost as good, but not quite. Margarita wondered suddenly when it had first hit Xia that she wasn't as good today as she had been yesterday. And what that had meant. One day—not soon but eventually—that day would come to Katrina.

I can go on forever. Margarita leaned her head back against the wall that divided atmosphere and vacuum, life and cold cataclysmic death. Unless her brain failed, and then she probably wouldn't care. Not so for Katrina. Talent would outlive ability. Dance is so *mortal*, Margarita thought bitterly. You could capture it on holo, but it wasn't the same. *It has to be live*, Katrina had said late one night when they'd gotten a little drunk together. *It's a symbiosis between audience and dancers, a living, breathing sharing. You can't record it. You can't really do it by yourself.*

Mortal. Margarita's holos didn't need her presence to work for someone; they'd be around long after she'd turned to dust. Yeah. Her lips twitched. If anybody gave a damn. Out on the floor Xia danced—the music's flesh and bone and mortal soul. For an instant her eyes met Margarita's, unseeing, full of fire and inward vision. And then she was past, whirling away, solo now; even the red-haired boob had retired.

Margarita went back to her table as the music and Xia's dance ended. Scattered applause rattled through the room, and a sudden pang stabbed her. A moth, Sorrel had said of Xia. Chasing a fire she couldn't know. Yeah, she'd seen that in

Xia's face. Why did Katrina dance? What did it *mean* to her? Margarita had never asked. She dropped onto her cushion and leaned her elbows on the scarred plastic tabletop.

"Want that brandy now?" Sorrel asked gently.

Margarita looked up to see compassion in his face. "Yeah." She nodded. "Thanks."

Xia appeared, flushed, her skin sheened with sweat. "Water," she said, and laughed. "Sorrel's getting me some, bless him."

She must have been incredible once. "You were really good," Margarita said, wincing at the awkwardness in her tone.

Xia raised one eyebrow. "Meaning, 'You don't do half bad for over the hill'? Is that a fair translation?"

Margarita tried to hold back her blush but failed utterly.

"Yeah, I am indeed good." Xia's eyes pinned Margarita, refusing to release her. "Once upon a time, I was better. I will probably be worse someday. I dance. I like to dance. Fuck you, Daughter." She looked up as Sorrel set three glasses down on the table, then picked up the largest. "Thanks, love." She touched his wrist. Then she drank half the water in quick thirsty swallows. "Are you about ready to head home?"

"You want to?" He glanced dubiously at Margarita.

"Yes, I do." Xia finished her water, taking his hand as she got to her feet. "Coming, Rita?"

"In a little while." Margarita touched the rim of her liquor glass and didn't look up. "I know the way."

Fuck you, Daughter. Margarita drank half her brandy, welcoming its burning rawness. She felt humiliated and hadn't a clue as to why. Which pissed the hell out of her. Out on the dance floor the red-haired dude was dancing again, strutting his ass, sillhouetted by sunlight reflecting from Earth's blue and white skin. Give Xia and Sorrel some time, she told herself. Give them some privacy before going back to the apartment. Although she had a feeling Xia didn't give a damn about privacy.

Maybe so, but she was damned if she was going to listen to Xia and Sorrel making love. Margarita finished her brandy and went to get another.

She didn't get drunk—not very, anyway. Another survival rule: never get drunk when you're on strange turf. But she drank enough to muddy some of the feelings that kept wanting to surface. Feelings about Katrina, and about Xia. Feelings she didn't want to face tonight and maybe didn't want to face ever. Michael Tryon was there, too, another face in the chorus. When the bartender offered her a dream patch, she was tempted.

But it wasn't her turf, and she'd never liked the helpless fuzz that a patch put you into.

Time to go, she told herself, and changed her mind about a last drink. The bar was as crowded as ever, but the faces had changed, all a little pale and strange in Earth's glow. It was as if there were no night and day up here, as if people lived out their own schedule of "day" and "night." Maybe they did; Margarita didn't know this world and didn't really care to know it. She threaded her way carefully between the crowded tables. The red-haired dancer had vanished, replaced by four or five tentative couples out on the floor. No more solos. No more show-offs.

Xia had been one hell of a dancer. No. Margarita's cheeks stung. She was *still* one hell of a dancer. That "fuck you" had been earned. Maybe mortality was part of the art form. Margarita thought about that as she left the Earthlight. Maybe part of what made each dance unique was the sense of present. Dancers translated music into a living moment of strength and sweat and weakness—of here and now. Maybe that explained Katrina a little; it was the present that mattered far more than the future. So she had paid Ari Yiassis's price because that slot was now, not because she doubted Margarita's talent. Because she loved Margarita, and she lived the moment, not the future.

Maybe Liza had cracked the sphere. Margarita paused at an intersection, suddenly unsure. The corridor was empty, so maybe people did follow some sort of night-day schedule up here. Frowning, she stared down the intersecting corridors. Her feet wanted to take her left, but it looked wrong. Footsteps thudded suddenly behind her, running but muffled, as if the runner was trying to be quiet. Running *at* her. Margarita spun, hard-wired reflexes bringing an arm up and dropping her into a half crouch. Something struck her with numbing force, exploding sight and consciousness into fragments for a bright instant. Margarita reeled backward, gasping as the corridor wall slammed into her back, and slid down into a heap on the floor.

Fingers raked her, yanking at her tunic. Fabric tore. Her vision was returning, chaos focusing into a blurry face. The hands touched her neck, slapped roughly down across her breasts.

No way, bastard. Summoning returning strength, Margarita lunged upward, her fingers reaching for eyes, punching for her attacker's groin. She connected, and a voice yelled hoarsely. The weight against her released suddenly, and she staggered to her feet, one hand on the wall. A small olive-skinned man crouched in front of her, a short wand in his hand, one eye half-closed. Teeth bared, he started toward her, then paused and shot a quick glance down the intersecting corridor. With a muttered snarl, he shoved the wand into a pocket, turned, and darted away. Margarita ran a step or two after him but halted as the corridor tilted beneath her feet. Uh uh. Not just yet. She leaned against the wall, eyes closed.

"Margarita!" Xia's voice. "What the hell is going on here? Are you all right?"

Margarita blinked as Xia appeared beside her. "I . . . think so." She touched her arm but felt no tenderness, just the memory of that numbing blow. "He used a stun wand on me." Set too low, so she hadn't quite lost consciousness. "Nice street crime you have up here." She straightened, her strength coming back fast now. "Do people usually go around raping in the corridors?"

"No." Xia frowned at a strolling couple wandering by. "Was that what it was?"

"I . . . don't know." Margarita touched the torn pocket of her tunic, remembering those rough, groping hands at her neck. "Maybe. Or maybe he was looking for something. Like the pendant." Coldness spread through her, starting in her belly, radiating outward. "I need to call Katrina." She brushed past Xia and looked up and down the corridor. "Damn it, where's the nearest public access?"

"Calm down." Xia's fingers closed around her arm, hard enough to hurt. "We'll go to the access and make sure your dancer is all right. And then we'll go back to the apartment and talk. Liza called me. Which is why I came looking for you."

"What's wrong?" Margarita stretched her legs to keep up with Xia, feeling gawky and awkward beside Xia's seemingly unhurried grace. "Slow down a minute, will you. If you don't want me to run. What did she tell you?"

"Nothing." Xia relaxed her pace a trifle. "She wouldn't, over local access. It was the way she didn't tell me that sent me looking. You've got a treasure." Xia gave Margarita a hard sideways look. "Or perhaps you know that? Perhaps you're much better at subtlety than I guessed? Maybe I am finally going senile."

"No." Margarita nearly collided with Xia as she halted in front of a corridor door. "I didn't know, damn it. Katrina didn't know, either." Damn Ari! Damn Katrina for letting him lever her. No, damn herself for not understanding, for not talking more to Katrina about her holoture, where it was going . . .

Too late for recriminations.

Margarita touched the door plate and then walked through the opening door. Inside, the large room was divided up into cubicles by transparent panels. Here and there men and women talked soundlessly to holos, seemingly surrounded by walls. The effect was mazelike, and Margarita hesitated.

"Look at the floor," Xia murmured.

A blue line led from the doorway, branching like a tree as it entered the cubicles. She followed it, passing a woman talking animatedly to a holoed man with bright green hair. After two more occupied cubicles, the next was empty. She went in, ears going cottony with the effect of the acoustic damping. The empty holostage yawned. "Access," Margarita said, and winced at the tremor in her voice. "Argent Zeladio." She blanked on his access for a moment before the letters and numbers came to her.

"Please recite your personal code now," a cool androgynous voice requested.

They didn't bother with a fancy interface up here. Margarita recited her code, aware of the video eyes that were recording her, comparing body language nuance to her personal file. Come on, come *on*. She clenched a fist, resisting the urge to slam it against the spotless transparent wall. Who the hell cleaned all these walls, anyway?

Opalescent light shimmered above the stage, flashed blue, then rippled through shades of teal, aqua, and yellow before fading to white. Argent appeared, his head and shoulders sharp and clear, the image dissolving to invisibility just above his waist. He had only screen access in his apartment, not a holostage.

"Margarita." He didn't sound enthusiastic. "I was wondering when you'd call again."

"Is Katrina all right?" Margarita snatched a breath, wondering why the air seemed so stuffy in there. "I don't have to talk to her, I just want to know that she's fine."

"Don't ask me." Argent glowered at her. "She was fine when she left."

"Left?" Oh, no. "How could you let her *leave*, Argent? *Damn* it. How do you know she really left? Maybe she got kidnapped." And killed, after she'd been forced to tell somebody where the pendant had gone? That was the reason for the attack in the corridor. "You *bastard*!"

"Bastard?" Argent flushed. "You listen to me, you self-centered little *artist*. You cost me my best dancer, and I can only guess what you've cost Katrina. A lot, I think. If you're going to call anyone any names, I think you'd better take a long look at yourself first. Yes, I know Katrina's in trouble, and so does she. Which is probably why she left, because she doesn't want to get anyone else involved. And maybe, just maybe, she's feeling a bit fractured, thank you very much, Margarita Espinoza. And yes, she left, because I took her down to the mag-lev myself, and no, I don't know where she went." Argent's expression was cold, unforgiving. "She's out of your reach, Margarita. And mine. Maybe you'll hear from her again and maybe you won't. Personally, I don't think you deserve it."

"Fuck you, too," Margarita said between her teeth, but Argent had already vanished. Light shimmered and died above the empty stage.

Gone. Katrina was gone, safe or dead, and she didn't know which. She might never know. Margarita slammed out of the cubicle, stumbling over the idiotic blue line as if it were an obstacle and not just paint on the floor. Xia, waiting for her beside the entrance, raised an eyebrow as she caught sight of Margarita.

"Liza will be waiting for us." She touched Margarita's arm: a light touch, full of gentleness. "I'm sorry." She palmed the door and walked out into the corridor.

Margarita followed her, unexpectedly comforted by that touch and lack of questions.

Liza was indeed waiting for them, perched restlessly on the corner of the small table, one foot flicking like a cat's tail. Sorrel had vanished. Gone to bed? Margarita wondered. It was late, but she didn't feel tired; she was full of a tight, restless energy.

"I didn't bring it," Liza said before the door had closed behind them. "I'm not done with it yet. What do you know about it, anyway?"

"It's valuable." Margarita shrugged, a little resentful of Liza's accusatory tone. "I thought you were the cracker."

Liza's whip-flick glare stung. She turned her attention pointedly to Xia. "This job's gonna take full-time work. Which I don't do for free. On spec? I get thirty percent of whatever we make on this baby, and I think we're gonna make a lot."

"So what's on it?" Margarita snapped. "Let's start there."

"Thirty percent," Xia mused to the ceiling. "That covers a lot of work."

"Yeah, it does." Liza hopped off the table and prowled across the room. "The front end is easy. I think I know who did it—reads like him, anyway. Two-bit hacker, good enough to get by, not good enough for big-time. And this is big-time. We're talking Net access codes and some heavy protection on the sphere. Back doors into primo space. This is the string into somebody's private labyrinth, and it smells real hot to me." She leaned her palms on the table, bouncing lightly on the balls of her feet. "Real hot. But it's gonna cost me some full-time effort to track it."

"Goddamn it." Margarita faced her across the table. "Before we talk profit, I want some answers. I want to know who's behind this, and I want to know it now. I'm not into this for the money, okay?"

Liza took a deliberate step sideways, then looked at the silent Xia. "Who is this child? Can we send her home to bed?"

"The info's hers, Liza." Xia shrugged. "Her lover's in the middle, so cut her a little slack, okay? You were that young once."

"Not me." Liza rolled one eye in Margarita's direction. "Not ever."

Margarita opened her mouth, then shut it tightly.

"Better." Liza nodded. "Just keep it in mind that you need me, honey. I want to *see* you remembering it."

"Yes, ma'am." Margarita bared her teeth. Because Katrina was out there somewhere, and she *did* need this bitch. "I'll remember. Promise." And screw you.

"You do that." Liza's amusement suggested that she'd read the subtext accurately. "The small-timer must have lucked out on this cache—I don't think he had the smarts to get through the protection. It's gonna take me a day or two." She straightened, looking at Xia again. "You agree? A three-way on whatever we get? And you get your names, whenever I have them." She gave Margarita a sour glance.

"Sounds good to me." Xia's face was thoughtful. "Watch yourself, Liza. Somebody up here knows Rita had it."

Liza shrugged. "I always watch myself. I'll let you know what I crack when I crack it." She paused at the door to wink over her shoulder at Margarita. "I'll give you a name to whet your appetite and maybe a guess about the other. The small-timer's a creep named Yiassis. Strictly a klutz ghost."

Ari. Margarita let her breath out in a slow sigh. Big surprise.

"I think maybe I know who our Minotaur is, but it might not be his style, after all." She leaned a hand against the door, frowning. "But I hear something's going on with him. He didn't make his squash game this afternoon, and nothing makes him miss. Plus that snotty boy of his brought home some guest or other. Very hush-hush. Maybe it's coincidence and maybe it's not. Some of the thumbprints on this file sure look like his boy's." She bared her teeth in a grin. "Stay tuned." She slapped the doorplate.

Snotty boy? Who'd brought home a guest? "Who do you mean?" Margarita snapped. "Wait a minute."

Liza looked back over her shoulder as the door closed, flashing another grin. "Gunner Archenwald-Shen. The power that moves the platform. And maybe Earth, too, who knows?"

The door whispered closed. Archenwald-Shen. Margarita stared at the blank panel, her thoughts racing. Maybe Liza was wrong and it wasn't Shen. And maybe she wasn't. Shen owned the gallery. And Zed had brought home a . . . guest?

So maybe his helpful little act had been just that—an act. What did Archenwald-Shen want with Michael? A chill touched her. Or did he want *her*, know somehow that she had Ari's pendant? And, dear God, *how* did he know? Did he think Michael Tryon would bring her running?

What if she had to choose? Michael or Katrina?

Fuck.

Margarita started for the door, only to gasp as Xia yanked her to a halt.

"Where are you going?" Xia's eyes were cold.

"To find Michael." Margarita tried to twist free. "To find out what the fuck is going on."

"You are my daughter, and I am not stupid. And Michael Tryon is not stupid, even if he is a fool." Xia's face didn't soften. "Which means you are probably not stupid, either. And this is a very stupid thing to do. Shen *owns* the platform. Liza wasn't kidding. Shut *up*." She waited for Margarita to close her mouth. "We will let Liza find us the key to Mr. Archenwald-Shen's very tightly locked front door, and then, only then, will we go knocking. Do you understand me? You don't know this world. If you don't do this my way, you are going to get hurt, and so will other people. Maybe your dancer, if she isn't already dead."

Margarita flinched. But it was the unrelenting honesty of that evaluation that hit her. *If she isn't already dead . . .* "Why?" Margarita met her mother's eyes. "Why are you helping me?"

"Because Liza thinks there's money in it, and I always need money." A shadow flickered in Xia's eyes. "And because you love someone, and I did, too, once. I guess I'm sentimental enough to think that's worth saving."

"All right." Margarita rubbed her arm where Xia had grabbed her. "I'll do it your way." For now. "So what next? What do we do now?"

"We go to sleep." Xia turned her back, heading for the dark bedroom. "You can sleep on the cushions." She disappeared into the other room.

For a long moment Margarita stared at the empty doorway, furious, groping for something to do, anything.

And came up with nothing.

"Crap," she said very softly, and began to pile the cushions together.

Chapter Thirteen

Gunner Archenwald-Shen maintained a lot of personal space up on the platform. Michael wandered down the carpeted, softly lit hallway, appreciating the distance between his shoulders and the walls. These rooms had none of the too-small feeling that had tickled him with subtle claustrophobia ever since he'd come here. Very expensive.

He touched a wall, savoring the slightly rough texture of hand-applied paint. Even he, uninformed about upside life as he was, knew that space had to be expensive up here. Very expensive. And these empty, spacious rooms were a statement, the way the Fechin House guest quarters had been a statement back in Taos. *I only tolerate the best.* Michael eyed the closed doors, guessing they were bedrooms. He hadn't seen Zed since they'd arrived yesterday afternoon. Zed had pleaded work, his eyes full of restless deception. Shen had simply vanished without bothering to give any reasons. If they were there, they had to be closeted behind one of those doors. Michael knocked lightly on the nearest one, rude and not caring, annoyed at this abandonment.

No, not quite annoyed. He wandered on, knocking on the next door. The silence in this place was eerie. Like the silence you'd hear in some abandoned town out in the desert heart of the country. He'd spent a week in one of those dead towns once, camping, listening to the small noises of wind and blowing sand and the voices of the dried-out crumbling buildings. Those voices had been part of a greater silence—a sense of absence, Michael decided. That same sense of absence filled these rooms. He reached the door at the end of the hall and touched the panel lightly. To his surprise, it slid open.

"Zed?" Michael peered into the room, then sucked in a quick breath. Three Stones stood on lacquered pedestals, showcased by light and space, glimmering with hints of color.

Dust and summer . . . a woman's laugh. Michael closed his eyes. Joy and gentle fatigue . . . the flash of dark hair tossed by a hot breeze . . . the feel of sandy desert soil between his fingers . . .

Dawn Stone.

Step by step Michael crossed the room to halt in front of its tall lean shape. A symphony of sun and love and human warmth. He closed his eyes and laid his palms against the Stone's surface, wakening it, letting the resonances close over his head like still water: faces, moments of peace, and rest, and love. It felt warm beneath his hands, live, living flesh, filled with memories of yesterday. That woven tapestry of memory had trapped him like a net, had let him deny the present.

Now Dawn Stone had the feel of nostalgia. Margarita had torn that net apart with her Xia eyes, her anger, and her wary, wounded pride. And with her art. He'd finally left the past behind. Because of her. Michael sighed and opened his eyes, lifting his hands from Stone's surface, letting it sink into slumber again. Yesterday was gone. Forever out of reach. I loved you, Xia. Michael touched Dawn Stone with one finger. I loved you, only I couldn't tell you. No, it wasn't even that. I couldn't even admit it to myself. I told myself I couldn't take even that much energy away from the Stones.

His love for Xia hadn't taken energy away from the Stones. It had added to them. By the time he had understood, it had been much too late.

Michael grimaced, sighed, and turned away from Dawn Stone. The other two weren't his. He stretched a hand toward the closest Stone but hesitated. Dangerous? He frowned, sorting through the resonances. No, he got no hint of that alien darkness. He didn't recognize the style, either. Eyes half-closed, he brushed his fingers against the Stone's squat curve, not quite waking it. Images of a bonfire's red light against black darkness, brief pain, panting breath that tightened his chest, the feel of sharp stones beneath bare feet . . . *Driven,* Michael thought. That was the theme here, woven with some subtle harmonies. Michael let his breath out slowly, his vision shimmering with a glimpse of naked shoulders brown and sculptured with muscle, black hair, a sunset like blood streaked across an orange sky, waves pounding bleached and broken shells on black sand . . .

They didn't quite come together, the images. A subtle dissonance jarred them, like cracks in a perfect porcelain vase. Didn't quite make it, but . . . almost. Oh, yes, *almost*, and if it did, if those images and resonances would just come together, they'd sweep you away. Michael turned his back on the Stone, fists clenched, breathing hard.

Not quite genius.

But so *close*.

He knew the style, or thought he did. It nagged at him like a sore tooth, feeling too familiar to be some newcomer. Michael bent, searching the pedestal for some kind of glyph, script, a name. Someone talented. Oh, shit, more than just talented. Michael rubbed his eyes, eyelids burning as though he were going to cry, but he didn't have any reason to cry. Except that this damn sculptor was *good*—or would be, would be spectacular. Not yet, but could be. Harness those dissonances, Michael thought. Make them work *for* you, and you'll do it the way I want to, the way I try to, and who the hell is this person, anyway?

Michael touched the Stone again, simultaneously jarred and entranced. He wanted to tell her . . . him. That the Stones were good. "Just in case you don't *know*," Michael murmured softly.

"Don't know what?" Archenwald-Shen's tone was amused. "You do get up early, don't you?"

Michael turned slowly, reluctantly away from the Stones. "Mr. Archenwald-Shen." He bowed, an intentionally stiff angulation from the hips.

"Oh, stop." The node grinned, revealing perfect teeth that were probably implants. "Don't ruffle your feathers at me. I've been rather appreciating your reactions, you know. Your art means something to you, but then you sell it." He wandered into the room, a real-silk robe belted around his thick middle. "Do you feel just a bit the whore, Mr. Tryon, primo artist? Do you sometimes lie awake at night wondering if you're getting enough for those pieces of your soul? Do you ever wonder if you'll hit bottom, if the well will run dry?" He smiled again, a civilized, demure grin that barely revealed the tips of his white, even teeth.

Michael pressed his lips together and looked away. Where had *that* question come from? It had hit too close to home, and he struggled to control his expression. "Actually, I pay more attention to what I'm trying to do." Michael glanced sideways at the humming dissonance of those flawed, powerful Stones. "Who did these?"

"Oh . . . a student." Archenwald-Shen waved one hand. "They were his first attempt at sculpting, I believe. I've lost track of him. If he exhibits, Zed hasn't liked his work enough to buy any. I trust Zed's judgment."

"You're kidding." A first effort, and they were this good? "Who *is* this guy?"

"A nobody." Smiling, Shen put a hand on Michael's elbow. "Would you care to breakfast with me? I brought up some Nova Scotia lox—farm-raised, of course. Certified toxin-free."

"No thanks." Michael shook himself free, then remembered Margarita and her lover's plight. "Well, maybe I will eat with you." He put a neutral smile on his face. A *student* had sculpted those Stones? "So what's his name?" He let the node guide him out of the room, submitting to a touch as proprietary and smug as a possessive lover's. "I can't believe I don't know him." He put cocktail party into his tone, figuring he'd get more that way and faster. "I think I'm jealous." And that should bring the name up pronto, Michael figured.

Archenwald-Shen tugged at one earlobe, grinning. "Promise me the next Stone you work on and I'll tell you his name."

When hell freezes over. "Gunner?" Michael used the node's given name, hoping for insult, but elicited nothing worse than a wider grin. "We need to talk about Vildorn BeltMining and about those tainted Stones."

"*You* want to talk about them. You're the one who claims the Stones are tainted. Personally, I'm happy with my return from the lease." The node opened one of the doors that hadn't opened for Michael, revealing a carpeted floor scattered with cushions and low tables. French doors opened onto a vista of manicured green lawn and pond, and marble ruins gleamed white on a distant hill.

"Please, help yourself." Archenwald-Shen gestured toward

an antique buffet table against the wall. "I never talk business before breakfast."

Play the game. Michael sighed. The main door wasn't locked. He could walk out into the corridor, flag down a taxi, and catch the next shuttle home.

With a nod, he walked over to the buffet. It was actually a kitchenwall designed to look like furniture. The wood grain looked real enough to fool any casual glance. Nice job. Frowning at a platter of translucent pink lox, he picked up a plate. If it wasn't china, he couldn't tell. He took half a bagel, ignored a bowl of what looked like cream cheese, and layered thin slices of fish with a slice of tomato and onion. Someone had told him that vegetables were cheaper up here than downside because of the hydroponic technology the platforms had developed.

The tomato looked better than any he could remember buying downside. He poured coffee that smelled as if it had been brewed from real beans, carried plate and cup over to one of the low tables, and settled himself onto the cushions. Beyond the leaded-glass panes of the French doors, peacocks strolled across the lawn, sweeping the perfect grass with their iridescent tails. Nice holoture—a wall projection with surprising depth. Better than the public park, Michael decided. Not as good as Margarita's work, but close. He caught sight of more white ruins and marble columns and glimpsed a statue within their shadow. They looked familiar. Some Greek temple?

It wouldn't exist anymore. Michael picked up his bagel and took a bite of salty fish and sweet-tart tomato. Greece had been through too many wars in the terror years. A lot of humanity's cultural treasures existed only in computer-generated holo or virtual now. Same with the environmental treasures. Michael leaned his elbow on the table, eyes on that distant, gleaming marble. Long ago we celebrated godhead with our hands, he thought. Then we tried to tear it all down. Cathedrals, paintings, rain-forest glades—so much had vanished beneath the tide of violence that had swept the world.

That was the soul of Margarita's work. Michael put down his half-eaten bagel, warmth stirring in his gut. She reached out to yesterday, to the world of forests and mountain meadows that had died or changed in the face of technology. It wasn't nostalgia, either. She looked at what had been and held it up like a mirror to reflect what was. And her audience saw itself through the lens of yesterday. There was so much strength in those flawed Stones, in Margarita's work. Artists let humanity search its own soul, Michael thought, and excitement filled him, expanding inside like spring. That's what art can be: a window into ourselves, into our deepest, most hidden places. And, yeah, he had done that. Maybe not as much as he wanted, but he had *done* it. Even if the darkness took him, it could never take that.

"You look pensive." Archenwald-Shen sat down beside him, setting his own plate on the table. "Feeling blue?"

"No." Michael picked up his bagel and took a bite. "You know, I thought once that we were nothing more than an envelope for our DNA, a vehicle for reproducing it. Maybe I've got it backward. Maybe our DNA is the yearning of the universe for art, love, war, culture." He smiled at the bagel in his hand. "I'm going to go out to Vildorn. I'm going to listen to the new Stones, find out why these deaths have happened. I'd like your help. The connection between the raw Stones and the suicides is going to occur to someone any time now. That's going to gut your little monopoly." He popped the last bit of bagel into his mouth, chewed, and swallowed. "If you aren't willing to help me, then I'll do it on my own."

"Will you?" Archenwald-Shen sipped at his coffee, his face pensive. "You're naive, downsider. Is it so important to you to know the face of your killer? What are you willing to trade for it? What's your price?"

Michael sipped his own coffee to cover his surprise. Archenwald-Shen believed him about the Stones' darkness. Which he hadn't yesterday, so what had changed his mind? "I don't know what my price is," he said, and the truth of those words stabbed him. "It's not just . . . wanting to know who kills me." He met the node's considering stare. "One of those Stones might kill a student like the one who sculpted your Stones. And she or he would never be."

"And that matters to you?" Archenwald-Shen wrapped a fragment of fish around a piece of onion and nibbled delicately at it. "Such a pretty piece of self-sacrifice. You know, people die in a thousand silly ways every day. They have heart attacks, walk in front of mag-levs." He wiped his fingers on a napkin. "Maybe your saved sculptor will get bored and go farm fish."

"Maybe." Michael pushed his empty plate away and stood up. "If a Stone kills him, I guess we'll never know, right? Are you going to help me visit Vildorn? Have you decided on a price yet?"

Archenwald-Shen raised his head slowly, his eyes cold. "I've considered it." He didn't smile. "I don't think you have anything that I particularly want. So, no, I don't think I'll let you visit Vildorn. Not that I have anything to do with it, in any case. Feel free to search any public database you wish. I don't own the operation." His smile bared only the tips of his teeth. "Zed was mistaken about my personal involvement, of course. Occasionally, even he makes mistakes. But only once. He has a steep learning curve."

The hard chill in his voice made Michael want to shiver. Zed had mentioned that Archenwald-Shen's ownership of Vildorn was very oblique. Maybe he'd gotten Zed into trouble. Maybe that was the source of his flinch yesterday when Michael had mentioned the mining company. And maybe Zed deserved it, because he had, after all, set up all Michael's legal headaches. "Did you know that Zed was bringing me up here?" Michael watched Shen's face carefully. "*Was* he just following orders?"

"Was he?" The node's smile didn't touch his eyes. "You decide. Or you can ask him yourself. But you might want to take his answer with a grain of salt. Zed lies very well whether he gets paid for it or not. It's rather a habit with him, and he's a very talented boy."

Michael saw a flicker of emotion in those cold eyes, but it was gone too fast to identify. He gave the node a cold bow. "I don't suppose it matters whether Zed was following your orders or not. Since I would have found my way here sooner or later, I suppose. Thank you for the breakfast, and I think I'll go find somewhere else to stay." I'm sorry, Margarita. Michael stifled a pang as he started for the door. I couldn't do anything for Katrina; it would only make things worse if I mentioned her name. He hesitated at the door, but Archenwald-Shen's silence was like a hand at his back.

With a sigh, he let it push him through the door and out into the corridor, and the ghost-town silence folded around him again, thick and stifling. He walked slowly down the hall, thinking hard about his next move. He was depressingly short on ideas. Without Zed's guidance, he would have to waste time fumbling for transport out to the belt mining operation. Without Zed's guidance, he would be at the mercy of local hostility toward downsiders. If Archenwald-Shen put the word out that Michael was persona non grata, then he could have a very tough time indeed. Michael had noticed the power Zed used so casually; Archenwald-Shen was obviously big up here.

But someone was always willing to play the maverick for pay. He'd find a ride out there eventually. And what the hell was he going to do when he got there? Kill the person or persons responsible for that deadly song with his bare hands? Michael closed his eyes briefly, remembering Danners's dark power, Lustik's lyrical poetry of the human soul, S'Wanna's evolution toward greatness. And that flawed student who might one day stand in front of another Stone and make it work. Yeah, if he had to, he would kill someone . . . because it mattered. His vision shimmered, motion stirring the darkness behind his closed eyelids, filling him with dark song as it had in Danners's studio, only stronger this time. Butterfly wings again, a touch like gentle hands cupping his face, drawing him into deep water, like a lover's lips against his, drawing him closer. *Let go,* a distant voice urged. Just let go and you'll understand.

No! Michael shaped the word, not sure if he'd spoken out loud or not. He was sagging, knees buckling, in slow-motion free fall to the carpeted floor. Stand *up*! He flailed, lost in darkness and light, his flesh dissolved into molecules of nitrogen, oxygen, hydrogen, dissolving in a million breathing moments of life, of eternity. His hand banged the door. The small, immediate pain shocked him, and he clawed at the solid surface, palm flat, focusing on the stretch of his fingers, the coolness of the door's surface. Hang on to that or you'll fall . . . down into darkness.

Eternity.

With a hiss of friction, the door opened, spilling him off balance and sending him staggering into the room. Adrenaline surged through him, banishing the darkness in the chemical wave of falling fear. His knees hit the floor, pain spiking upward into his groin, heart thundering in his ears, half-blind in the light. "Stop," he whispered. No Stone, not this time. This time the darkness had come from everywhere—and nowhere. It had come from inside him. Zed was right. He blinked, trying to focus, and found himself on hands and knees beside a small holostage. The floor was real wood: satiny rectangles of soft beige and magenta set in a zigzag brickwork pattern. What appeared to be handwoven carpets were scattered across the floor. Slowly, Michael raised his head.

A chair stood beside a small table—a comfortable lounger covered in soft suedecloth. Pictures hung on the walls: watercolor scenes of city streets and hurrying umbrella-carrying pedestrians dressed in twentieth-century style. On the far wall was a bright abstract. Originals? Michael laughed shakily. He would never have guessed that the node was into pre-twenty-first-century art. It wasn't the in thing.

That terrible, familiar darkness had almost claimed him. Michael closed his eyes briefly, then snapped them open in sudden fear. What would he have done? Wandered Archenwald-Shen's domain until he'd found a knife somewhere and slashed his own throat, the way Danners had done? Found an air lock and let himself out into vacuum? He had almost accepted it this time. And maybe—maybe that had saved him. Perhaps, if he'd fought it, only pain would have come through. Because pain is what we know best, he thought with terrible clarity. Pain and isolation. So that loneliness and agony would have come crashing in like a feedback howl, and maybe he would have killed himself to stop it. Maybe Danners had done just that.

I understand. Michael shivered and scrambled to his feet. And realized suddenly that he was in a bedroom. The bed stood at the far end of the room; it had been hidden by the chair and table until he stood up. More pictures hung on the far wall—surreal city scenes, mostly. He didn't pay them much attention, because Zed lay sprawled across the tumbled spread, dressed only in a pair of black tights. His loose hair streamed across his tawny shoulders and hid his face. Asleep. Michael flushed, automatically embarrassed at his invasion of this obviously private space. Or was he asleep? Even as he turned to leave, Michael hesitated. Zed also responded to that dark song. What if it had seized him, too? Whatever it was. He walked slowly over to the edge of the bed, afraid of what he might find, remembering Danners's glazed, empty eyes.

Blood. Michael caught his breath. It stained the white comforter beneath Zed's face, rusty and drying. "Zed!" Michael grabbed his shoulder, fingers snagging in Zed's long hair. "Zed, are you okay?"

"Hunh." Zed hunched away from his hand at the same moment Michael's brain registered warm flesh. "Who?" He peered up at Michael through the tangled curtain of his hair, then levered himself onto his elbow. "What are *you* doing in here?" he asked thickly.

"I . . ." Michael looked away and swallowed. Even concealed by Zed's hair, the damage was ugly. One eye was swollen almost shut, and his face was blotched with darkening bruises. Shen's doing? "I saw blood on the spread. I thought . . ."

"Hey, it's nothing out of the ordinary." Zed's voice was bright and bitterly mocking. "Just the usual little games. I got a nosebleed." He sat up and shoved his hair back over his shoulders, grimacing with pain as he did so. "Actually, this *is* a little out of the ordinary." He touched his lip, fingered the crusted blood, and winced. "Gunner doesn't usually do much visible damage. He has more restraint than you might think. No, Mr. Tryon. This is my pink slip." He stared up at Michael from his one good eye. "I tried to keep one foot in the door while I played hunt-the-ghost with you. I would have done better to just cut and run. I think he'd have been less pissed at me, and he sure as hell would have had a tougher time catching up with me."

"This is my fault, isn't it?" Michael let his breath out in a slow sight. "Because I mentioned Vildorn to . . . your boss."

"It's my fault for telling you anything." Levering himself stiffly off the bed, Zed limped past Michael and through another door. "I do know better. Maybe I gave myself the pink slip."

Water ran in a sink, and Zed made a small controlled sound of pain as he splashed water on his battered face. Michael leaned against the wall beside the door, giving Zed his privacy. "I'm sorry," he said, raising his voice to be heard over the water sounds. "I was so busy trying to convince him to listen to me that I didn't think. You should have told me what I wasn't supposed to give away. In words of one syllable, probably."

"Yeah, right, well, next time I'll do that." Zed emerged from the bathroom, blotting his face gingerly with a towel. "You gonna leave now? I think our business is about finished."

Mocking, superficial words. Beneath that bright surface lurked hurt, like deep muddy water. "We still need to find out what's going on." Michael held Zed's bitter stare, forcing himself not to look away. "I'm going out to Vildorn. One way or another. Zed, it nearly ate me just now. Out in the hall. It can take you, too."

"Maybe I'm not as sensitive to it as you." Zed brushed past him, opened a closet, and took out a tunic. "Maybe I don't care. I don't think Gunner has decided whether he's through punishing me or not." He paused, tunic in his hands, his expression thoughtful. "I've never seen him lose his temper before. Not really. It's always an act, and it wasn't this time. I don't know why." He caught Michael's eye and put on a smirk. "You know, I think he's more pissed about that than about my letting some outsider in on his business affairs. That I made him lose his temper. I don't think he's ever going to forgive me for that." He shrugged. "Hey, getting eaten by your ghost might be the better deal."

"Why didn't you leave him before this?"

"A little disgusted, Mr. Tryon?" Zed pulled the tunic on over his head. "I told you in Taos. I liked what I get, and if I'm willing to pay the price, that's my business."

"Is it worth that much to you?" Michael turned away because he *was* a little disgusted, and it probably showed on his face. "It's his power and money, not yours. Is the money so important? You could have made out okay on your own."

"Yeah. I could've made out. You know, once upon a time I knew what I wanted to do with my life." Zed smoothed a fold in his tunic, his frown distorted by the darkening bruises on his face. "Did you wake up one morning and know exactly what *mattered* to you? What you wanted to *be*?" He shrugged. "I did. And I discovered that I can't do it. I can want it like hell," he said softly. "But I can't *do* it. Not the way that matters to me. You know, you're the first to get that out of me." The smile was back, bright and bitter. "You're talented, Mr. Tryon.

Or persistent. Hey, money and power make a pretty decent second choice, even if they're not exactly mine."

And suddenly Michael understood. "You did those two Stones," he said softly.

"No!" Zed's shoulders jerked.

"Yes, you did. I knew they felt familiar. I figured I'd run into one somewhere else, but that's not it. They're *you*. That's what felt familiar." *The warp is strung from the sculptor's soul* . . . "They're good."

"Not really." Zed looked away. "I was playing around. I'm not sure why Gunner hangs on to them. Because he thinks it hurts me, I guess, but it doesn't." He lifted one shoulder, then let it drop. "Yeah, I did them, so you know, all right? It was fun, and I found out that I'm no sculptor."

"Yes, you are." Michael reached for his arm, then withdrew his hand as Zed's expression hardened. "They're not perfect, but they're good. Don't you understand? *Damn* it. You've got a hell of a lot of potential."

"Fuck potential." Zed's voice was soft and low. "You just won't lay off, will you? You're gonna keep pushing and pushing, because you're so sure you know it all, aren't you, Mr. Tryon?" His eyes held Michael's, full of shadow, full of fire like distant buried coals. "You're so sure anybody can just *do* it, all it takes is your decision, huh? A little practice, like playing the piano? Oh, I can do it. I can wake up a Stone; I can layer in some model's lust, or pain, or mellow attitude. And then I stand back, and you know what I get? I get *me*." His voice dropped to a whisper. "That's all I'll ever get. I'm like Danners, only worse. I'll use the models, sure, but the Stones will always be me. And don't tell me how I can learn to do it right, because learning's not part of it, Mr. Tryon, and you're not God. You don't *know*, and I do. I looked the truth in the face a long time ago. Did you ever do that? Do you know how much it hurts?" He turned his back on Michael and began to comb his hair. "Good luck with your ghost hunt. But don't count on getting out to Vildorn on your own. Gunner keeps a much tighter hold on things around here than you realize. He'll rather enjoy watching you try to scrounge up transportation."

"Zed?" Michael hesitated. It's *there*, he wanted to yell. Talent—real, solid *talent* with those Stones. You can do it. You can make it work. "We're the ultimate exploiters," he said finally. "We use our *selves*, our own souls, ruthlessly. Estevan told me that, and he was right. You've got to reach inside and rip your guts out to do this, and it hurts like hell." *The warp is strung from the sculptor's soul.* "Maybe you can't be that ruthless."

Face turned away, Zed might have been carved from granite.

Michael sighed, his shoulders drooping. "Look, I'm sorry. For a lot of things, I guess. And you know yourself and I don't, but . . ." He shook his head because there weren't any words. "They're good Stones." Michael turned his back on Zed's silence and walked out of the room. As the door began to close behind him, he realized that he was holding his breath, waiting for some sound from Zed, some word to stop him, bring him back.

The door whispered closed. Why does it matter to me? Michael asked himself in the quiet carpeted hallway. So what if he doesn't want to do Stones or can't? His choice.

But it mattered. Because the sculpting mattered—what it *did*, what it meant.

Maybe it *had* to matter. To Michael, at least.

And did it matter to anyone else? The way he wanted it to matter? Maybe. And maybe not, and he was deluding himself, hiding from the cold reality that what he did wasn't any different from the work of some virtual game designer.

Head down, Michael walked along the corridor. There was no sense of darkness now, but hey—he laughed a single bitter note—would he even notice right now? "What are you?" He paused in front of his bedroom door, looking up at the spotless ceiling. "Who are you? A ghost, like Zed says? My own brain short-circuiting?" And perhaps he had pulled Zed into his own insanity, because Zed was a sensitive and they were somehow operating on the same wavelength. Everything comes in through our senses. We have no reality check. Maybe we create it as we go. Michael stared at the closed door. He hadn't brought anything up with him, had left nothing but rumpled sheets in the room. Gunner could deal with those. He turned his back on the door to walk down the hall and out into the overdecorated living room.

Time to go wander around the port bars and see what kind of transport he could scrounge up. If nothing else, Mr. Archenwald-Shen would get his entertainment.

If that Stone darkness wasn't his own insanity, it wasn't anything left by some twisted sensitive. Michael looked up at the ceiling again, wondering how far to trust those unchecked human senses. That darkness was *someone*. Back there in the corridor he had felt a vast, incomprehensible attention.

Which was perhaps more frightening than the possibility that the darkness came from within. Maybe humanity wasn't quite as alone as it thought. Michael laughed softly, palmed the main door, and walked out into the public corridor.

Chapter Fourteen

Sorrel walked with her through the crowded daytime streets. Margarita forced herself to slow down, clenching her teeth in impatience as Sorrel's pace seemed to slow even more. Xia had intended to accompany her, but at the last minute Sorrel had offered. And Xia had meekly stepped aside.

Xia was *never* meek, but what the game was, Margarita couldn't figure out. She realized she was leaving Sorrel behind again and paused, swallowing exasperation as he peered into a shop window full of baked goods. Damn Xia for letting this man play guide.

"You're a very energetic lady." Sorrel finally caught up, giving Margarita a sleepy, somewhat apologetic smile. "Sorry if I'm slow. I never was good at hurrying."

It was probably lucky for him that he was a good cook. Margarita pressed her lips together, hoping that Archenwald-Shen's fancy house wasn't too far away. Sorrel noticed her expression and smiled again. "It's right down here," he said, turning down a side street. "Just on the other side of Hawkins Park."

Hawkins Park turned out to be a VR amusement park done in fake gravel paths and a holoed garden full of silvery spheres the size of large cars. Customers paid their money, climbed into the appropriately styled seats inside, put on their goggles and gloves, and went for one hell of a ride. Kids hung out around the spheres in tight groups, preteen mostly, giggling and watching the scatter of adults and older teens who were buying into the rides. They reminded Margarita suddenly and sharply of the kids in the barrio, hanging around the flea markets, keeping close and accurate track of the serious business of gang turf and trade.

What magic could one find in this sterile, fragile bubble of life? Margarita watched a dark-haired Asian girl twirl complicated patterns on the grass-carpeted ground. Ritual of the unconscious turned into play? What gods and demons ruled this space beneath the curve of the sky that was nothing but a skin between vacuum and air, life and death? How would it work as a holoture? The scent of metal and ice, a hint of warmth like midnight sheets in a cold room . . . Maybe she would set the stage with light and black shadow, beneath a steel sky. A sun like a beach ball, fringed with static flames. Plants? Margarita eyed a staggering couple as they exited a sphere. Maybe lichen. Soft, layered flesh that hid tough survival.

Excitement shivered down her spine. Arrow, wait till you see this. Oh, *yes*, it'll work, and it'll make all those people who walk around under that blue sky so damn *uncomfortable*.

Sorrel cleared his throat, nodding toward the far side of the park. "Over there; that garden court."

Margarita blinked, flushing. "Sorry. I was thinking about something."

"So I gathered." His sleepy smile broadened as he led the way out of the park.

The neighborhood on this side of the park was very Middle Eastern. Ornate walls, brick or stucco, hid the faces of the houses from the street. It wasn't real brick, of course, but it looked real enough.

"Refugees from Syria or Jordan." Sorrel didn't look at her. "They had enough money and foresight to escape up here before the Backpack War turned the Middle East into a desert. You know, when you've been up here awhile, you're different. You don't belong downside anymore, and you know it. You can't really leave, because you'll be an alien down there." His voice was soft, as if he were musing to himself. "So you stay. And you work for whatever the companies pay, because you don't have much of an option—and that's what everybody else gets, anyway. There wasn't much for them to go back to, even after all these years." His swift sideways stare lanced her. "And up here you don't like downsiders much—they've got a hell of a lot more options than you do, and they don't give a damn."

So you didn't have many choices. Was that what he was saying? Margarita eyed a tiny mosque at the far end of the street. Its dome gleamed copper in the bright light from the fake sun. Children laughed from behind an ornate latticed wall, and Margarita caught a glimpse of a brown face peering out at her. A girl, dark-eyed and solemn. She vanished as Margarita raised her hand to wave.

How would you do that—include that sense of limits? A touch of claustrophobia? Steel walls leaning in over you? Cupped hands that could trap or crush or cradle gently? A tall hedge enclosed Archenwald-Shen's yard. A real hedge; Margarita touched the crisp, shiny leaves. A wrought-iron gate closed the gap in the well-trimmed foliage. The house was white stucco with narrow, shuttered windows. Very ethnic.

Margarita pushed against the gate. Nothing happened. The bars felt like real iron, cold and lustrous beneath her palm. She raised her head. "Margarita Espinoza, here to see Gunner Archenwald-Shen." She enunciated clearly for the pickups that had to be focused on her. "I have an appointment." She shouldn't have said that; it made her sound anxious. His house system would know she'd made an appointment.

Because of Liza's little key. *Mention Procenium Productions,* Liza had said. *He'll invite you in.* And she had been right.

Or sort of right. For all the earlier on-screen invitation from a thoughtful Archenwald-Shen, the gate didn't open. Sorrel was watching a couple of adolescent boys toss a ball back and forth down the street, his expression dreamy. He wasn't much help. Margarita let out a gusty sigh, then grabbed the gate and shook it. To her amazement, it rebounded away from her grasp, crashing back against the hedge, showering the neat concrete walk inside with leaves and bits of debris. It wasn't iron, after all; it was much too light.

"I guess we can go in now," Sorrel said mildly.

No shit. Margarita stalked through the gate, struggling with anger. So Shen was going to play cute games. Great. Wonderful. She drew a deep breath as she reached the door, squashing the anger down inside her. This was no time for her damned temper to break loose. It could cost her Katrina.

If Katrina wasn't already dead.

The near certainty of that loss chilled her, turning her anger to cold ashes in an instant. She lifted her face to stare into the door's video eye. "I'm here," she said. "Margarita Espinoza. Can I come in, please?"

The door opened inward, hinges creaking a little as if this were an ancient house from some back street in Damascus or Baghdad. Although neither city existed anymore. Upsiders resented anything and everything Earth yet preserved their own version of Earth so carefully. Love and hate? Need and rejection? Show that in dissonance, maybe woodwinds and percussion . . . Margarita walked through the open door, blinking in the dim light, and halted as she recognized the man waiting to greet her.

"Zed?" His face was swollen and ugly, blotched with bruises. Who had he pissed off? she wondered. "I didn't expect you."

"Gunner's off at his regular squash game." His smirk distorted his swollen mouth. "We've got half an hour." He turned his back on her and walked through an archway into a carpeted living room.

"Wait a minute." Margarita followed him to the archway and leaned against the plastered wall. Sorrel had come in before the front door had closed itself and was standing in the middle of the foyer, looking lost. Margarita let out an exasperated breath. Carved wooden screens, cushions, and richly patterned carpets continued the Moorish theme in the big room. "I came here to talk to Archenwald-Shen, not you," she snapped at Zed. "I made this appointment with *him*. What do you mean he's off playing squash? Where's Michael?" She glared at Zed's back. "What the hell are you up to, Zed?"

"You didn't talk to the boss. He doesn't *do* random access. I handle it. That's my job, sweetheart." He lowered himself to a tasseled cushion.

He moved stiffly, without his usual grace. Oh, *yes*, someone had done a job on him. Mouthed off to the wrong person, had he? "I *thought* I was talking to him." She kept a tight hold on her temper. "You wear his face, too, huh? Not just his power?"

He looked up at her, his expression enigmatic beneath the swelling. "Yes, I do. Like I said—it's my job."

"Fine." Margarita plunked herself down on a cushion opposite Zed. "I'll just sit here until he comes back and talk to him in the flesh. You can't wear *that*, can you?"

"You know, you do very good holoture. *I* do the Worldweb for Gunner." His eyes held hers, unreadable as polished stones. "He's kept me on because I'm good at that. I'm as good as you are at your art. Maybe better. You came here because you've got some inside information that you want to trade for your dancer's protection. If you mention Procenium Productions to him, you'll blow the whole deal. And he may very well have you killed. Because he won't be sure who you might be connected to, and Gunner never takes chances. That's how he got here: by taking the minimum number of risks. This is a gift from me to you, Margarita Espinoza." Was that true? Margarita shivered, looking away from him. He could be a damn good liar, but she didn't think he was lying. Not this time. "Why the free advice?" she asked bitterly. "And why should I believe anything you tell me?"

"You don't have to." He shrugged, then leaned one elbow on a low table. "Do what you want. But your little tidbit . . . intrigued me."

"Did it?" First Liza with her cryptic hints about the profitability of the data on that damned pendant and now this. She was tired of hints, tired of being made to feel like an uneducated little kid. "Tell me in basic English or shut up," she said between her teeth. "You want what I have, you tell me what you get out of it."

"I'm not sure what I'll get out of this." Zed straightened, his posture suddenly attentive. "Right now I'm out on my ass, never mind appearances. No one should have access to what you gave me. The implication is that you've got yourself quite a cache of serious leverage. Once I've taken a look at it, I might be able to use it to buy my way back into Gunner's good graces. Or maybe not," he said softly. "Maybe I'll just indulge myself in a little vengeance. It might be worth the price."

Light gleamed and vanished in his eyes as if someone had cracked the door of a furnace. Yeah, Zed might be a bad enemy if he ever decided that his own skin didn't matter. He might be a very bad enemy indeed. She wondered if Archenwald-Shen knew it. She drew a quick breath. "You can take a look at what we've got." And too bad if Liza bitched. Margarita held his stare. "I need to find out who wants the file—probably the same person who killed Ari Yiassis. Possibly the same person who attacked me in the street last night. I need to make sure that they leave Katrina alone. That's the price of the information. Katrina's safety. And I have no idea where she is, so that's going to be just a bit difficult." Or it was already too late and it didn't matter. "Give me that guarantee and you can do whatever you damn well please with the data." And too bad if you and Xia don't like that arrangement, Liza. Margarita drew a deep breath. "Do we have a deal, Zed?"

"You're going to have to trust me, but you already know that." Zed's eyes glittered with that buried fire again. "Why are you willing to do that?"

"Because you're ruthless. And you're honest."

"Honest?" Zed raised one eyebrow and gave her a crooked smile. "I don't know if anyone has ever called me honest before."

There was a lot of bitterness in that smirk. "But you are, aren't you?" she asked softly.

Again that flash of flame. "Yes." Zed held her eyes. "I am very honest. I'll find your lover for you. And I'll deal with the person who's leaning on her. Do you want me to kill him or her for you if your lover's already dead?"

He said it so casually. "Yes." She met his shadowed eyes, her own voice just as casual and as full of death. "Yes, I do."

An eye for an eye. A hot rush centered like lust between her legs and rose slowly into her chest. Tooth for tooth . . . We've created our gods in our own image, Margarita thought. It's one hell of an image. She'd add that to her platform holoture—because that vengeful God existed up here, too. She got stiffly to her feet. "I'll go collect the pendant. A cracker friend of Xia's has been working on getting into the files on it, but she's not making much progress. She's not going to like my giving it to you, but I don't give a shit."

"I don't think I'm going to have much trouble cracking the files." Zed looked up at her and bared his teeth. "Tell me about this attack on you."

"Someone stunned me on the street last night." Margarita rubbed her arm reflexively. "I think he was looking for the pendant, but maybe not."

"What did he look like?"

"Muscular." She frowned, trying to remember. "Dark hair,

olive skin—downsider, I think. He didn't look soft enough for up here."

Zed laughed a soft, dry note. "Not Thomas. One of his helpful cousins, I'll bet. They're quite the family. That's probably why Gunner went for a loner when he hired me." He laughed again at Margarita's uncomprehending expression. "Thomas Ariades. My predecessor. Oh, no, I'm not Gunner's first boy. I'm not that old, sweetheart." He bared his teeth at her again. "Thomas was very slick, maybe a hair better than me." He considered briefly, then shrugged. "And then again, maybe not. But I am, as you noticed, honest. Gunner values that. Thomas was a little . . . greedy. He was good enough to sneak a few things by Gunner, and Gunner's ego is very sensitive. He doesn't like it when his employees let him see that they're smarter than he. He hires you to be smarter, *expects* you to be smarter, but he doesn't want it in his face.

"So Thomas got canned. Apparently he took a few things with him. He's the one who got Yiassis his job, by the way. Maybe he was another relative. I don't know." He shrugged. "If it *was* Thomas who set up the file, I should be able to crack it. I learned quite a bit about how he works in the Net when I took over here." He got to his feet, stretched, and winced. "Call me," he said as he ushered her to the door. "Like I said, I deal with any and all access. Make it soon, okay?"

"Okay." Margarita hesitated. His smile was warm, genuine, his face the perfect picture of polite and civilized friendliness. But you could still see it down there in those murky green depths: a flicker of fire, like smoldering coals. "I'll do it soon." She walked ahead of him into the foyer.

Sorrel leaned against the wall near the front door, eyes on the ceiling. "Nice tile work." He pursed his lips. "Custom job?"

"Yeah." Zed looked up at the mosaic ceiling, then gave Sorrel a quick disinterested glance. "Very primo artist."

"Thought so." Sorrel shambled through the opening door. "Very pretty." He waited for Margarita, then hurried ahead to hold the gate open for her.

Jeeze. She stalked through and didn't wait for him. All she wanted to do was get back to Xia's apartment, get the pendant, and get it to Zed. And how long would it take him to locate Katrina? If she could be located.

"In spite of what Xia may think, *I* think you've got a lot of solid sense under all that anger." Sorrel caught up with her suddenly and fell in beside her. "You trust Zed." He pursed his lips. "I wouldn't, myself, but I assume that you know him better than I do."

His easy, bumbling manner had vanished. Margarita shot him a quick sideways glance, catching a gleam of amusement on his face.

"Yeah." She frowned, not sure she could explain, or wanted to, or that there even *was* a rational explanation. Maybe it wasn't trust so much as desperation. "I guess I have to trust him."

"Okay." Sorrel nodded. "So we'll believe that the dude who nailed you last night wasn't working for him or for Shen. Hmm." His face took on that sleepy hick look again, and he wandered over to a street vendor to peer hungrily at the mound of steamed buns being offered for sale.

Strange dude. She wasn't sure whether he was smart and playing dumb or just plain dumb with the occasional flash of brilliance to confuse you. Maybe she'd ask Xia. Margarita looked over her shoulder, but Sorrel had vanished; he wasn't hanging over the vendor's cart and wasn't anywhere in sight. The wide street—street, not lane—was busy. Vendors hawked food from small pushcarts, and a slender woman danced with a drum. She had no bowl for collecting money, not that anyone even used cash up here. Margarita wondered how she got paid for her entertainment. Or was she dancing in public just for fun?

Margarita took one last look around and gave up on Sorrel. Big deal. She strode down the middle of the street, refusing to yield to anyone, aware of the glowers she was getting. No, I don't know the rules, she answered silently. And I don't care. She reached the intersection with the street that would take her to Xia's apartment. A translucent plastic wall blocked her path. Margarita detoured toward the pedestrian gate at one side of the street. It opened for her, releasing a breath of moist, earth-scented air. A second door formed an air lock of sorts. As the outer door closed the inner door opened, the earth scent grew stronger, danker.

This was one of the platform farms. Margarita breathed shallowly, her nose adjusting to the heavy smells filling the moist air. Green overwhelmed her eyes after the sterile streets, lush and crowded. On each side of the expanded mesh walkway that led through the farm, fruit and vegetable plants lifted their leaves into the sunlight, growing from nutrient-filled troughs. Tomatoes trailed leaves onto the walkway nearby, and a woman picking brilliant red fruits looked up and waved as Margarita passed. Farther on, corn rustled in the gently circulating air.

All the produce was genetically tailored so that every last fiber was edible, full of vitamins, or protein, or whatever was needed. Very efficient. Not like messy, chaotic, random Earth. Nothing here was without purpose. Margarita walked a little faster, claustrophobic suddenly, finding the damp air thick and hard to breathe. Banana trees grew along this section. They crowded the walkway, their broad, damp leaves at head height, brushing her shoulders as she walked past and soaking her tunic. Thick stems of green bananas hung down nearly to the ground. It was so quiet in here. She hadn't noticed it before, but now she heard only the sound of her feet on the walkway, the drip of water, and the soft rustle of the banana leaves.

Suddenly that silence felt eerie. Margarita picked up her pace again. Relax, she told herself. They're just plants, nothing more. She was behaving like a little kid, running from ghosts in the dark. Her stepbrothers would give her *mucho* shit. With a smile, she slowed her pace. Up ahead, another path intersected this one. A cart full of coiled hose and various tools stood directly in the middle of the intersection. Careless. Trying not to brush against too many wet leaves, Margarita edged past. A shape moved suddenly in the concealing shadows. Margarita recoiled but had time for only a single indrawn breath before hands clamped on her arms from behind and yanked her backward.

Struggling for balance, she stumbled and went reeling across the pathway. Her toe snagged on the mesh, and she fell hard on one knee, palms burning, face nearly in the water at the base of the banana plants. Skin twitching, expecting the slam of a stunner any second, she scrambled to her feet and dropped into a crouch.

No attacker. Instead, a familiar figure was straightening up from the banana trees' shadows on the far side of the intersection. Sorrel. "What the *hell*?" Margarita eyed him, not sure whether to run or go punch him.

"Sorry." Sorrel smiled gently. "If I'd given you a chance, you'd probably have decked me." He looked down into the muddy shadows beneath the bananas. "I figured he was going to jump you in here somewhere. If you gave him the chance. That's why I brought you this way this morning."

"What?" Margarita edged away, watching him closely, rubbing her stinging palms on her tights. "Whose side are you on, anyway?"

"My own." His expression was pleasant. "But I'll help Xia's kid out if it doesn't cost me too much."

"Thanks." Margarita relaxed slightly. She wasn't ready to trust him completely. Not yet. Rubbing the elbow he'd twisted, still keeping an eye on him, she glanced between the trunks of the bananas. Her attacker from yesterday lay wedged between the banana stems. She recognized the olive skin and profile.

"Don't," Sorrel said as she bent to touch him. "He's dead."

Dead? Margarita straightened slowly, the barrio rushing in to fill this leaf-shadowed space with a cold new context. "It's an act." She met Sorrel's sleepy eyes, giving him a thin smile. "I'd have known you down in the flea markets—one of those sleepy-eyed harmless dudes, too dumb to be trouble, just waiting for suckers to trust them. Are you going to tell me what's really going on here?"

"Well, it never hurts to let people underestimate you." Sorrel spread his hands and smiled. "I thought I saw this guy on our heels this morning, figured I'd like to pick the spot if he was going to try something. You don't get much privacy on public turf upside, so I brought him through here. He was from downside, didn't know his way around. I figured he'd jump at the offer. I got a good look at him in one of the shop windows and noticed he was carrying this." He extended a closed fist, then opened it. A tiny tube lay in his palm. "An injector." He stuck it into his pocket. "Some kind of bioweapon, probably. I don't like bioweapons."

Margarita shivered at the cold new light in his eyes. No, she did *not* want to find herself facing this dude in a fight, thank you.

"If he'd been carrying something else, I wouldn't have had

to kill him." Sorrel stripped off transparent skintight gloves. "Let's keep strolling on."

"Wait a minute." Margarita glanced up and down the deserted path, tension pulling her shoulders tight. "This guy's *dead*."

"Yeah." Sorrel stuffed the gloves into a pocket, smiled gently, and took her arm. "Security is rather poor up here, you know. This is a consensus society, something that you downsiders don't really understand. Maybe because we're all stuck inside this tin can together. And then there's the local Net—sort of a public gestalt in a way. We all look over each other's shoulders, even when we piss. Which can drive downside immigrants nutso in a very short time." He chuckled. "This'll get discussed. If the popular consensus is that the murderer ought to be punished for this guy's death, then there will be plenty of people who will remember that we took this route at this time. But this is a downsider." He gave her a gentle smile. "We don't think much of you downsiders. If this dude's the nobody I think he is, the consensus may be 'who cares?' I didn't leave enough of a trace to make the local police force do anything they don't want to do."

Margarita shivered again. "I don't think I want to live up here."

"Probably not." Sorrel didn't smile this time.

"Does Xia . . ." Margarita blushed, because she had been musing out loud, and what she had almost said was *Does Xia know that you're like this?*

"Xia fits in up here." Sorrel's smile softened his expression. "She isn't really a part of this world, but she understands it, and it doesn't bother her. As for you—" His smile disappeared. "You need to finish your business with Shen's boy and get off the platform. If Shen's involved and *he* decides to off you, you're dead."

Now Margarita understood why Xia had deferred when he had offered to come along that morning. Lips pressed together, she walked along in silence. "I've got to get the pendant to Zed. He thinks he can crack the file."

"Liza's going to throw a fit." Sorrel nodded. "She's proprietary. I'll handle her."

He wasn't offering, he was *telling* her. No, this man was no casual lover, tolerated by Xia only because he was a good cook. Margarita had been as wrong about him as she'd been about Zed. And about Katrina. She let her breath out in a slow sigh, wondering suddenly if she saw *anyone* clearly. She flinched as Sorrel put a hand on her arm, but it was a warm gesture, surprisingly full of comfort.

"Thanks," she said, and meant it, understanding suddenly what Xia saw in this man. Strength, yes: frightening strength. But understanding, too. She sighed again as they reached the end of the farm, where something leafy and tall grew. She pushed the lock door open and exited into dry cool air that raised brief goose bumps on her bare arms.

They were in a street that emptied into the holoed park where she had first spotted Xia. The daffodils had almost all gone by, Margarita noticed. And the breeze smelled more like summer today, tinted with the scent of grass clippings drying in the sun. Nice detail work—the artist was talented with scent. She wondered suddenly how important seasons were to the human soul. Maybe one day upsiders and downsiders would evolve into two separate species. A man lounged on the bench, hand stretched out to the holoed squirrel. Michael. He turned his head as if her start of recognition had been a shout.

"Margarita!" He got quickly to his feet. "Where did you *go*?" Noticing Sorrel, he nodded. "Hello." He held out a hand, his expression uncertain now. "I'm Michael Tryon."

"Sorrel." Sorrel touched Michael's palm briefly.

Margarita wondered what Sorrel thought of this meeting with Xia's old love, but whatever it was, he wasn't giving it away. "What happened?" she asked Michael. "I thought you were on your way out to the asteroid belt."

"I got Zed in trouble with his boss." Michael's shoulders slumped. "That sort of blew our trip. I was on my way down to the port to check out freelance transport for myself. Zed doesn't think I'm going to find any."

He looked bad, as if he were aging at an accelerated pace. Suddenly, intensely, he reminded Margarita again of Arrow. Pain squeezed her chest, hard and hurting, an angry stab of . . . betrayal. Betrayal? The intensity of it shocked her, filling her with sudden shame. Arrow hadn't betrayed her; he had *died*.

It had felt like a betrayal. Because she had needed him so much. Margarita bent her head, struggling to hold in sudden, burning tears. I was so angry at you, Arrow. Because I doubted myself, and you were the only person who could tell me I was wrong. Or right. Is it worth it, Arrow? All the pain? All the hurt I've caused Katrina, caused others?

You could have told me, but I didn't ask.

And maybe now I'll never be sure.

Michael hadn't betrayed her, either. Margarita let her breath out in a slow sigh and touched Michael on the arm. "Are you all right?"

"Not really." He managed a smile, then reached tentatively for her hand. "I'd better get on with my ship hunting. I don't know if Zed can get you any time with Archenwald-Shen. I'm sorry I couldn't do anything for Katrina."

"I'm dealing with it." Sort of. No need to mention that a man was lying soggy and dead among the banana trees a few hundred yards from there. Margarita closed her fingers tightly around Michael's hand. "Come back to Xia's apartment with me, will you." She couldn't keep the urgency out of her voice. "Maybe she'll know somebody who can get you out to the belt."

"What's wrong?" Michael focused on her face. "Are you in trouble?"

"I'm always in trouble." Bitter words, edged with truth. She shot a quick glance at Sorrel, but read nothing in his bland, pleasant expression. Oh, shit. "Come *on*."

"Are you so sure Xia is going to welcome me?" Michael looked at Sorrel, the surmise clear on his face. "For that matter, I'm not so sure that *I* want to meet her again. I really need to work on this transport thing."

He was going to walk away. "No." Margarita's tone made Michael blink. "Damn it, you walked into my life and started kicking things loose. You come with me, because I'm not sure that I'll ever see you again after today, and you owe me that much, Michael Tryon. Do you hear me?"

You owe me . . . Margarita shook her head, dizzy suddenly, not sure where the hell these words had come from.

"I'm coming." Michael's eyes were on her face, full of shadows and emotion that she couldn't identify. He reached for her hand. "I can spare that much time," he said softly. "I'm just a little bit afraid. Xia's going to show me a reflection of the Michael Tryon she knew, I think. I'm not sure I want to see that man. I'm not sure I want to face him."

Yes, he *did* remind her of Arrow Frome. That was something Arrow might have said. He was holding her hand gently, ready to release her. She didn't pull away. "I was angry at you," she mused as they walked across the park. "All my life, but it was worse when I knew who you were. You were what I wanted to be. And you . . . weren't there when I was a kid." Abandonment. Betrayal. And she had never let Katrina get too close because then it wouldn't hurt so much when she left.

Did I create my own abandonment, Arrow? My own betrayal?

He could have told her that, too. If she had let him.

She realized suddenly that Sorrel had quietly vanished again. To set up another ambush? And whose side was he *really* on? Margarita glanced up and down the busy street, then shrugged. She would possibly find out. "This way," she said to Michael, and laughed. "Xia is probably expecting us."

Michael gave her a strange look, but she didn't explain and he didn't ask.

Xia was curled up on one of the floor cushions when they walked into the apartment. She was dangling the pendant so that it caught the light, her face thoughtful. "Liza didn't have much luck with the file," she said as they came through the door. "She left it here when she went on-shift." She looked up and noticed Michael for the first time. "Hello." Her eyes widened just a hair, and she got gracefully to her feet, dropping the pendant into her tunic pocket. "Michael?" She smiled softly. "How are you?" She held out both her hands to him. "It has been a very long time."

"It has, hasn't it?" He stepped forward stiffly, hesitating as if he didn't really want to touch her. "I'm . . . sorry, Xia. For the way I treated you. I've wanted to say that for a long time."

"Have you?" She laughed, her head tilted slightly back, her gray braid hanging down between her shoulder blades. "We were who we were. We couldn't have been anything else, Michael." She looked at Margarita, half smiling. "I wondered if you would shake him loose from his Stones. I thought I would give it a try."

Margarita felt herself gaping but couldn't help it. Michael

looked a little pissed himself. "I wish you'd told me a hell of a lot earlier," she said. She met her mother's amused glance, angry, her face getting hotter. "Things might have been a lot different."

"Do you think so?" Xia lifted one eyebrow. "No, Rita. What good would it have done? You were my kid, even if I knew better than to keep you. Michael was still lost in his Stones." She nodded at him. "It wasn't time yet. I wasn't sure it would ever be time." Her face took on a pensive expression. "I almost didn't tell you. But you were so serious about your holos. So serious that you could hide from Katrina in them. You reminded me of your father. So I decided it was time that you knew him. Maybe you'd see yourself in him, and maybe not." She smiled at Michael. "She's like you, even if she didn't inherit your face."

"She is." Michael's voice was hoarse, although his eyes were dry. "I know it's way too late for might-have-beens, but I want you to know how much I loved you."

"I know." Her smile lit her face like sunshine. "And I loved you, Michael Tryon, but you loved your Stones more. I'm very possessive. I have to be first." She reached suddenly to take his hand in hers. "Nothing is forever." She brought his hand to her cheek, but her eyes were on Margarita's face. "Remember that, Rita. This moment is precious because it will be gone in an instant. You save us some of those moments in your holos, but the rest vanish."

"Xia, I . . . missed you." Michael's fingers tightened around hers. "I didn't realize how much until recently. I'd like to get to know you again."

"Would you?" She shook her head. "I'm not the same woman you loved. But I think you'll want to see her in me. You've been working with your Stones too long, Michael Tryon. You capture bits of the soul and turn them into something unchanging and static. Life isn't like that—it's growth and change. I am alive."

"I think maybe I am, too. Finally." Michael sighed and took his hand away. "Maybe you're right. I'm not sure I could ever stop seeing the Xia I knew every time I looked at you. I'm not sure I could let myself know *you*."

The door opened and Sorrel lounged in. "Yo." He went to the kitchen wall and served himself some water. "I dropped into the Net for a while. Some downsider got offed in Brightside Farm." He drank thirstily, then refilled his glass. "Seems he was a flesh-time enforcer for some midlevel web node. Discussion's running to the opinion that maybe he's no loss and not our business. It'll be a while before it's settled, though. Later tonight, I'd guess."

Sorrel had recited this for her benefit. Margarita went to get her own glass of water, disturbed by the speed with which this platform society reacted. He hadn't been kidding about everyone looking over everyone else's shoulder. It made her think suddenly of a beehive. One wrong move and the whole hive reacted.

It was Alien space up here. She looked at Xia over the rim of her glass, wondering how she could stand it. No wonder the platformers didn't go in much for Earth artists. I'm not even sure we speak the same language anymore, Margarita thought, and wanted to shiver. That's what she would bring to her holo: that sense of alien.

The First Tuesday crowd would probably hate it.

"I think we should let Archenwald-Shen's boy crack the file," Sorrel said.

"Why?" Xia's chin lifted. "He's not as good as Liza."

"He knows the code." Sorrel put his glass into the cleaner. "Someone tried to kill Margarita on the way home. Time counts."

Both Xia and Michael were staring at her, Xia with narrowed eyes and a considering expression. Michael looked shocked. And worried.

"I don't think this is the place to unravel our little treasure trove." Sorrel reached into Xia's pocket, kissing her lightly on top of the head as he withdrew the pendant. "Somewhere else might be more healthy." He dangled the tear-shaped lump of petrified tree sap from its cord, lips pursed. "Liza did a neat job of removing the chip. You can barely see the scar."

"She put it into a standard disk." Xia handed him the small translucent disk of plastic. It could hold one memory sphere or a hundred and would fit into any reader.

"Zed is at the door," the House intoned softly. "He wants to come in."

Zed here? The skin tightened between Margarita's shoulder

blades. "I didn't tell him where I was staying," she said quickly.

"Doesn't matter." Sorrel didn't act worried. "He could find out."

Barrio mentality showing up again—you *never* gave away your home address. Margarita let her breath out in a sigh as Zed walked into the room. He had a carryall slung over his shoulder and moved quickly, nervously, glancing here and there as if he expected people to be hiding behind the furniture. Michael was frowning at him, his brow furrowed.

"What's wrong?" he asked.

"Michael." If Zed was surprised to find Michael here, he didn't show it. "No luck down at the port, huh?"

"I didn't try yet."

Zed didn't answer; he just gave Xia and Sorrel a brief distracted bow and turned to Margarita. "I think Gunner was listening in on our conversation. I'm not entirely sure, but when I reviewed the security files, I found some discrepancies. Gunner is the only person besides myself with that kind of system access, although he never uses it." He frowned, tossing his hair back over his shoulder. "It's a very bad sign that Gunner listened in like that. And that he kept so quiet. I think you and I need to leave the platform as quickly as possible. With the file. Did that body in Brightside Farm have something to do with you?" He gave Sorrel a sharp, doubtful glance, then turned back to Margarita. "It seemed a bit coincidental."

"Yes, it had to do with me. It was the same man who stunned me. He was going to kill me this time." Margarita walked over and reached for the disk in Sorrel's hand. A little to her surprise, he handed it to her without comment.

Sorrel's expression was unreadable. If this dude didn't want you to know what he was thinking, you just didn't *know*.

"That's it?" Zed couldn't quite keep the excitement out of his voice. "Let me have it." He held out his hand.

They were all watching: Xia, Sorrel, Michael. Slowly, Margarita dropped the disk onto his outstretched palm. Eyes blazing, he pulled a clunky handheld access from his carryall.

"This is a secure archive—no direct Net access. Absolutely safe." He slipped the disk into the port and touched the screen to life. Scowling, he leaned against the table, shoulders hunched, focused on the small glowing holo that materialized above the handheld.

Margarita caught a glimpse of colors, shapes, a few cryptic words. Zed touched here, there, then swept two fingers through the holo. "Yes." Suppressed triumph vibrated in his voice. "This is Thomas, oh, *yeah*. He thought he was such a hotshot on the Net—better than me, anyway. At some things he was better—but not *this*, sweetheart." He stabbed with an outstretched finger, and the holo blinked off. "It's going to take me some time to figure out exactly what he's got here." He spoke only to Margarita, as if everyone else had vanished while he had worked on the file. "Judging from what's going on, it's very big. I think we'd better do our figuring out somewhere else. And fast."

"Liza would gut you for even saying that." Xia's tone was mild, but her eyes were coldly thoughtful.

Margarita watched Zed shrug, obviously unconcerned.

It concerned *her*. She was through underestimating people, thank you. Margarita looked at Sorrel. He met her glance and smiled gently. "I'll handle Liza."

"You looking for a little challenge in your life?" Xia rolled her eyes. "Your choice. I don't think I'm up to it."

Sorrel shrugged. "So where do you plan to go to ground?" He looked at Zed. "Got any particular destination in mind?"

He wasn't using his hick manner. Zed shot him a quick, troubled glance while he stuffed the archive back into his carryall. "Downside, I guess. I can do a solid disappearing act in New York or Dallas. Dallas is better—Gunner doesn't have any close interests in Dallas."

"How about the asteroid belt?" Michael said.

"Forget it." Margarita glared at him because she didn't have any choice anymore; she had to stick with Zed and the file, had to get Katrina out from under this shadow. "Can't you give up this crazy death quest of yours? Can't you just let it *alone*? Oh, never mind." She rubbed her eyes, tired suddenly, tired to the center of her being. "I know you can't. It's your life. Okay, I'll stop, but—I wish you'd come to Earthside with us."

"Actually, I think Michael's right." Sorrel raised an eyebrow. "It's pretty hard to sneak a ship through downside airspace without somebody spotting it. Oh, you can buy a hole—pay off the right people to not see you—but you've got Gunner Archenwald-Shen on your collective asses, remember. You better make sure of your bought hole or Shen will know where and when you landed just about the time you touch down. But there's plenty of room to lift *outward*." He shrugged. "Nobody much cares. It's the incomings that get noticed."

He knew how to do this. Margarita understood suddenly. Sorrel was a freebie—she'd bet her next holo on it. He took some kind of ship out to the belt, dropped asteroids into unpopular orbits, and sold them to some miner who would strip out the ore and ship them Earthside, thus bypassing both the platform and Earthside tariffs. Nice work if you could survive it. Both platform and Earth governments were greedy for their cut of the riches to be found out in the belt.

"Great." Michael was nodding. "We still need transport. Or do you know someone?"

"You'll lift us." Margarita showed her teeth at Sorrel. "That's what you're telling us, right?" And that way, he'd get to keep his eye on whatever might be in Katrina's file. "Don't worry." She smiled into his sleepy nonchalance. "I'm never going to underestimate you again."

Sorrel nodded, amusement in his smile. "Yeah, I'll lift you. The cost is seventy-five percent of whatever you can get out of that file. Liza is going to expect her cut, and not even I am going to short her on that." The amusement vanished from his face. "Deal?"

If they took it, they were committed. Margarita had a feeling that backing out of a deal with this man would be a very bad idea. She looked at Zed, who was glowering at Sorrel but would probably agree. Michael didn't care. Excitement glossed his face. She took a step closer so that he had to look her in the eyes. "What do you think you're going to find up there?"

"Someone." He met her stare, his own eyes full of strange light. "That someone is trying to tell me something, only I don't know the language. Maybe that's what it was trying to do with Lustik and Danners and the others—communicate."

"An alien?" Margarita swallowed an urge to laugh. "Is that what you're saying? That you're hearing alien voices now? I like the layered-in-insanity idea better myself." It all added up to the same bottom line: he was going to die, as Arrow had.

I'm tired, he had said to her not too long before he died. *I've lived a long time, and I've done a lot of changing over the centuries. That's what life is all about, isn't it? Growth and change? I don't think I can do much more changing.*

Xia had said something about change just now. Margarita crossed her arms tightly. About change being life. "Okay, Sorrel. Are you going to lift us? I guess we'd better get moving if Gunner Archenwald-Shen is on our butts, right?"

"Right." Sorrel smiled his sleepy hick smile at her. "Any time you're ready."

Chapter Fifteen

Sorrel's ship was docked in a local bay not far from the apartment. Margarita followed the three of them, hanging back a little. Where was Katrina right now? No, don't think about that. She closed her eyes briefly. The scenes she kept coming up with were ones she didn't want to see. They were passing warehouses, functional, sterile blocks designed to hold the most stuff in the minimum of this expensive space. Margarita hunched her shoulders, uneasy. Except for the farm, she had seen no real plants. Holos, yes. But beneath her feet the street was sterile and gray: no trash. No weeds growing up through the cracks. Even in the newest of the cities weeds made their way through sidewalk cracks and straggling potted plants perched on front steps or windowsills.

It felt sterile, she thought, but she was from downside. Maybe it was order that mattered up here. Control. If you didn't control your environment, you died.

If you didn't control your life, you died. Barrio rules. Maybe these places weren't so different. Put that into your holo. Margarita shivered, nearly walking into Michael, who had slowed to wait for her.

"Are you all right?" He looked concerned.

"This place bothers me." She looked up at the windowless face of a building.

"It *is* different, isn't it?" He nodded. "I think humanity is evolving into a new species up here. Pretty soon we'll diverge entirely."

"That's just it . . . that it's *not* different." Margarita hunched her shoulders. "It's like the barrio in some ways. I can do this place, I think. If I can come up with the lex."

Michael was looking at her with an odd expression.

"Yeah, I know it sounds weird." She shrugged, a little pissed that he didn't get it.

"No, it doesn't sound weird at all." He didn't smile. "I think you're even better than I guessed." He lifted his head, nodded, and turned away before she could speak.

They had reached the end of the street, where a pair of pedestrian doors flanked a big vehicle port. Sorrel and Zed waited beside them: Zed twitching like a cat, Sorrel in hick mode with his arms crossed, his eyes half-closed. Margarita stepped away from Michael as one of the doors opened and a couple strolled out, dressed in identical brief outfits of melon and brilliant green, their buzzed scalps inlaid with identical fiberlight work.

None of the colors really came from nature. It hit Margarita suddenly. All the brilliant clothing, even the pastels of walls and floors and furniture—none of it matched any living plant or animal she could think of. You think you aren't us, don't you? She looked at the woman as the natives shuffled past, getting twin glares and a hostile lift of their shoulders in return. But you are, even if you don't want to see it.

Upsiders wouldn't like her platform holo any more than the First Tuesday crowd would. Margarita followed Michael, Zed, and Sorrel through the door, full of buzzing excitement. Bubbles of air falling through cold, endless night, filled with children's magic, whispering ghosts, and bright colors. It was taking shape in her mind, scored by flute and percussion, with the distant murmur of violas. They had entered another lock; the door opened ahead of them, and Margarita blinked. Big space, harsh light. Quite a few lumpy little ships stood in tight ranks. They didn't need to be sleek and birdlike up here; there was no atmosphere to require wings and aerodynamics. Environment shapes us, Margarita thought as she followed Sorrel between the ugly, alien ships.

"These mostly belong to the freight companies." Sorrel ambled along, playing tour guide with a genial smile. "They do the pickups on the asteroid drops, haul the rocks over to the sling for downside transport. They shunt a lot of cargo around, but they aren't very fast." He jerked his head sideways at a set of three-fingered metal talons nestled into a recess on one ship's hull. "Some of the really hot rock-jocks can untie your shoelaces with those things."

"Like you, Sorrel?" Margarita lifted an eyebrow, wanting to needle him suddenly, make him show those shark teeth of his. "Can you untie someone's shoelaces?"

"I never saw anybody outside wearing laced shoes." He smiled an aw-shucks smile. "If I ever do, I'll sure try." He stopped beside a small steel and blue craft and touched a lock plate. "This one can make the belt at a good clip. Esmee drive, maneuverable, not too big. Make yourselves at home. I'll call for a taxi to haul us to the launch lock."

A big cargo door opened like an unfurling wing from the ship's side. Margarita could see a ramp beneath the deck, but it didn't descend. Sorrel hopped lightly up into the dark cargo bay, and lights immediately glowed in the ceiling. Zed climbed easily after him, then offered Michael a hand. Margarita touched the bright blue paint that striped the side of the ship. It gleamed, depthless and rich. She had thought that the ship was new, but up close she could see the small dings and scratches that meant it wasn't. So Sorrel kept his ship pretty. That didn't surprise her. Margarita scrambled up onto the deck, the sound of her feet echoing a little in the empty bay.

Michael and Zed were looking through the door into the tiny bridge. She joined them. It was nothing more than an unaesthetic bulge on the front of the tubby ship: one padded seat with a VR hood and gloves laid out on a console. No windows. No obvious viewscreen. "How do you see out? Just the VR?"

Sorrel raised an eyebrow at her. "Yeah." He sounded slightly disdainful, as if her question had been an incredibly stupid one. "Kelly?" he said. "SR232 requesting taxi to the gun."

"Pronto." A clear, boyish voice filled the bridge space. "It's on its way, boss."

"Kelly?" Michael picked up the VR hood, frowned at it, and put it down.

"My ship system." Sorrel slid into his seat and began to tug on the gloves. "You gotta talk to somebody out there." He shrugged, pulled the hood over his head, and made a stabbing motion with one hand.

Behind them, the cargo doors closed. A moment later a solid *thunk* shivered through the ship's hull.

"Have a seat." Sorrel's fingers danced over invisible controls. "We hit a window in traffic. That was the taxi hooking up."

Beneath their feet, the deck jerked sideways. Margarita staggered slightly, and Michael caught her arm. They were moving, being towed into the launch lock, she assumed.

"Sit down." Zed had pulled a padded seat down out of the wall and was strapping himself in. "The launch'll knock you off your feet if you don't. This is no passenger shuttle." He sounded like he'd done this before.

Margarita discovered that four seats had been built into the bulkhead. She pulled one down and strapped herself between Zed and Michael. She hadn't noticed any wheels on this ship, so the taxi must have picked them up somehow. She had a sudden image of an enormous steel crab with the blue and silver ship clasped in giant pincers. A giggle tickled her throat, but she swallowed it. Nerves, she thought, and they'd hear it in her laugh. She wanted to *see*, never mind that it didn't make any difference, that Sorrel had a hundred eyes spotted all over the ship's hull. She wanted to know what was out there.

"Claustrophobia?" Michael touched her knee lightly.

"I don't think so." Margarita gave him a sideways look. He was sharp. "I just don't like traveling blind."

"It *is* a helpless feeling, isn't it?" He leaned his head back against the hull, his expression dreamy. "It knows I'm on my way. Whatever it is. I can *feel* its knowing. It's waiting for me."

"You're giving me the creeps." She scowled and scooted a few inches away from him. "What about you?" She glared at Zed. "Are you hearing alien voices, too? Or do you hear anything at all?"

"I hear what I hear." Zed stared at the far wall as the ship jostled beneath them. "Aliens? Why not?" He looked at her at last. "Maybe it's the voice of God, Margarita Espinoza. Talking to me and not to you. Did you ever think of that?"

He was kidding . . . maybe. A reflected glimmer gleamed in his eyes, and Margarita looked away. Maybe he wasn't kidding. I don't do people, she thought. She dealt with people through externals. Maybe if she had been a little more sensitive to the internal landscape, she and Katrina would have been able to talk.

Yeah. Maybe.

The ship jolted to a halt. "Brace yourselves," Kelly announced brightly. "You got about thirty seconds to launch. It's rough. And then the Esmee kicks in, and that's worse, guys."

She hated that teenager voice. Margarita braced herself, copying Zed. Michael was copying him, too. Without warning, the ship shuddered like a dog shivering. Then it leapt forward. Even braced as she was, Margarita's back left the bulkhead behind her, and she slammed against the straps. She heard Michael's grunt of surprise but couldn't look. A moment later the slingshot acceleration slackened abruptly, and she slammed back against the wall. "Ouch." She rubbed her bruised spine. Michael looked a little shaken, too. Zed was grinning. Of course.

"If you don't tense up, it's easier to ride." Zed winked. "It's kind of fun, you know."

The ship was rotating. Suddenly they were lying on their backs, growing lighter by the second as their acceleration slackened.

"Get ready." The ship voice snickered. "One, two, three . . ."

Weight. Crushing the air from her lungs, squeezing her heart, driving it down onto her stomach, down into her pelvis. Finally it eased. Margarita gasped, frightened by the effort it took to push air in and out of her lungs. Nausea sat like a stone in her belly, and clammy sweat slicked her skin.

"That's all the excitement, ladies and gentlemen." The ship system sounded as if it had a grin on its nonexistent face. "You can walk around, take a dump, do whatever you want. It'll take us five hours to get out to Vildorn, even with my new tune-up. Take it easy. You guys all gained a little weight."

Wiseass teenager voice. Margarita got to her feet, wincing at her bruised back, appalled at her heavy, clumsy body. Why pick a snotty kid for a system voice? Acceleration was bad enough. She made it across the empty cargo bay, exhausted by even this small amount of movement, wondering if they'd be like this for five hours. What did Sorrel smuggle through his bought-and-paid-for holes? Raw ore? Manufactured stuff from the zero-g factories? That stuff got hit with the heaviest tariffs, so it was probably worth the most effort. Maybe she'd ask. And maybe not. She glanced at the sealed bridge. She didn't know his rules yet, didn't know where the boundaries lay.

"Bored?" Zed wandered up, managing to make his movements look normal. "I'd heard rumors that Sorrel had a nice ship. I guess they were right." He fingered a shallow gouge in the padded wall. "I also hear he's quite the success."

Margarita shrugged. "Do you really hear God, Zed?" She raised one eyebrow, wanting him to just go away and leave her alone because she weighed about two hundred pounds and felt like shit. "What does God say to you?"

"Are you really asking, or are you just being a bitch?" His green eyes were steady on her face.

"I'm being a bitch." Margarita flushed, because she owed him quite a bit at this point. "I'm sorry. What *do* you hear?"

"I don't know." His smile vanished. "Maybe it's God. Maybe it's your dad's aliens talking to me. Maybe I've finally decided to go happily gonzo and I'm imagining all of you." He studied her face, one corner of his mouth lifted into a mocking half smile. "That last choice might be the easiest to deal with. Hell, it might be fun to be truly nuts." He fished in his pocket. "You didn't ask for this, but I think I'll let you hold it."

Margarita stared at the sphere he dropped onto her outstretched palm. "What's on it?" She closed her hand around it and stuck it deep in her tunic pocket. "You know, don't you? Or you're pretty sure."

"I've got an idea." Zed nodded, his expression sober. "I'm probably right, more or less. Gunner's a strange guy." His stare turned inward, darkening. "His security isn't all that tight on a lot of web deals. Tight enough to keep the rubes out, but not airtight. It's like he doesn't care if the hot crackers get in. Not that he'll take serious pirating lightly." Zed smiled a thin, mirthless smile. "He doesn't waste time with the law. He contracts a punishment team, and the cracker doesn't fuck with him twice. That's how he hired me." His smile turned mocking. "Caught me in a file and tracked me back. I had a hit team on the doorstep before I could say shit. I thought I was dog meat when they hauled me up in front of him. Instead, he handed me this contract, all filled out and ready to sign. Not exactly in my favor, but with two muscle boys breathing down my neck, I figured I could live with that." He shrugged. "It's had its compensations. I could've done worse."

Examining his swollen face, the scabbed-over cuts, Margarita raised an eyebrow.

Zed shrugged again, lips twisting. "Anyway, I sort of stumbled into this little scam of his last year. I think these are the numbers that prove it." He nodded at the pocket where she'd tucked the sphere. "He lets the top crackers break into his space. But not because he can't afford the talent to keep them out. I think he *wants* them there. I think he's got hooks planted in his filespace that are too good for even the hotshots to notice without a careful sweep. And they sweep, but he's got plenty of high-end hooks that you *can* find, so they figure they've got 'em all. Only they don't." Zed laughed softly.

"So they do their thing and go waltzing out of there patting themselves on the back for being so slick and clever. Only they're wearing a string, and they don't know it." His grin bared his teeth this time. "So then they go into somebody else's Net space. And maybe they get tagged, and maybe they don't, but that string sticks. And later, Gunner slides right down it and into that file." Zed shook his head. "All those hotshot crackers are his unpaid help, and they don't even know it." He smirked. "I bet that bastard's got an in with half the nodes in the web. No wonder he always comes out on top of any deal he gets into."

"You admire him for that."

"You don't approve, huh?" Zed raised one eyebrow. "Yeah, I admire him for that. He's good. He's smarter than any of the other sharks out there—smart enough to take what he wants without getting carried away. Without getting too greedy, like Thomas did. And yeah, he beat me up sometimes." Zed tossed his hair back over his shoulder. "I knew what the price was when I signed on. He made it real clear." His tone was cold. "I could have settled for less, for some kind of number job. Good pay, limited ceiling. I was just twenty, with a public ed from the Net and the best university Net degree I could afford, which wasn't much. My ceiling anywhere in the web was going to be pretty midlevel without some kind of an in. I didn't want to be midlevel."

His eyes glittered. "If I'm going to do something, I'm going to be the best. So I knew what I wanted from Gunner

Archenwald-Shen. I wanted to learn how to do it *right*, the way Gunner was doing it. Don't think it's just the power trip. Don't ever think I *like* wearing someone else's clothes." His voice had dropped to a whisper. "It's the skill I'm after, and I'll do whatever it takes to be good. I'm gonna be the best. Or nothing."

Passion. Margarita looked away from his taut face. "I . . . so what's in the file?" She winced at her lame tone. "How come Shen wants it so badly?"

"It's probably some kind of proof that these strings exist." Zed spoke with resigned patience, as if he were talking to a child. "If word got around the web that this was how he was doing business, everyone would start looking for those strings. And they'd find them, because you can find *anything* if you know where to look. And then his sweet little run would be over. And everybody would be keeping a very close eye on him for a while, so he'd have to play things very straight. Which would cost him serious money on a lot of fronts. Gunner hates to lose money. Zed shrugged. "I'd guess Ari did some of the digging for Thomas. That's probably how he got a copy of the file. Thomas knows that if Gunner finds out, he's dead meat. He's got to be pretty damn desperate."

More reason to believe that Katrina was already dead. Thank you, Zed. Margarita leaned her head against the cool, slick padding. Money, she thought bitterly. Money, which is really power, shapes everything and everyone—or its lack does. It even shapes the environment, which maybe shapes the human soul. The root of all evil—wasn't that what the fundies called it? I'm like Zed, she thought, and there was bitterness in that admission. She wanted to be good, but she had also seen money when she had first looked at Arrow Frome's holoture. It wasn't the *reason*, but it was part of the art. It was a way out of the barrio, a door into a world that had been closed to her as a child.

Arrow had known, never mind how hard she tried to play the pure artist. Late one night he had come unexpectedly to the studio, where she had been changing a piece she'd already finished, because a midlevel web node had said he would buy it if she changed it. She had stood there, cringing inside, waiting for Arrow to pass judgment on her, because the piece had been good before.

You're not a whore, he had said, running through her changes. *Not unless you do it only for the money.*

That was all he had said, the only judgment he had passed. She had gotten a lot for that piece. She had bought a second-hand Brunner scent generator with the money.

Now she was going to look at the barrio again, look at the platform, and find enough similarities to curl the lip of every one of the bored First Tuesday aficionados. What a change, Arrow. Did you think this might happen? Margarita laughed softly and opened her eyes. Michael was standing behind Zed, his expression hesitant.

"Sorrel showed me the water tap." His eyes were full of questions. "There's some food, too, if you're hungry—some kind of high-energy bar. You should probably sit down. I'm no medic, but this kind of plus-g ride can't be too good for your heart."

"It isn't. That's why you don't see too many old smugglers. That and other reasons." Zed shrugged. "You eat emergency rations if you want. Me, I'll stick with water. You don't have to show me the tap." He walked past Michael, still moving as if he were oblivious to the acceleration.

"He knows his way around everywhere, I think." Michael stared after him, lips pursed. Then he turned back to Margarita. "You look upset."

"I was remembering something." She looked at him sideways. "I don't know why you remind me of Arrow. He was dark, like me. You don't look like him at all, except that you're both old." Her cheeks warmed. "Sorry, I didn't mean it to sound like that."

"It didn't," Michael murmured softly. He was looking at her strangely, a shadow on his face. Margarita looked down at her clasped hands.

"Maybe it's the way you feel about . . . what you do. About how much it matters. I don't know." She shrugged. "Maybe that's why I've been so pissed at you. I mean, I'm *not*. I think maybe I was mostly angry at Arrow."

"No, it's me, too." Michael touched her arm. "He died and left you, but I was never there."

"Maybe. Maybe it's just that—that I thought art meant something different for him than it did for me. He never told me what that difference was, and I thought he was . . . disappointed in me. For not understanding." She blinked rapidly, eyes burning, tearless and dry. "I think I was wrong."

"I think you have enormous talent and enormous soul." Michael covered her hand with his. "If I don't come back from this trip, I want you to know this. That I believe in what you can do. And I love you."

"I can't say that to you," Margarita whispered. She turned away from him, weight dragging at her heart, sucking the strength from her. "Not when you're going out there to die. I don't want to hear it from you."

"I don't think it wants to kill me." Michael put his arm around her and drew her gently against him. "I can almost see it sometimes. Like invisible butterflies in the air, or heat waves. I'm not sure that I'm actually *seeing* that. Maybe that's the only way my brain can interpret whatever is happening."

"So why not tell somebody if you're so sure this is some kind of first contact?" She had to stretch for that possibility; the old barrio distrust of cops and authority was something she'd never quite shed. "Why do it yourself?"

"Who's going to believe me?" Michael asked gently. "Anyway, I don't think I have the option." He frowned at something she couldn't see. "I think if I turn aside or even think about backing out, this . . . being, thing, whatever . . . will simply come to me." He laughed softly. "I don't know, maybe Zed's right and it's the voice of God. It doesn't feel like it to me, but I'm not sure I'd know God if I was introduced." He sighed. "I made a will." He touched her face gently, sorrow in his fingers. "You get it all if . . . anything happens. The income from my unsold Stones. The lease in Taos. Which is probably worth more than the Stones." A trace of bitterness seeped into his smile. "It's not a lot, but it should keep you working for a while. It'll give you the option to say no to a gallery offer if you don't like it."

"Me?" Margarita sucked in a quick breath, feeling as if he had just punched her in the stomach. "I mean, you never even checked the DNA profile I gave you. Damn it. You're so sure you're going to die." She had been angry once; now she was simply sad. "I'm sorry," she said slowly. "I would have liked to . . . do another holo with you. It was—" Fun, she had been about to say, but that wasn't it. That sharing had been more than just fun. "It was good," she whispered.

"You really are my daughter." His arms went around her, and he stroked her hair as she leaned her face against his chest. "I don't need to read the DNA scan. I'm sorry, too. That we didn't know each other earlier." He kissed her gently on the forehead. "You're very good," he said. "You've got a lot of life ahead of you to do what you want to do. Just keep growing. Don't let yourself stop. That's the mistake I made. That's when I truly started to die."

"I won't stop." Margarita straightened suddenly, and he released her.

For a moment they simply looked at each other, each waiting for the other to speak. But there was nothing left to say. Not really.

"Will you tell me about your . . . growing up?" Michael spoke finally, awkwardly. "Will you tell me about Arrow Frome? I'd like to hear."

"No." Margarita met his eyes, groping for the reasons behind that quick and certain refusal. "Not now. You can't really . . . know me. Not now, not when you think you're about to die. It won't really matter, and it needs to matter." She looked back at him, seeing the hurt in his face, feeling it in her own gut and not sure why it should be there, why it should hurt so damn *badly*. "If there's time after all this," she said harshly, "then I'll tell you."

He didn't say anything as she hauled her too-heavy body back over to her seat and strapped herself in. Zed looked from Michael to Margarita but said nothing. For a moment their eyes met. Compassion? He turned away too quickly for her to be sure. She sighed and leaned back against the padding, waiting to reach Vildorn.

Chapter Sixteen

"We're here." Kelly's voice, bright and a little bit excited, made Margarita jump. She had been half drowsing, oppressed by her weight, watching Michael because she couldn't shake her nagging fear. She believed in his alien voice, no matter how much she wanted not to.

"Where's *here*?" she asked the ship voice, not addressing it, not expecting an answer. "All I see are walls."

"So stick your head through the door." Kelly's tone carried all the scathing disdain of a fourteen-year-old for a stupid adult. "We don't waste visuals on cargo, lady."

Brat, Margarita thought. She *hated* systems with cute personalities. Affectation. Stupid affectation. She stood up and stretched, shocked because her weight was back to normal—maybe a little less than normal. Michael gave her a glazed, preoccupied look and said nothing. Zed was hunched over his handheld and didn't even look up. She wondered if he'd cracked the scam yet. Sighing, she opened the door to the control cubicle. And gasped.

No walls. Empty space yawned on all sides, studded with the icy burn of stars. Rocks floated, lumpy and dead. There was no up, no down, only the hard glitter of those distant suns, so different from the twinkling stars in Earth's night sky. Margarita clutched the door frame, fear tearing at her. If she let go, she'd fall forever.

"Fuck!" She focused on Sorrel, faceless beneath his VR helmet, his chair seemingly hanging in the middle of a vacuum.

"Be glad the system compensates for our spin." A smile colored Sorrel's tone. "I thought you wanted to see where we are."

Yeah, this guy could live with that system brat voice. "Thank you," she said between her teeth. Very good holo, this wall projection. Very precise compensation for curvature and surface distortion. She wondered if this kind of expensive accuracy was necessary or a matter of ego, like the bright new colors on the ship's hull.

"It looks rather empty out here." Michael crowded into the doorway beside her, his face full of subdued excitement. "I expected . . . I don't know. More rocks, I guess."

"Not here. This is fringe and sparse, even for the fringe." Sorrel stretched out one gloved hand and made a twiddling motion with his fingers. "That's why Vildorn got the kind of lease they did. Nobody else was stupid enough to think they could make a profit in this sector. So they were wrong." He shrugged.

"So where is it?" Margarita looked around, not quite so afraid of falling now, although she didn't let go of the comfortingly solid door frame. "Vildorn itself, I mean. Headquarters. Office. Whatever."

Sorrel and his system voice snickered together. "It's very expensive to lift stuff up here. You bring the minimum hardware up and drop the rocks down to the refineries. The hard crews up here don't live a very luxurious life, let me tell you. You got to be a little twisted to make it on a hard crew." He pointed left and down. "That's the home office right there, behind that big 'roid."

She looked but didn't see anything but a lumpy mass of rock floating at an unguessable distance. And then she spotted something small and black. A ship? It looked like a discarded can. Her perspective shifted suddenly, making her a little dizzy. That was a ship. The rock was *big* and farther away than she'd guessed.

"That's it? Just that ship?" Michael peered over her shoulder.

"That's the mother. I think Vildorn uses a couple of little tugs to do the collecting. You don't know much about this end of the business, huh?" Sorrel turned his blind, hooded face toward Michael. "From what I hear, they're just loose out there. Your Stones. Floating around. Once the hard crew snares one, they ID it, register it, and drop it down the well. It gets collected, foamed up, and shipped downside in a pod."

"You know a lot about Stone mining," Michael said softly.

"Yeah, well." Sorrel lifted both hands in a "dunno" sort of shrug.

"I'd imagine some of those dropped Stones must go astray," Michael mused. "It's a long way from here to there."

"Could be." Sorrel reached out to touch an invisible icon. "Don't ask me."

A warning there. Hearing it, Margarita gave Michael a quick sideways look. He nodded and winked; he had read it, too.

"So, can we go knock on the door?" he asked Sorrel.

"I gotta call them." Zed pushed past, shouldering Margarita's arm aside. "You don't just walk up and ring doorbells up here. That's why Sorrel's hanging out here, out of range." His lips pulled back from his teeth. "Patch me into the talk net."

Margarita half expected Sorrel to pin Zed's ears back, but he merely grunted, his fingers doing whatever they needed to do on the virtual console. "Okay," he said mildly. "Talk."

"Yo, Vildorn." Zed leaned against the invisible hull of the bridge, his eyes on the distant black ship. "This is Zed calling. The boss sent me up with a present for you. Want to turn off the hostilities so we can dock?"

Silence.

"Maybe they didn't hear," Michael said.

The urgency in his voice bothered Margarita. It had a sharp, brittle feel to it, like thin, stressed glass on the verge of shattering. His face looked strange, as if his skin were hardening into porcelain.

"They heard." Sorrel crossed his arms and leaned back. "They're checking everything out nine ways from Sunday. Zed's voice trans, visuals, ID on my ship. You don't take any chances. Not when you're making money on a lease. They've put a lot of their profit into some pretty heavy-duty weaponry. We'll just wait for an invitation."

Michael made a soft, impatient sound in his throat.

"Michael?" Margarita touched his arm, but he didn't react.

"Sorrel?" A thin voice spoke from everywhere and nowhere. "When did you get into the ferry business? You losin' your touch?"

"Ferrying?" Sorrel laughed softly. "When the sun goes out,

honey, and you know it. How you getting along, Tonik? Haven't seen you down the well lately."

"Cause we're short. It's just Juniper and me, and that don't give us a lot of time off. Juniper's out hunting Stones right now. Okay." The banter vanished from the woman's tone. "You can bring Shen's pet bookkeeper on in. You read okay."

Margarita glanced at Zed, but the woman's dig hadn't evoked any visible reaction. Maybe everyone *did* know everyone else up here. She had a feeling that for all the friendly repartee, if Sorrel had made the wrong move or if Zed hadn't been along, this Tonik would have blown them apart. Friendly place, this. Maybe worse than the barrio. Maybe just different. She frowned as Sorrel touched them into motion.

"We're going to match with their spin," he told her. "Brace yourself, okay? If you've got to puke, don't do it in here."

"Thanks." Margarita grimaced. Movement made the endless vista suddenly less bearable, and her stomach flip-flopped. She retreated quickly into the nice, safe cargo hold, glad now for the windowless hull.

It didn't take Sorrel long to do his maneuvering. A solid *clunk* made her start. It was followed a moment later by scratching noises and a rasping hiss. Normal sounds? She eyed Zed and Michael, still leaning into the door, sharing Sorrel's view. They didn't seem particularly upset. Which was probably a good sign. The light flickered, and the engines shut down. Margarita touched the padded wall. She hadn't noticed the tiny perpetual vibration from the drive but she noticed its absence now. She staggered a little as she moved. Up and down were still in place, but she felt strange—too strong or too light. She tried an experimental jump and nearly banged her head on the ceiling. Shit. She recovered quickly, feeling stupid, as Michael stuck his head back into the cargo bay.

"We're here." He held out a hand to her. "We're going out through a lock up front."

"How can you be so excited when you think you're going to die?" There was no heat in her voice; she was beyond anger. "Michael, what does this mean to you?"

"I don't know." He smiled gently. "It's pulled me here from Albuquerque. Sometimes you have to stop being careful and just leap."

"Right from the cliff edge? Yeah, okay, end of lecture."

Margarita squeezed his hand briefly as she edged past him, squashing thorned emotions down into a tight ball inside her. She would deal with them later. Blessedly, the walls were blank again—no more of the holoed forever. A hole had opened in the ceiling above Sorrel's empty pilot's chair, and a flat-runged ladder extended to the floor. Margarita caught a whiff of dirty socks and wrinkled her nose. "Me, I'd like to be sure I've got wings before I jump." She peered up into dim light, glimpsing grimy composite walls and a door.

"How do you know whether you have wings until you try to fly? Once I was willing to find out." Michael nodded at the ladder. "Sorrel went that way."

Okay, so jump and to hell with it. Margarita grabbed the rungs and climbed quickly up into a small, close room. Michael followed her, crowding her on the ladder.

So eager to meet his aliens. His death.

"Maybe it's redemption," he said softly. "Estevan was right about the warp being strung from the sculptor's soul, and I ran out of soul. It was my own fault. I was scared of tomorrow, so I tried too hard to hold on to today, and today turned into yesterday. I stopped growing. I turned to stone in my own garden. Maybe this is the way to become flesh again."

Dead flesh, maybe. Margarita shivered because Zed was waiting in the lock with Sorrel, and his face was full of the same shadows that darkened Michael's eyes.

"Let's go." Zed tossed his hair back from his face. "They're waiting to cycle the lock."

"Coming." Planting both hands on the edges of the hatch, Michael levered himself lightly up and onto the lock floor.

Margarita backed up, banging her shoulder blades on the wall. Some kind of accordion-pleated material joined Sorrel's ship to the air-lock hatch on the miners' mother ship. Only a thin skin of molecules stood between her and frozen death. Margarita gasped for air, suffocation fear twinging through her as the floor hatch irised closed with a wavering squeal. Great. Sounded in *wonderful* repair. But it was too late to stay behind. She pressed back between Zed and Sorrel, grateful for the warm touch of their flesh. A bell shrilled. Good thing Andy wasn't along. Squeezed by bodies, she almost smiled. He would have come unglued in here. A light turned green, and the bell shrilled again. Her ears popped as part of the wall slid aside.

"Clunky hardware," Sorrel mused. "Got to be a century old at least. Hope they've overhauled the seams lately."

She didn't want to hear that; had he said it for her benefit? Margarita drew a deep breath and nearly gagged. The dirty-sock smell was overpowering in the narrow corridor beyond the lock, overlaid with the scent of cooked food. Dank and warm, the air felt sticky on her face and bare arms, felt almost dirty. It sure smelled dirty. Margarita stepped gingerly through the lock and into the corridor. A normal step nearly propelled her into the wall, and she stumbled, catching herself ungracefully.

"Watch it," an unfamiliar woman's voice came from behind her. "Use those downsider muscles of yours too hard and you'll bounce off the ceiling."

Margarita turned to see a small, skinny woman standing in the doorway at the end of the short corridor, fists planted on her narrow hips. Her sleek, hairless scalp was tattooed in red and purple whorls, and her dark eyes and tawny, stark profile reminded Margarita a little of Xia. And of herself. But she looked . . . wrong. Subtly, disturbingly wrong.

"Tonik." Zed stepped past Margarita and bowed a minimum bow. "This is Michael Tryon, the Stone sculptor, and his assistant, Margarita Espinoza. We're getting contaminated Stones in our downside shipments. Tryon here is trying to spot the entry point of the contamination."

Smooth speech—nicely confident I'm-the-boss manner, authoritative but without his usual posturing. Huh. Maybe some of that boy-in-man's-clothing stuff was a put-on? Maybe he paid attention to who reacted to that bit of posturing and how. Margarita wondered about that suddenly, about what that implied about Zed's depth and subtlety. A lot, if it was true.

"What the fuck do you mean, contamination?" The woman's face darkened, and she started down the corridor, jerking her head at them to follow. "You know we score the goose egg on all your fancy tests and always have. Don't give me 'contamination.' " She led them into a cramped, cluttered room.

A couple of recliners stood in front of an outdated touch-panel control deck below a big wall screen. No state-of-the-art ship, this. The rest of the room was taken up by a table with built-in benches, a terminal, cupboards, and a small exercise gym that seemed to serve mostly as a clothesline. Food wrappers littered the floor, and the smell was even worse in here. Margarita swallowed a twinge of nausea.

Sweeping a battered reader and a dirty tunic off the table, Tonik perched herself on one corner. "Nobody touches those Stone babies except us before they go down the well. You came out here for nothing, Tryon."

Tonik was ignoring both Zed and Margarita, as if they were invisible. If upsiders didn't think much of downsiders, these belters obviously thought even less of anyone from the bottom of the well. Margarita studied the woman, frowning: soft-looking muscle, and not a lot of it. And her bones looked bird-like, too long and slender to be human. Maybe that was the source of that wrongness. No human could be that delicately built. Margarita wondered suddenly if Tonik had been born out here, if she had grown up in this environment.

"How do you handle the Stones?" Michael was standing in front of Tonik, close enough to be rude. "How do you know you've found one?"

"This is your business?" Tonik swept him with one quick head-to-toe glance, jittering, backing up until the table stopped her. "They don't look like nothing else. You know 'em." She tossed her tattooed head. "But we bring 'em in and run a mass spec. They don't emit like anything else out there, you better believe. While we got 'em onboard, we scope 'em and ID 'em. Just in case one gets . . . lost. Sometimes they sort of get lost on a drop." She shafted Sorrel with a razor-edged glare. "Sometimes they get found, sometimes not. We don't get paid for the ones the tugs don't catch."

"Not my problem if you guys got bad aim," Sorrel mused to the ceiling.

"Fall down the well, platformer." Tonik's eyes flickered from Sorrel to Zed to Michael, and her lips drew back from her yellow teeth.

You're pushing her, Margarita thought, and it worried her that Michael didn't notice. Or didn't care. Most of the smell was coming from Tonik. How often did she bathe, anyway—once a year? Margarita edged over to Zed and touched his arm. "What did you come up with on the trip up? From the sphere?"

"What I told you." He sounded disinterested.

"This is your vengeance, remember?" She leaned close, her voice a hissing whisper that didn't cover her sudden fear. He had cracked that sphere back there in the cargo hold, but she had no idea if he'd left her any kind of clues, or entry, or anything. It came to her suddenly that Zed was about to die. He knew it. And she knew it, too. Death—that was what made the air hard to breathe. And it was too late for Zed or Michael to turn back. "I've got to have something I can use, Zed." She clutched him, squeezed by a sense of catastrophe that filled her with animal terror. "Zed? Can I find it? The stuff to lever your boss with?"

"It's not on the sphere." He shrugged, moving away from her. "You've got to get the hard details from the Net. The sphere just gives you the entry points. When I get onto the Net . . ."

You aren't going to get onto the Net, Margarita wanted to scream at him. You're going to commit suicide up here.

"Do you have any Stones onboard?" Michael was asking. He sounded feverish, excited, not like himself at all. Something was happening here, and it was happening too fast. Margarita struggled for breath, barely noticing the stink now, and wondered if there was enough oxygen in the air. She had a sudden image of the three of them sliding down a chute that was getting steeper by the second, and there was no turning back, no stopping now. What was at the bottom, anyway? Darkness wavered at the edges of her vision, vanishing when she turned to look directly at it. Am I about to faint? she wondered shakily.

I'm feeling it, too, she thought with a spurt of panic. The way she'd felt it in Danners's studio, only there it had been darkness, deep and black enough to drown her. Now it was a glossy, breathless excitement that glazed the corridor, blurring people and walls to meaningless patterns.

That could still drown her, was drowning Michael and Zed. Her twinge of panic washed adrenaline through her blood, contracting blood vessels, increasing her heartbeat. Fight-or-flight response. Primitive. Useful. The shadows at the edge of her vision were thinning, washed away by the adrenaline surge. The corridor refocused.

"Yeah." Tonik's eyes gleamed with suspicion. "Juniper just

dumped one off. Not too big, but big enough to class out as a Major. I tell you, nobody's touched it yet, so you ain't gonna find nothin' that wasn't already there. But I guess you can look." She jerked her chin at a set of double doors. "If you want to. You gonna leave after that? Like right away?"

"No!" Margarita ignored Sorrel's suddenly narrowed eyes. "Michael, *listen.*" She grabbed his arm, digging her nails in hard. "You don't want this. It's coming from outside; it's like Danners's studio. You'll die. It'll kill you just like it killed Danners." *It.* Being, or layered resonance, she could feel it like a million volts of electricity crackling in a downed power line, waiting for someone to touch it. "Michael, don't do this. You're not doing it because you want to."

"Yes, I am." He shook her off with seeming gentleness, but she staggered with the force behind that deceptive motion.

"I can feel it, too." Her voice was going shrill, too loud. She wanted to calm down, speak rationally, but she had no power, no control. Sorrel and Tonik were staring at her, but they looked flat and unreal, as if a thick sheet of glass separated her from the corridor. "I can feel it, do you hear me?" She clutched the front of Michael's tunic, panting again, unable to get enough air. "Fight it, Michael, just *fight* it."

Zed had gone back into the corridor and had palmed the lock on the doors Tonik had indicated. Darkness lay inside, as dark as Danners's studio. He started into the room. Michael tried to follow, but Margarita hung on to him, that siren song beating in her head until she thought it would explode. *Michael,* somebody screamed, and she realized with vague shock that that distant voice was her own. Light glowed on, and she caught a glimpse of the Stone, padded on a bed of frayed, dirty foam.

Michael shoved her, and the violence in his thrust tore her grip loose and sent her staggering. She would have fallen if Sorrel hadn't grabbed her. He wrapped his arms around her, pinning her arms to her sides. "Let *go*, bastard!" She slammed her elbow into him and almost broke his grip. Then she slammed him again, but this time his fingers closed on her arm just above the joint. Margarita gasped as white, blinding pain flared upward through her arm to explode like lightning in her head.

"Stand still," Sorrel hissed in her ear.

Stand still—that was all her muscles would let her do. Cold sweat bathed her, and the room receded to a bright distance. Across that vast distance Michael walked into the storage room where the Stone lay. "Don't," she whispered through the pain. "Don't let him . . . in there."

"It's his choice." Sorrel's tone was implacable. "Not yours."

"Bastard," Margarita whispered, and braced herself for worse pain. It didn't come. In the corridor the door whispered shut on Michael, Zed, and their Stone. Sorrel relaxed the pressure of his fingers very slightly. Margarita closed her eyes, willing herself not to tremble.

"If we're all in there, we're all in on whatever goes down," Sorrel said patiently. "This way there's maybe three of us left over. Enough to clean up the mess."

"You're not my mother." Margarita started to move, but froze as those merciless fingers fractionally tightened. "What's it to you if I want to go see for myself?" she asked bitterly. "How come I get special treatment?"

"It would hurt Xia if you died."

"Shit on that. Ah, *stop*." Margarita closed her eyes and sucked in a ragged breath.

"Maybe she knew her limits, Margarita. Maybe she did the best she could by letting your aunt raise you," Sorrel breathed in her ear. "She never says, but I can read her pretty well. She's proud of you. A little sad sometimes, but proud. Because you're who you are, not because you're her little piece of work. And sometimes you hurt her, but she doesn't dump that on your head, either. She loves you like she's never going to love me—or anyone else, I think. I want you to know this because I don't think she'll ever tell you herself. She figures you don't want to hear it."

Xia, proud of her? Loving her? Margarita closed her eyes, muddy inside, not sure what the hell she felt.

With a small grunt, Sorrel released her and stepped smoothly out of reach. "Rub your arm." He nodded at the mark his fingers had left. "It'll help quiet down the nerve."

Margarita rubbed at the red marks as the ache faded slowly from her shoulder. "Can we go look now?" she asked him bitterly. "Can we see if they're dead?"

Sorrel simply held her gaze for a moment, his expression

enigmatic. "I think Tonik can take an electronic peek for us, right, Tonik?"

"Sure." The belter rose lithely from one of the recliners and stretched like a cat. "You two are all done feuding, right?"

She had a weapon in her hand—no stunner, either. Margarita looked at it and raised her face to the woman's utterly cold glare. "We're all done," she said. *She loves you like she's never going to love anyone else.* No, Margarita thought bitterly. I didn't want to hear that. "Can we see what's going on, please?" She crossed her arms on her chest. "Right now?"

Zed had stopped beside the Stone, not touching it. Michael went over to stand beside him, the Stone's song beating like a million wings inside his skull, pulsing through his veins with every beat of his heart. Shoulder to shoulder, flesh brushing flesh, they stared down at the Stone. Threads of teal and silver shimmered in the smooth gray skin, drawing their eyes deeper until they felt they were staring into the heart, the center of the Stone.

Alive. Michael let his breath out slowly, aware of Zed's slow tandem sigh. The song filled him: darkness, yeah, like in Danners's studio, but light, too, a light so unbearably bright that merely to look at it would incinerate him, turn him to ashes in a second. A voice, oh, yes, a song in a language that he couldn't understand, could only *feel.* And he knew that the beauty would kill him, that the darkness would sweep him away, dissolve his bones like acid, but that wasn't important, didn't matter, because he'd have touched it.

He would be *part* of it.

Michael took a step forward, excitement like lust hot in his groin, spreading upward through his chest and arms. Immortality, he thought, and wanted to laugh. Beyond death, beyond this terrible isolation of the flesh. Yes . . . He reached out, arms opening to embrace it.

Light exploded inside his head, and Michael spun sideways, staggering, stumbling frantically for balance. He hit the wall hard, palms slapping down too late, then slid onto his knees, his head full of static.

"You don't get this." Zed's words came to him faintly through the song and the buzz of static in his ears. "I don't have your talent, and I never will. You do what I wanted to do, and I'll never do it, and that's just how it is. But you don't get this, too." His voice was fierce. "I go first, and you can come after me if you want to. If *you* can stand being second, Michael Tryon."

"Wait." Thick-tongued, his head full of fuzz, Michael struggled to his knees. "Zed, *wait*."

Green fire dancing in his eyes, hair loose on his shoulders, Zed slowly knelt. He stretched out his hands, palms hovering scant inches above the Stone's mottled, depthless flank.

"Zed," Michael whispered.

Face rapt, as if he were seeing God, Zed laid his hands reverently on the Stone.

For an instant he was still, eyes widening, full of agony or ecstasy. Then his head snapped back, his spine arched, and all his muscles spasmed at once. He screamed, shuddered forward, then arched violently backward again.

"Zed!" Michael staggered to his feet.

Zed's palms stayed flat on the Stone as his body convulsed.

Michael flung himself down beside Zed, his head full of invisible wings fluttering, shivering, trying to break free. For an instant he hesitated, fear and that bright terrible music making him tremble. Then he grabbed Zed by the shoulders and tore him free of the Stone.

He wasn't dead. His eyes opened, and his arms went around Michael. Green eyes, green as cracked glass, windows into . . .

. . . somewhere . . . somewhen . . . someone. . .

With a cry, Michael fell through those fractured anguished windows into . . .

Forever.

Time began, and galaxies coalesced from nothing/everything, rushing outward into infinity in a cascade of silent light and whirling dust. Stars were born into light, burned old and cold and died. Space and time folded back onto each other, piling into rumpled heaps of eternity that gathered stars like dust, became contemplation, consideration, *self* . . .

He remembered it all.

He had been there, was there, would be there in a million years and remembered that, too. "We don't know," Michael whispered. "We don't *understand*."

Human words, so brief, so finite, so utterly meaningless. So full of our own terrible blindness.

"I'm sorry." Michael closed his eyes and let himself dissolve into forever.

"Sure, we can take a look." In the main room Tonik gave Margarita and Sorrel a tight, wary look but didn't put away her weapon. "Why the hell should they be dead? What're you holding out on us, huh?" The weapon moved just enough to make its presence felt. "It's a clean Stone. You tellin' me there's something wrong? There's nothin' wrong. I *handle* those suckers. Juniper, too." Keeping one eye on them, she edged up to the console and touched a quick succession of buttons. "I think you guys are shitting me. You're outa here. Like now."

Behind her, the screen shimmered to life, showing the storage bay from a viewpoint above the doors. The Stone lay on its padding, taking up the center of the floor, with the squat box of a mass spectrometer on a stand beside it. Between the door and the Stone, Zed and Michael lay in a tangled embrace. Unmoving.

Margarita spun on her heel and darted toward the door. Sorrel made a grab at her, but she chopped his arm aside—thinking, You're not the only one who knows street moves, baby—and swung herself around the doorjamb to the lock plate of the storage bay doors. Tonik could have locked it, but no, it was opening. Everything seemed to have slowed to half speed. Margarita fidgeted while the doors slid ponderously apart, then squeezed through the widening gap, scraping her rib cage.

Michael lay on the floor, his arms around Zed, just as she'd seen on-screen. It was such an intimate pose, as if they were lovers. Margarita dropped to her knees beside Michael, thinking in the split second before her hands touched him that maybe touch was how this thing killed.

She didn't care.

"Michael?" She took his face between her palms. His flesh was still warm but slack. Damn, damn . . . Pulse? Her probing fingers found it. Steady. Strong. "Michael, can you hear me?"

She'd found Arrow. He hadn't meant that to happen, surely. He had simply overestimated the strength of his heart, how long it would last. He had been lying in front of the holostage, his head pillowed on one arm as if he'd simply fallen asleep, had maybe felt a little tired and had sat down for a brief nap as he sometimes did, planning to get up and finish the damned piece.

Only he never had.

Margarita swallowed, remembering the taste of that morning's coffee on her tongue, the sensual touch of the sun on her shoulders. She had walked so blithely through those Vancouver streets, so sure of her talent, so sure of her future. Yeah, Arrow wasn't happy about something, but they'd work it out.

She would ask him.

The lights had been on in the studio, but sometimes, groggy with a late night, he left them on.

"Michael," she whispered. "Don't. Damn it, *please.*"

He stirred, his eyelids fluttering. "Mar . . . garita?" His eyes met hers, pale as morning sky, clear, without shadow. "Stop them. The Stones. Stop them." His lips quivered, and a ripple of pain crossed his face. "Please? No more Stones . . ." The ripple of pain became a spasm that twisted his face and stiffened his body beneath her hands.

Frightened, Margarita pressed his shoulders down as his back arched and his heels scrabbled on the dirty floor. Then he went limp, his face relaxing suddenly. Margarita sucked in a quick breath and groped for his pulse again. Still there. She touched Zed's throat, knowing before her fingers registered the absence of a heartbeat that he was dead. A part of her mind wondered how she had known—some subtle difference in muscle tone or skin color? Or because he had come up here looking for death?

"What happened?" Sorrel stood behind her with Tonik, his face wary rather than concerned.

Margarita noticed that he was staying far enough away that he wouldn't accidentally brush against her; he'd figured the contact angle, too. "He's still alive." She looked up at him. "It's not contagious. You either die in seconds or not at all, I guess." Maybe. Or you kill yourself later, as the other sculptors had? Zed was simply dead, without a mark on him.

Believe me, Sorrel, Margarita urged him silently. He could walk out on her right now if he thought she was any kind of risk to him. And she had no doubts about what the belter's reaction would be then. "I've got to get him back down to the platform." She tried for confidence, because only confidence would mean anything to Sorrel. "Zed gave me the key to the scam we're going to peddle to Shen. If I can get into the Net, I can unravel enough hardcopy evidence to be worth a lot. It's not in the archive." His veiled, considering stare scared the hell out of her. It wasn't just her life on the line here; it was Michael's, too. "Zed told me how to crack it, but he didn't record it." She hoped he believed her.

"I'm not going to dump you." Sorrel nodded. "What killed Zed?"

"An alien." The words came so easily, loaded with truth even though they sounded silly. "I don't know how it did the killing. Michael can tell us when he wakes up." When, not if. This happened before, she reminded herself. In Danners's studio. He'll be fine.

Sorrel sighed. "I guess there's no reason for us to stay here." He smiled into Tonik's hard, suspicious face. "We'll let our sculptor file a report with the boss when he wakes up."

"Nobody touched that Stone." Her expression didn't soften. "You review the log. You'll see." She turned on her heel and stalked back into the main room. "Fuck you both."

"Belters," Sorrel said under his breath. He stared down at Michael and Zed. "She's not going to touch them, either." He let his breath out in a slow sigh. "I sure hope you're right about this stuff being some kind of alien weapon and not a nasty bug." He sighed again and squatted beside Zed. "What I do for love." He grabbed Zed's arm, slung his body over one shoulder, and stood with a grunt, staggering a little. "See if you can wake him up, okay?" He jerked his head at Michael. "I don't want to lug him, too."

"Sorrel?" Margarita licked her lips, smelling her own sweat. "Thank you."

He grunted again and shuffled through the door. Zed's head and shoulders hung down Sorrel's back, hair streaming across his arm, limp hand swinging with Sorrel's movements.

"Michael?" She bent over him and slapped his cheek lightly. "Michael, wake up."

His breathing didn't falter. She lifted one eyelid, revealing a white gleam of eyeball. His pupils were even. Pinching an earlobe hard got her a twitch of reaction, but not much. A tiny fear had wakened in her belly and was trying to grow. "Michael? *Michael.*" Shit, what if this *wasn't* the same thing that had happened in Danners's studio?

"Still out, huh?" Sorrel reappeared in the doorway, breathing a little fast but otherwise unperturbed. "I think we get out of here now," he said softly. "Tonik is getting restless. Belters can be a little unpredictable."

"I can't wake him up." Squashing her fear down into her gut, Margarita laid Michael's head down gently and got to her feet. "I'll help you move him."

"Forget it." Sorrel grimaced. "He's limp as a rag. It's easier to do it this way. Just give me a hand, okay?" He squatted beside Michael and grabbed his arm.

Margarita helped him lever Michael over his shoulder, steadying him as he got to his feet. The strain showed on Sorrel's face in spite of the low g here; Michael weighed more than Zed. She hurried ahead of him but stopped as Tonik blocked her path.

"Here." The belter held out a clenched fist, her face hard and angry. "You take this back to your boss. Tell him to review it, okay? We didn't touch the damn Stone. It's all there, with a security seal to prove that we didn't fuck with the copy. You got a problem, it's not with us."

A bright, crazy light glimmered fitfully in Tonik's eyes, and her shoulders hunched with tension. The back of Margarita's neck prickled. Who would know if this belter killed them both, then sent Sorrel's ship on an out-system course? If anyone asked, Tonik could play innocent. Margarita would bet that the ship's video log would show only what the belters wanted it to show.

"Thanks." Margarita smiled and held out her hand. "I'll make sure he takes a look at it personally. Actually, we suspected that the contamination is a natural phenomenon. This just confirms it."

"Yeah." Tonik's face didn't soften. "Sure." She hesitated a second, then dropped a cased memory sphere onto Margarita's palm. "You do that."

"I sure will." Margarita hoped she was loading her tone with casual certainty. She didn't want to be threatening here, no way, no, ma'am. With as much nonchalance as she could manage, she turned her back on Tonik and palmed the lock door open for Sorrel. Could Tonik do something while they were inside? Muscles twitching between her shoulder blades, she stepped into the cramped space. Zed's body lay in the corner in a crumpled, undignified heap. Like a pile of discarded rags. "Everything okay?" She looked back at Sorrel, hoping to hell he was thinking along the same lines.

He nodded and edged in beside her. "It's all right," he murmured as the door shut off Tonik's hostile stare. "I checked the safety. She shouldn't be able to blow the lock on us."

Shouldn't be able—that didn't comfort her much. Margarita let her breath out in a long sigh as Sorrel eased Michael to the floor. Her knees wanted to tremble. "She's crazy."

"Yeah, a little bit." Sorrel slid onto the ladder as the floor hatch irised open. "All belters are a little crazy or they wouldn't be out here." He gave her a doubtful look. "If I climb down, can you ease him down to me? He's heavy."

"I'll manage."

Sorrel shrugged and disappeared down into his ship. "Okay." His voice rose from below. "See what you can do."

Margarita was already squatting beside the hatch, wrestling with Michael's limp weight. At least he didn't weigh as much as he would on Earth. Mostly, it was just awkward. She eased his legs over the edge. One foot snagged on the ladder, and she swore softly as she tugged to free it.

"Hang on." Sorrel reached up, grabbed Michael's ankle, and freed his foot. "Slide him down slow, okay?"

Teeth clenched, she slid him carefully over the edge. For a moment her hand slipped, and she thought she would drop him.

"Got him."

The sudden relief as Sorrel took Michael's weight nearly toppled her over the edge. Carefully she eased him downward, flattening onto her belly, guiding his slack body down into Sorrel's arms. He grunted and shuffled back from beneath the hatch. Margarita scrambled to her feet and grabbed Zed's body by the tunic.

"Get down here."

"I'm getting Zed."

"Forget it." Sorrel's voice cracked like a whip. "He's dead, and we're still alive. Get your ass down here before Tonik makes up her mind."

Hard, cold words, but too full of truth and death to ignore.

"Shit," Margarita said softly. It was so damn easy to die. The flesh deserved a little respect before you tossed it aside to rot. She tried to close Zed's eyes, but they opened slowly, fixed in that glazed stare. "Sorry, Zed." What more could she say? Go in peace?

Yeah, right. Margarita grabbed the rim of the hatch, swung herself over, and dropped. Above her, the hatch closed and she heard the hiss of air as the lock cycled.

"Kelly?" Sorrel's voice had an edge. "Get ready to blow out of here."

They'd made it. Tonik hadn't offed them, anyway. Or maybe she'd tried to and couldn't get past the safety. The air in here smelled almost like a summer meadow after the belter's thick space. Margarita drew a deep, grateful breath as she opened the cargo bay door for Sorrel. He maneuvered Michael through the narrow door and eased him into one of the seats. No change. No twitch of response as she strapped him in. Sorrel had already disappeared up front. Kneeling beside Michael, she pressed her fingers against his carotid. His heart was beating, and he breathed. He could wake up at any minute.

The floor vibrated gently beneath her. They must be easing away from the belters' ship. This time, without the stomach-wrenching distraction of the view, she was aware of the ship's movement as it spiraled away and assumed its own independent spin.

A sudden shift threw her against the bulkhead. She yelped as she banged her bruised elbow. "What's going on?"

"We're playing a little hide-and-seek." The ship's voice sounded excited. "Just in case Tonik decides to play rough with that nasty hardware of hers. She packs some big guns."

Gee, thanks. Margarita braced herself against the bulkhead as the ship lurched again. "You're having fun, aren't you?" She lifted Michael's head onto her lap, trying to brace him against the next violent course change.

"Sure. Why not have a little fun?"

Up yours, kid. Sometime maybe she'd ask Sorrel why he'd programmed this adolescent ship system, anyway. She smoothed wisps of gray hair back from Michael's face and found herself searching for her own genes there. He didn't really look like her. She had inherited Xia's jutting Mayan nose and high cheekbones. Maybe the shape of their brows was the same.

Margarita stared at the blank wall of the cargo bay, wondering what Tonik would do with Zed's body. Kick it out the lock, she supposed. Maybe he would orbit up here for a good chunk of eternity, he and the Stones that had killed him, keeping each other company until the sun finally went nova and cremated them all. What a spectacular funeral. He'd probably appreciate it.

Zed had come up here to die. More than Michael, he had been looking for death. She closed her eyes, leaning her head back against the padding. And what about Michael? Would he simply wake up in a few minutes or hours or days? Sure, of course, so why did she feel so *uncertain*?

Because she'd felt it—that alien presence. And it had scared the crap out of her.

The ship wasn't bouncing around anymore. They must be out of range of Tonik's big guns. She had nothing to do now but sit back and wait. And figure out how to pull Zed's information out of the Net. Maybe ask Liza?

"It's gonna be a longer trip back." Kelly sounded gleeful. "Vildorn and the platform were lined up pretty good when we lifted. Not anymore."

This time Margarita didn't even bother to answer it.

Chapter Seventeen

Zed sat on the other side of Michael, one hand resting lightly on Michael's shoulder. He wore a hint of a smile, as if something amused him and made him a little sad at the same time.

"You're dead," Margarita said. "We left you behind because you were dead. I'm dreaming." She had to be dreaming because it would upset her a lot to be talking to a dead man, and she felt so calm. She reached across Michael suddenly to grab Zed's arm.

Flesh—warm, solid flesh. She shuddered and let go. "I am dreaming, right?"

"I don't know." He smiled at her. "I guess you could call this a dream. That's something you made up, you know—dreaming. You don't really let yourselves understand what it is. I'm not sure." He frowned. "I think maybe you don't want to understand."

"You're not Zed. Are you?" She looked into his eyes. Windows into space. Into infinity. Distant stars glittered there, and she had the sudden, dizzy certainty that if she just stretched a little, she could pass through those windows, step onto the planets that circled those stars, turn around and see Sol shining in the heavens. Her muscles spasmed in a clutch of falling fear, and she jerked upright, bruising her shoulder blade on the hull.

It hurt. "Are you really here?" She rubbed her shoulder, her voice wanting to tremble. "Who are you? *What* are you?"

"Zed. And yeah, I'm really here." He grinned his familiar Zed grin. "And I'm orbiting Earth with Vildorn, because, yeah, Tonik dumped me out of the lock. And I'm in bed with Gunner, and I'm watching you and Michael create together on that stage in Danners's little kingdom." His voice had gone low and soft. "All me, all at the same time."

"I don't understand." Her words came out as a whisper.

"Maybe dreaming is a peek. The boundaries are your own doing, you know. They keep you safe." He frowned, his eyes focused on some invisible scene in midair. "It's too big for you, yet. That's why the others died." He looked at Michael, sighed, and touched his cheek lightly. "I understand now, and I'm sorry."

"Are you?" She couldn't choke it out: *Are you the Stone voice?* An alien? A creature?

"I'm Zed." He looked puzzled, as if she'd spoken out loud, after all. "You know, time isn't a highway." He raised an eyebrow. "It doesn't start under your feet and run forward and backward. Every instant exists at the same time, every possible instant. *You* travel from here to there. *You* create the path."

"How's Michael?"

Sorrel's voice made her jump, sending a rush of adrenaline crashing through her bloodstream.

"Hey, are you all right?" He squatted beside her and laid two fingers across Michael's throat. "Still alive." He gave her a sideways look. "Sorry. I didn't mean to wake you up."

"I don't—" Zed was gone. "Was I asleep?" Of course, she told herself. Dreaming that she was awake.

"I thought you were asleep." He shrugged. "When we dock, I'll message Xia. She can meet us with a mover."

And maybe . . . she hadn't been sleeping. Margarita swallowed, light-headed. What if time wasn't linear? Then Zed sat on the other side of Michael and he didn't. At the same time. And if she wanted to see him, if she *chose* . . .

He smiled at her, his expression bland. As if he'd been there all along. And he had. She sneaked a look at Sorrel. *He* didn't see anything. Boundaries, Zed had said. Sorrel had different boundaries, and Zed didn't exist inside them. This train of thought was getting scary. Margarita let her breath out slowly. "Xia needs to meet us with a doctor." She got the mundane words out with an effort. "We need to get Michael to a clinic right away."

"I don't know about that." Sorrel frowned.

Margarita swallowed her hot words. Sorrel's manner had

changed subtly. He wore a new hardness like a suit of armor. "Sorrel, he's hurt. Or something." The note of pleading in her voice surprised her.

"Or he could wake up fine in a few hours." Sorrel's expression was implacable. "I think the two of you are an incredible danger to anyone around you right now." He got to his feet, his expression unchanged. "I'd better get back up front. Kelly's pretty good at flying this ship, but he's still learning the finer points of piloting. Here." He held out a wrapped package. "I figured you'd be hungry by now."

Margarita took it. Food. Sorrel was the kind of man who would feed you even if he decided that it was in his best interests to dump you later. Her lips quirked, and she lifted the food in a half salute. "Thanks, Sorrel."

Halfway through the door, he looked back, one eyebrow rising. "You're welcome."

And he was gone. Margarita settled back against the wall, keeping an eye on the slow, steady rise and fall of Michael's chest. She wondered suddenly how Sorrel felt, risking his neck for Xia's ex-lover. Had Xia really loved Michael once? Could Sorrel see that in her, that someone had mattered to her in a way that he wanted to and maybe never would? And still he helped Michael. Because he'd get seventy-five percent of that precious file?

She didn't want the money to be Sorrel's only reason for helping them.

Zed had vanished from beside Michael. Hallucination? Ghost? Alien in human form? With a sigh, she unwrapped the food package: a sandwich, a juice packet, and a bar of something sticky and chocolate-colored. She turned the sandwich over but didn't unwrap it. If Zed was real, if he was right about time and forever, then Arrow sculpted holoture in his midnight studio, talking about life and creativity to an angry young barrio girl. And Katrina stopped beside a street-corner exhibit and said, "Hi, can I buy you a drink?"

There was grief in those images. And comfort. "I'm sorry." Margarita put the food aside. "I really am."

As she counted Michael's slow steady heartbeat, it occurred to her that she didn't know who those words were meant for: Michael? Arrow? Katrina?

Or had she been speaking to herself?

* * *

Docking was much smoother than their launch had been. Sorrel must have taken over from Kelly. Margarita shifted Michael's head from her lap as the subtle engine vibration died, then got stiffly to her feet and stretched. She hadn't talked to Zed again, but he was *there*. Part of the universe, the way air was part of it, and planets, and cats.

"Xia is on the way." Sorrel stuck his head through the door. "I've made a reservation for you and Michael on the next Earthside shuttle run."

"What?" She blinked at him. He looked tired, but his eyes were hard. "Michael needs a doctor. What the hell are you talking about?"

"He made it this far; I don't think he'll die during a shuttle trip." He didn't react to her anger. "The trade-off is that whatever you get out of that file you get to keep, Margarita. Once you're off the platform, you're safe from Liza, but I wouldn't come back up here." He didn't smile. "Liza holds a grudge forever, and I'm going to cover my own ass by giving her yours."

"What if I tell you to fuck yourself?" Margarita narrowed her eyes. "What are you going to do about it?"

"Kill you. And him."

She'd learned to read serious threat before she was twelve. He meant this. Margarita swallowed her anger, as poised for violence as she had ever been in the barrio. "Why?" she asked, watching his face.

"I don't understand what went on up on Vildorn. I don't understand why one, maybe two men died, and I don't like not understanding. I don't want Xia messed up in it." His eyes flickered. "If you stick around, she will be."

No, he hadn't been ferrying them around just because of the money. "It's not Xia's problem." Margarita lifted her chin. "And *I* don't want her involved." Was that truth or a lie? Suddenly she wasn't sure, and it wrung a frown from her. "Look, I know my mother. She's not going to get too involved in this."

"*Do* you know her?" For a brief instant those hard, unreadable eyes held hers. "You're so sure?"

Margarita looked away, because the pain in his eyes had such a private feel. "So get us onto the damned shuttle." There was nothing else to say. She touched the memory sphere in her pocket. If they made it down, it would be easier—and safer—to dig Zed's hidden files from the Net Earthside. That was all she had left—that file. Katrina's salvation and doom both, in one razor-sharp double-edged blade. Who was going to get cut? She could already smell the blood. Margarita jumped as the cargo door popped.

"So that's why you wanted the mover. What the hell is going on here?" Dressed in a soft green singlet that managed to look elegant compared to the neon colors most upsiders wore, Xia stepped back as the ramp extended smoothly, her eyes fixed on Michael. "What happened?"

Calm tone, calm posture, but her face twitched, just enough to see. "He's in some kind of coma." Margarita faced her mother, wondering what was going on behind that mask of a face. Maybe nothing. Maybe she was misreading. "He didn't hit his head as far as we know."

"Why didn't you tell me?" Xia gave Sorrel one quick look. "I would've brought a paramed team."

"He's on his way downside." Sorrel crossed his arms.

For a long moment Xia met his stare. Margarita rubbed her arms, her hair prickling as if the air were charged with electricity. She half expected a blue arc of lightning to leap between Xia and Sorrel, frying them all. But it didn't happen. Xia turned away. Silently she brushed past Margarita and bent over Michael, feeling for his pulse, peeling back his eyelids, probing here, there. With a small sigh, she straightened.

"Let's get him out of here." Her face was as expressionless as Sorrel's now. She fished a small remote out of her pocket and touched its controls.

So. Not even Xia would cross Sorrel. Margarita's neck prickled, and she was suddenly *very* glad to be here, alive. A small mover was trundling up the shallow ramp and into the cargo bay. It looked like a hospital gurney. When it reached the three of them, they hoisted Michael onto the padding and strapped him down. His pulse and breathing were still strong and steady, as if he were asleep.

Margarita looked away from his slack, aged face, stricken by a vision of Arrow's body on the ambulance gurney. The paramedics had been at the end of their shift that early morning. They had been laying bets on the next soccer game, discussing odds and some player's pulled hamstring. Delano. She remembered the player's name, could remember that but couldn't remember what Arrow had said to her when she'd left the studio on that last night. Tears burned suddenly behind her eyelids, freezing her with the fear that they'd spill over, that Xia and Sorrel would see.

Sorrel took the control pad from Xia. "It's the only thing to do," he said.

"Yeah?" Xia studied his face for a minute, looked down at Michael, then frowned. "You're probably right." She shot Margarita a quick glance. "You got a decent Net contact down there?"

"Yes." Andy Rodriguez might be good enough, assuming he wasn't through dealing with them forever. She looked at Xia. So calm. She was just going to wash her hands and walk away again. "No problem, Xia." She didn't try to temper the bitterness in her voice. "I'll do fine. I always do." She could feel Sorrel's stare but didn't give a damn.

People made way for the mover, paying no more attention than if it had held a load of crates. Private space was so sacrosanct up here. Margarita let herself drop back, chilled by that eerie isolation. No wonder Sorrel had been able to murder and get away with it. If that scum had really tried to rape her in the corridor, would anyone have stopped him? Maybe not, since they were both downsiders. You're not so different from me, she told the colorful, oblivious pedestrians silently. You just *want* to be different. Maybe I'll show you how alike we are.

Yeah, let me show you your own fears and ours: our fragility protected by only a thin shell, our fear of alien, especially when it's us. I'll show you in color and shape, in shadow and steely light, in the smell of upside, in the sound of flutes and drums like a nervous heartbeat, in scalding words.

You'll see it, and maybe you'll hate me.

Because you'll see yourselves, and it'll be *us*.

She was ready to get out of there. Margarita stared into the carefully unseeing faces, a flute line evolving in her mind, violas coming in slowly. The street they were following ended in the familiar holoed park. Illusory children rode past them on their bikes, weaving and yelling in some wild game of tag or chase. Margarita had the sudden giddy sense that they *were* looking at Michael, were staring with all childhood's curiosity and enthusiastic lust for disaster.

Maybe the park's nameless designer had a talent that went far beyond mere scent.

That designer might appreciate what she was going to do.

They passed through the big doors into the main port itself, into noise and bustle that struck Margarita as forcefully as it had the first time. It came to her suddenly that Sorrel was very alert, despite the fact that he was doing the upsider no-look thing very well. Watching for danger? It wasn't alien Stones she had to worry about. It was people. Margarita suppressed the urge to look over her shoulder, her vision overlaid by images of that sprawled body tangled in banana roots.

More uneasy than ever, she found herself looking at everyone, never mind how many icy glares she earned. Sorrel led the gurney into one of the partitioned waiting areas, then talked with a uniformed security guard. She waved them through with a jerk of her chin—life was so much easier up here when you were buddies with one of the natives. Following Xia, Sorrel, and the gurney, Margarita gave the woman a cold stare. What do you think? she wanted to ask the blond woman with her gene-selected Aryan face. Is he a sick friend? Dying relative on his way back down to his birth planet? Do you care? She probably didn't, because she'd most likely guessed he was a downsider, could probably *smell* it.

The shuttle wasn't loading yet, and Margarita found herself looking around for a terminal. It would be a hell of a lot cheaper to check her mail downside, and what did a few hours matter? Then she spotted a public terminal on the far wall of the waiting room, not too far from the gurney. Fuck the cost. Maybe Katrina had left her a message. Margarita went over and touched the screen to life. It wasn't much of a terminal: screen-only with a nonsecure privacy hood. Don't say anything you don't want the whole platform to know. She palmed the screen at the ID prompt, then recited her code. The pickups scanned her, ran a visual comparison with her on-file image, and let her in.

"Mail." Margarita frowned at the queue of junk waiting for her: ads from firms whose designers had defeated her selective interface. A couple of gallery announcements. Something from Yamada in formal business format—probably a cancellation notice for the rest of her show. She didn't call it up. Nothing from Katrina. Or from Argent. "Send mail," she said between her clenched teeth. "To Andy Rodriguez, address United States, western region." Vague enough, but she didn't know where he actually lived. How many Andy Rodriguezes lived in the western quadrant of the United States?

"Three listings for Andy Rodriguez," the terminal answered her in a cheerful young girl's voice. "More details, please."

Was this juvenile-voiced interface thing another upsider idiosyncrasy? "Age . . . uh . . . early twenties." She thought hard. All three probably had dark hair. "Paramedic." She didn't know *shit* about this guy. Try all three, and to hell with the expense?

"Messaging Andy Rodriguez."

Well, the Net thought it knew which one she wanted. Okay. Margarita drew a deep breath. "Andy?" She tried a smile for the screen. "This is Margarita Espinoza. Could you message me as soon as possible? I need to talk to you about something . . . advantageous." Advantageous? She swallowed a bitter laugh, keeping her face smooth. Two men dead, one in a coma. Oh, yeah, this was a very advantageous deal she was offering. Although Zed and Michael's encounter didn't have any direct connection to the sphere. "I'd better talk to you on a secure access, okay?" Margarita thought about deleting that, then decided to risk leaving it. It should get his attention, if nothing else.

And, of course, it flagged this conversation for anyone who might be listening in. It meant she knew something valuable, or she wouldn't want the secure access. But it was better than having him ask awkward questions if the wrong person was listening in. Can't have it all your way. Margarita exited the access, then stared briefly at the blank screen. No word from Katrina. She wouldn't do this, punish Margarita with this kind of silence. Unless—

She flung herself away from the terminal, nearly colliding with Sorrel. He looked like a cop on his way to make a bust. "I'm coming." She let her breath out in a rush. "I'm not trying to duck out on you."

"I didn't think you were." His eyes doubted her. "It's lift time."

She wanted to be angry at him. But this came from love.

His love for Xia, never mind that she might never love him back. Margarita swallowed a sigh as he escorted her back to the mover. How come you don't blame her? she wanted to ask him. How come you still care?

She didn't say it.

Passengers trickled along a green-outlined path on the floor that led to the shuttle. They were mostly business types on their way back from flesh-time conferences with their upside plant managers, Margarita guessed. She swept them with a quick glance, searching for any familiar faces that might mean trouble. More women than men, mostly a little rumpled and out of sorts. Didn't get the warm welcome, did you? Margarita thought at them. They don't like us up here. They don't give a shit if we die like flies, did you know that? She glanced back at Sorrel. Standing a little apart from the mover, his arms folded on his chest, he wore a strange expression.

Loss? Margarita's eyes narrowed as Xia bent and pulled a carryall from a storage cupboard built into the gurney. "I'll need the remote, and who does this belong to, anyway?" Margarita touched the gurney. "What do I do with it at the other end?"

"It belongs to Ensminger Transport." Xia's face wore a strange, transcendent expression. "They'll take care of it downside." She slung the carryall over her shoulder. "The control pad is in my pocket." She started walking toward the green-lined departure lane.

Margarita gaped as the gurney trundled ponderously after her. She realized suddenly that the waiting area was empty; the tired business crowd had taken their chafed egos aboard. Comprehending suddenly, she looked for Sorrel. He was walking back toward the park with a swinging, angry stride that was fast enough to earn him a few irritated glares. The security guard was watching her with a self-satisfied smirk held firmly in check. It hit Margarita suddenly that she was about to miss the shuttle lift. Sorrel had vanished. Margarita turned to dash after Xia and the gurney.

She caught up with them at the elevator tube that coupled the shuttle to the platform. Unlike the local ships, the big winged shuttles docked outside the hull. A pair of uniformed stewards hovered at Xia's elbow. They peeled away as Margarita approached, scattering like startled rabbits. Xia's tongue? Margarita smiled in spite of herself.

"I thought you'd changed your mind." Xia lifted one eyebrow at Margarita.

"What are you *doing*?" One of the stewards looked back over his shoulder, and Margarita lowered her voice. "You can't come."

"But I can." She gave Margarita a tranquil smile. "I knew something was wrong when Sorrel messaged me about the mover. I had a suspicion that he might lean on you to head downside, so I checked the reservation database. Sure enough." She sighed as they dropped. "Sorrel is a little too much the upsider at times," she said softly. "Which I suppose is only reasonable, since he's third generation. But I'm not."

"But why—" Margarita broke off as the elevator doors opened to reveal the shuttle cabin. The surroundings were considerably nicer than the corporate freighter they'd ridden on the way up. Margarita looked down the narrow aisle. Plush carpeting on floor, walls, and ceiling cut noise to a minimum. There wasn't much space for moving around, but the recliner seats were wide and comfortable, with built-in screens and phones.

Huge holowindows in the hull showed a panoramic vista of alpine wildflowers and distant mountain slopes beneath a cloudless sky. A powerful scene but done so poorly that it had no impact. Margarita stalked after Xia. A steward was tethering Michael's gurney carefully in place behind the last row of seats, his face a professional blend of sympathy and neutrality.

The passengers stared surreptitiously at Michael, full of downsider surmise and curiosity. Margarita slid into one of the seats in front of the mover as Xia tossed her carryall into the cargo bin beneath her recliner. She didn't sit down right away but leaned over the back of the seat, staring down at Michael's face.

Margarita found herself looking away from the tenderness in that pose. She remembered Sorrel's fast, controlled stride through the port crowds. "Why did you come along, anyway? Sorrel loves you."

"Yes, he does, and I *am* sorry about that. I'm not the involved type, am I, Rita?" Xia settled herself into her seat, a gentle sadness on her face. "That's always been true, for the most part. Loving costs you a piece of your soul. I tell that to people who want to love me."

"Is that what you gave Michael Tryon?" Margarita asked softly.

"A piece of my soul? Yes." She bowed her head. "I began something with him, and I never finished it. Loving him." She stared at the tasteless windowvista, frowning. "You can't walk away and leave love unfinished. It haunts you. So I need to finish this."

I did that, too, Margarita told herself, and shivered. I walked away from an unfinished love. She reached for her harness and pulled it into place. "Where are we coming down, anyway?"

"In the Frisco Drop Zone." Xia gave her a closed, preoccupied glance. "There wasn't a lot of choice, actually. Is that a problem?"

Back to San Francisco. It seemed as if years had passed since she'd walked out of the gallery and taken the elevator up to Andy's hotel room with her DNA scan in her pocket. She had been so full of righteous anger, so sure that she knew this man and what he meant to her. What had happened to all that certainty and anger? Touching the curve of her cheek, Margarita turned to look down at him. His face looked peaceful, relaxed. As if he were asleep. Was he there, somewhere, or was he . . . gone?

"Margarita?" Xia looked at her, then looked at Michael. "I need to be honest with you."

Margarita, not Rita? She turned to Xia, full of sudden dread. "He's not my father. That's what you're going to tell me."

"I think he is." Xia frowned, her face full of memory. "You're so *like* him. But there was one night. With Estevan, when I needed comfort and he gave it to me. You need to know that it's not for sure."

"I . . . see." She traced the curve of her own brow and cheekbones, her eyes on Michael's face. Like him? Not physically. It would be such a bitter irony if she wasn't his daughter, after all. "You threw a father at me," she said bitterly. "And now you're taking him back."

"No, I'm not." Xia folded her hands in her lap. "I'm giving you the chance to refuse him if you need to do that."

"Need," Margarita said softly. "You're offering escape. That's what you did, wasn't it? When you left Michael?"

"I needed to escape, yes." Xia stared into a landscape visible only to her. "It was the right thing for me, if not a good thing. Right or wrong, you have to make your own choices." She faced Margarita at last. "If you need to walk away, you don't have to leave a father behind."

"Like you left a daughter?" Margarita turned away, Xia's answering silence loud in her ears.

Maybe human lives could be defined by what got left behind. Danners had left his room full of Stones. Who inherited them? Who would get his state-of-the-art holoture system? It occurred to her with a jolt that the autosave feature might have been on while she and Michael had composed their impromptu duet onstage. If so, that duet was stored in some data sphere or in the Net. Would someone discover it one day and assume that Danners had done it?

If Michael never woke up, it would be the only electronic memory she had of him. Margarita leaned over the back of the seat to touch one of his limp hands. *Are you my father?* He had her gene scan. If he compared it with his own, he could tell her.

Michael . . . Katrina . . . father . . . lover. Margarita squeezed her eyes closed. Love cost so much. Maybe the easiest thing was to simply run away, as Xia had run. I *was* running, she thought. From Katrina's love.

From Arrow's.

And maybe he had understood. Maybe that was why he had given her so much space, had stood back to let her find her own stumbling way. Because he had respected her fear.

Margarita shoved her hand into her pocket, clenching Zed's sphere in her fist. If Katrina was dead, she would have only flesh memories of her. *You don't do people,* Katrina had said when Margarita had grudgingly offered to include her in a piece. *I don't want you to do it just for me.* And she hadn't done it, because Katrina had been right; she *didn't* do people. But if she had done it, she would have that much. Margarita closed her eyes. She had been working on an alpine scene at the time, like the crap on the shuttle walls pretended to be. It had been good. And Katrina, with her lithe grace, her sun-bright hair and pale skin, her enthusiasm for life, would have fit.

But she hadn't done it because she didn't do people. And because if she had done it, it would have meant . . . what?

That Katrina mattered to her?

Had Katrina understood that refusal for what it was? Had it hurt her? I *told* her I loved her. Margarita buried her face in her hands, dry-eyed, the ache in her soul too deep for tears. She had said it in words, yes, but she hadn't let it really happen, had been scared to let it be real. And now Xia was offering her another chance to run from love.

The floor shuddered gently beneath her feet. The shuttle must be launching. Margarita felt Xia's fingers on her arm but didn't raise her head. Maybe Andy could find her, maybe Katrina was still alive, maybe they could heal what needed to be healed.

A handful of maybes. They slipped through her fingers like dust.

"Ms. Espinoza?"

She lifted her head to discover one of the uniformed stewards in the aisle. He nodded brightly, smiling. "An e-mail message came in for you with a priority routing. But it came through just as we launched, so it downloaded to hard storage automatically." He offered a small handheld. "If you need to reply before landing, we have a terminal in the service area. You can contact any of the crew." He smiled and marched off up the aisle.

"If you have to reply before we touch down, I hope you made a lot of money on your last showing," Xia murmured.

Margarita made a noncommittal noise, heart pounding as she touched the screen to life. The message was from Andy Rodriguez. Disappointment stabbed her, a tearing pain that closed her throat. Just Rodriguez—a couple of brief lines only: *Come talk to me.* And an address.

Oakland. Well, at least they didn't have far to go. Great. Margarita leaned back in her seat, trying not to look at the flat, unreal alpine meadow. It sounded as if Andy might be interested in her little package, anyway. Margarita slid her hand into her pocket and touched the memory sphere again. Deal with this. If she couldn't find Katrina, she could maybe stop anyone else from finding her and hurting her.

Beside her, Xia had turned a little sideways in her seat. She was watching Michael, and her eyes were full of soft shadows, like a desert hillside gentled by evening light. You were very beautiful once, Margarita thought, beyond anger, even beyond resentment. Xia was still beautiful. It showed through her aging skin and softening flesh like light shining through a paper lantern or a polished shell.

It came to her suddenly that she could see it if she chose—the young Xia, the dancer. She existed, yesterday, today, tomorrow. All she had to do was let herself look. "Zed's right," she murmured.

"Zed?" Xia looked at her, eyebrows rising.

And she was young, Margarita's age, a dancer who loved and feared and ran. "He told me that yesterday is never over." Dizzy, Margarita reached out and took her mother's slender young hand. "I'm afraid, too," she said. Maybe fear was part of love.

"It's part of being human," Zed said.

Margarita looked but didn't see him. "What *are* you?"

"Zed. You. Xia." His voice murmured in the air, in the hiss of the ventilation. "What do you want me to be?"

And for an instant the shuttle became less solid—it was here and not here, was at a million million points between the platform and Earth. And she remembered Gunner watching Zed sculpt his Stones, remembered the touch of a young Michael's arms on a hot summer afternoon, remembered love and fear, and touched . . . infinity.

"Part of being human," she murmured.

"Who are you talking to?"

Margarita closed her eyes, still holding Xia's aged/young hand. "I think I'm talking to everyone," she said. "And no one."

Chapter Eighteen

Ensminger Transport, in the guise of a polite and hard-eyed steward, refused to let the mover depart the gate area after the shuttle had landed.

"I can order a private paramedical service for you." The steward, in his twenties and very sure of his authority, folded his arms across his chest.

"A taxi will do." Margarita resisted the impulse to cross her own arms, trying to keep her posture neutral and pleasant. It wasn't easy.

"I'm sorry." The steward's smile revealed perfect teeth. "He'll have to leave here under some kind of medical supervision. Insurance, you understand." He shrugged delicately. "Since the gentleman boarded in this condition, I can't legitimately call emergency services." Disapproval shaded his tone. "I'd be afraid to transport *anyone* without monitors and biomed support. If they were in that condition, I mean."

And fuck you, too. Teeth clenched to keep the words in, Margarita glowered up at his supercilious Scandinavian face. Gene-selected prick. Blond must have been very *in* twenty-some years ago. She'd bet the upside end of this operation didn't give a damn if you hauled dead bodies around, as long as they were downsider bodies. Insurance, her *ass.* It would cost a lot to order private medical transport. You could tell just by looking at this jerk that if they tried to sweet-talk an ambulance crew into picking up Michael, he'd see it as his civic duty to interfere and set the record straight about Michael's emergency status. And the fine would undoubtedly be higher than the private-transport fee.

There was something to be said for upsider hostility. Getting a firm grip on her temper, Margarita bared her teeth in something that probably wouldn't pass for a smile. "We'll deal with this. Don't worry. We won't try to run off with the gurney." She turned her back on him and stalked off to a terminal to check out transport rates.

"If you *did* try to remove the equipment," the steward called after her in a helpful tone, "its security chip would set off an alarm."

Margarita ran down the list of all the things she wanted to call him but kept her mouth tightly closed. Even though Michael had been cleared of murder charges, the cops undoubtedly wanted him; you didn't piss off the cops the way he had and not pay for it. They were probably going to run smack into that mess when they hit a clinic, but no sense in starting now by picking a fight with this jerk. She stopped in front of the public screen, debating.

"Just pick a name from the directory." Xia sounded tired. "We need to get him to a clinic pronto."

"Maybe I can do better than that." Margarita touched the screen to life and entered Andy Rodriguez's code. He was a paramedic.

"Well." His face blinked into existence, and he smiled from the screen. "You got down here fast enough. And since this isn't a secure access, maybe you should just give me a hint about what you wanted to talk to me about. Or come on over, since you're in the area." He grinned.

"I need medical transport." Sometimes abruptness was better. "For Michael. Who do you know?"

"What happened to Michael?" His smile had vanished.

"He's . . . in a coma." To hell with security. "We kind of got kicked off the platform, and I need to get him to a clinic."

"Is this the same thing that happened in Danners's studio?" Andy's face had gone thoughtful and cold.

"I think so." She hoped so. "Can you give me a name?"

"I'll pick you up." His smile didn't quite warm his eyes. "I'm working up here now. I used to live here. Before S'Wanna." His tone was casual; his eyes weren't. "You and your dad owe me. For staying behind and stalling the cops. It was not a lot of fun."

"We do owe you." A sense of urgency tugged at her. "Come

get us and we'll talk about it, okay? We're at the shuttle terminal, at gate seventy."

"I'll be there." The screen blanked.

"You trust this guy?" Xia frowned, one hip propped against the gurney, her hand resting lightly on Michael's shoulder.

"More than anyone else. He was sort of in on this crazy chase for a while. And we *do* owe him." Margarita looked at Xia's hand—so much language in the curve of her fingers. "Did you really love him?" she asked softly. "I want to know."

"Yes." Xia's eyes held hers, dark as midnight shadows. "I thought it was forever. I thought it was something unique." She smiled finally, shoulders lifting and dropping as if she'd sighed. "It *was* unique, that feeling. But it wasn't forever, because I'm not a forever person." She looked away. "Michael was the first, and I think that made it different. It was all so new, and I didn't know all the things I know now. I don't think I'll ever feel quite like that again. I don't think I *can.*" She tilted her head, her smile a little sly. "Is that what you wanted to hear, Rita? That your conception was something special?"

"My probable conception?" Margarita met her eyes.

"Your probable conception. Well, it was special." Xia looked down at Michael again, silent for a minute, her expression enigmatic. "I don't think I realized that until Michael showed up again. And I thought nothing could take me by surprise anymore." She laughed softly. "See? Even I can hide things from myself, Rita. Even I can be wrong."

"You're in luck, ladies." Andy's voice interrupted, amused, edged with a trace of anger. "I happened to be in the neighborhood. Your ride is here."

They looked around together, *exactly* together, and Margarita wanted to laugh because they couldn't have done it more smoothly if it had been a computer sim.

Andy stood behind them, a remote gurney trailing at his heels. He grinned at them, his teeth bright and white in his dark face. Yeah, he was pissed beneath that smile. His white uniform tunic made his dark skin look even darker than it was, and he carried a stun gun and comm link on his hip. "I'm on-shift in an hour. Contract work for Sisters of Mercy." He jerked his chin at the hospital patch on his shoulder. "So let's go."

Margarita's surge of relief startled her. She hadn't realized how vulnerable she'd felt ever since they had landed. Because of Michael. She did *not* like being vulnerable. "Thanks for coming," she said, and meant it.

"You're welcome." Andy looked mildly surprised. "Actually, if you'd called Sisters of Mercy, they'd have sent me out here whether I wanted to help you out or not. But I did want to give you a hand." He grinned. "See? I'm not *too* pissed at you." The grin faded as he looked down at Michael. "What's the diagnosis? How long has he been out this time?"

"There isn't any diagnosis." Margarita clenched her fists, fighting fear. "I told you we got kicked off the platform. It happened yesterday."

"Shit." Andy threw her a swift, hot glare, then bent over Michael.

Ignoring both women, he lifted Michael's eyelids, shined a light in each eye, pinched hard between two of Michael's fingers, and grunted softly to himself as Michael's hand twitched. People stared at him curiously as they strolled by, slowing down to make sure they didn't miss anything. Feeling like a stupid kid, totally inadequate in the face of Andy's angry competence, Margarita glowered at them. The ones who noticed her expression picked up their pace considerably.

Andy was taking off one of Michael's shoes. He stroked the sole of Michael's bare foot with one thumbnail, nodding as Michael's big toe curled inward.

"What's that for?" Margarita leaned over his shoulder.

"Babinski." He glanced at her irritably. "If he has upper motor neuron damage, his foot would have arched in the opposite direction."

"So this is good?"

"You could say so." He shoved the shoe into her hands. "You put it back on."

"What do you think?" She heard the tremor in her voice and fought to get it under control.

"I'm not a doctor, remember?" He gave her a quizzical look. "Oh, hell, I'll quit being pissed at you. I can always walk away this time, and I probably should." His lips quirked into an almost-smile. "What happened to *you* up there?"

"Me?" Margarita blinked. "What do you mean?"

"Nothing." He gave her a sideways look. "Anyway, I don't know about Michael." His expression grew thoughtful. "It could be some kind of catatonia. I don't think it's neuro-damage, but I could be wrong. I can hook him up in my van, do an on-the-run EEG and a few other little tests. Or I can take you in to Sisters." He glanced at his watch and grimaced. "They'll give you the pro treatment. If he's got coverage. Technically, I'm in violation of my contract if I *don't* take him there." He sighed. "Just keep your fingers crossed that I don't get a legit call while we're trundling around." He snapped his fingers for his own gurney. "You can tell me about this little item of interest you mentioned so carefully."

"I will." Margarita nodded, touching Michael's shoulder. "Will you do the tests first?"

"You really are worried about him, aren't you?" He turned to Xia. "By the way, since introductions seem to have gotten lost in the shuffle, I'm Andy Rodriguez."

"Xia Quejaches." Xia inclined her head. "Margarita's mother. Yes, she is worried about him." She sounded thoughtful.

"You inherited *her* face, anyway." Andy lifted an eyebrow at Margarita. His mobile gurney had lined itself up beside the mover, and Andy slid his arms beneath Michael's body, shifting him easily onto the gurney. He flipped webbing straps across his torso, secured them, and snapped his fingers. "The van's parked right outside."

The gurney trailed him like a dog, one wheel squeaking. The sound set Margarita's teeth on edge—or maybe it was the prospect of tests or what Andy might tell her before they even got to the hospital.

Andy's rig was as battered as the body carts that had run the barrio streets, picking up the losers in the perpetual turf wars. Patches showed on the oxidized red paint, and the right side was crumpled from some past collision. Margarita peered doubtfully through the rear doors, eyeing a tangle of leads, tubes, and impressive electronics. It looked like he had a lot more than just the basics required to keep a body breathing all the way to a clinic. She wasn't sure any of that stuff would help Michael. But it might keep his flesh alive.

The gurney crawled up the shallow ramp and settled itself into the high-tech jungle. Andy began to patch remote leads to Michael's scalp, chest, and arm. "Okay." He sealed a wide black collar around Michael's neck and stood, straightening the tubes and leads that connected it to a humming monitor. "He won't die between here and there unless he tries awfully hard. In a few minutes we'll know a whole lot more about what's going on inside him." The corner of his mouth quirked. "You're getting the high-end treatment. I usually charge big for this kind of service."

He was teasing her—and he wasn't. "I'll pay you." She sighed. "The information I've got is worth more than this."

"You keep on surprising me." This time a flicker of genuine warmth showed in his smile. He shut the rear doors and led them to the front of the vehicle. "I'm not supposed to carry passengers under this contract, but I never look in the jump seats." He ambled around to the driver's side of the rig.

Xia gave Margarita one sharp, questioning look.

Margarita nodded. They could trust him. More than anyone else she could think of. She climbed into the cramped jump seats behind the driver's seat. Xia climbed in after her and pulled the clunky manual door closed. The hinges squealed worse than the gurney's wheels. Interesting mix of old and new, here. Margarita sat down on one of the two pull-down seats, her knees touching Xia's. No window connected to the back, where Michael lay, but part of the dash was taken up by screens. Numbers skipped across them in various colors. Monitors, she guessed. A glint of metal caught her eye. A seat-mounted holster held a gun—one of those small, squat automatics. That particular model was the primo gun in the barrio—ugly and accurate, even on full auto.

Andy slid into the seat and started the engine with an actual key.

Yeah, this clunker was old. You couldn't hear yourself think over the engine noise, and it smelled of sweat, some kind of musky aftershave, old upholstery, and lunchtime burgers. Trying not to breathe too deeply, Margarita leaned her head back against the wall, the vibration soothing her muscles in spite of her anxieties. *Unique*, Xia had said about her love for Michael. Margarita closed her eyes, remembering Xia's face as she'd uttered those words, and felt a sudden piercing sadness for Sorrel.

Did I ever feel that way about Katrina? Sure, she told herself, but it was a lie.

I don't do people, Margarita thought, and her sadness increased. She didn't *let* herself do people.

Arrow had said something about that. The night before he'd died. She opened her eyes, frowning, because that was what she'd forgotten. It had made her angry. Well, everything had made her angry back then. Frustrated, she shook her head; the more she struggled to remember, the farther it receded. Maybe it would come to her one of these days. And maybe it wasn't all that important. Suddenly the rig accelerated and swung into a sharp right turn.

"Hey!" Margarita grabbed for the back of the seat, nearly pitching into Xia's lap. "What're you *doing*?"

"Hang on." Whistling tunelessly, Andy changed lanes.

This was the old part of town, and traffic moved sluggishly, bogged down in the narrow, outdated streets. Andy accelerated again to veer into the last meters of a left-turn lane, then braked so hard that Margarita's shoulder banged the seat. The tires protested as they swung left on the yellow light.

"Interesting." Andy peered at the dashboard screens, nodding. "Michael's doing okay back there, by the way." He gave Margarita a quick over-the-shoulder glance. "Why the tail?" His voice was hard. "What am I into *this* time? Tell me quick."

"I have this data sphere." Margarita ignored Xia's hiss of warning. "People are willing to kill for it."

"Thank you, Margarita." He rolled his eyes. "I should have known."

He turned right again, not so fast this time, and laughed deep in his throat. "The cowboy tailing us isn't even trying to be subtle. He's so sure of himself." He grinned. "This guy needs a little lesson in humility."

Xia growled something inaudible.

"Go for it." Margarita leaned forward. "This information is worth a *lot*."

"So Zed told you," Xia murmured very softly.

"I *know*." And she did. It shocked her a little that Zed's knowledge was so available.

Andy didn't say whether he believed her or not, but he began to whistle again. He was driving more cautiously now, trundling along with the flow of traffic. "Let's let him get nice and comfortable back there. I worried him with those turns, and we don't want him worried."

Margarita clutched the back of the seat, skin tight between her shoulder blades, hating this ride. Andy was in control, and she wasn't. That bothered her a lot. A part of her squirmed, wanting to tell him to let her out, that she'd deal with this on her own.

You can do it all on your own, Margarita, a voice whispered in her head. *You're very competent. But you can let people help, too. Sometimes you need to let people help.*

Arrow's voice. Memory stirred—an alpine meadow at sunset, something about *people.* And then it was gone again.

"Okay." Andy grinned, braking gently. "We're here. Sisters of Mercy took over this old department store."

The rig bumped over a low curb and into the entrance to an underground parking garage. "Hey." Margarita leaned forward as he accelerated fast down the ramp. "You sure about this?" She squinted into semidarkness. "Anyone could live down here."

"Sisters pays security. Local goons. Told you it was upscale." He grinned at her and winked. "I know the back door, and by the time this guy feels his way down here—" He stopped talking and used both hands to fight the rig around the tight spiral of the ramp; engine roar filled the concrete space like a jet taking off. "—we'll be long gone."

Maybe. Square concrete pillars flashed by, scrawled with layers of graffiti like cave paintings, stained with smoke. Trash drifted like old leaves in the corners: plastic, the tattered remains of sleeping bags, moldering clothes. Before the local goons ran them off, this must have been a squatter camp. A dozen cars were parked in the shadows beyond: a skinny woman was smoking a joint or a cigarette, dressed in tank top and jeans, a battered Uzi under one arm. She wasn't quite pointing it at them but didn't quite point it away. The rig bounced up a short, steep ramp. Sunlight dazzled her as they exited onto a narrow street, and Margarita blinked, squinting in the bright light. "Won't your local down there point them in the right direction?"

"Nah." Andy fished under the seat and came up with a handful of bright jelly beans. "Angele likes me. So she didn't see us." He popped the handful in his mouth and chewed. "Want some?" He fished up a plastic bag.

Margarita shook her head. "Thanks, Andy. For shaking that tail."

"That's twice." Andy gave her a sharp look.

"Twice what?"

"Twice you've said 'thanks' to me." He swallowed some candy and grabbed another handful. "From everything I can see on-screen here, Michael's in some kind of catatonic state. Vitals are good, reflexes normal, pupils reactive, and no decerebrate posturing." He jerked his head at the dash. "Reasonable EEG."

"What does that mean?" She clutched the seat back.

"He means Sisters probably can't do much for Michael." Xia narrowed her eyes. "Except catheterize him, plug him into a drip, and wait for him to wake up."

"They'll zap his muscles once a week so they don't shrivel up. They could do more than that, but he's only got midlevel care. I checked that, too." Andy shrugged as he swerved around a dawdling jitney. "So they won't. I'm a little more than just an ambulance driver, you know." He gave Margarita an over-the-shoulder grin. "I'm not as picky about care levels as the fedmed clinics."

He was a flea-market doc. Hands-on training, probably—no diploma, no license. That explained the tech in his van. Margarita nodded, because that was about all there was in the barrio. He would take black-market cash or trade for his services. No wonder he carried the gun. Margarita banished a sudden image of Michael's face as he worked out the lex for their duet on Danners's stage. "Someone has to do *something*." She heard the note of panic in her voice and tried to control it. "Take us to Sisters, I guess."

"No." Xia sat forward suddenly. "You do that, plug him into the machines, and he'll never come back. That's not the way, Rita."

Margarita stared at her, taken aback by her intensity. Andy was looking, too, watching her in his rearview mirror.

"Sisters can't do anything, but Michael is *there*," Xia went on in the same fierce tone. "I know it. He's hiding, and I don't know why. If we let him, he may hide forever. No." She crossed her arms. "No clinic. I'll take care of him." Her eyes went to Andy again, glittering. "I'll need a power chair. He'll need to be catheterized, and he'll need a nasogastric tube for feeding. Yes." She grinned at Andy. "I was in the same line of work. You do the tubes, I'll maintain them."

"Whatever you say." Andy sounded respectful.

She was right. Margarita threw herself back in the seat. But Michael's helplessness terrified her. Maybe because she had been so helpless herself as a child. In a way, love was a state of helplessness. Was that why she couldn't let herself love Katrina?

"One chair, coming up," Andy said cheerfully.

"Good." Xia sat bolt upright, hands on her lap. Her stark profile might have been that of some ancient goddess, carved from agate.

Full of strength that she might never have. Margarita sighed. "After we take care of Michael, we need Net access," she said. "And I'll give you this datasphere."

Andy took them to his condo. In the ambulance, Margarita watched him settle Michael into the power chair Xia had rented and strap him in. Slightly reclined, he looked like her infirm grandfather, perhaps, out for a stroll in the nice summer weather. The collection bag from the catheter was out of sight beneath the seat of the chair, the tube hidden by the sheet tucked across Michael's lap. Andy shoved open the bay doors and the chair crawled slowly down the ramp.

"Thank you," Xia said to him. "For everything."

For a moment, head lifted, her face full of calm and strength, she was young again. Andy was silent for a moment. Then he bowed, reached for her hand, and kissed it lightly. "You're welcome." He turned away from her, a look that might have been regret on his face. "It's not much of a place." He jerked his head at the scabby apartment building that pushed the edge of the sidewalk. "But it's cheap, and I can leave the rig in the street. For a small fee paid to the local gang." He grinned and touched his personal code into the antiquated screen beside the bombproof security door.

The apartment was old, built of stone and retrofitted for today's urban life. Which meant no glass windows on the first four floors, for security's sake. The residents would have their choice of holoed landscapes. Margarita wondered suddenly what each person had chosen. Environmental demographics: if you lived here, working a crappy time-clock job, what did you want to see from your window?

The door clicked and swung inward. Xia and the chair followed Andy into the doorway, but Margarita hesitated for a minute, her fingertips brushing the gray stone blocks of the building. Tiny flecks of mica glinted in the sun. How old was it? A million years? Something that old would have such *unconcern* about humanity. It would be nice to be a stone. She followed the others inside.

The scent of moist earth, rotting leaves, and a hint of rose closed over her, thick as stagnant water. Margarita paused, surprised. The old building had been gutted and renovated into an attempt at a miniarcology. A nice idea, but it hadn't been kept up. She squinted in the uncertain light. Big halogen floods spotted the high ceiling—an expensive way to mimic sunlight, even with every square inch of solar collector allowed by law. A lot of the floods had burned out and hadn't been replaced. Spindly, light-starved plants twined around the nearly leafless trees, and the paths between the free-form beds were littered with dead leaves. More leaves choked the small stream that wound across the floor, and green algae scummed the still pools.

That rose scent tickled Margarita's nose, and she paused by a small concrete basin choked with dead leaves, where a tiny green frog no larger than her fingernail perched on a rumpled, submerged condom. "Andy, I owe you for staying behind at Danners's studio. I owe you for today." She poked a finger gently at the tiny frog and watched it leap away. Rings dimpled the still water, expanding to the rim of the basin. "Zed told me that this sphere contained the entry points that would let someone expose a major web scam. Something Archenwald-Shen is up to. Anyway, it's all yours."

"I wondered if Zed was part of this." Andy had stepped up close behind her. "How come he's not using it? And how do I know he didn't make a backup?"

"He's dead." The frog had vanished into the shadows. Margarita looked up into Andy's face. "He met the—the voice that he and Michael heard. It killed him." Or his flesh, at least. "It killed S'Wanna and the other sculptors. It really is an alien. Or something."

Andy's face was expressionless.

"You don't have to believe the alien part. Zed thought the file was worth a lot." She fished in her pocket and pulled out the sphere. "He thought he might even be able to hurt Shen with it."

Andy knew what that meant. She could feel his excitement like lust as he stared at the sphere in her hands. Xia was watching her, too, her thoughts hidden behind the still mask of her face.

"I'm only asking for two things." She met Andy's eyes. "Find Katrina Luoma for me. And . . . take care of Michael until I get back."

"No." Xia's voice made them both jump. "The sphere is a thing between you and Katrina and Archenwald-Shen. I am going to take Michael back to Taos." Her eyes seemed full of shadows. "He had a garden there. A Stone garden. I think it will still be there even though he's left. And it will be full of yesterdays, like echoes. I think perhaps those echoes may call him back."

Her face might have been carved from polished ivory, its lines pure and implacable. Watching her, Margarita felt the protest die on her lips. Yesterday still existed, and yes, in Michael's garden it would be easy to touch. An emotion between grief and envy seized her. That yesterday excluded her. "All right." She forced a smile, then nodded. "I'll come to Taos. When this is over."

"If you want." Xia held her eyes for a long moment, then looked down at Michael. "I think we'll go tomorrow. I'm going to book us on a flight out tonight."

"The cops would very much like to meet Michael Tryon," Andy mused to the halogen-lighted ceiling. "They're not happy with him."

"I have a few resources." Xia nodded. "I think we'll do all right."

"Xia?" But Margarita fell silent, because what Xia had said was true. And she and Michael would actually be safer without Margarita.

"I hope Michael hears those echoes." Andy met Xia's eyes. "I hope he wakes up. He was . . . good."

An epitaph? It was the one Michael would have wanted.

"Why are you doing this, Xia?" Margarita's voice was low and soft. "Why does it matter to you now?"

"I told you." Xia rounded on her suddenly, her dark eyes flashing so that Margarita took a quick step backward. "He could hide forever if someone doesn't call him back." She glanced away. "I owe him that much. Who do you love, Margarita?"

"Arrow." The name shocked her, and a part of her wanted to call it back, deny it. I love Katrina, she thought, and that was true, too. And she had run from both of them. Margarita turned away from Xia. "If we're going to crack this thing, let's go do it."

"This way to the elevators." Andy nodded. "I'm on ten."

The thick, humid air settled over Margarita like a blanket as they made their way slowly along the littered path. The lush growth and humid air reminded her unpleasantly of the hydroponics farm up on the platform, and she looked uneasily into the shadows beneath the unpruned shrubs. The elevator shaft, at the center of the building, was formed of giant steel columns, their shiny finish dulled by green and brown smears of algae. Beyond it an overgrown thicket of roses sprawled in a thorny tangle. The halogen fixture above the roses was still working, and small red blossoms studded the topmost canes. The scent wafted to Margarita on the humid air, a brief crimson thread in a dark tapestry of earthy decay.

The light was out over the path, and thick shadows pooled beneath the tangled, sun-starved growth. "That's new." Andy stared upward and sighed. "Pretty soon we're going to need flashlights in here."

A branch had fallen across the walkway, large enough to stop the chair. Margarita bent to pull it aside.

"Don't make any sudden moves," Andy said softly. "We've got company."

His tone raised the hair at the base of her neck. Margarita straightened very slowly. A shadow had detached itself from the leaves and stems of some overgrown bushes, stepped into the light, and become a small wiry man with a carefully tousled head of black hair and a taut face.

Andy was watching the weapon in his hand. So was Xia. A cap pistol—too upscale to see much use in the barrio. Old handguns were cheaper and easy to get. This thing would fire a tiny capsule loaded with a fast-absorbing carrier. And whatever drug the gun wielder wanted to deliver.

"Very still, please." A trace of an accent marked the man's voice, and he smiled a perfect white smile. "This is a curare analogue." He waved the small gun at them gently. "Very fast. No trace left for the lab."

Margarita met his eyes, and a small shiver crawled down her spine. She remembered eyes like that from the barrio: smart, in control, and utterly without compassion. If he needed to kill them, he would.

"The sphere, please," he said. "Now, or I will shoot you all and take it."

"You're Thomas Ariades." It was a guess, but Margarita caught his small, revealing start of surprise. "You worked for Shen before Zed. You killed Ari Yiassis." And Katrina? She couldn't say it, because it would show on his face, and then she would know. "Zed took your scam farther than you did." She had to improvise, say *something* to put him off balance and buy them some time. "He gave me a message for you, for when you caught up with me."

"He didn't come back from the belt with you." Ariades's face was impassive, but Margarita caught the tiniest flicker in his eyes. "He's dead."

"Oh, no." Margarita smiled, riding on the crest of this instant. "He's here right now."

"Behind me, correct? Please. I am not stupid."

"Yes, behind you." She smiled, because this was truth, and he heard it in her voice.

He almost looked, and Xia leapt at him, fingers stabbing at his eyes. Ariades pivoted, the muzzle of his gun tracking her, taking his time.

Margarita threw the sphere at him.

It bounced off his temple, and he jerked. As she flung herself at him, she saw Andy charging in from the corner of her eye. Not enough time, she thought, and felt an instant's despair.

But Ariades hesitated, his eyes tracking the sphere for a precious second as it bounced off the path. Margarita brought her left arm up and slammed his gun hand aside. He gasped as her shoulder hit him, then struggled to recover, to bring the gun to bear on her. She slugged him in the belly but hit too high, ribs bruising her knuckles. Then Andy grabbed him and spun him sideways. The gun went flying, and as Ariades went down, Andy brought his clasped hands up hard beneath Ariades's chin.

Street fighter, Margarita thought.

Ariades's head snapped back on his neck, and he gave a single mewling cry. Arms splayed, he crashed backward into the undergrowth, groaned once, and lay still.

Panting, Andy grinned at her.

"Not so fast," Xia said softly. And pointed with a bleak lift of her chin.

Margarita turned, her triumph shredding into weariness. Of course the bastard hadn't been there alone. Her eyes widened.

Archenwald-Shen stood on the path.

"Very pretty." He smiled at Margarita. "You would have made a good dancer. Like your mother." He bent his head briefly to Xia. "Ms. Quejaches, you will please pick up the sphere and hand it to me."

He wasn't holding any kind of weapon that Margarita could see, but she wasn't stupid enough to think he was anything but very well protected. Neither was Andy, because he stood very, very still.

"No," Xia said softly. "Fuck you, node." Her head was up, eyes full of darkness. She was looking at Shen, yes, but seeing more than that. Seeing what? A lifetime of running, from which this was the final escape? Suicide, Xia? Yes, Margarita thought. I can feel it in you, the way I can feel Zed. He had been right when he'd told her that it was all there to touch—past, present, and future. For one dizzy instant, she could touch it all: Xia and Michael's love all those years ago, Zed's hidden hurt as he stood in the shadows and watched Michael and Margarita create together in a way he couldn't. I can be anyone, Margarita thought. Because of the Stones, or their touch. Or maybe she *was* everyone. That thought frightened her, as if she'd looked over her shoulder and found herself poised over an infinite gulf. Desperately she focused on Zed, on the memory of his face, his yearning, his anger. She hadn't been lying to Ariades when she'd told him Zed was here.

"Stop!" she said.

Xia and Shen both flinched and looked at her, still teetering on the brink of violence.

"I'll get it." Moving very carefully, so as not to worry Shen's invisible bodyguards, she bent, groping among the rotting leaves. For a panicky instant she thought she couldn't find it, but then her fingers brushed the small, cool sphere. "Here." She straightened and tossed it lightly to Shen. "It's all yours." She met his cold eyes, smiling. "Go ahead and destroy it. It doesn't matter."

His eyes narrowed. "Why not?" Careful words, very slick with threat.

"Because *I* got into Ariades's files. And I downloaded all the information into several nice, secure places. You'll never find it all." She smiled at him. "And if you kill me, the right people will get the proper pieces of it. They'll have proof that you're in their filespace, and your lucrative little scam will be over."

"I don't believe you." His eyes held hers, considering. "I've been keeping very close tabs on you, Ms. Espinoza. You haven't done any Net time other than e-mail since your lover walked out on you."

He knew so *much.* And so little. "*I* didn't file that information. You're right." She smiled at him. "But I'm Zed, too. And Zed did." From Sorrel's ship, in a single, secure burst of compressed data. Because Zed covered all his bets. "I remember you, Gunner." She stepped up to him, letting herself remember as Zed. There really weren't any boundaries if you didn't let them exist. Zed's memories, his past, were as clear as her own. "I remember when I first touched a Stone. And you were there. That's when you started to love me and hate me, wasn't it?" She brushed his cheek with her fingertips, the way Zed did. "Because I could do it, and you wanted to, and you couldn't. You couldn't really touch it—what the Stones offered. But you could touch me. Love and hate. They're part of the same whole, Gunner."

He flinched violently away from her hand, his face for one instant a mask of desolation. "I don't believe you," he said hoarsely.

"I read the whole file. The Malaysian Free-Market Web. Arce-Moreno Mineral Exploits, Tanaka-Pacific—"

"Stop." He tossed the datasphere in his palm, frowning at it. Then he flipped it into the pool. It landed with a small plop and sank instantly, trailing a few bubbles. "So we have a stalemate." He stared at her, his face unreadable. "I would not presume to push it too far."

"I want two things." She met his eyes. "No more Stones. And safety for Katrina Luoma."

"Why no more Stones?" His twitch of surprise showed.

"I promised Michael that I'd stop them from being imported. You can do that, because you're the only real importer."

He didn't deny it. "Why?"

"They killed Zed." She held his eyes and for one brief, terrible instant touched his grief. We can be so twisted, she thought sadly. Love, hate—it's when we try to separate them that we do ourselves the most harm.

"So he is dead." The node looked away.

What was he remembering? "His body is in the same orbit as Vildorn, or close to it. And he's me, Gunner." Her voice came out as soft as the brush of her fingers. "And he's you, if you could let yourself understand."

Archenwald-Shen's face twitched, then hardened once more. No, he'd never dissolve any boundaries.

"The Stones stop until the first item leaks from that file," he said coldly. "Safety is a subjective thing. I can't guarantee that your lover will always be safe, and neither can you." Ariades groaned; Shen glanced down at him, no emotion in his face. "But *that* won't bother either of you any more." And he walked away.

Margarita sighed and slumped, her knees beginning to tremble. If Katrina was still alive, she was safe. I could know if she's alive, she thought numbly. If I let myself, I could *be* her.

But if she really did that—let the boundaries dissolve—perhaps *she* would dissolve, too, into a sea of humanity. Was that what had happened to Michael? Margarita shivered.

"What the fuck just happened?" Andy let his breath out in a gusty sigh. "That was some performance." He glanced at the pond. "And you were shitting me about that sphere being the only copy. I'd call you a bitch, but I think maybe you just saved my ass. So I won't."

"It wasn't a performance, was it?" Xia spoke softly, watching her closely.

"No." Margarita wondered if she was going to faint. We are so isolated . . . By choice, she thought sadly. By necessity.

"Zed made the copy. I didn't know until just now." The Stone consciousness had touched her, and somehow it had made his memories accessible, had dissolved *those* boundaries, at least. But she wasn't ready for more. Not now, maybe not ever. "Zed never takes chances," she said.

Xia bent and plunged her hand into the scummy pool to retrieve the datasphere. "Do we need this?"

"No." Margarita met her mother's eyes and saw comprehension there. "You spent time in Michael's Stone garden. You felt them, didn't you? Their voices?"

"You really do have Zed's memories, don't you?" Xia said softly.

"In a way, I *am* Zed." Because for the Stones, all human pasts blended into a single past. "I do know where he hid all the copies, anyway."

"Well, I don't understand. Oh, crap." Andy jerked his head toward the entrance, sighing. "I should know better than to hang around with you, Espinoza."

Cops were coming in the front door. A little distraction in case they decided to follow Shen?

At her elbow, Xia sighed. "I hate cops."

"Me, too," Margarita said, and laughed softly. "Maybe it's genetic."

Chapter Nineteen

Margarita sat on the hard cot in her cell, staring at the pale yellow wall. Fingerprints smeared the doorjamb, and video eyes stared at her from the corners of the ceiling. The cell stank of old piss, a trace of vomit, and the sour, musty odor of despair. The red-tape morass had been worse than she had anticipated, and she had anticipated a bad time. The cops were quite annoyed at the disappearing act she and Michael and Zed had pulled. And they very much wanted her to give them Michael and Zed's addresses.

She had been more than willing to tell them where Zed was. Where his body was, anyway. But they hadn't believed her. Childhood had sneaked up on her, and she had acted barrio enough that they hadn't been particularly polite. Or gentle. She rubbed the tenderness of a bruise above her left elbow. The cheap lawyer she'd hired hadn't sounded very worried, but he got paid whether she went to jail or not.

She wondered if they had let Xia go. She wondered what they had done with Michael.

No one was going to tell *her* anything.

The video pickups stared down at her like unblinking glass eyes. She didn't look up at them but stifled an urge to give her invisible observer the finger. It was so easy to fall back into childhood patterns, the old self-defeating behavior. Arrow had taught her better; it never hurt to play the game if you came out with what you needed in the end. And if the price wasn't too high.

She had never shared much about her childhood with Arrow, and now she felt a sudden piercing regret for that willful silence. He would have understood if anyone could. But he had respected her silence, had been careful not to trespass. She wished he had, suddenly and intensely. Maybe his insight would have helped, would have let her touch some of the hurting that had kept her so distant from Katrina. Margarita tucked her feet under her, suppressing an urgent need to get up and *move.* Her silence with Arrow had been an angry thing. Like her refusal to tell Michael about her past.

Margarita's lips twitched, and she squirmed on the hard cot. Ultimately, Arrow had accepted her anger. As Katrina had. And she had lost them both. Margarita stared up at one of the round, glassy video eyes. There probably was no observer. The whole system would be watchdogged by an autoroutine that would analyze inmate behavior against certain movement parameters and set off some kind of alarm if anyone did anything suspicious. The system had gotten pretty damn automated, she thought bitterly. Plug people in at one end, and eventually they got spit out at the other end. Nobody much had to handle them in between. Except a few rubber-gloved guards willing to risk the latest virus stewing in the city's dirty corners. Everything else—arraignment, bail hearing, trial—could take place on-screen, nice and safe and clean.

Maybe she'd put that into a holo, after she finished the platform one—mix a nice montage of clean mountain visuals with bits of urban decay, like scuffing through pretty fall leaves and kicking up a carcass of a dead mole with its eyes full of maggots. That would be a new direction. Yeah, her ecophile audience would probably like it about as much as the platformers would like her platform piece. She grimaced. If she got that darkness to resonate just right with the light, maybe it would make them look at the world a little differently.

Could she afford to make her audience uneasy? Holoture wasn't a street-corner art.

But excitement fizzed in her blood like bubbles in champagne and wouldn't go away. Do it. Take the chance, because it would be *good.*

The lock clicked. "Espinoza." The gloved guard wasn't wearing a mask, and he looked bored. "Let's go."

"Let's go where?" She stood, not expecting an answer, keeping one wary eye on him even though he'd left his stun wand hanging on his belt.

To her surprise, he answered her. "Out. You can pick up your stuff at the front desk."

So the lawyer had leaned on them hard enough, or they'd gotten tired of waiting for her to provide addresses. Relief washed through her, because she had never trusted the machine. She let the guard usher her down the dim hall, very anxious to get out of this place.

A bored woman at the front desk handed her a sealed plastic bag with all the things they'd taken from her when they'd arrested her. Which wasn't much. Margarita ripped the bag open and dumped the contents onto the desk, earning an annoyed glare from the woman. She had obviously bought a cosmetic workover, Polynesian style with a subtle touch of African—wide, high cheekbones, coarse black hair straight as a horse's tail, and slightly too-full lips. It was today's fad, all over the street. Margarita wondered how much of her salary went to paying off the maintenance.

You could wear youth almost forever—for a price. Margarita wondered suddenly if this woman would ever dare let go, let the years catch up with her. Maybe that youthful face had already hardened into a stone mask, trapping her. She felt a sudden pity as she pocketed her ID card. And she felt a sudden respect for Xia's aging face. Looks could possess you if you let them.

A folded leaf of hardcopy had fallen out of the bag with her ID card and folded scrip. Now she picked it up and unfolded it. It was a handwritten note in a strong, sweeping script.

> Rita,
>
> Michael and I are in Taos. Your lawyer says you'll be released, and he doesn't seem like too much of a sleaze, so I believe him. I saw on the news that one Thomas Ariades died in a freak traffic accident. Your dancer is safe. I'm glad. See you next time we cross paths.
>
> Xia.

Margarita crumpled the hardcopy slowly. So. Ariades was dead; Katrina was safe. Xia hadn't said that Michael had wakened. *See you next time we cross paths.* That was Xia—a wind that blew through Margarita's life every so often, leaving nothing behind.

Instead of anger, she felt a sudden piercing sadness. Xia had never pretended to be anything else. And she had never apologized for it.

The woman behind the desk was staring at Margarita with bored hostility. I'm on this side, you're on that side, her glance said. Margarita looked down at the wad of paper in her fist, tossed it into the recycle slot on the desk, and smiled gently. "You look very nice." Turning her back on the woman's wary surprise, she walked through the doors and out into the street.

Exhaust from the expensively licensed private cars tainted the air, mixed with the concrete and grime smell of the city. The scent of frying food tickled her nose, and her belly rumbled loudly. Somehow she'd managed to miss mealtimes inside. Or they had forgotten to feed her. Maybe they fed you only after you were sentenced.

She followed her nose to the food seller in the next block: a woman who fried falafel over a cart-mounted burner and sold it wrapped in pale triangles of thin bread. Margarita traded a leaf of her reclaimed scrip for one of the sandwiches, spooned a mint and yogurt sauce onto the crispy balls of falafel, and took a huge bite. The falafel burned her mouth, but it tasted wonderful. Still eating, she headed for the public booth on the corner. This time hope was only a faint flicker when the slightly British-flavored terminal voice told her she had one piece of mail waiting.

Oh, yeah, the Yamada letter. She'd forgotten about that. Margarita sighed as Delia's on-screen smile and nasal tones filled the booth. What did Ari's assistant want? To cancel the rest of the show?

"Margarita, dear, I don't know where you've disappeared to, but I certainly hope you're working. I've been reviewing our schedule, and frankly, I'm not impressed with Ari's lineup for the coming year."

Yeah, here it comes. Lips tight, Margarita almost cut her off. Why listen? Maybe she should just e-mail Delia a note to tell her to stick the stage into the storeroom and she'd collect it eventually.

"I've taken over his position, and I'd like to continue you as one of our featured artists. At least for the next six months. You do have something else that we can put in place after this one? I'm really looking forward to seeing it, Margarita. Let me know if this is all fine with you. Here's the contract." Delia's face vanished, to be replaced by white lettering on a blue background. "Look it over and get back to me so we can get the catalog online, okay?"

Margarita stared at the lines of legal language, her mind refusing to register any of it. Another piece? Featured artist status? Automatically she was looking for a catch, sniffing around this unbelievably amazing message for the kind of price Ari had asked for. Which might be part of this deal but not the bottom line, or Delia wouldn't have uploaded the contract. Now she would be open to legal action if she withdrew the offer without cause.

So maybe—just maybe—this offer was genuine. Or mostly genuine, anyway. "Exit." Staring at the featureless screen, Margarita shook her head.

Featured artist.

She could do the platform piece. Margarita drew in a slow breath. Bright sun dazzled her as she exited into the street once more. No word from Katrina, but Archenwald-Shen had his sphere, and Ariades was dead. Xia was right—she was safe. Margarita opened her hand slowly and stared at the lines in her palm. *Whore.* It was a terrible word, and she had flung it in Katrina's face. There was no reason to expect any messages from her.

Margarita closed her hand into a fist. Down the block the falafel seller was dishing out sandwiches to the lunch-hour crowd. A voice rose shrilly, and the small cluster of customers scattered, bodies moving with jerky, anxious rhythms. A slight, blond figure dashed down the sidewalk, skinny legs flying. A kid. Margarita stepped back as he dashed past her, face intent, legs pumping. He clutched a fistful of the falafel seller's bread in one hand.

For an instant he looked up and his eyes met hers, wary and ready to dodge. But beneath that wariness she caught a glint of light—laughter? This food snatch might be survival, but hey, it was fun, too, this game of chase, and besides, the kid was winning.

Then he was gone, darting into the mouth of an alley, and the sound of his running footsteps was fading on the noon air.

The owner of the stand had given up the chase after a few steps and had turned back to her customers. She looked briefly over her shoulder and shook her fist at Margarita—for failing to grab the thief, probably. Margarita shrugged, then peeked into the now-empty alley as she walked past. There had been desperation in that skinny, running body, yet also that hint of fun. He reminded her suddenly of the skinny, mangy coyotes that lived in the dry hills above the barrio, raiding the 'burbs' Dumpsters and yards for garbage and cats. She'd met one once. It had lost a front paw to a trap, but it had grinned at her, poised on its three legs, its yellow eyes full of sly amusement at her surprise. And then it had vanished into the weedy lot behind it.

She would put this coyote kid into her urban holo. The one she was going to do after the platform piece.

"You know, Arrow?" Margarita said softly. "I think maybe I *can* do people. I think maybe I need to." She turned a corner, and it came to her suddenly that she was on her way to the bus station. That she was on her way to Taos.

She was going to listen to the Stones in Michael's garden. Maybe she would talk to Xia again or just sit with Michael for a while. Maybe she'd talk to him about Zed, about time and the past and how nothing was really over. Maybe she would find Zed there, in the Stones' song. She walked faster, her blood singing with an echo of sage and dry heat. The Southwest was full of neat environment, where it hadn't dried up and blown away. Maybe she could come up with something for Delia. Rocks, this time around. Desert. Lizards. Or maybe not, but it wouldn't hurt to go see. Taos tugged at her, the way the moon tugged at the sea.

The bus station took up the end of the block, fronting a big parking lot that was mostly empty. Three buses stood on the asphalt-paved lot. She had a feeling that one of them would be heading for New Mexico.

It was a destination, never mind where that sense of urgency had come from. And it would put off any new decisions for a day or so at least. Margarita hurried into the terminal, already fishing for her ID card.

She couldn't get to Taos directly, Margarita discovered; tourist-supported Albuquerque had managed to establish a death-grip monopoly on Taos-bound traffic. If you wanted southwestern ambience, you could find a more culturally upscale version in Santa Fe. If you wanted Taos, you had to go through Albuquerque. Margarita leaned back in the expensive, air-conditioned tour bus, waiting impatiently for the Taos perimeter guards in their Federal Historic Registry uniforms to finish scanning the bus for recording devices. She sipped at the iced tea that the steward had served, wondering who got the payoffs for this lovely little monopoly and how much of her money would end up in their pockets.

It wasn't really the price of the tour that bothered her, although the expense was painfully real enough. It was the suffocating sense of illusion that depressed her. Albuquerque and the Historic Registry had decided what was important, and they weren't about to let the real world contradict them. The hostel she'd stayed in the previous night had been a prime example, designed as an adobe village, a simulated Taos pueblo, complete with wooden ladders leading to the roof, barred with chains and warning signs. Margarita had always used illusion to attempt truth—her perception of truth, anyway. Beyond the clean bus window a yellow dog lifted its leg against a fence post. The Historic Registry used illusion to perpetuate illusion—history retrofitted to current-day perceptions.

She had wandered around the too-pretty buildings of the hostel this morning, killing time until her bus was ready to leave, and had discovered a weathered old man with a leathery, sun-dried face and milky UV cataracts hoeing weeds out behind one of the units. Or rather, he had been hoeing. About all he had been digging up was dirt; the weeds were pretty much untouched. At first she had blamed his bad vision. But as she watched, she had realized he was carefully avoiding them. After a while a man with a slick, managerial demeanor had shown up and scolded the old man, gesturing at the weeds. As he had stomped back to his air-conditioned office, the old man had turned to Margarita and given her a gap-toothed, conspiratorial grin. And had gone back to digging dirt.

When she had pressed two leaves of scrip into his hand, he had drawn himself up to his five-foot-plus height, affronted.

"A gift," she had said quickly. "Because I like weeds, too."

"Wait," he had called after her, and when she had paused, he had shuffled over to press a dusty bouquet of the freshly picked weeds into her hand. "For the cough." He had coughed for her, a hard, hacking sound. "Make tea." And then he had gone back to his hoe, his posture proud in spite of his cautious shuffle.

A gift requires a gift.

Yes, she could like this man who let the weeds grow and knew their value. A gift for a gift. If you didn't give a gift back, you would be saddled with a debt, an obligation. Arrow had given her a gift of his talent. Margarita looked through the window, barely registering the sage-covered hills beyond the Taos perimeter fence. Michael had given her the gift of life, even if he had done so without knowing. And Katrina had given her . . . love.

And she owed them all. Margarita shivered in the cool air-conditioned air, oppressed by that sense of debt. Maybe that was what she had been hiding from behind her wall of anger.

Maybe it was too late for gifts.

The Registry people had taken their scanners off the bus, and it was moving now, rolling slowly through the gate, into the static yesterday that was Old Taos. The adobe on either side of the street was real. Some of it. Some of it was concrete adobe but old enough to be validated by a Registry medallion. Jeans-clad locals, many with faces as Hispanic as her own, wandered the streets. She wondered if they lived here or if they only played a part and went home to an air-conditioned apartment at night to do VR and ski the Alps. The dress code seemed a little too consistent to be real.

Mostly, tourists crowded the streets—a lot of tourists, although the Registry strictly limited the number allowed inside the gates at any one time. Small galleries, jewelry and clothing shops, and restaurants lined the main street and the small side streets and plazas. The bus was scheduled to stop at the Taos Hotel. Margarita watched a dark-skinned woman dressed as a local in a striped shawl and dowdy flower-print dress haul a cranky toddler up to the curb. The child suddenly broke free and darted into the street in front of an oncoming bus. Passengers exclaimed, and Margarita hunched, expecting impact, the shrieks of mother and onlookers.

But a small blond woman leapt from the curb, scooped one arm around the child's waist, and swung him gracefully back onto the curb. Margarita gasped, her throat closing at that familiar, heartbreaking blend of strength and grace. "Katrina!"

The bus was rolling on down the street, and already the scene of the near accident was half a crowded block behind them.

Margarita snatched up her carryall and ran down the aisle. "Driver, let me out here." Heads were turning, annoyed, curious, or simply bored. The steward was looking her way from the back of the bus, his expression disapproving. "Right now, please."

"Sorry." The driver, young and sullen, didn't sound sorry. "I just make the one stop. At the hotel."

She clenched her teeth and fumbled her last leaf of scrip from her pocket. "Quick, before the uniform gets here." She dropped the leaf into his lap. "Tell him I'm crazy and I threatened you with a knife."

He grinned, eyes full of unexpected mischief, and opened the doors as he braked for the stop sign on the corner.

"Hey!" The steward hurried down the aisle.

Margarita lifted a hand to the driver and swung herself off the bus, clutching her carryall.

The sidewalk jarred her from the soles of her feet to the top of her head. The bus accelerated with a mumbling roar from its electric motor. It was *hot*. Margarita drew a gasping breath, hoping that the driver didn't get into too much trouble. Sweat immediately coated her arms and face, and her armpits prickled. She shaded her eyes, searching for Katrina on the crowded sidewalk. No sign of her. Urgency seized her by the throat and sent her hurrying down the sidewalk. The mother and kid had disappeared. Tourists eddied along the shop fronts, eyeing silver, licensed leatherwork, beads, and the ethnic foods that they would probably contemplate with horror if they weren't an upscale fad.

Damn. Margarita pushed her way through the throng, straining to see over the forest of shoulders and fancy western hats. What had brought Katrina to Taos? Maybe it hadn't been Katrina, after all. Maybe it had been someone else, a chance look-alike.

But it had been Katrina. She *knew* it with a kind of cellular conviction that had nothing to do with logic. Margarita scanned a small, shop-lined alleyway, biting her lip with frustration. Katrina could be in this store, that tavern, buying a blouse or ordering a beer and not giving Margarita a single thought. Go look? Or check the next street? She hesitated, her gut churning, because how did you find someone in a town full of tourists? Unless she could bribe someone into searching the Registry's visitor database, she could spend a week asking at every hotel, bed and breakfast, or fancy rooming house. And what if Katrina left tomorrow? She could go anywhere.

Katrina was alive.

Margarita broke into a run, her shoes slapping the pavement, drawing almost as many startled and hostile glares as she had up on the platform. Urgency seized her as it had back in San Francisco and wouldn't let her stop and peer into stores. She dashed around a corner, nearly flattening an elderly couple. The man yelled something after her, his voice cracking with outrage. The street ended in a tiny plaza where a fountain spouted real water into the hot dry air.

And she was there, sitting on the stone bench that edged the fountain, arms crossed on one raised knee, staring at the water. Her hair, almost silver in the intense sun, was coming loose from its thick braid. It hung forward, half across her face, and the clean lines of cheek and hair nearly stopped Margarita's breath.

Dear God, she was so beautiful.

"Katrina?" The word caught in her throat, snagged on something thorny, and shredded into a whisper. But Katrina heard and turned, her head coming up, hair falling back over her shoulder in a river of light. For an instant terror seized Margarita, and her muscles twitched with a burning need to flee.

Then she was running across the cracked stones of the plaza, throwing her arms around Katrina, pulling her close, harder, holding her so tightly that her own ribs wanted to crack—no, that was Katrina, holding her just as tightly. "I was so scared." The words came out in breathy bursts, rough with tears. "I didn't know where you were. I thought you might be dead. Trina, I am so *sorry*."

"Me, too." Katrina, who never cried, who was always so balanced, was crying.

For a while there was no space for words, no need for anything but the warmth and tightness of arms, rib cage, smell and feel, and *presence*. People stared, or averted their eyes, or giggled, and Margarita didn't care.

"I can't ever take back what I said." Margarita pulled back

finally, blinking, dazzled by the sun and Katrina's eyes. "I can't ever say I'm sorry and make it go away."

"I know." Katrina touched her face lightly. "I was so sure it was over when I took off. I wasn't good for you, and you weren't good for me."

"No!"

"I was afraid." She turned her face away, the curve of her cheek stark against the fountain's stone. "It hurt you, what you were doing. And I couldn't get at the *why*, couldn't make it stop hurting. I was scared that if it didn't work, if you didn't start making it in the galleries, that you'd just take off. Run away from it. And I'd . . . lose you anyway."

"I *was* running away." Margarita leaned her face on Katrina's shoulder. "From Arrow, from you—because I loved you. And I was running from my own talent, too. Trina, I love you." She breathed the words against Katrina's neck. "And I'm afraid."

"I love *you*, Mar." Katrina's arms tightened around her. "I tried not to, but I do."

Margarita laughed softly, a sense of lightness growing inside her; it was fragile yet but growing stronger, sweeter by the minute. "What are you *doing* here?" She pushed Katrina away and held her by the shoulders. "Do you know how crazy it is to run into you *here*?"

"I came to listen to Michael Tryon's Stones." Katrina's smile was tentative, as if she expected Margarita to get angry. "I thought if I got a sense of who he is, maybe I'd understand you better—or what hurt you, anyway. It felt *right*, as if I'd already done this, come to Taos to listen to Michael Tryon's life, as if I knew that I'd find you here. As if the Stones were calling me." She laughed, the sound catching in her throat. "Anyway, here I am."

"Maybe—they were. Calling you. It was never you who hurt me." Margarita leaned her head on Katrina's shoulder. "Did you know that someone was trying to . . . find you?" She put her arm around Katrina's waist. "Some very ugly people were after that pendant."

"What happened?" Alarm tightened Katrina's face. "Margarita, did they come after you?"

"It's not a problem anymore." At the cost of three lives. No, make that four, including Yiassis. And Archenwald-Shen would go smugly on about his business. She'd *use* that. Margarita let her breath out in a slow sigh. Oh, yeah, all the smug, complacent people out there, comfortable with their nice illusions. Let her put all this into image and sound and scent, and she would *really* show them a few things.

"I was afraid to change things, Trina. In my art. In my life." Margarita grinned suddenly, that lightness pushing up inside her like an expanding bubble. "Not to change is to die."

Katrina took her hand, her expression tentative. "Come on. I'll buy you lunch, or at least a beer, and you can tell me everything."

"Everything?" Margarita let herself be tugged along, grinning now, full of crazy happiness. "That's some story, and I'll tell you every bit of it. You know, I really like Xia. She's an amazing woman."

"You *have* changed." Katrina laughed—a happy sound, even if that tentative note was still there. "Look." She nodded. "That's the gallery where Michael's Stones are displayed." She gave Margarita a cautious sideways glance. "I was . . . impressed by them."

"He's here. I need to find him." Maybe Xia was right, and the past would reach out to him. Rescue him. "Let's go in. Maybe they know." Tickled by that unexplained urgency again, Margarita tugged Katrina toward the gallery. It was made of what looked like real adobe. Bits of golden straw sparkled in the mud plaster. They came from dung, the guide had told them, added to the adobe mixture to give it strength. Tiny bells tinkled as she opened the warped wooden door.

She had expected dim light, a cavernous feel. But the sun streamed in through the front window, blending with the artfully focused floods that highlighted the paintings and sculptures. Michael's Stones took up the center of the floor. They stood on polished wooden pedestals, displayed against off-white linen flats: a tall Major and a trio of Minors.

Oh, yes, they were his Stones. A gentle symphony of summer sun, sweat, and pleasant contemplative weariness murmured at the edges of her mind, like a rich melody heard at the limit of hearing. Visions flickered in her head: glimpses of rocky, sage-green slopes, a dry arroyo, a laughing brown face, a woman with dark eyes.

Xia.

Recognition jarred her from her reverie. Xia was part of that Stone. A young Xia. Michael's lover. His soul was engraved on this Stone, too. This was the Michael Tryon who had fathered her with Xia one night, or morning, or afternoon.

This was the Stone that would call him back. He'd hear this one, oh, yes.

"I'm sorry." Angry words from the back of the shop. A woman's voice. "The subject is closed. I will not discuss it with you further."

Margarita blinked and focused on the hard, slightly shrill voice. A desk stood in the far corner of the gallery, half-hidden by a twining sculpture of shaped polymer. Two women stood in front of it, oblivious to Margarita, their postures rigid and tense.

One was Xia, head back, chin tilted aggressively. The other woman was young—not much older than Margarita—with Xia's height and build but as fair as Katrina. And she had the power here. You could see it in the way she stood, the way Xia's shoulders drooped a little.

"So." Katrina leaned her shoulder lightly against Margarita, her eyes on Xia and the blond woman. "So what do you think of Sun Stone? I was really impressed."

Her voice was too loud for the small space. Intentionally loud, because Katrina never raised her voice, not even when she was angry. Both women looked up.

"I'm sorry. I didn't hear you come in." Smoothing away her frown, the blond woman hurried up to greet them. "I'm Christine Neiman." She extended a square strong hand, her smile bright and professionally warm. "Yes, Sun Stone *is* rather impressive, isn't it?"

"Yes." Margarita touched the gallery owner's hand lightly. "It is." She looked beyond her at Xia's tight face. "What's wrong?"

"You know each other?" Christine's smile faded as she examined Margarita's face. "Oh, I see." She looked at Xia, then back to Margarita. "You must be the one who wrote to him. To Michael." She took a single step backward, hostility tightening her face. "You told him you were his daughter."

"I am." Maybe.

"I'd like to see the DNA work to back it up." Her eyes met Margarita's, ice blue, unreadable as chips of broken china.

"I gave him my scan." She didn't ever know if he'd looked at it or compared it to his own. But that shook the gallery owner.

She frowned and looked away, licking her lips. "Well, it's not my affair. I only handle his Stones."

For a moment this pale cold woman reminded Margarita of Sorrel when he talked about Xia. Do you love him? she wondered. Do you blame me because he left? "Where is he?" she asked Xia, no longer angry, only a little sad and not sure why.

"Ask her." Xia's face was closed, all emotion hidden. "She petitioned to become his legal guardian, and the court granted it. I don't know where he is."

"He's in a private clinic here in town. Receiving the best care possible." *Better than you gave him*, Christine's manner said. "The doctor suggested that we limit visitors for the time being." She gave Margarita a challenging look. "Any claim against him would have to be backed up by genetic proof, of course."

"What do you think I'm after?" Margarita asked softly. "His money? Or do you think I'm going to take him away from you?"

For an instant the gallery owner's eyes looked bleak and empty. Then she shrugged and tossed her head. "Whatever you're up to, you'll have to do it through a lawyer. If you'll excuse me—"

"No." Margarita stepped in front of her as she tried to retreat. "Do you know what happened to him? Did Xia tell you?"

"Nothing I believed. Now, please, I have my billing to attend to." She glanced at her terminal, drawing her professional manner around herself like a cloak.

Close enough to the Stone to touch it, Margarita had a misty vision of a young, black-haired Xia leaning against a twisted tree trunk with a sun-bleached skull on her lap. Smiling. Her face tender. And then it vanished in a gentle wash of sun heat on skin, sand grating beneath boot soles, the cool touch of wind on a sunburned cheek . . . She turned toward the Stone, touched it. A strange texture: neither cool nor warm, or maybe both at the same time. Not quite the feel of stone, not quite petrified flesh. Vision and emotion washed over her in a gentle tide, sweeping her into a space of youth, and dusty sun, and love . . .

"Excuse me." Christine's hand on her wrist was barely gentle. "Please don't touch the Stone. Unless you *know* you're not a sensitive."

"I'm not." She took her hand away anyway, dizzy with the rush of sensation that had just poured into her. "I can't wake a Stone. I didn't inherit that from him." Or much of anything. What if she was this Estevan's daughter? I don't want that, she thought, and sudden pain took her by surprise. "I want to see him."

"Do you?" Anger abraded Christine's tone. "He was happy here. He was doing what he wanted to be doing. Until you came along. Why the hell did you have to send him that letter?" She spun away from them and stalked back to her desk, her shoulders tight, almost hunched.

Love could be such a burden. "I'm sorry," Margarita said softly. "I am. He's hurt, you know. I'm not sure what hurt him, but it did. If someone can't touch him, help him, maybe he'll never come back. Maybe he'll hide forever."

"Come back from *where*? He sustained some kind of trauma. The doctor said so." Christine leaned both palms on her desktop, refusing to look at them. "So how about if you tell me what happened."

"Some kind of alien consciousness touched him. It touched me. Maybe Katrina and Xia, too." Margarita drew a slow breath. "I think it brought us here for Michael. Will you help me try to reach him?"

Zed was sitting on the desk, one foot tucked under him. He nodded at her, lips quirked in a lopsided smile.

"Please?" Margarita met Christine's eyes and saw tears there, beneath the surface. "Because you love him," she said softly.

Christine looked away.

"For him." Xia touched her shoulder, her voice full of sadness. "I'm not your competition. I never was."

Christine jerked her head sideways in an angry arc. "I'm not sure it even matters if he wakes up. He can't sculpt Stones anymore. Some mining company is claiming that they've cleaned out the belt, that they've harvested the last Stone.

That's all Michael cared about—his Stones. It's going to destroy him."

From the desk, Zed smiled at Margarita, his eyes full of distant stars and their circling planets.

"No more Stones?" Margarita whispered. Shen had done it, then; her bluff had worked. "The Stones aren't everything to him anymore," she said softly. She could see love in Christine's face, and hurt, too. "It's true, Christine. Will you bring Michael here?" She reached out to brush Sun Stone with her fingertips, evoking echoes of distant, sun-struck days. "I think maybe there's a part of him here that he's been trying to find. I think maybe he'll hear it."

For a long moment Christine's expression didn't change. Then she looked aside, her hostility draining away, leaving her face pale and full of grief. "All right." Her shoulders slumped. "We'll bring him here. For whatever good that does."

You do love him, Margarita thought with piercing clarity. Enough to risk losing him. She reached out suddenly to take Christine's hand in both of hers. "Thank you."

"Don't." Christine turned her face away. "I'll call the clinic and make the arrangements." She laughed a single broken note. "They're going to think I'm crazy. And maybe I am." She pulled her hand free, turned her back on them, and retreated to her terminal.

Michael had never mentioned this woman. A tremendous sadness welled up inside Margarita. I am sorry for you, she thought, and bowed her head. The first tear came as Katrina put her arms around her and drew her close.

Chapter Twenty

It was summer—hot and dry like all summers. Michael sat on the bank of the Hondo, the sun on his shoulders, the hum of insects in his ears. On the far bank of the muddy early-summer trickle Xia sat with her back against a dead juniper, brushing dry clay from the skull she'd found. It was from a goat, the curved horns still attached, the eye sockets staring with a strange wisdom. How long ago did it die, and why? Michael met its silent stare. Disease? A coyote?

How long had it lain in the soil, first covered, then uncovered by rain and flood? It hadn't changed much in all that time.

You're right. The empty sockets contemplated him. *Life is change. The end of change is the end of life. You should know that.*

The goat skull spoke in Zed's voice. It spoke in the Stones' voice. It isn't my fault, Michael tried to say, but the words stuck inside him like dry riverbed pebbles.

Your fault as much as anyone's. Self-imposed isolation is no excuse. You're very young, your race, but you can grow up. If you want to. You imposed your memories on us; you ended our ability to share, to change. You killed us.

"It was art." Michael looked away from the skull's accusing eyes. "It mattered. And we didn't know."

The skull merely stared at him.

It was right to accuse him. Because he'd known they were alive from the first time he'd touched one. Remorse squeezed Michael. I knew, and I imposed my self on them, overlaid a soul with my human memories, my past, my loves and fears and needs. *The warp is strung from the sculptor's soul.* And the Stones could no longer share, change . . . live.

He had killed.

Mistake for mistake, the skull said with Zed's smirk. *You are so fragile.*

Remorse gripped Michael again, but this time it wasn't his own, and it was so vast that he nearly cried out with the pain of it: the Stones' remorse.

We also ended change. Life. There is no balancing of greater against lesser evil. Evil is simply evil.

Compassion bathed Michael, banishing the pain.

An eye for an eye? Yes and . . . no. *You are so fragile,* the Stone soul had said. Yes, fragile. For the Stones, time did not exist. Now was a single infinite instant that had no beginning, middle, or end. I can't grasp it, Michael thought, and shivered. S'Wanna hadn't been able to grasp it, either. Or Lustik, or Danners. They had been lost. Death had been the only anchor to their humanity.

Death was such a *human* thing.

Across the Hondo, Xia cradled a goat skull in her lap. Michael buried his face in his hands. We killed. We destroyed souls in the name of creation. He stood slowly and turned his back on the Hondo, on Xia's face, so full of compassion.

The Stones' compassion? For this crippled, isolated race.

We are so *alone.* Dear God, what we lack.

The landscape wavered, and he realized that it wasn't real; it was only a backdrop, a flimsy curtain of illusion. In a moment it would tear, and he would look through to see the enormity of his sin. So many souls were out there—so much beauty shared among them. Sage and sand ended behind him, becoming the shore of an endless sea of darkness. That darkness was human, without sharing, silent and empty. Death. He would be safe there. Forever. He took a step into that welcome darkness, then another.

"Michael?"

Xia, calling him? He looked back, hesitating. She was standing on the riverbank, holding out her hands to him.

"I can't," he whispered.

"Yes, you can." Xia's eyes were soft, full of love and tears. "You're not finished yet."

"But I am." Anguish twisted him, and he took another step into darkness. Let go and the pain would stop.

But there was something he had wanted to tell her. Something important. He struggled to remember it as a thunderstorm massed on the horizon. The first gust of wind struck him, whipping his clothes, stinging his face with grit. Suddenly he was in his Stone garden, and Xia sat against Sun Stone, her long hair blowing in the wind. The safe darkness had vanished. He looked around for it, panic seizing him.

"Wake up, Michael." Xia stretched out her hands. "I love you. I always have, and I need you to come back. Wake up," she sang with the Stone's voice.

He remembered now what he had to tell her, what mattered, what had mattered all these years. "I love you," he whispered.

The words crashed like silent thunder, shattering sage and dust, shattering the Stone and Xia's reaching hands. Light blinded him, and he tried to turn his face away. His head was too heavy, as if he himself were turning to Stone. Hands touched him, and it *hurt*.

"Stop." It came out a garbled croak.

"Michael? Michael, come *back*."

Xia's voice, but not her voice. Not quite. Old, he'd dreamed of her old, with gray hair—no—not a dream. Memory was seeping back in bright bits of vision, like drops of water oozing through a cracked vase. A woman opening a door, young and wary . . . not Xia. Margarita—his daughter. They had traveled up to the platform, and he'd found Xia again.

Sun Stone? The memories were thin transparencies overlaid on the dark music of—the Stone's eternal dying.

What have I *done*?

"Michael!" Xia's voice, sharp as a claw, snagged him, yanking him from darkness forward into the harsh, hurting, abrasive light. "Stay here, with us. Michael? Wake *up*. Now!"

His eyelids fluttered, scattering photons, feeling each and every one of them, aware of fat molecules of oxygen and nitrogen bouncing off his skin like tiny rubbery balls. He opened his eyes, because Xia was right. He *wasn't* finished. Someone groaned in the distance—his own voice. A pale balloon shape wavered in front of his eyes, coalescing slowly into a face.

"Xia?" The light was dimming, or his eyes were adjusting.

It *was* Xia. The Xia he remembered from the platform, not the vision of Stone-remembered yesterday.

Behind her, Sun Stone sang its unending song, murmuring of the Hondo and sun and a goat skull. Dying, forever. He groaned again because he'd done this, *he*, Michael Tryon.

"Michael? We're here. It's all right. You're in Taos. In Christine's gallery."

Margarita's voice? My daughter, he thought, and suddenly wanted to cry. *My daughter.* Will you judge me, too? He struggled to sit up, shocked at his weakness, at the instant tremble of his muscles. He felt arms behind his shoulders, voices like birds chirping in the dawn bushes outside his window. No, that was before, the bird voices. In Taos, before he'd left.

The room revolved slowly around him. He recognized the gallery, recognized Christine's face—she looked so worried—and knew where he was. Another part looked at all this with a stranger's eyes. It was a weird schizophrenic state of mind: native and newcomer both inside the same soul. What a beautiful thing, a soul. Was there any crime greater than its destruction?

"Can you hear me?" Margarita was sitting beside him, one arm supporting him with a strength he unabashedly needed. "We were so worried." Her voice faltered. "I . . . was so worried. What happened, Michael? Up at Vildorn?"

Vildorn. The Stone—that Stone. Terror seized him. "Did they send it downside?" The words came out in a whisper, as if he'd forgotten how to speak. "Did it get sold?" He struggled to sit upright, light-headed. "I've got to find it."

"Somebody sent it out of orbit. It didn't get sold, Michael." Her urgent tone cut through the fog in his head. "No more Stones are coming down." Her cheek brushed his, her breath warm on his face. "It's over, okay? No more Stones."

She was so afraid. Of what? He blinked, his eyes focusing finally, and discovered tears on her face. For him? "Is Katrina all right?" He wiped her cheek.

"She's safe. She's right here." Margarita took his hand and held it tightly. "Michael, I was scared."

"We're so . . . alone." His words came out as a whisper, squeezed by the sheer immensity he remembered. "We're so shut off from everything. There are a billion beings out there, and . . . they share. They're a billion minds and . . . just one.

At the same time." He swallowed, struggling for words. "That *sharing*; it . . . sings the universe. I mean *everything*. I think maybe it is the universe." Except us. He closed his eyes, wanting to give in and mourn but knowing that he'd never come back if he did. "It's scattered among the galaxies, and every bit knows every other bit. And the Stones are part of it. We impose so much on them." Life, love, pain . . . yesterday. "We make them *alone*." They had always seemed so alive beneath his hands. "They can't change," he whispered. "They're dead. No, that's not it. They're *dying*. Forever. Trapped in our isolation." If I hadn't sculpted Sun Stone or Silver Stone—if Estevan hadn't sculpted Tree Stone—they would have lived. They would have evolved to become part of this vast song of joy.

Ah, Estevan, I'm glad you didn't live for this.

"I know, Michael. Some of this, anyway. Zed told me." Margarita had her hands on his arms, steadying him as he tottered to his feet. "You didn't know." Her face was turned up to his, and her eyes were full of pain.

She understood. He shook his head, nearly overwhelmed by that understanding. *Zed told me* . . . But in the end it didn't matter whether he had or hadn't known. Blame wasn't the issue here. Ignorance meant nothing. He had done this.

He had destroyed souls. Twisted them. Deformed them.

He swayed as black spots swarmed across his vision. Margarita held him upright. She was a strong woman, his daughter. He touched her face, needing her to know this, know how he felt. Willing her to know. He took another step, closer to Sun Stone, that symphony of yesterdays beating against him like afternoon sun on his face. Xia's love, his own, the soft sweet afternoons in the shade along the Hondo . . .

He had tried to hoard yesterday like gold. Pain twisted him, and he leaned on Margarita. He had been trying to hold on to it forever. He wanted the world to stop changing.

To stop changing is to die.

He lunged forward to slap both palms against the smooth, cool flesh of the Stone, shuddering as its dying, frozen soul writhed beneath his hands. For a second he ceased to exist, became only a gateway. *The warp is strung from the sculptor's soul.* And it bound the Stone. With a groan, he embraced it—

damage, memories, responsibility. And tore that warp into a thousand shreds.

There was no sound, nothing but terrible pain. A distant voice cried out, and then his vision cleared once more. He stood with his arms around a lump of stone—pretty stone, shot through with buried veins of silver and gold.

It was just a stone.

"What did you *do*?" Christine's horrified voice.

"I let it go," he said softly. That vast alien sharing grieved, and that terrible tide of grieving had driven him into darkness, had turned S'Wanna's hand against herself, and Danners's, and Lustik's. He would have died, too, perhaps, if Zed hadn't touched the Stone first. The Stones had comprehended Zed.

Because he was who he was? A twisted, genius soul. "I need to let them all go," Michael whispered.

Christine and Xia looked shocked, uncomprehending. But Margarita understood. She was staring at the empty Stone, a mix of horror and pity on her face. "You'll be a great holoturist," he said to her. "One of the best."

And he fainted, dropping back into a darkness that resonated with vast, inhuman compassion. And humans could be compassionate, too. We *are* alone, Michael thought.

And then he slept.

Chapter Twenty-one

Yamada Gallery was empty this late at night. Margarita stood just inside the door, listening to the small sounds of the old building's slumber. Here and there dim floods highlighted the shadows, picking out the dangling chains, the stark mesh of the balcony levels. Did Ari Yiassis's ghost haunt this space? Did he rattle that chain elevator, mourning his lost years? She listened but heard only the tick of metal contracting in the nighttime chill.

There was so much death in the world—in the barrio, in the ugly little wars that didn't even make the prime-time news anymore. How much do we ignore? she asked herself bitterly. How much, because the sob of one man or woman weeping gets lost in the white noise of so many tears?

The Stones had killed Danners and the other sculptors by accident, Michael had told her. Because the Stones hadn't understood the fragility of the human brain. It was Zed who had finally let them—it—understand. By becoming Zed. Or perhaps Zed had become the Stones. Margarita walked slowly across the shadowed floor. Michael grieved for the dead sculptors and the Stone soul he had damaged, both.

Arrow would grieve, if he were alive. He had cared, too. Perhaps too much. Margarita paused in front of a light sculpture by a popular new artist—shut down now so that only the dark pedestal bulked in the dim light. She had never let herself know this about Arrow before: how much he had immersed himself in people, their pain, and tears, and joy. He had cluttered his holoture and even his old-time movies with them.

And they had worked, never mind that they pissed people off or made the critics sneer sometimes.

They had worked because Arrow had cared about people, and that caring had come through in everything he did. He had cared about Margarita, too, and had hidden it behind that calm, aged face so that she didn't have to know it. He had given her space to grow into caring. Or to deny it if she needed to. Margarita closed her eyes, remembering Zed's proud cringe in Danners's dome and the young-old gang faces she'd grown up with. Remembering Arrow.

A soft sequence of taps at the locked door sent her heart leaping into her throat. Katrina's rhythm. She hurried across the floor to palm the lock, a bright, scary surge of love—and fear—turning her instantly shy. The door whispered open to reveal Katrina, spangled with raindrops.

"Hi. Rosita, that new dancer I told you about, twisted her ankle." She stepped through the door, bringing in a gust of damp wind and the wet-asphalt scent of new rain. "Gods, I'm soaked." She laughed and shook back her damp, loose hair. "I told Argent that Rosita couldn't handle the solo, that she was trying too hard. So when she fell, he got pissed." She rolled her eyes and gave a breathy sigh. "So he sent everyone home, and here I am. Is it okay?" Her smile faltered. "If I watch you compose?"

They were still a little careful of each other, still testing new ground. "Yes, it's okay." Margarita took her hand, a thousand unsayable feelings crowding her chest. "You can come watch. You can watch anything I'm working on. Before, I—" The words faltered, awkward and full of discomfort. She stopped at the base of the chain that led to her level, looking up into the shadowy space. "I wanted to keep you separate from what I did. Because then I could tell myself that you weren't really important, that you could walk out of my life and it would be okay. And you *could* walk out—I've given you enough reason. But I need you." And she'd never said that to anyone before.

"I thought about leaving," Katrina whispered from behind her. She put her arms around Margarita and kissed her shoulder gently. "You're trembling, Mar. I decided I didn't want to leave. You know, you're a great holoturist."

"I'm not great yet." Margarita leaned back into her embrace, tears pressing against the back of her eyelids even though she wasn't sad at all. "Maybe I will be, one day." She said the words gently because they were a promise to herself and Katrina together. "And if so, you're part of it." Gently she stepped away from Katrina's embrace, then bent to touch the chain elevator to life.

Its rattle was shockingly loud in the darkness. Margarita grabbed it and swung lightly onto a step. She wasn't afraid. In the last weeks mortality had taken on a new meaning for her. It wasn't that life meant less; life meant *more.* Suddenly death seemed almost trivial.

"What Michael said about the Stones." She looked down at Katrina, who was rising through the shadows beneath her. "You know, if time really isn't linear, then I'm still a kid." Young enough to know the backyard jungle of the project buildings as a wonderland, back before she'd started to learn the streets and the rules. "And in the future I'm dead. I want to touch them both," she said softly. The kid with an eye for the wonder that could lurk even in barrio shadows—and death. "I want to bring them together, make them . . . touch. They're not really separate."

Katrina reached up from below to touch her ankle lightly, as if she'd read Margarita's pain. And maybe she had.

Art had so many prices: the price you exacted from yourself and the price it could exact from the people whom you loved or who loved you. Prices within prices, like lacquered boxes nestled one inside another. And in the center, a gem?

I don't want to tell the media, Michael had said when he had told her about the Stones and his strategies for freeing their tortured common soul. *They won't listen, or they will, and it will become a circus. Who's going to believe me?*

So he was doing it himself. A trail of stories in the media—reports of silent Stones in museums and galleries around the world—marked his progress. In reaction, museums and private collectors were beginning to take extreme security measures. How long would it be before Michael ended up in prison or some psych ward? He knew what he was risking, Margarita told herself. No. It wasn't a risk, it was an inevitability.

Each release hurt him. She'd seen the pain he'd tried to hide as he emptied his own Stones.

What price art? What did it cost to toss a lifetime of creativity into the air like a handful of ashes? Michael wouldn't let her come with him. *It's my job*, he'd told her. *And two people attract a lot more attention than one.*

She had acceded because he had been right and because he didn't want her to see his pain. But a part of her had hurt. Abandonment again. She grimaced as she stepped from the swaying chain onto her balcony and held out a hand to Katrina. Maybe a part of her would always expect to be abandoned, to stand apart and play it safe. Even from the people she loved.

She bent to touch the holostage to life. Opalescent light shimmered above the platform, and she caught hints of rose, fresh grass, and hot metal as the generators warmed up. "You know, when we were on Sorrel's ship, I hated his ship voice. That teenage wiseass kid. You know what Xia told me?" Margarita picked up her console and ran the archive index. "She told me the voice was his son. He got killed in an accident, and Sorrel paid for a brain peel. They got enough to run a ship system. Xia said he told her once that Kelly could still learn and had a sense of humor and that for him, that meant Kelly was still alive." She paused. "I got a message from Xia today."

"You didn't tell me." Katrina ran her fingers through Margarita's hair.

"I just got it." Margarita frowned at the index, running an eye down the list of milieus. "She was on her way back up to the platform. Back to Sorrel, I guess." She touched the console, then watched the high-altitude greens and granite tones of an alpine meadow take shape on the stage. "Maybe she'll let him love her. Maybe she's ready to stop drifting." And maybe she would never be able to stop.

Tiny flowers shimmered among the green blades, trespassing on the weathered gray bones of the mountain. "Arrow once said that I couldn't put real people into my work until I could accept myself." She looked sideways at Katrina. "I'd like to put you into a piece one day. You'd be perfect for this winter cityscape I have in mind."

"City?" Katrina's eyebrows rose. "That's a change."

"Yes. It is. There are flowers in the city, you know. Weeds bloom."

"Yeah, I guess they do." Shadow and light softened Katrina's face as she nodded at the stage. "I think I've seen that before. Is this an old piece of yours?"

"No," Margarita started to say, because she'd pulled it out of the archive. But Katrina was right. "Yes," she said softly. "Oh, yes, it is an old piece."

How had it gotten *here*? She must have misfiled it. Or maybe Arrow had. She stepped slowly up onto the stage, the balcony fading, banished by gentle alpenglow. A breeze touched her cheek with a thread of cool urgency, a sigh of coming night that stirred the top of a single pine. She took a deep breath, struggling against a pang of nostalgia. She'd had to save it fast, once, because her interface had been trying to crash. She must have dumped it into the archive and then forgotten.

For an instant her fingers hovered over the console, ready to touch the meadow out of existence. Arrow hadn't been happy with this piece, and she'd never been quite certain why. And she had never really finished it, even though she'd had a buyer. Now it resonated with all the incompleteness that Arrow's death had left inside her. Her fingers stroked the console. It was good. But, so hungry for mastery, she had wanted him to tell her it was great. And, of course, he hadn't. She had been angry. Hurt.

"*I* had to decide," she said softly. "I had to know what was good and what was bad. That's what you wanted me to learn, wasn't it?" Margarita bowed her head, tears burning behind her eyelids.

So much ego went into this thing called art—and so much hurt. You had to open yourself to both, embrace both—the yin and yang of creation. A flute whispered beneath the rustle of grass and the distant evening cry of a hawk. It was a wandering note, thin as the mountain air and full of regret. Margarita walked quietly across the stage, sheltered by fir and pine. The stone beside the brook invited her to sit. It would be armature in a finished piece—a solid, rigid-foam shape to hide beneath the illusion of weathered granite. Here it was illusion only. She squatted beside it and frowned into a brook that was a waterless creation of light and cold. Illusory water chilled her fingers, and the breeze caught a loose strand of hair, teasing her, tugging gently.

Yeah, something was missing. Margarita brushed hair out of her face, tears smearing on her cheeks. Not great but good, and Arrow would be proud of her, only he was dead.

But he wasn't really dead. Not according to Zed or the Stones. Bracing the console in her lap, Margarita brought up the holo sketch she'd made of Zed so long ago and planted it on the far bank of the stream.

She didn't do people, and it showed. He looked worse than a mannequin, without life, without that *pose* of his. She touched in a few basic commands: walk, turn, stoop, rise, shrug. Had Zed ever shrugged? She tried to remember, but his face, his posture, that rakish, wary glint in his eyes—it was all slipping away. Fading. She scowled and hit *delete.*

Zed didn't go away. His face shimmered a little, shifted subtly, and somehow it really did look like him. So she hadn't done too badly, after all, but a chip was going if she'd lost her delete function. Hissing softly to herself, she tried again, thinking she'd better save before the whole system crashed.

"Forget it." Lithe, wiry, his insecurities almost invisible beneath that graceful, strutting walk of his, Zed splashed through the stream. "Sorry, lady, you can't delete me."

Zed. Not a holo sketch. "You know, you've never told me." Feeling strangely unsurprised, Margarita took her hands away from the console. "Are you a ghost? Or the Stones wearing a human shape?"

"I'm me." He tilted his head, trying for a profile view as he stared at his reflection in the stream. "I'm here, and I'm dead. I'm you, too." He grinned at her. "Which you should have figured out in that overgrown jungle of Andy's, but you didn't."

She winced, and Zed laughed.

"Get rid of that flute, okay?" He jerked his chin at her console. "It's a drag."

"Forget it." She glowered at him because he was so much . . . himself. Right down to the attitude. "You don't sound like an alien. Arrow liked the flute line."

"I'm not an alien." He eyed her. "Who's Arrow?"

"I am."

Margarita turned slowly, her heart hammering, and there was no need for that kind of adrenaline rush. Because Arrow had holoed himself a lot.

Gray-haired, 136, he smiled at her, his face the same weathered map of decades that she remembered from the night he had died. This was no holo; this was memory turned into . . . reality. Margarita sucked in a gasping breath, fingers reaching for her own face, touching, as if she needed to be sure of something. Was this why Danners had suicided? And Lustik and the others? Because all of a sudden they'd turned around and there were all the people they'd loved and lost?

"No, that's not quite it." Zed raised an eyebrow at her, then grinned at Arrow. "She hasn't quite got it yet. But maybe you can't before you die."

No, no she wasn't ready, not for Arrow. Margarita doubled over, clutching the console to her, seeking comfort in the hard reality of a corner pushing into her belly, hitting *delete* again and again, struggling against tears that burned like acid. A touch on her shoulder, and her flesh recognized it: warm strength, delicate old fingers. She drew a shuddering breath as the angular dryness of his cheekbone touched her temple.

"It wasn't on purpose." His whisper was soft in her ear. "I didn't try to die. I didn't mean to. It just happened."

She felt him, felt flesh. With a choked cry, Margarita leapt to her feet and spun into the holoed brook. Cold. An explosion of water, spattering her thighs with ice . . . She scrambled out, her tights soaked, her shoes full of icy water—*water*, not illusion. Zed had been flesh up on Sorrel's ship, but this was different. She stared back at Arrow, shivering and not just from the cold, still clutching the useless console. "What's happening?" she whispered.

Arrow waded across the stream, moving hesitantly because his joints were giving him trouble again. He reached for the console, his eyes on hers, loamy brown and startlingly clear. "I don't have to be here. If you don't want me to." He tugged the console free of her white-knuckled grip and touched voice control. "End it."

"No!" Margarita grabbed for the console and slapped the *cancel* button. "Arrow, don't go," she whispered. "Please?"

The alpenglow shifted, ready to give way to the chilly gray of a mountain evening. "I only have a moment." Arrow glanced back at Zed. "You, too. You never heard this in life, so come hear it now. It still may matter sometime, somewhere." He sat down on a fallen log near her and waited for Zed to amble up.

Margarita looked at the log, knowing it was illusion but chilled by her wet tights and sodden shoes. She took a half step toward it, then hesitated. "Does this mean I'm dead?" she whispered.

"I don't think so." Arrow's eyes twinkled, and Margarita laughed suddenly. Hell, dead or alive, sane or crazy, so be it. Maybe anything could happen, anything was possible. She hadn't felt this way since she was little and the barrio had still had its magic corners. And, yeah, she could look over her shoulder and find that kid grinning at her. With a soft laugh she sat down on the log—solid wood with crumbly, just-starting-to-rot bark—feeling Arrow's silent smile like sunshine on her face. Zed had crossed the stream to sit down beside them.

"The world lost something when it lost you." Arrow touched Zed's shoulder briefly.

"Sorry to disappoint you, old man, but I didn't mean to die any more than you did."

"Oh." Arrow sighed. "I didn't mean that." He frowned, considering. "The world lost you long before you died. Perhaps that's why you *did* die. Because a part of you was already lost."

"And maybe that's why I'm here." Zed stared at the flowers between his feet.

Margarita watched him: Zed, man and more than man, dead and more than alive. The ruddy light was like his intent, pervasive and clear. The cool breeze carried his mood, so that he *was* this scene and it was his soul. If she could only do it like this . . .

"And I *am* here. As alive as I've ever felt, for all I'm dead, too. You tell me, old man." Zed looked at Arrow finally. "What stood between me and the Stones? It kept me from really touching them, and then I think it let me become . . . what I am. Part of the whole, and not part of it. But what was it?"

Arrow looked past them, out into the softening light, and began to speak.

Each of us dies alone. When we learned this, we began to die. We feared the aloneness more than death.

He looked at Margarita. "Sorry. I don't have your feel for lex. Excuse me if it's rough."

He really was apologizing. Margarita couldn't stop the tears this time.

We touched life, imagining that we seized it, that we could weigh it against death, imagining that we understood death, too. We wove a blanket to cover the corpse of our dread.

Once we were young.

Once we saw the morning sun caper through curtains, across blankets our parents put on our beds; and we never saw the cheapness of the cloth; we never feared a sun that might steal our sleep or our play.

Each of us wove ourselves from immortal things, the sun, the good things we were fed when we were small. We created until we, the weavers, knew there was nobody.

Zed glanced away, head bowed, and Margarita thought she saw tears glimmer in his green eyes. Alive and dead, now and forever, his body frozen and unchanged until the unchanging sun went nova. Whatever lived had to change. So did this mean that immortality was death, after all? That death itself was simply another change, not an ending but another aspect of life? She touched her face, fingertips sliding in the tears that slicked her cheek. Who are you? she wanted to ask Zed. What are you? Can we go on living only by dying?

And me? What am I? She opened her hand and stared at the gleaming trace of tears on her skin. A piece of her soul had broken loose. Should she cling to it now or let it go? And what would she become if she did that? What had Zed chosen to do?

Night comes. The distance between skin and the chill: name it. What did we know when we were new? And when were we cold for the first time?

In remembering we fail. And in forgetting. Perhaps this is the world to come, the heaven: to remake each moment as it returns, setting it alone in imagination. In life we forget, or remember, and imagine little, recollecting the cold.

Arrow's whisper filled the deepening dusk, soft, dry as the rustle of grass blades, the wind's voice.

Once we were new, each of us measured against nothing except the distance between sunlight and the warmth it taught us. We were so tall, like the sky.

Night comes. Rock calls out as it cools in shadow. Grass bends in the breeze. We were so tall. For a moment we still reach, plucking the evening star from the horizon, setting it in our hands to drink.

Blanket, curtain, veil: we are married to imagination. There is no death. There is no beauty. Our hands are only cupped to drink water and the night.

Margarita opened her eyes, not realizing she'd closed them. *Night comes* . . . and it had, as if she'd brought it on by closing her eyes. She squinted in the near darkness. Arrow was gone. Zed sat on the log and wept. She moved silently closer and put a hand on his shoulder. He didn't shake it off, and she sat there with him, silent, as a full moon crept above the plateau to the east. Huge and yellow, it shed enough light to brighten Zed's eyes when he finally looked up.

So much light was there in those eyes, and so much darkness. The black cold of empty space gripped Margarita, but it offered shelter, too. *Blanket, curtain, veil* . . . was *she* married to imagination? Doomed—or privileged—to ride each fragment of her soul into darkness, and into sunlight, if she would just let those fragments go?

And were they living things, those fragments? Were the Stones living things, or were they beyond life? Zed's shining eyes had become the night itself. He was gone, and she was there alone on the face of the mountain with nothing but the chill and the yellow moon.

" 'There is no death.' " The low voice came from the darkness, was part of it. " 'There is no beauty.' "

Michael's voice. Margarita turned slowly, fear clutching her. He was standing on the far side of the stream. Dead? Had someone killed him as he released a Stone? Was that why he was here? "Please," she whispered.

Please.

A prayer, that single word. The dialog of a lost lifetime in a single syllable. "Michael?" How did she ask, "Are you alive?" Especially when she wasn't sure what the hell that meant anymore.

"I understand why Arrow means as much as he does to you." Michael bent and retrieved the console that Arrow had left on the bank. "I see why you're so good. I wish I could have known him." He touched the console, his face almost as folded and aged as Arrow's. "And I could have. It's a bitter irony that we can be so close in the physical world and yet so far apart. I—touched it. That sharing. Up in Vildorn." He looked through her, into a space she couldn't see. "It was . . ." He shook his head. "We are so *alone.* What would we be if we weren't? Not human, perhaps. Margarita?" He held out his hand to her. "Doubt is going to be part of what we do. Because of our isolation. Even if we reach into the darkness, we'll never be sure. But we have to reach. We have to keep changing, growing."

"That's what Arrow was trying to teach me." She waded through the stream; it was just illusion this time, just generated cold and air currents that felt like water if you were seeing a stream. "How much of what we know is like this stream?" She hesitated, one foot on the bank. "How much of the world is our own illusion, created so that we don't really have to see? Arrow was *here*. And Zed. They were real."

She wasn't asking a question, despite reality, despite science, despite definitions. "They were here. I'm Zed, if I want to be." And Arrow? That still frightened her—that she could be Arrow and know herself, his gifted student.

Michael folded her into his arms, his heart a thud of cells and muscle fiber beneath her ear.

"Why?" Margarita leaned against him. "What do the Stones want?"

"Want?" His shoulders lifted with his shrug. "I don't know. I think concepts like 'want,' 'curiosity,' and 'intention' are far too human and limited to apply." He laughed softly and a little sadly. "Who knows? Zed is part of it now, the Stones' sharing. You've felt it." He smiled down at her, a tentative movement of his lips beneath eyes that were windows into vast spaces. "Maybe Zed brought you and Katrina back together."

" 'We counted,' " Margarita whispered, repeating Arrow's lex. " 'We were special in more than death.' " You were special, Arrow. And when I couldn't forgive you for dying, I shut you out. I ended that specialness. For both of us.

I'm sorry.

She buried her face against Michael's chest, cloth against her cheek, smelling his skin, a hint of sweat, the warm, physical life of him. Feeling *him*, Michael, a soul stretching backward and forward in time, spreading out in all directions, encompassing the bright spark of other, distant suns.

And she began to cry. For her cousin who had died at nineteen in the barrio, for her mother, who would never let anyone really touch her, for the nameless man whose body she had seen beneath an LA pier. All here, now, alive and dead both, in this folded, Möbius moment of forever. The sobs came from some deep well within her, shaking the flesh on her bones as they unwound, emptying her. She cried for her holos—for what they were, for what they weren't, and for what they would be. She cried for Katrina and for love that could never be perfect, no matter how hard you tried to make it so.

For the first time in her adult life she didn't fight the tears.

After a time—long or short, there was no knowing—she began to emerge from the storm of grieving and memory and became aware of Michael's arms tight around her, his tunic wet and rumpled beneath her face, his cheek pressed against her hair.

A forever soul, touched by the Stones as Zed had been touched, remembered by them.

Immortal.

Like Zed, changed and changing, beyond death. She hadn't thought of it like that. The first hazy glimpse of a holo began to take shape in her head. Towering city spires, stark and lonely, isolated . . . that was where she'd start. Margarita drew a shuddering breath and lifted her face from Michael's chest.

His eyes met hers, full of warmth as vast as the universe. "I think you can let us touch it, at least. What the Stones are. I think you can bring us as close as we can get." He kissed her gently on the forehead. "I think Arrow will be very proud of you."

"Oh, I always was." Arrow lifted his hand from the far bank of the stream, a vague shadow in the mountain night. "I always knew you'd be better than me."

"Will I be?" Margarita squinted, but mountain darkness had dissolved into the shadows of the gallery and the pale gleam of the empty holostage. "No." She shook her head, smiling. "I'm not really asking you to tell me." She *was* better than he—and she wasn't—and maybe she had never even tried to be. All were possibilities, all existed. She sighed, felt her nose running, and wiped her damp, swollen face on her sleeve. "We'll always doubt ourselves sometimes." She pushed her hair back. "That's just part of the process, right?"

"I think so." Michael nodded, then took a breath.

To remember without regret,
to dream without embarrassment
of love more wise than our old loves,
but more passionate in knowing
that all has passed in the certainty
that even eternity is brief:
before you go through the doorway, wait
and see how the moon (less perfectly bright than sun)
lets her shape be seen in perfect change.
Go like her, but let these things return
to you and learn what I feel for you.

Michael sighed, silent for a moment. "That came to me while I was waiting to get into the Chelert Gallery in Paris. You got me started writing lex." He smiled, then dug into his tunic pocket and handed her a folded sheet of hardcopy.

It was the printout of her gene scan.

"I didn't check it against mine." He met her eyes. "I can, if you want."

"I might not—" The words stuck in her throat. "I might be Estevan's daughter."

"Perhaps." Michael's eyes were full of soft light. "He would be very proud of you. And you would still be mine. In pride, not possession." He kissed her again, the warmth in his gaze like afternoon sun on her face. "We shared a lot, Estevan and I." He looked over his shoulder, down onto the shadowy main floor. "Katrina's waiting for us. She came down to let me in—don't ask me how she knew I was out there. I had just stopped to look through the doors and see if I saw any sign of life. I was lucky she came down."

"Katrina's perceptive." Margarita smiled. "I think she knew you were there." Maybe she, too, still felt the touch of the Stones; maybe she *had* known he was there. "Michael?" She powered down the stage, then reached for his hand again. "Isn't there any other way to release the Stones?" She searched his face, hoping for hesitation. "You're going to end up in prison." And I'll finish the job. The knowledge came to her suddenly. She would. Not just for Michael but because she understood.

"I don't think I'll end up in prison." Michael stretched out a hand, his fingertips just brushing the rattling chains. "I seem to be getting help." He looked down at her, half smiling. "From Gunner Archenwald-Shen, no less. I'm finding the job . . . possible. Where it shouldn't be possible. He has a lot of connections."

"Shen?" Margarita blinked. "Why? What's in it for him?"

"The obvious answer is that since he can't import any more Stones, he'd like to increase the value of the few he owns. Maybe he thinks I'll leave them alone, or maybe he plans to sell them before I get to them." Michael stared out into the shadows. "The Stones don't matter to him, but I think Zed did. Maybe not Zed himself, but Zed's talent. I think maybe Gunner Archenwald-Shen has his own talent. Enough to recognize that Zed could have been a genius. I don't know." He shook his head. "It's envy, and admiration, and a twisted love, I think. Maybe he's just decided that if Zed can't sculpt Stones or be tortured with his own decision not to try, then nobody else gets to do it, either." He looked back at Margarita and gave her a thin smile. "Whatever, he's keeping my ass out of jail."

"I appreciate that," Margarita said dryly. She stood back as Michael grabbed the chain and swung himself onto a descending step. She followed, sinking slowly through the shadows down to the main floor. Those glimpses she'd had—of platform, of city—they were expanding, solidifying. The safety grid jarred the soles of her feet, and she stepped quickly off, Michael's steadying hand on her arm.

"Working on something?"

He sounded almost wistful. "Yeah." She watched his face. "What are you going to do? When you've dealt with the Stones?"

"I don't know." He looked briefly away as they walked toward the entrance. "Wander around for a while, maybe. Think about things. Spend some time with Chris."

Maybe the world would never look quite the same for him now that he'd looked at it through the Stones' perceptions. " 'To dream without embarrassment of love more wise than our old loves,' " she quoted softly. " 'But more passionate in knowing that all has passed in the certainty that even eternity is brief.' " She drew a deep breath. "Your lex—fits something I'm roughing out. If you wanted to do it with me, I would like it very much." He heard the awkwardness in her words. She shook her head, angry at herself. "I mean it. I don't see things like you do, and I probably never will. It might make that holo really work."

He stopped then, looking back at her, hesitant, and pride struggled with something like yearning in his face. "I would like that. When I have time." He closed his eyes briefly, then opened them and gave her a tentative smile. "We could at least find out if we could work together."

"We could find that out." Margarita wanted this and didn't want it, and neither of those feelings had anything to do with right here and right now. Things had changed. *She* had changed. "I'd like that a lot," she said, and meant it. "I don't have a clue as to whether we can work together."

"Me neither." He laughed softly. "It'll be an adventure."

And then Katrina was coming toward them, her smile lighting her face; yeah, she was perceptive. And Margarita opened her arms, her throat closing into a knot, because love was never perfect and couldn't do everything for you, but it mattered. If you let it matter.

"Ready to go home?" Katrina tossed her hair back over her shoulders. "I invited Michael to come by for a late supper."

"I'm ready." Margarita twined her arm through Katrina's. "Let me tell you about this piece, this platform thing." She palmed the lock on the front door and breathed fresh, rain-washed air, wet asphalt, and night. "It's going to be really different. Almost surreal, like a Gaudi cathedral, but more so. And ugly in places. So that . . . it's beautiful."

"I think I'm going to head back to my hotel." Michael touched Margarita's arm, his eyes gentle on her face. "I'll see you."

"I'll see you." Margarita returned the touch, smiling, because she *would* see him. And they'd work together for a while and see how that went or didn't go.

"I like him," Katrina said as Michael made his way down the street. "Did the gene scan settle everything?"

"*We* settled everything." Margarita looked back as the gallery's glass door closed, catching a glimpse of a figure in the shadows. Arrow? She lifted a hand in thanks, and he returned her salute.

I'll see you, too, she promised silently. And she would—in every holo she did.

"I brought some curried chicken from that little stand down on Market." Hefting her carryall, Katrina tilted her head and grinned at Margarita. "Want to pick up a bottle of wine on the way home? My treat?"

I think this is where I came in, Margarita told herself. Only this time we'll do it right. "Yes," she said, and laughed. "Let's definitely pick up a bottle of wine on the way home."

EXPLORE THE WORLDS OF MARY ROSENBLUM!

"Rosenblum is one of the best new writers of the nineties."
—GARDNER DOZOIS, Editor,
Asimov's Science Fiction

THE DRYLANDS

After years without rain, disaster lay ahead for the Pacific Northwest—unless the strange talents born of the drought could stop it.

• • •

"In straightforward but evocative prose, Rosenblum builds a convincing picture of a disintegrating society in an increasingly barren landscape . . . *The Drylands* is a first-rate debut." —*Locus*

"THE DRYLANDS marks one of the strongest debuts in recent science-fiction history. Clearly the work of a major new talent." —LUCIUS SHEPARD

• • •

Drought had come to the twenty-first century, and the land was dying. Crops failed, refugee camps overflowed, and riots raged across the country—and the Army Corps of Engineers had the dirty job of rationing what little water was left.

Carter Voltaire, a Corps officer in charge of the Columbia Riverbed Pipeline, had orders to stop a group of desperate farmers sabotaging the Pipe—at any cost. Nita Montoya, a Drylands woman burdened with a strange mental talent, knew the farmers were being framed. She could help Carter expose the real saboteurs—but only by exposing her own abnormal ability.

In the Drylands, the few people strangely altered by the drought were feared and persecuted if their mutations came to light. But if Nita couldn't trust Carter with her secret, there was no way to stop the wave of violence that would sweep their lives away . . .

CHIMERA

Virtual reality was both toy and tool for millions. But who knew what was virtual, what was real—and what was beyond them both?

• • •

"A dazzling second novel that draws into the VR nets several compelling, complex characters . . . Engrossing, principled, compassionate, vivid—a hell of a book." **—*Feminist Bookstore News***

"Mary Rosenblum paints a fascinating future landscape with all the skill of a true artist. CHIMERA is a book to savor and enjoy over and over again. **—PAT CADIGAN**

"The nineties wave is here, and Mary Rosenblum is riding its crest."
—WALTER JON WILLIAMS,
author of *Hardwired* and *Aristoi*

• • •

Born a privileged corporate scion, David Chen had severed his ties to his strict Chinese family to become a virtual-reality artist in the Net—and he was one of the best.

Jewel Martina had escaped the violent, dirt-poor 'burbs by becoming a medical aide. But she was determined to make it as a VR deal broker in the economic network that spanned the world.

They might never have met. But then Jewel saved the life of David's partner—only to find that someone powerful had wanted him dead. Mysterious trouble was brewing in the Net, and Jewel and David were caught in the middle. So they searched for the answers—in the Net, in the flesh world, and in their own unhappy pasts. Nothing was ever as it seemed in the Net, where illusion was the rule of the game—but for Jewel and David, the difference between real and virtual was a matter of life and death . . .